WHAT PEOPLE ARE SAYING ABOUT

The Micah Judgment

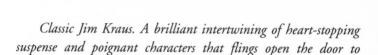

Classic Jim Kraus. A brilliant intertwining of heart-stopping suspense and poignant characters that flings open the door to ancient secrets ... and the compelling power of love.

RAMONA CRAMER TUCKER,
FORMER EDITOR, *TODAY'S CHRISTIAN WOMAN* MAGAZINE
AND SENIOR EDITOR, TYNDALE HOUSE PUBLISHERS

In The Micah Judgment *I experienced what doctors already know about the possibilities of a global pandemic. A thrilling and expertly written read.*

BETH LARSON, MD

THE MICAH JUDGMENT

A NOVEL

JIM KRAUS

RiverOak®
Good News in Fiction

COOK COMMUNICATIONS MINISTRIES
Colorado Springs, Colorado • Paris, Ontario
KINGSWAY COMMUNICATIONS LTD
Eastbourne, England

RiverOak® is an imprint of
Cook Communications Ministries, Colorado Springs, CO 80918
Cook Communications, Paris, Ontario
Kingsway Communications, Eastbourne, England

THE MICAH JUDGMENT
© 2006 by Jim Kraus

Published in association with the literary agency of Alive
Communications, 7680 Goddard St., Ste. 200, Colorado Springs, CO
80920.

Cover Design: The DesignWorks Group, Inc.

This story is a work of fiction. All characters and events are the product
of the author's imagination. Any resemblance to any person, living or
dead, is coincidental.

First Printing, 2006
Printed in the United States of America

1 2 3 4 5 6 7 8 9 10 Printing/Year 10 09 08 07 06

All Scripture quotations are taken from the King James Version of the
Bible. (Public Domain.)

ISBN-13: 978-1-58919-074-0
ISBN-10: 1-58919-074-2

LCCN: 2005937984

PROLOGUE

ISRAELI/JORDAN BORDER (JUNE 1973)—The hills far outside Jerusalem were blanketed in a tense darkness, a fierce midnight blackness filled with small crawling sounds, the hiss of cloth against sand and dirt.

Two men crouched low in the darker shadows, near to the dusty earth. They carried dark canvas packs, each filled with C-40 explosives and a single detonator. The men knew their mission. They adjusted their turbans and scarves, slipped their arms through the wide straps, and lay down in the warm dirt. They began to crawl to the west, toward a small rise in the landscape. That rise was host to a squadron of Jewish soldiers arranged in a semicircle around a half dozen David tanks. The massive armored vehicles were parked, almost hidden, in the thickness of an olive grove.

"The war will begin tonight. We will set the match," Musfa Yemant whispered. "We'll push the Jews back into the sea. It will be a glorious day for us."

The other, much younger soldier didn't speak. Salim Fadhil, seventeen, would waste no words before tonight's attack. He looked up for a moment and his dark eyes narrowed. He barely noticed the stars. No more than a thousand yards lay between him and the Israeli tanks and soldiers. He brushed back an errant strand of his thick black hair, then continued to slither, as a serpent, toward his prey.

With his eyes closed, he crawled forward, dirt and sand collecting at his belly. He felt the heat of the rocks and sand against his neck and hands. He closed his eyes for a moment and thought of home, of his childhood, of watching his mother slowly perish. There had been food to be had, but Salim was worse than poor. He was poor—and powerless. He thought of that moment when she had breathed her last. *That night had been as dark as this night,* he thought. And through that darkness, as he had held his still warm mother in his arms, had come the sound of a ship's horn in the gulf.

It had been the call of an American tanker filled with millions of dollars worth of oil.

His mother had starved to death while others grew fat and rich.

"Salim."

He snapped back to the task at hand. Musfa was a dozen yards ahead. The Israelis were now no more than a hundred yards distant. Both men froze and stared at a faint flickering of light.

Salim sniffed the air. A cigarette. An American cigarette, he was sure. The acrid smoke was unmistakable.

Musfa raised his hand in the night air and wagged his hand in a signal. Salim saw the glow of Musfa's watch in the brittle darkness. At that same moment, he heard a scuffle from the direction of the Israeli camp.

"Over there," an Israeli soldier called out in a harsh whisper.

"I saw it too. Use the lights," another replied.

Suddenly the night was split with the blaze of floodlights and headlamps. Musfa, lying on a small raised dimple of sand and rock, was silhouetted perfectly against the night behind him. Salim sank farther down in a small depression, flattening as deeply as the earth would allow.

"Who are you? Identify yourself!" a soldier shouted.

In an elegant and dignified stretch, Musfa rose into the night and began to run toward the Jews and their tanks and rifles and machine guns.

"Stop or we will shoot."

Musfa didn't slow a single footstep.

A Jewish soldier jumped to the top of a tank. Salim heard the sound of a gun being chambered. He heard the footfalls of Musfa as he ran toward his enemy. He heard the nervous clumping of the Israelis as they took positions of defense.

Then he heard the clatter. It was a deadly clatter, a ballet of tracers and shells and bullets. Musfa was hit, perhaps with the first bullet fired. With leaden, dying feet, he stumbled forward, then turned, as a pirouetting dancer. Another bullet found its way to him, tore into his pack filled with explosives, and turned the night sky to daylight.

Rocks and bloody debris rained down on Salim as he rolled from his pack and away from the explosions. He crouched and ran back toward the darkness, toward his own lines. A clatter of shells spangled about his feet.

"Jews firing American bullets," he cursed. "Allah should not allow such perfidy."

He dove into the deep trench, nearly a mile from where the vaporized remains of his brother-in-arms lay whispering to the cooling desert sand.

And at that moment, staring into the dark void above him, he vowed that the nights of his enemies would never again be peaceful.

LUXOR, PENNSYLVANIA (JUNE 1973)—Outside Luxor, a small, pleasant but misnamed community in western Pennsylvania, the single three-acre park had remained lush and green all summer—thanks to the constant hiss and chirp of the irrigation system.

One corner of the park was fenced and lined and raked. The Luxor Community Baseball Field was alive with the sounds of cheering and shouts.

The Luxor Tigers were facing the Herminie Spartans, a team consisting of ten- and eleven-year-old boys who seemed larger than most boys, and stronger, walking with an angry swagger.

At the end of eight innings, the score was tied at three runs apiece. The hometown crowd murmured their hushed appraisals of the action. The whispers all agreed the Tigers had been lucky so far. A few balls hit a couple of feet farther and the game would have been a rout.

Hays Sutton crouched behind home plate, nearly hidden by the complex set of protective gear he wore. He lifted his catcher's mask and brushed his dusty-blond hair from his forehead. He blinked his blue deep-set eyes as he tried his best to appear intimidating to the opposing batters.

His mother had laughed at him. "Handsome don't make a soul scared, Hays."

He tightened his jaw muscles again and lit into his bubble gum with a big-league attitude.

His catcher's mask back in place, Hays nodded and signaled to the pitcher, wiggling two fingers for a curve ball. Bob Stotler nodded and slowly tilted backwards, going into his long windup. The ball came spinning toward him. He closed his eyes as it made a leathery slap in his mitt.

"Strike one."

Hays smiled and tossed the ball back.

He stared at the pitcher. He nodded. He watched as the batter, one Barry Bioggio of Herminie, flexed and coiled. Then the batter simply unwound in a tight, aggressive arc. There was no leathery slap this time, but the hard crack of wood against the leather cover of the ball.

As the batter took off, Hays leapt to his feet. The ball bounced a few feet in front of the far right field fence that separated the park from old man Holtzer's back pasture. The base runner was fast as well as big. Within a few breaths he had turned the corner at second as the right fielder found the ball. He was at third when the first throw was made. He was charging for home as the cut-off man was leaning back to throw to the catcher.

Hays stood on the base path, blocking home plate. He watched the arc of the ball. He heard the footsteps coming closer. He turned for a moment to stare at the runner. He looked in his opponent's face and saw the angry sneer, his powerful disdain. Hays couldn't help but close his eyes. The ball arrived at his mitt at the same moment that the base runner collided with him. Hays held the ball for a second—and then it squibbed free and rolled on the ground. The impact of the collision sent him sprawling as well. He had flinched. He'd let himself be intimidated.

"Safe."

Hays heard the quiet chuckle. "Nice try, wimp," his opponent sneered, mocking and soft.

The Herminie Spartans scored twice more and defeated the Tigers by three runs.

The taste of defeat was metallic and bitter. Hays hardly even listened to his coach and his admonition that they would "get 'em" next year.

He walked home alone. At the corner of Hardwell and Woodlawn, he stopped and stared at his feet. He felt the tears come, tears over his mistake, his error, his fear.

In his mind he saw the galloping runner again, grinning as he ran head-first toward him. He knew that Bioggio had a reputation of hard plays and thrown elbows.

He knew why he had dropped the ball.

With the sharp sting of tears on his cheeks, he wondered what it would take to face that sort of fear again—with eyes open, not shut tight from fear.

Then he sniffed, dragged his sleeve under his nose, and trudged home.

1

THE VALLEY OF AGA BIN SARTHE, IRAN (THE PRESENT)—A nicked and battered pry bar slid into the gap between stones. The metallic scraping echoed across the narrow desert canyon. Thomas Stough wiped his forehead with his sleeve. He adjusted the pry bar again and grunted, pulling up, the tendons and muscles in his arms and back straining. His University of Pittsburgh hat was stained with sweat. Summer in Iran, in this lonely and forsaken valley, was brutal.

He often wondered if the ancients who once lived here were constructed differently to better stand the misery of the climate.

Tom was praying hard that a career-making discovery lay hidden behind these crumbling blocks of yellowed stone. Western archaeologists hadn't set foot in this valley for decades, not since the Ayatollah Khomeini and his revolution had closed the doors to digging. Even though the current political climate was somewhat more hospitable, few, if any, researchers wandered these desolate pitches and flats.

Armed with lucrative grant money, Tom had managed to purchase the rights from the University of Iran to spend a summer digging in the nearly inaccessible foothills. He had picked a particular northern valley—the valley of the Aga Bin Sarthe—a rabbit warren of dry riverbeds, dusty washes, and remote, isolated villages.

This day, he dug with urgency.

Where there is great fear, there is great reward.

Those words had been carved into the mantel of a great stone gate in the village of Tash-ka-gheddi. It was only four miles from where he now toiled. He toiled nearly alone. Most of his crew had taken this day to rest and worship in that small village. Tom took no time for such foolishness.

Tash-ka-gheddi, once a stop for the silk caravans, now lay nearly empty, worn and abandoned. That morning after breakfast, in the muffled quiet of the streets, he had come upon a blind man begging for coins in the deserted market. Tom had tossed him a handful of change—considering the local currency nothing more than ballast. The blind beggar had eagerly felt each coin to ascertain its value, smiling, nodding as he did.

He'd chattered away, his useless eyes darting in different directions. "Thank you."

Tom offered a reply in the native language.

The old beggar tilted to the side, talking and scrabbling in the air with a nearly wizened hand, his words a thick badgering of Farsi and English.

"You the crazy man digging in Aga Bin? Near the bitter spring—the ravine they call the Mal kin Meer?"

"I am," Tom replied.

The blind beggar whispered a few words. Then he gathered up the coins Tom had given him, and tossed them in the dust beyond his feet.

"What are you doing?" Thomas asked, angry.

The old man spit out a torrent of words, edgy, bitter, scared.

"Only death awaits. A man who disturbs that ground faces judgment. Allah has cursed this land for a thousand generations. Your money is cursed. You are cursed."

"Don't be crazy, old man. The money is good," Tom replied and left the blind beggar muttering to himself, assuming he would gather the coins later.

And now, the noon sun glistering, Tom worked under the shade of a shaft of granite. He was a stone's throw from the bitter, sulfurous spring that he had found in a cleft in the rock face. He brushed away a thickness of dust with a soft, smoothing stroke.

An entrance to a tomb lay beneath that dust. No other structure would be built in this manner.

Tom wedged the pry bar in deeper. One more push and the keystone would tumble out.

The rock shifted and groaned. With a dusty harrumph it slowly fell backwards, a *whuff* of dust exploding around the rock as it hit the floor.

He grabbed the flashlight and clicked it on. The opening revealed a small room, no bigger than a child's bedroom, strewn with objects, stacked waist high. A sarcophagus leaned in one corner. Chairs, tables, goblets, boxes, vases, and statues lay in a muddled jumble—as if whoever built this tomb had packed it in a great, panicked urgency.

Tom blinked, trying to see through the darkness. He saw, and knew at once, that he was gazing on the object that would make him famous.

In a small alcove, cut into the rock, rested a golden skull, grinning at him from across the darkness and the centuries.

SHADYSIDE, PENNSYLVANIA (THE PRESENT)—Hays Sutton stood at his front door and jiggled the key in the lock. The old mechanism would hardly deter a determined thief. *I should change this,* Hays said to himself, as he had done every time he unlocked his door.

His apartment consisted of the entire second floor of the old Victorian house set in the nearly exclusive Shadyside district east of Pittsburgh. He could afford the place precisely because of quaint defects like the outdated and needing-to-be-replaced front door lock.

The gingerbread trim needed scraping and painting. The water pressure was almost adequate. He was forced to use the second bedroom as a closet, but there was a fireplace in every room. There was a leak above the bay window in the living room, but that only happened during serious, daylong rains.

Hays had returned from church this quiet Sunday morning and tossed his keys onto the front table. They slid along the polished black surface and stopped with a metallic nick against the single empty vase on the table.

He quickly changed from his formal khaki church trousers to his casual, everyday khakis. He pulled on a University of Pittsburgh T-shirt and added a University of Pittsburgh sweatshirt on top—all purchased with his faculty discount—a discount offered even to adjunct faculty. He stopped for a moment and stared at the small cluster of pictures, each in a flat black frame, on the shelves of the small alcove to the right of the front door.

There was a picture of his parents, smiling at each other, basking in a glorious sunset. The photo was snapped on a fortieth wedding anniversary cruise. He could never look at it without feeling a small twist just under his heart. Within six months of the photo, both were dead. They had died within minutes of each other—his father from a heart attack and his mother in a car crash on her way to the hospital. A terrible, painful serendipity.

In the far corner stood a black-and-white photo of a tall, serious-looking young man in a military uniform, blond hair cut short, strong chin, eyes set deep. Hays smiled as he looked at it. It was a photo of himself wearing an Army Ranger uniform, doing his best to appear intimidating. He sighed, realizing it had been many years since he last wore that outfit. He knew he was fifteen pounds—perhaps twenty—from ever fitting in it again.

Close to the front was a picture of Hays grinning widely, his right arm around a young woman and his left around a dark-haired young man whose sharp features were softened by a three-day growth of beard. The girl was Norah Neale, his girlfriend and then fiancée for almost five years and his ex-fiancée for the past one. She was pretty, dark-haired, petite, with dark, intense eyes, and full lips—a fragile, breakable beauty. She lived three blocks away from Hays. They both worked at the University Medical Arts Building, separated by one floor. The young man in the photo was Dufhara Quahaar. Duffy had been his best friend since the two of them mustered out of the Rangers together.

He knew he should replace the picture, but it was hard for him to give up so easily on his past.

No one saw him smile as he rearranged the pictures once again, making sure all were equally distant from each other. It was a small affectation; he did the same thing nearly every time he left the apartment.

He locked the door, slipped the keys in his pocket, and snagged the door closed, taking comfort in the clicking of closed tumblers.

"Mr. Hays, so nice to see you. Your usual spot?"

Hays nodded and Mr. Davos handed him a menu, and with a sweep of his arm pointed to the booths by the front window. "You have your pick this morning. Weather is too nice. Keeps everybody outside. Rain is much better for business. I hope it rains soon."

Hays didn't need to see the menu. He had eaten at the Davos Grill at least once a week for the past four years. It was a simple, neighborhood place, burnished with a patina of thousands of simple meals.

He flipped open the menu and pretended to read it.

"Two eggs over easy, hash browns, bacon almost crisp, Greek toast, coffee, hot sauce on the side, right?"

Hays did not appear surprised as he nodded at the server. "Emma, you know me too well. Better than any woman since my mother. I'm not sure I like that."

She scowled at him. "You're telling me something I don't know?"

She poured a coffee and retreated into the kitchen, growling at several patrons perched like old molting birds on the stools at the counter.

Hays unfolded the newspaper. He loved Sundays when the paper was as thick as a man's forearm and filled with so much news that no one could ever take it all in. An article on the third page of the second section grabbed his attention.

"Ancient Burial Vault Unearthed by University of Pittsburgh Team"

The grainy picture above the headline showed a handful of men, some in turbans, some in baseball caps with the letter *P* on them, in a ragged line around an ill-defined hole in the ground. Rocks were strewn about like debris from a bomb crater. Hays stared closer, bringing the page six inches from his eyes.

The fellow in back with the loopy grin was Professor Thomas Stough.

He found a lost tomb? He can't even find his car after a faculty meeting.

"You are growing old, my friend, when you have to smudge your nose in a newspaper to read the print."

Hays recognized the voice, of course. Dufhara Quahaar slid into the booth opposite him. He wore a jogging outfit—and it actually appeared he had been jogging that morning.

"That's not it at all. I just couldn't see the faces in the picture."

Duffy laughed. "Faces, pictures, small type, menus, signs on the road—it is what happens to all men as they age. The body is the truth; don't let it betray your heart," he said.

Hays folded the paper and took a sip of coffee. "Ancient Lebanese wisdom?"

Duffy laughed again, showing his white teeth. "No. I read it on a billboard for the new fitness center they're building over by the nursing school."

Duffy took a piece of bacon from Hays' plate and then pointed to the open paper. "I saw that article, too. Can you believe Tom was in on this discovery? He gets lost leaving your office."

"I know. The story said the tomb had been hidden and sealed for four thousand years."

Duffy chewed thoughtfully. "Think he'll find his way home?"

Hays shook his head with a smile. "Tommy? No. I think he's gone forever."

UNIVERSITY OF PITTSBURGH—Duffy leaned against the wall as Hays pulled out his massive ring of keys. The door to the lab jangled with three sets of padlocks the size of cats. A broken door or forced entry might mean someone had added an unknown variable to the rats' diet—and that alone could negate a year's worth of research.

Duffy looked down at his watch glowing brightly in the dark corridor. "You're not going to spend all Sunday here, are you? I want to get home to watch the ball game."

"I thought you Middle Eastern types didn't like baseball."

Duffy snorted with a laugh. "No, it's apple pie we don't like. Mothers … well, motherhood is okay. Everything but apple pie."

Hays snapped on the lights. A long bank of fluorescent bulbs flickered on, and both men could hear the rustle and start of nearly two hundred lab rats, all housed in neat little cages lining both sides of the long laboratory. Besides the scratching, there was the hum of ventilators pulling out stale air and bringing in fresh.

The two men walked down the middle of the lab. At the end of the room was a plastic trash bin on wheels. Duffy slowly made his way up one side and then back, carefully removing what was left of the rat's food and dumping it. Hays followed behind, a little slower, carefully adding a measure of pellets to each cage's food slot.

Feeding the rats was not a particularly difficult task; the mindlessness of it made the work tedious.

But then there was the fear.

Most of the rats simply cowered in the back of the cage when a human passed by, then would scurry out and sniff at the new food. Some rats would be at the feeder as he was adding the pellets, eager to see what was on that day's menu—even though it was always the exact same thing.

But there were a few rats that Hays had begun to recognize, that would crouch at the rear of the cage as he neared, waiting until Hays placed his hand on the feed tray, then would launch themselves in a furious leap at the cage door and his hand. No matter how he steeled himself, he always wound up gasping and nearly falling backwards from their surprise attack.

"A cornered rat is a mad rat," Duffy always said.

"But why not all of them? Why only a few?" Hays would ask.

Duffy would shrug. "Maybe it's the few who know their ultimate end. Best to go out in a flame than to simply die an ember."

"More Lebanese wisdom?"

"No. That's from a Hallmark card you sent me."

Duffy picked up a clipboard and scratched at it with his pen. He shook the pen several times, then tried again. "Is there another pen on the desk?"

Hays smoothed the pile of papers. "No. Wait, here's one." He tossed it toward Duffy.

Duffy caught it. "I'll sure be glad when our new assistant starts."

Hays snorted. "She's my assistant—not yours. Don't expect her to do work you should do."

Duffy looked wounded. "Never. I have more honor than that."

Hays shook his head. Roberta Dunnel, his new hire starting the next day, was indeed a very attractive young woman. "And remember, I'm not hiring assistants as a dating service."

Another wounded look crossed Duffy's face. Then he smiled. "And you get no ideas either, right? You have not been out with a woman for a long time. How long has it been? Since Norah?"

Hays dismissed him with a perturbed wave of his hand.

Hays sat at his desk and wrote in the large gray lab journal that he kept locked in the top drawer of the desk. When he finished with the notes, he returned the journal to the drawer and turned the key. Then he sorted through a half-dozen letters that were in his in-box from the late Saturday mail delivery. One drew his immediate attention.

The return address and eye-catching logo was familiar. It was a stylized eagle with what Hays thought was a sheaf of wheat in its talons, flying over the globe. Duffy said he thought the eagle carried thunderbolts.

Huber/Loss, headquartered in Frankfurt, Germany, was not the largest pharmaceutical company in the world. Far from it; it ranked well below the giants in the drug world. However, while not huge, it was noted for its willingness to fund new and innovative research. Hays' research was funded by one of their research and development grants.

He slit the envelope silently and unfolded the single-page letter.

"News from our German benefactors? Good news, I trust?" he asked.

Hays' expression didn't lighten.

"What? Is it bad news? What?"

"They're threatening to eliminate our funding."

Duffy was shocked. "But they said 'no strings attached.' They said three years to payoff. It's only been eighteen months."

Hays folded the letter and slipped it back into the envelope. "Apparently, they changed their minds."

Norah Neale, one flight up from Hays and his friend Duffy, sat in her office overlooking the Cathedral of Learning—a 1930s brooding Gothic master-piece, the spiritual center of the university. She enjoyed the way the light played off the granite facade during the day.

She turned to her task at hand—a stack of papers in a neat pile in front of the computer screen. She picked up the top sheet, matched it to the computer file, and then updated the information on the computer. She then filed the single sheet of paper in the corresponding folder in the large black file cabinet behind her.

As director of research funding, she could have entrusted this task to a lower-level assistant, but she enjoyed it—and it kept her familiar with who spent how much on what.

The university had dozens of medical researchers—professors, instructors, and technicians—undertaking a wide variety of research, from cancer research to studies in nutrition and genetics. No university could afford to fund all that work, so drug companies and government agencies were also part of the funding mix.

Halfway through the stack, she came upon a familiar name: Hays Sutton. She smiled as she held the report. She set it back down for a moment and pulled out the typewriter drawer on her old desk, wondering if anyone used a typewriter anymore. The shelf was decorated with snapshots. In the upper corner was a photo of herself and Hays—holding hands, standing in front of the fountain at Point State Park in Pittsburgh. They were both smiling. He was at least a head taller than she was, but he had often told her they fit together well and that his arms went around her as if it had been designed.

It was a happier time for both of them.

She shook her head to clear her thoughts and picked up Hays' report again. There was a long list of expenditures. She tapped the numbers into the computer. Hays had spent a fair sum of money over the last year and a half. His research focused on viruses, and he was using a genetically altered West Nile virus to explore the manner in which viruses appeared to "learn" how to exploit a new weakness in the host's body.

She turned and filed the report in Hays' folder.

She looked once again at his face in the photo, staring back at her.

She sighed and slowly slid the drawer back into place.

Even on a bright Sunday afternoon, Marzelli's was dark, with angular, sharp shadows. The bar opened at noon, along with the restaurant. Roberta Dunnel sat down, her back to the entrance. When the door opened, a stream of sunlight would pour in with a swirling of fresh air, sweeping both the smells of garlic and beer out of the corners. She flipped her long auburn hair back behind her shoulders every time the door let the wind inside.

Roberta adjusted the stool closer to the bar. It was her favorite spot, the last stool on the far end. Initially, she had hesitated to sit at a bar alone. But Roberta felt lost in a booth by herself—and more alone. Seated at the bar she could talk to the bartender if she chose or read her book by the light of the Rolling Rock beer sign behind her and the shaft of sunlight straining through the small window. The bartender brought her the usual tumbler of Chianti.

"Linguine with a red clam sauce is the special," he said. "Smells real good."

She grimaced. "Not today. Not after last night."

He offered a knowing grin.

"A plate of white spaghetti. A lot of butter. And a lot of cheese. And a small salad with the house dressing. And a glass of water with a lime slice."

He nodded. "Coming right up, Miss Dunnel."

She felt the light from outside pour around her shoulders.

A man entered and blinked several times in the unexpected dimness.

She stole a glance at him. Tall, dark curly hair, an intense look in his eyes—from what she could tell. He glanced at her, catching her looking at him.

He offered a dazzling smile.

She could do nothing but smile back and, without intending to, include an almost imperceptible nod.

He hesitated only a moment, then took a seat two stools away. She returned to her book.

After a moment, he turned to her. "Good book?"

His accent was thick and liquid, the sound of honey.

She shrugged. "I've read better." She looked at her hands for a moment, than back up. "Where is your accent from? I just love it."

"It is a very small country. You have never heard of it."

Roberta laughed. "Try me. I'm a smart woman."

"Quadare."

"You're right. I have never heard of it."

"Not many have. It is a small country. It lies on the Persian Gulf."

The young man looked at her hard, staring deeply into her eyes. She felt lost. And then she closed the book, knowing she was done reading for the day.

QUADARE CITY, QUADARE, PERSIAN GULF EMIRATES—At that moment, on the other side of the world, another man drew a newspaper close to his face.

"Another looting of a grave in Iran," he said, his words angry and venomous. "Americans are not even content to leave our dead in peace."

Salim Fadhil closed the newspaper and rubbed the bridge of his nose. He knew he needed glasses but wouldn't admit to the weakness. His beard had gone gray years earlier. His hair had turned gray at his temples in the last two years. His face was deeply lined from years spent in the harsh desert sun.

Glasses would make me look too old, too soft, he thought.

"More tea, sir?"

A servant sidled close to Fadhil's desk, holding a large, elegant silver samovar. "Yes. You may pour another."

He looked at his watch. It was late and he was tired. The servant filled his cup with the dark tea. A swirl of steam gathered at the top.

Fadhil scratched out a note, signing it with his full title as Director of Security, Quadare, and handed it to the servant.

"Give this to Hameed. Tell him I want information on the burial site they discovered in Iran. I want him to find out why Americans are digging there. Do you understand?"

The servant paled. Fadhil was quite certain that the young man from Quadare's desert interior couldn't read.

"Yes, sir. I do. The note goes to Hameed. I will deliver it now, sir."

As the servant scuttled out of the room, Fadhil returned to the stack of letters, cables, and reports on his desk. One letter caught his eye. Slowly he removed it from the stack.

On the envelope was a black and green logo—an eagle flying over the globe, holding a sheaf of wheat in its talons.

Fadhil grinned.

He liked to imagine that the eagle was a Quadare falcon, holding thunderbolts between its razor-sharp claws.

PITTSBURGH INTERNATIONAL AIRPORT—The belly of a jet opened and a young man hoisted himself from the roof of his motorized conveyor to the dark interior of the plane.

Tom Stough stood on the tarmac peering up, shielding his eyes from the sun.

Five suitcases spilled out first. Then he saw the crate.

"Be careful with that," he called out.

The wooden crate, the size of a coffin, edged out into the sun, then tilted down to the black, moving conveyor belt. At the bottom, Tom grabbed at the wooden slats on the side of the crate. Another luggage handler came up and took the other side.

"It's going in that van," Tom called out. "The white one over there."

There was a University of Pittsburgh decal on the back window.

The young man from the inside of the plane shouted, "That hasn't cleared customs yet. It's gotta go through customs, you know."

Tom waved back.

"I know. I have the paperwork right here. Special cargo. Very fragile, you know. Bones of the dead."

The young man recoiled a step, back into the darkness of the plane.

Tom showed the folded forms to the worker on the ground, who grunted and then turned to catch the next suitcase on the belt.

The archaeologist climbed into the van, put it in gear, and drove slowly along the runway. As he turned the corner, he drove at a slow speed past the customs area and headed toward the in-flight freight offices. There was a stop sign at the end of the runway access road. He stopped, waited for traffic, smiled, and then merged quickly with the speeding traffic on the freeway heading north, heading toward Pittsburgh.

2

PITTSBURGH, PENNSYLVANIA—Roberta was impressed with the car. Ayman Qal Atwah drove the sleek two-seater Mercedes fast, slipping in and out of traffic with hardly a glance in the rearview mirror. Unnerved at first, she leaned back into the supple leather seats and watched as buildings and houses seemed to speed past her window.

"You always drive like you're on your way to a fire?"

"Fire? Why would anyone drive fast to a fire?"

Roberta smiled. "I mean fast. You drive fast. That just means you drive fast."

"Does it scare you?"

Ayman turned to face her, almost ignoring the traffic. He smiled at her and she felt dazzled by the light of his smile.

"No. A little. Maybe. I like it."

Ayman downshifted and shot between two cars, keeping the center-line under the center of his vehicle. Perhaps no more than an inch remained between the mirror on the passenger side and the rear panel of the truck beside them. Roberta held her breath and closed her eyes. She waited a second and felt the press of acceleration. She heard no metal scraping or breaking glass. When she looked up there was no one in front of them.

She took a deep breath and laughed out loud.

Ayman looked over again. "What makes you laugh? Something I said in error, perhaps?"

She shook her head. She felt her heart beating faster. She felt giddy.

"No. I'm laughing ... well ... because I'm happy. It was a wonderful meal, good conversation, and now, the most amazing ride home I have ever experienced."

Her street was only half a block distant. She pointed to the right. "Over there," she said.

He jammed on the brakes and swung the wheel, shooting across the other lane, missing a city bus by inches, and then zooming down the narrow side street.

"The red brick building on the left," she said, her words breathless.

The tires squealed as he slid into the empty loading zone in front. The car stopped with a lurch and Roberta let herself be bounced back into the seat. She loosened her grip on the armrest and took a deep breath.

"Thank you," she said. Her tone was charged with a pent-up energy.

Ayman turned in his seat so he faced her directly. He took her left hand in his two hands and held it tight.

"I, too, have enjoyed myself this day. I'm glad that Allah brought us together. Perhaps we will see each other again?"

She had already told him her phone number and now he knew where she lived. "I hope so."

Ayman grinned, like a fox grinning at a flightless chicken. "Perhaps … this evening?"

A wistful look crossed her face. She nervously nibbled on her lower lip. "I—I wish we could, Ayman." It was obvious that she was tempted—very tempted. "But I start my new position tomorrow with the university. I'll be joining a medical team working on viruses. I need to be there early."

She gathered up her purse, opened the door, and slipped out. She crossed in front of the car and leaned down to the window. "I had a wonderful time. Call me."

Then she straightened up and adjusted her blouse to a more modest level.

She heard the screech of his tires as he sped away and closed her eyes, remembering the warmth she felt as he held her hand.

Norah half dozed as she watched the late local news on television. She jerked awake. She had recognized a face.

The shot went back to the female reporter talking breathlessly into a microphone. She was standing on the west lawn of the Cathedral of Learning. It was the same view Norah had from her office.

The camera shifted again. It focused on Tom Stough, wearing a jacket that might only be appropriate in the jungle, his arms crossed in manly style across his chest. He looked hot and sweaty and uncomfortable.

The camera pulled back. Norah saw the large wooden crate at his side. He patted it as he spoke.

"It was an amazing discovery, Kay. Imagine a tomb sealed for four thousand years—never seeing the light of day. Filled with the secrets of the ancients."

"And you were the first Westerner to find this spot?" the reporter asked.

A smug look crossed Tom's eyes. "Yes. It was amazing."

"And some of your finds, your discoveries, are in this crate?"

Tom nodded. "And I'll be revealing them at my lecture next Wednesday evening at the Archaeology Center at seven o'clock. Tickets are on sale at the Student Union. These secrets are more than forty centuries old."

The camera turned back to the glossy reporter, Kay Westbrook. She offered a knowing smile, and stared straight into the camera. "Not unlike his more famous predecessor, Indiana Jones, Thomas Stough will share with the world the secrets in this crate."

The camera zoomed out to include both people. Kay spoke again.

"There's no chalice of Christ in there, is there? Like the Holy Grail in the Indiana Jones movie? Wasn't that a chalice or a cup of some sort? You don't have a cup in there, do you?"

Tom just smiled.

Then Kay turned and faced the camera straight on. Her face filled the screen. She offered a final dazzling smile and concluded. "You'll have to wait until Wednesday to find out for sure. This is Kay Westbrook reporting."

And sitting in her large chair, Norah shook her head, wondering how Tom had ever found his way home.

QUADARE CITY, QUADARE—Fadhil stormed about his office, whacking his desk with the papers he held rolled up in his hand.

"Infidels," he said, his words angry, as he smacked the rich wood. Hameed didn't flinch. Over the last two years Hameed had grown accustomed to Fadhil's rages. "How dare they."

Hameed waited. There was a pause. He heard the loud tick of the old French grandfather clock in the corner. Hameed waited until he knew that he was expected to answer and then spoke evenly.

"I'm told that a substantial payment was made to the university in Tehran. Enough to pay the salaries of many teachers for a year. Expediency, I believe, was the author of the decision."

"Expediency. Selling off their ancestry for a few dollars."

"I heard it was one hundred thousand dollars."

Fadhil threw the papers across the room. They fluttered down to the ancient Persian rug that nearly covered the floor of his office. "A pittance. From a Westerner. They should be ashamed."

Hameed allowed himself the tiniest of nods. "It was a site that showed little promise, they thought."

Fadhil paced to the window, clasped his hands behind his back, and stared out at the city and the gulf beyond. The lights of a tanker reflected off the oily waters.

"And it was cursed, so the locals say," Hameed added.

Fadhil spun about. A smile lit his face for the first time the entire meeting.

"Cursed?"

"It is the legend of the valley of Aga Bin Sarthe."

"Cursed? What is it that they say? What is the legend? Cursed? Truly cursed?"

Hameed straightened the line in his carefully creased trousers. He adjusted his feet so the heels of his shoes clicked together.

"They say that from the time of the pharaohs the land has been cursed. Before then, the village was a stop for caravans of traders in silk and spice. Now the land is only desert and rocks—a valley of starvation, they say. The curse is that anyone who breaks the sanctity of the tombs will suffer same death—a death by wasting away amidst plenty."

"Death?" There was a lilt to Fadhil's voice. "Amidst plenty? How could that be?"

"Only the barest of rumors make up this legend, Fadhil. There are so few people who live there that no man can be sure where legend ends and reality begins."

"But surely there is more." Fadhil sounded disappointed.

"Well, they say that men will starve with a bowl of grain and honey in their hands. They say the curse is the reason only death exists there." Hameed cleared his throat softly. "But, it is only a local legend."

Fadhil grinned widely and began to pace the room. "Ahh, my friend Hameed. In every legend, there is truth. Perhaps the curse will follow these infidels back to their home."

Hameed nodded slightly again and waited.

"Where were they from?" Fadhil asked.

"A place called Pittsburgh. The university there, in the state of Pennsylvania."

Fadhil stopped midstride. "The University of Pittsburgh?"

Hameed allowed himself a smug, congratulatory smile. "Yes."

"Ayman?"

Hameed cleared his throat again. "Yes, Ayman is there. As a student, of course. And I have taken the liberty, sir, of passing on to him a brief instruction."

"Instruction?"

"I have told him to pay attention."

Fadhil smiled again and walked back to the window. "How excellent. How excellent indeed."

As he turned his back, Hameed's smile disappeared, to be replaced with an empty look that hovered just at the edge of evil.

PITTSBURGH, PENNSYLVANIA—Tom Stough paced about his office. The crate, featured in this afternoon's television interview, was back behind his desk. He didn't like the feel of it there. He pushed it to the far side of the office, the wood squealing.

He stepped back to his desk and pulled off his jacket. Dark rings of sweat stained his underarms and back.

Tom sat down and pretended to go through the papers on his desk. Even though he had been back in Pittsburgh for nearly two weeks, the stack of memos and letters remained as high as when he first unlocked his office. He hadn't even turned on his computer, or attempted to read through his e-mails. With pen in hand, he stared at the same memo for a long moment. The type appeared to swim in small circles in front of his eyes. He dropped the pen, rubbed his forehead.

He was still sweating. He reached for the fan on his desk and switched it on. The breeze ruffled the stack of paper, making a ghostly rippling sound. The breeze didn't cool him, but made his skin clammier than it had been.

He stood again. He took a long swallow from a water bottle on the bookcase. The water was no cooler than room temperature, and he swallowed hard.

He looked over at the crate again. He scowled.

What was I thinking?

Nothing had changed and everything had changed. The crate hulked in the corner, almost as if it were mocking him, mocking his ability to remain unaffected.

Slowly he stepped toward the crate, each step leaden and shuffling. He wanted to push the crate out into the hall, down to the elevator, and into the basement—or even out to the loading docks and into a van—but did none of those things. He rested his hand on top.

He thought he felt the coarse, splintery wood vibrate. He told himself it was the air-conditioning in the building, or the heat, or the traffic outside on Fifth Avenue. He pushed at the wood.

He cursed under his breath, as if he didn't want anyone to hear him.

He bent to the combination lock fastened to the hasp on the crate, tight, almost as if in prayer. He spun the tumbler one way, then another, and then back again. The lock opened with a whispery click. He didn't want to open the lid. He placed his fingers under the small cleft. He waited. He resisted, counted to ten once, and then again. He closed his eyes tight, then opened them.

The only illumination in the office came from the streetlights below. It was enough, he thought—more than enough light to see it. He lifted the lid. A velvet cloth the color of midnight lay crumpled in loose cuffs on top, as if bedcovers had been tousled by a night of dark and evil dreams.

He grabbed the edge of the cloth unwillingly. He counted to ten three times. Then he took in a rapid gulp of air, filling his lungs. He exhaled.

With a snap he yanked the cloth from the crate. It slipped away as light as a moth descending into a flame.

And there it was, in the box, grinning at him—at him and his office and all that he had worked for. Grinning.

It was the golden skull he had found in the tomb in the valley of Aga Bin Sarthe, in Iran. It was the skull that had guarded that tomb, a silent, mute sentinel for so many centuries.

Now it stared back at him.

Larger than a human skull, the carved artifact was both a magnification and a reduction of the human form. The eye sockets were deeper set, the jaw line softer, the forehead more pronounced, the nape of the neck almost childlike, birdlike. There were round disks of obsidian for eyes—black and dead, yet translucent in imaging the darkness of whatever was inside the skull.

He didn't want to pick it up; he didn't want to touch it again. He counted to ten five times in a row, slowly, with his eyes closed. Then at number fifty, he opened them and bent to the skull, twining his fingers behind it.

He lifted it up out of the crate.

The skull was heavy—heavy like gold—heavy with secrets.

The workmanship was the most amazing thing Tom had ever seen. It had been polished to a high sheen and had held that luster for centuries. Circling the skull, just above the eye sockets, was a thin line, as if the skull could be separated into two pieces—unscrewed like a bottle.

He felt his stomach growl.

He shook the object.

From inside, from the hollow core, came a rattle, a dry rattle of dust, of stone, of the darkness of the past.

There was something in there—something malevolent—something that had been hidden from the light for all these millennia.

He felt a shudder and couldn't hold the skull any longer. He pushed it back into place, pulled the midnight velvet overtop again, slammed the crate shut, and fumbled for the lock. He snapped it shut, stood, and backed out of the office, banging into the wall by the door.

Tom stepped into the hall, and as fast as he could walk without truly running, he made his way to the street below.

A dry, deathlike rattle echoed in his ears as he ran, sweating and panting, to his car.

3

PITTSBURGH, PENNSYLVANIA—Roberta steadied herself and placed her hand on the doorknob to the lab and hoped for the best.

She was nearing thirty and had yet to hold a job for more than a year. She wasn't sure why, exactly, but when a task grew unpleasant or boring, she would simply leave. Afterwards, her joy would be replaced by depression or panic and she would vow that the next job would last. During the many periods between jobs, Roberta would audit classes at random, or several classes, sometimes auditing almost a full course load, without the worry of tests and papers and tuition. She lived simply—and had a small inheritance as a cushion. During her sporadic college tenure, she spent three years with the ROTC, earning a small stipend—yet avoiding full-time military service because of an erratic heartbeat.

Last semester Roberta had been attending an advanced molecular biology class when she first met Hays Sutton. He was subbing for the tenured professor, and he mentioned that he was looking for an assistant. In her many forays into other disciplines, Roberta had almost gathered enough medical course work to qualify as a premed student.

The lab was larger than she imagined, stretching almost the entire width of the building. To her right were the cages—hundreds of them—partitioned off by a glass wall.

To her left was a long run of countertop, with centrifuges, microscopes, burners, scales, laptop computers, cables, beakers, a couple of huge sinks, several hooded and glassed ventilators, incubators, and banks of locked cabinets above and below.

At the end of the counter was another wall of glass. Behind that smudged wall she could see at least two isolation chambers, each with long, limp arm-length rubber sleeves and gloves gusseted into them, plus fans and filters and airlocks.

Hays sat behind his desk and rose quickly, wiping his hands on his smock. "Good morning, Roberta," he said, trying his best to appear composed. "I'm glad you're here. Welcome."

"Roberta Dunnel, this is Dufhara Quahaar; everyone calls him Duffy."

She offered him a small wave and a smile. Duffy stood and walked toward her.

Good heavens. He's handsome, she thought.

Duffy took her hand and held it gently. "At last we have some civility here. You are a civil person, are you not, Roberta?"

"I am. At least I try to be."

Duffy offered her a wide, warm smile and then a wink.

She recognized the gesture, and its intent.

There was a moment of silence as both men stared at her. She often got that reaction.

"Well, then," she said firmly, "I guess we could start by someone showing me where to put my purse."

By the end of the day, even by the end of lunch, Hays knew that he had made the correct decision when he'd offered Roberta the job. He had spent an hour showing her the sort of research that they were involved in and how she could help—by maintaining records and updating computer files and databases.

At day's end, the lab appeared better organized than it had in the last eighteen months. Without asking, she seemed to sense what needed to be done and the best manner in which to do it.

She had presented Hays with a list of supplies she needed. Some were technical—a larger and faster external hard drive and the latest update of their database software, and some as simple as paper towels and cleaning supplies.

"Thank you," Hays said as he held the door for her at the end of the day. "I think this arrangement will work out well."

She smiled and nodded. "I enjoyed today. To be honest, that never happens to me on the first day of a job. I think it will work out, too."

As Hays locked the top padlock, a shadowy figure pressed itself against the inside of the frosted glass of the door. "Hey. Wait a minute. I need out of here."

Hays slapped his forehead and unsnapped the lock. Duffy popped out of the dark interior.

"A day. One day with a new employee and you forget about me."

Roberta grinned and Duffy gave her a mock glare.

"One day, and you have bewitched him. I have worked with this man for nearly five years—and he forgets me like this. I would have starved in there—locked away in the dark with a thousand rats around me."

Then Roberta laughed out loud. It was a musical laugh, Hays thought.

Duffy placed his hand on Roberta's arm. "Do you need a ride home?" he asked. "Being your first day and all."

Hays turned back just in time to see Duffy offer her his most dazzling smile—all the while his hand remaining on her forearm.

"What about me? You promised me a ride home," Hays said, pretending he was hurt.

"You? Who gives rides to people who forget their friends so easily?"

The three of them laughed as if they had been laughing together for years and then made their way to the elevator at the end of the hall.

Duffy easily negotiated the narrow streets of Pittsburgh. He made his way from Oakland to downtown by zipping through the Hill District, a less than savory part of town. "I'm impressed," Roberta said as he sped over the bridge past the new ballpark. "Most everyone else gets nervous when I mention living on the North Side. Go past the stadium and it's like a foreign country."

Duffy shrugged. "All of this town is a foreign country as far as I'm concerned. There is no rhyme or reason to any of it. Hills and rivers and bridges."

"Then why aren't you nervous? Or lost?"

Duffy looked at her as if he were oblivious to traffic and his driving. "I abandon all logic when I drive here. I never become lost. I'm Lebanese. We are born with a wonderful sense of direction. Beirut—my hometown—is an old-world maze—but it is as wide open as Kansas compared to this town."

He spun the wheel and headed down a narrow cobblestone street.

Roberta stared at her new coworker. "Is Hays married?"

Duffy didn't look away from the road, but she sensed the question might have surprised him.

"Why do you ask?" Duffy answered. "He is not that handsome, is he? I know he is not rich. You can see that by the manner of his dress. Tell me it is not his looks. Please."

"No, it's not that," she laughed.

"And why do you not ask if I'm married or not? To me, that question is the more valid of the two," Duffy said, sounding slighted.

Roberta shook her head. "I know you're not married. You're too handsome."

Duffy didn't know whether the comment was meant as an insult or a compliment. "No. Hays is not married."

"Then who is that dark-haired woman in the photos he has on the typewriter drawer of his desk? Small woman—very pretty—oval sort of face with dark eyes. He had his arms around her in one photo—and she clearly isn't his sister."

"He still has them there? Really?"

"You learn a lot by cleaning," Roberta said in explanation. "Who is she?"

"That's Norah Neale. They were engaged up till last year. She works in our building. She's the director of research funding."

"Engaged? Really? What happened?" Roberta asked, then added softly, "I don't mean to pry, but I don't want to say anything insensitive in front of him—you know what I mean."

"I don't know what happened—really. I liked her. Still do. When Hays' parents passed on, it was a very sad time for him. He was ... I don't know ... sort of away—lost. Something inside was just missing from him. Then, all of a sudden, he was back. Happy, like the person I knew. He was back to being funny and laughing."

"What happened?" Roberta asked.

Duffy braked the car hard to avoid a city bus. "He said he found God. Said he had been going to church and found God. Like God was lost."

"So what does that have to do with being engaged?"

He pulled into the empty driveway of her red brick two-flat. "I don't know. One day, out of the blue, he tells me that he called it off. He just backed out of the engagement. She put up with his being sad and depressed, but he said she couldn't accept how he had changed—you know, about finding God."

"And he broke up with her for that? Really? About going to church? But she is so beautiful."

Duffy shrugged again. "That's what I told him. I mean, look at him—he is expecting someone better? But there is no arguing with God, now is there?"

Roberta climbed out of the car, then leaned down to the passenger-side window and smiled. "Thanks for the ride. I'll see you tomorrow morning."

Hays blinked, staring at the clock. Only a few minutes remained until midnight.

The persistent phone had roused him. He fumbled for the receiver.

The voice trembled.

"I need a favor, Hays, a special favor, and I don't know where else to go. I mean, this is a special favor and I know we aren't the closest of friends, but I just don't know where else to go. I mean, I think you can do what needs to be done. I think you can. I mean, I saw your lab that one day."

Tom's words poured out like marbles on a metal slide, clattering and ricocheting in the phone.

"Meet me at your lab in thirty minutes. Please. I mean, really … please." Hays heard the urgency in Tom's voice and agreed before thinking what it might mean.

Tom was the last person he would have expected to call him for a favor—any favor. Hays dressed quickly and within thirty minutes exited the elevator and headed to his lab.

Tom was already there, pacing. Hays sniffed the air. There was an acrid scent of cigarettes.

"You can't smoke in here," Hays said softly. Tom nearly jumped into the wall. His eyes were shadowed, his hair uncombed. His hands trembled.

"Listen, smoking is the least of my worries."

"But not in the lab. The rats will go crazy."

Startled, Tom spun around as if there were rats behind him.

"In the lab," Hays said again, calmly.

Tom nodded, swallowed, and with a twitching hesitation, reached down and picked up a squat black nylon bag.

"Can we go inside?"

Hays snapped on the lights. Tom nearly stumbled in the brightness.

"You have isolation chambers here, don't you?" His voice was agitated, at the edge of panic. "I thought I saw isolation chambers on that tour I took last year. Please tell me you didn't get rid of them?"

Hays had never seen Tom act this way. He'd never seen anyone act this way—as if a darkness loomed over them.

"No, they're still here. Down this way."

The two men walked the length of the lab. Hays unlocked the door to the sterile chambers.

"How do you put something inside?" Tom asked, his eyes darting about.

Hays didn't answer but unlocked a separate small door.

"You place the item on that tray. I lock this door. The air is vacuumed, filtered, and sterilized. Then the tray slides to the next chamber, and the process is repeated. After that, the tray automatically enters the larger chamber there—the chamber with the gloves. We use it sometimes to look at organs we cut out of our lab rats. Just in case they are more contagious than we thought. The whole process takes just a few minutes."

Tom nodded, his eyes haunted. "Here," he said, unzipping the bag. He pulled out a large, heavy object covered in dark-blue velvet fabric. "I'll put it on the tray."

He didn't unwrap it.

"What is it?" Hays asked.

"Just start the process. I'll tell you then. I'll be able to think better once it's behind a locked door."

Hays shrugged, closed the thick Plexiglas door, and pressed the button that initiated the process.

When the vacuum pumps whirred into life, Tom sagged, took a deep breath, and almost fell against the wall opposite the isolation chamber.

"Finally," he whispered.

Hays turned to him. "Now tell me—what is it?"

Tom stared at his feet. His voice seemed to rattle from somewhere deep inside him. "It's death. I'm sure it's death. They said it was cursed and I didn't believe them."

"Death? What are you talking about? Who are 'they'? You're a scientist. You don't believe in curses."

Tom shuddered. "Yeah—I know. That's what I would have said. Curses? But … well, you have no idea."

In the briefest of narratives, Tom told his story—of finding the golden skull in an ancient tomb, of being warned that the land was cursed, of smuggling the objects past customs officials, of not having had more than an hour's uninterrupted sleep in the past month.

"I keep thinking about what that beggar said to me. Now everything I taste is bitter. I'm always hungry, I'm always eating, and I'm still losing weight. There's something inside that skull, Hays. You have to open it. You have to find out what it is."

Hays was surprised. He hadn't noticed before Tom mentioned it, but Tom was noticeably thinner than he had ever been.

Tom stood up. The machinery began to whine, and the tray rattled as it made its way to the last station. The doors slid back into place. The pumps whirred into life for a moment, then grew silent.

Hays stepped toward the glass and slipped his hands into the rubber sleeves and gloves. He reached out and gently took the fabric. The dark-blue folds fell away, and Hays nearly stepped back and out of the gloves in surprise.

The gold skull, still burnished to a glistering finish, leered back at him. Over his shoulder he could see Tom slink farther into the shadows, farther away from the glare of the golden reflection.

He reached out and touched the metal.

It was cold, colder than he could have imagined, even through the thickness of the protective gloves.

He had done no more than uncover it that night. He noticed the thin blue line that encircled the crown of the skull.

"Does it unscrew?" he asked Tom. "Does it come apart?"

Tom shrugged from the shadows.

"I don't know. It looks like it might. I was going to try—but then ... I couldn't. I just couldn't."

Hays stepped back.

"Then we'll wait until tomorrow. I have to send the tools through the same decontamination process. I'll do it tomorrow."

Tom's eyes continued to dart about, but his body sagged, as if in great relief.

"It's hollow. I know that. There's something in there, something behind those black eyes. It rattles and whispers. Like death."

Hays took a deep breath. He wondered what had driven Tom to this point. It couldn't be the carved skull. It was an inanimate object, after all. And if something was inside, it certainly couldn't have escaped through solid metal.

"Well, whatever it is inside, we'll find out. And it will be safe here for tonight," he assured Tom. "Nothing is going to get through this safety glass. It filters things as small as a virus. In the morning, I'll try to open it."

Tom didn't turn his back to the isolation chambers as he exited the room, and kept glancing over his shoulder the entire way to the elevators.

"It will be fine," Hays said. "I'll take care of it tomorrow. Now go home and get a good night's sleep. It looks like you could use it."

Tom mumbled a thank-you. Hays watched as he pulled his shoulders up and straight, and flexed his fingers, as if he had just completed a hard task. He brushed at some imaginary crumbs on his chest.

"Okay, then," Tom said.

Hays watched as Tom walked away, slowly, with a forced dignity, refusing to look back, until at the very end of the hall. Then he secreted a glance over his shoulder and Hays caught the frightened look in his eyes.

QUADARE CITY, QUADARE—The sun stood directly overhead. The air felt hot, nearly dangerous. The birds grew silent. Only the soft, liquid sounds of the fountain in the courtyard below broke the stillness of midday in the desert.

Hameed stood in the cooler shadows of the second-floor arcade. He had never been comfortable in the traditional attire of Quadare men, but also realized that Western dress, with suit coats and ties, was even more impractical. Instead, he met the traditions somewhere in between—a short, loose *dashiki* worn over Western-style trousers and sandals. He always selected solid dark fabrics—never a print or a pattern.

He looked at his Rolex watch. The gold band glistened, even in the shadows.

Two minutes till twelve.

He would wait until five minutes after twelve before walking down the last corridor to Fadhil's suite.

To arrive on time risked being thought of as obsessive. Five minutes late was the correct time to arrive, he had carefully calculated. Even though Fadhil was his superior, Hameed took great pleasure in controlling the flow of events.

At five minutes after twelve, he arose, took a deep breath, and walked to the great double doors—carved from a single cedar tree—and tapped with the point of his gold fountain pen.

The door swung open. A servant bowed back into the shadows. Hameed didn't even turn his eyes. He walked to the second set of doors, inlaid with mosaics of gold and ivory. He didn't tap, merely lifted the latch and walked in.

Fadhil looked up. He took great purpose in looking at his own Rolex watch. He neither smiled nor frowned. Fadhil gestured to the chair in front of the desk.

Hameed sniffed the air. Then he saw the gold tray and plates—olives, cheese, bread, a small tumbler filled with what appeared to be tea but could have been wine. He knew that Fadhil wouldn't offer him lunch. If he had, he would have refused.

"So tell me, Hameed, what have you discovered? Have you been successful in your attempts?

He folded his hands in his lap, making his movements slow, deliberate, and serene. He waited almost a full sixty seconds to respond.

"I have discovered the name of the American teacher who desecrated the tomb."

"Delicious," Fadhil said, rubbing his hands together. "So, Hameed, what should we do now? How will justice be meted out?"

"He should be punished. It should appear that the curse has claimed a victim from beyond the grave. It can be done."

Fadhil looked across the desk. Hameed watched his eyes dart to the food waiting for him on the thin, delicate plates.

"The tomb carried a curse. I can make it appear as if the curse claimed the man," Hameed said.

Fadhil glanced at his lunch again as if he had more important decisions to attend to.

"Then, Hameed, I ask that you make it so. And may the Lion of Quadare grow in stature."

Hameed nodded.

He so often heard that oath that it ceased to hold meaning anymore. He stood and walked out. As he neared the door, he saw the reflection in the mirror over the door of Fadhil reaching out and grabbing a handful of olives, popping them into his mouth.

PITTSBURGH, PENNSYLVANIA—Norah picked up the letter with the green and black eagle in the corner. The letter opener hissed along the slit. She pulled out the single page. It was in regard to the research grant of Hays Sutton.

She blinked her eyes.

Dieter Rollens, the American managing director of all research funding for Huber/Loss, was scheduled to visit the university in two weeks. He was requesting a time with Norah to review all of Sutton's expenditures over the past eighteen months.

She knew Rollens. He had been in Pittsburgh several times before, the first when he announced the grant to Hays some two years prior.

She remembered him asking her to dinner during his last visit—a business dinner, he had insisted. She also remembered that his definition of business and her definition of business came from two different dictionaries.

At the bottom was a hand-written note.

"I would love to get together with you on this visit—the eighteenth is best. You name the place. We have much business to discuss. Dieter R."

She laid the letter on the desk and smoothed it out with her hand.

If Hays loses his funding, then he'll probably have to leave the university. Then I will never see him again.

She sighed and looked out the window for a long moment. Then she turned back to her desk, opened her calendar. On the eighteenth she penciled in the name "Dieter" and added "dinner."

4

PITTSBURGH, PENNSYLVANIA—Hays pulled his keycard from his pocket and opened the side entrance to the medical research facility. There were only a few lights on, spilling their hazy, round pools of lights on the dark marble floors. Despite having only a few hours of sleep last night, he was wide awake. He took a deep breath as he stood in front of the door to his lab.

He felt more than wide-awake. The feeling was something deeper and darker, almost a premonition … a premonition of something undefined, yet malevolent.

Hays knew he couldn't let Duffy or Roberta see Tom's ominous golden souvenir—at least not yet. This was not just proprietary knowledge; this was deeper and darker.

He was certain Tom had taken the golden skull without legal authority to do so. No country would allow such a treasure to be taken by outsiders.

Hays walked toward the isolation chambers, slowing as he came closer. He wasn't sure if it was fear or simply guilt that slowed his footfalls. He hitched up his resolve, and in a moment he was in the dark, silent chamber.

The emergency exit sign filled the room with a reddish glow. It was enough light to enable him to see. Hays slipped his hands into the rubber sleeves and pushed and wiggled his fingers into the gloves. His hands were big and it was always a snug fit. Then he looked directly at the skull. Bigger than a human skull by a third, Hays imagined it followed the human anatomy in a general sense. The eye sockets were deeper and filled with a round black stone that he guessed was obsidian. The jaws seemed clenched, and when Hays looked to one side, the skull seemed to twist its frozen expression into a sneer—or perhaps a mocking laugh.

He squinted and looked more closely at the thin teal blue line running the circumference of the skull just above the eye orbs. It appeared as if the line was some manner of enamel or glazed pottery band, fitted into a recess the width of a pencil lead. There appeared to be no reason for it. It looked out of place—as if it were added after the object was created. Hays peered closer. He still hadn't turned on any lights.

I'm sure this comes apart. Why else would it be there?

He put his right hand on the top of the skull and held the lower half with his left. He twisted it. He thought he felt an ever-so-slight give, no more than a breath.

He placed the skull back on the tray. He covered it completely with the midnight blue cloth. He waited a moment then pulled his hands out of the rubber sleeves and gloves.

Now what do I do?

Hays placed the skull on the tray and moved it to the far end of the chamber. Unless one knew what to look for, it might go unnoticed. He did not yet want to attempt an explanation to Duffy and Roberta. He could not yet explain it to himself.

Hays' footsteps echoed loud in the empty foyer. Other than Franklin, the security guard, he might have been the only other person in the building on a Sunday morning. He had made a point of coming in the main entrance. He didn't want Franklin investigating any odd noises or activity and scaring them both in the process.

Hays offered a small wave and a smile as he walked past the guard station in the lobby.

"It's Sunday, Mr. Sutton. You working on a breakthrough?"

Franklin had been at his post for years and knew that if researchers came in early on Sunday their presence might portend some impending discovery.

"No, Franklin. I don't think so. Not today. I'm just catching up on a few things."

This morning, Hays snapped on the lights and bustled about, fixing a pot of coffee, turning on the radio, making it seem as if it were just an ordinary morning. The image of the skull had commandeered his thoughts ever since he had first set eyes on it. He had spent a second sleepless night wondering if it indeed had some secret hidden inside, hidden from prying eyes for so many centuries.

He didn't for a moment think it was death or a curse or any other illogical and far-fetched flight of fancy. But it was a secret, and it was overwhelming poor Tom.

He decided he would prove there was nothing in the skull—nothing hidden inside except a few pottery shards or parchment fragments. And after he opened the skull, he would do all he could to encourage Tom to return the object to its rightful owner.

He had spent several hours on the Internet and printed out a few dozen pages concerning subjects ranging from Tom's archaeological trip to Iran—posted on the university's Web pages—to preservation techniques of the Egyptians, to penalties for disturbing or removing antiquities in several countries. He learned, to his dismay, that in a few Middle-Eastern countries a man might lose a hand or arm to the ax for "desecration of the resting place of an ancient."

He sipped at his coffee, almost as if to announce his nonchalance with what lay hidden in the isolation chamber. If he didn't rush to it, nor run from it, then it had no power over him.

The keys to the isolation chamber in his pocket jangled softly as he walked. He stepped up to the door and carefully, slowly unlocked it. He stepped inside and snapped on the lights. He pulled a stool to the window, slipped his hands into the gloves, and looked over to the second tray. He had sent a full complement of tools into the inner chamber after work the day prior. There was a set of drill bits and a portable drill. On the tray was a battery-powered jeweler's saw. A handful of delicate chisels. A small hammer. A set of jeweler's snips. Old dental tools. It was an odd assortment. He laid out the tools in an arc around the skull. He positioned the magnifying lenses close to the glass.

He turned to his left. The door was locked and the blinds closed. He wouldn't be disturbed.

And with that, he took hold of that blue velvet fabric and gently unwrapped the golden skull.

The size of it surprised him again. Though he had only seen it for a few minutes, he had remembered it as larger than it was. Up to this moment, he had imagined it to be at least a third larger than a normal human skull. But now, holding it in his hands, he realized it was nearer to life-size. Large, to be sure, but not a gross exaggeration of human proportions.

He looked closely at the eyes. The stones were obsidian, perhaps Black Sea obsidian. The blackness of that stone was unsettling.

He drew the skull closer to the glass, trying to ignore the power of those black eyes. He examined instead the thin teal line. He realized it was not enameled metal or pottery at all. More surprising, it was a form of anodized metal—most likely copper. Looking at it closely, touching it with a dentist's probe, Hays discovered that the metal would flake off under some pressure.

They sealed the skull with a copper band, he thought to himself.

He tapped at the line once more. Another flake came off, tumbling to the tray below.

They sealed it with copper and then used an acid to form the oxidation. Once the acid dried, the oxidation would swell to fit the channel and form a permanent seal. What was on the inside would stay on the inside. A perfect solution.

He placed the skull back on the tray.

But why would they want it sealed? Like this—almost a perfect anaerobic seal. Oxidized, it would stay perfect in that desert environment for ... well, for centuries, I imagine.

"Why would they seal it like that?" Hays said aloud. "Copper acid oxide would offer no protection at all. A thief would break through it in a moment."

But what if ... what if they were trying to protect something that was precious ... or simply deadly?

Hays stood away from the glass. The skull, from this angle, appeared to be leering, almost maniacal, nearly evil. Hays told himself it was a trick of angles and light. Whoever fashioned this object must have been skilled. The cold dead eyes were unsettling, malevolent, virulent.

That's what I saw in Tom's eyes. That's what's been troubling me since that night. Tom looks like a man who is being chased by demons.

Hays shook his head, trying to clear these runaway thoughts.

I want to see what's inside. I want to see it.

He stepped back to the glass and slid his hands into the tight rubber sleeves and nearly pressed his face against the thick glass that separated him from the black stare of the gold skull.

Hays turned the skull around several times, holding it close to the magnifier.

"There it is."

He picked up the dental pick again and nudged at a thin crack where a small bump protruded. The copper band relaxed, pinging as the joint broke apart. It had been pounded to the thickness of paper and it came away like ancient skin. Hays carefully laid it on the tray next to the small sample jar filled with blue oxide.

He peered in closer to the skull. Behind the copper lay a thin line, a separation between the top and bottom.

Laying the skull back on the tray, Hays took another deep breath. He felt as if he hadn't breathed deeply all morning. He heard the whir of a fan pulling in air, and then a filter switched on.

He took a second gulp of air. It felt sanitized, as if everything had been stripped from it and there was nothing to taste.

He placed the skull on the tray and held the jaw with his left hand. With his right hand, he attempted to turn the top half of the skull. It was neither tight nor hard. With that first twist, Hays felt the two halves give way slightly, a few fractions of an inch. He twisted it carefully in the other direction and the two halves slipped a few more breaths apart.

Hays shut his eyes for a moment, then refocused. He grabbed the top of the skull again and pulled up. He felt absolutely no resistance. The top of the skull simply separated from the bottom in a fluid movement. And then the skull was in two pieces, just like that, with an elegant and surprising lift.

Hays felt no different after opening the skull. He had thought he might. But no demon rushed out to claim his life or run rampant through the lab and the city. Hays smiled at the thought and took a deep, relieved breath. He felt a hollow laugh in his throat, the kind of laugh that happens after a near miss with tragedy, a narrow aversion of panic or injury.

He laid the top half of the skull on the table. He blinked and then tilted the bottom half of the skull toward him, praying he would see nothing. When the skull was fully tilted, he turned it from one side to the other.

With his right hand, he took a large glass container—the sort of dish one might use to bake a casserole—and placed it in front of him on the tray. Then he slowly tilted the bottom of the skull further.

A whispery hush of something white and powdery began to pour into the dish. Then a handful of what appeared to be grains of wheat or barley slipped into the dish. And then finally, two small objects slid out and into view. Hays first thought they were two small sections of twine or rope. He set the skull down and with a hemostat picked up one of the fraying bundles.

He held it close to the magnifier.

He blinked in surprise.

He was holding a nearly perfectly embalmed and preserved mouse. Its eyes had been sewn shut, as well as its mouth. There were the tiniest of beaded silk coverings on its four paws. And around the small neck was the most delicate of items—a small chain, with individual links no bigger than a speck of sand, forged out of gold.

Hays laid the small dead creature in the tray, carefully set the hemostat down, pulled his hands out of the rubber sleeves and gloves, unlocked the door and walked out, locking it behind him.

He continued to walk until he got to the drinking fountain down the hall from his lab. He took a long, noisy drink, feeling at once both normal and disconnected.

He slowly returned to his lab, entered it, and locked the door behind him again.

Why would they have done that … to a mouse?

It took Hays nearly an hour to separate all of what was once inside the skull. He placed each mouse in an individual glass container, with a screw-down lid that made it hermetically airtight. He thumbed each container closed and labeled them with a grease pencil as *One Mouse* and *Two Mouse*.

He carefully and painstakingly lifted each grain fragment from the tray individually. He picked each one up and tapped the side of the tray in an attempt to remove all the white powder. He guessed he had at least a thousand grains in the container when he finished.

He sealed up the copper band and blue oxide flakes in a container.

By this time, his back was beginning to throb.

The white powder was a different problem altogether. Using a wide scraper—one of his dental tools—he managed to get most of it collected and placed in a small dish, worrying that some small part might escape. Hays thought all his precautions verged on being paranoid, but one could never be too careful.

In the stack of papers on his desk was an article on a researcher at Oxford who had come down with hemorrhagic fever while inspecting a nearly forty-year-old carcass of an African chimpanzee that had been stored in freezers all that time—until the researcher defrosted it.

Viruses were ruthless and could lie in wait for years. Perhaps not for centuries, but Hays knew it wise to be more cautious than less.

He placed the two halves of the skull together and covered them once more with the midnight velvet fabric.

He stepped back from the gloves. There was now too much evidence of activity in this isolation unit.

He would have to tell Duffy and Roberta—at least part of the story. He might leave out some of the details, such at the object having been stolen and Tom's near hysterical behavior.

He exited the isolation chamber, locked the door, checking it three times, and returned to his desk. He leaned backwards in his chair, his back and the chair making popping, cracking noises.

He clasped his hands behind his head and shut his eyes for a long moment.

I'm sure there's nothing to be worried about—nothing at all.

5

PITTSBURGH, PENNSYLVANIA—Ayman drove like a man possessed, or perhaps more accurately, Roberta thought, like a man pursued. His sporty Mercedes neatly fishtailed around a corner, its tires squealing in elegant complaint. Ayman didn't look at her, but grinned, staring straight ahead, one hand on the wheel and one hand on the polished wood gearshift. The lapels of his soft leather jacket ruffled softly in the wind.

He had the top down, despite a gray scud of clouds overhead. Roberta leaned back and let the speed and wind wash over her.

Downtown Pittsburgh never looked more beautiful than at night. The darkness hid imperfections and the lights along the river looked like jewels, she thought. He raced over the bridge that spanned the Monongahela River. The steel supports whipped past her eyes, and she felt a loose laugh begin to bubble up in her throat.

"You are happy?" Ayman turned to face her. "You are even more beautiful when you laugh. I find it charming that you can be so open with a man. American women, well …"

His words trailed off in silence as he negotiated another tight corner.

"American women are what?" Roberta asked as the car jabbered over a course of cobblestones, a relic that the city boosters called charming and motorists cursed.

Ayman shrugged and smiled at her, a warm, passionate smile.

"American women … are free. They express themselves in such wonderful ways. Women in my home, they don't laugh like you do. They don't show their beauty with such grace, with such openness."

She reached over and touched his forearm.

"Why thank you, Ayman. You are very sweet."

He nodded, and Roberta left her hand resting on his forearm until they arrived at the restaurant a few moments later.

"This is not true Quadare food, but it is as close as one might find in this town. I suspect there is no authentic Quadare food anywhere—outside of Quadare, that is."

Ayman reclined against a stack of silk pillows that encircled a low table standing only a foot or so off the floor. Roberta had wished she had worn a longer skirt when she saw the seating arrangements.

"I would have never guessed this place was a restaurant, let alone one that specialized in Quadare food."

"Close to Quadare food," Ayman corrected. "Only close. To truly taste the sweetness of my land, one must take a journey. One must eat the evening meal in a tent in the desert with the howl of the Quadare jackals in the distant hills."

Roberta looked around the exotic, softly lit room filled with Oriental carpets, warm candlelight, and walls draped with heavy silk. Each panel bore rich colors and was embroidered with intricate patterns—like those in the Oriental carpets.

Tonight nearly every table was occupied. A hum of foreign voices filled the room, and in the background, the unmistakable pitch of Middle Eastern music.

She leaned close, her voice a whisper, "Are all these people from Quadare?"

Ayman laughed easily.

"No. Some are. Those men there are from Kuwait. The couple there is from Bahrain. See the shoes on those men? They are from Yemen. It is how one can tell. No American faces, though. Few Americans have knowledge of this place," Ayman said firmly. "And we prefer it that way.

"Now you must try this," Ayman said, holding a golden bowl, letting the steam flush at his face. "I would tell you the name but you will never be able to pronounce it. The name means 'Allah's gift.' Lamb, grapes, rice, and secret ingredients and spices that one only finds in the desert."

Ayman took a small piece of pita bread, scooped up a bit of the brown mixture and brought it to Roberta's lips. She opened her mouth.

The food was spiced and warm, the lamb pieces full of fat and flavor. She chewed and swallowed. "You're right. That is delicious."

Ayman nodded knowingly. "And that is not the only Quadare dish that you will find delicious."

Roberta watched his eyes. And it was now that they lingered longer. She bent toward the table and reached for another bite.

"Allah's gift always makes one hungry for more," Ayman said.

At the end of the meal, both Roberta and Ayman leaned deeper into the pillows.

"I have eaten too much," Ayman said. "But such is the way of the desert. One must eat when the season favors. The desert is harsh and may snatch Allah's offerings in the night.

"We will have Turkish coffee now," Ayman said. "I don't like the Turks—they are a nation of thieves and bandits—but they make such wonderful coffee that a man cannot refuse it, especially following a meal such as ours."

Ayman lay on his side and rested on his elbow. "So you must tell me, Roberta, about your work. Women in Quadare don't work like you do. I'm interested in your profession and how you live."

Roberta rolled to her side. "Really? You want me to talk? And not nap?"

Ayman held out a small cup filled with a dark, brooding liquid. "Taste. You will have no need for sleep."

She didn't question and took a delicate sip. The coffee was thick and sweetened with honey. She took another sip. He smiled at her.

"You would make a wonderful Quadare woman. I have never seen a Western man or woman take this drink without their faces tightening and a whimper escaping their lips."

"I like it," she said, finally placing the cup in its small saucer on the table. There was only a hint of coffee remaining.

She felt the dark liquid warm her stomach, and like the heat from a blazing flame, she felt it fan out through her body and into her arms and legs, and finally she felt the coffee shake at her fingers and toes. She was certain that she grew flushed.

Ayman reached out and touched her forearm. Her flesh shivered from the delicate touch.

"Tell me about this new boss of yours. Tell me about this job."

She was surprised. As with most men she had known, she would have guessed that Ayman had no real interest in her life. She imagined that Ayman, like most men, was truly interested in only one thing.

So she began to talk, and for the next forty minutes she explained what she did and what Hays did and what Hays was attempting to uncover through his research.

"Viruses," Ayman said. "I don't like such things. You must be most careful. No harm should befall you there."

He reached out and took her hand in his. His hand felt warm and powerful, insistent and intimate.

"No, it's not those sorts of viruses," Roberta explained, feeling protected.

With his free hand Ayman signaled to the waiter to bring another Turkish coffee.

Then she grew silent.

"Well … most of it is safe. Except … well, I'm not sure … I mean none of us are sure about this latest test. But Hays is very strict. It's all kept in strict isolation. There's no danger. None of us are allowed much to do with it."

"Danger? What manner of danger?"

Roberta adjusted herself into a more upright position. The coffee had stirred her and she felt wide-awake, almost powerful. Roberta decided then and there that Turkish coffee was truly a gift of heaven. Words poured from her lips. She felt a wonderful freedom.

"No danger, really. I mean, I never go into that room. Hays does, mostly. And this past week, he's just been setting up. Getting ready for some sort of test. He did show me the skull, though. Creepy looking thing—even if it is pure gold. To think Mr. Stough found the horrible thing and brought it back. I would have been scared to take it—but I heard Duffy say he didn't exactly go through customs, if you know what I mean."

Ayman didn't stir. "I think I saw him on television. Has he been on television?"

Roberta picked up the coffee cup. There was a slight tremble in her fingers.

"Why, I think he was. Something about his amazing discovery, about what he had dug up. He came into the lab this week and just looked terrible, though. Skinny. Bad skinny, not diet skinny. He said it was a bug he got from the water over there. Is Quadare like that? Is the water good there? Or do you have to drink bottled water? That's what I usually drink. Even here. I drink bottled water at work. There are too many rats around to feel good about the water in that building."

She took a breath and then another sip. She exhaled slowly.

Her thoughts and her words came like a flood.

Ayman smiled as he watched her swallow. He smiled as he watched her cheeks grow flushed again. He smiled as she offered him an inviting smile in return.

MOUNT WASHINGTON, PENNSYLVANIA—Norah selected the most expensive and exclusive restaurant she could find. It had been Duffy's recommendation. Set on a high river bluff overlooking Pittsburgh from the south, Richard's, with its understated elegant ambience, commanded a spectacular view with all of Pittsburgh spread out before it. The stadium on the North Side glowed from the lights of a baseball game. A string of barges plied their way down the Monongahela. She was sure the prices on the menu matched the views.

"This is very nice," said Dieter Rollens. "I'm so glad you agreed to have dinner with me."

Norah felt his hand on her back as he helped lead her to a table by the window. His hand lingered too long, she thought, and became too familiar.

She looked up at him and smiled as sweetly as she could. "Why, it's no trouble at all. I'm always happy to discuss funding."

Dieter placed his palms flat against the table. His blond hair was carefully combed back from his forehead. Norah imagined he had sprayed it in place. In the soft light the cheek line and square cut of his jaw appeared even more prominent, more angular and chiseled. He appeared to be happily perturbed.

"No business tonight. Well, at least not yet."

Norah sighed, then pursed her lips.

"But you wanted to see an accounting of several projects. I have them with me," she said, leaning over to extract a manila folder from her bag. "You said that Hays Sutton's research grant was in jeopardy. I think that's a serious matter."

Dieter shook his head.

"My dear Norah. Let's have a drink or two. Then dinner. We can talk about all of this later."

"But the Sutton grant … I mean, I know he's close to a breakthrough. He told me that himself. And he's not a man given to idle boasts."

She hoped her lie was convincing. True, Hays was not a man given to idle boasts, but he had never told her about being close to a major discovery.

Norah felt that she had to protect him. She wasn't certain why, exactly. After all, it was Hays who had walked away from her and a wonderful relationship. It was Hays who had said good-bye—because of God, he'd said. Her smile eased a fraction.

"A breakthrough?" Dieter laughed. "I do not think so. I have reviewed his work. I don't see anything of promise. I did not even see the hint of a promise. Viruses might be a compelling study—from a strictly educational standpoint. But Huber/Loss is not in business to simply learn things. We are in business to sell things. Hays tinkers with the mechanics of viral transmission. Interesting, yes, but not marketable."

A tuxedoed waiter swooped down to their table with a bottle of wine chilling in a silver ice bucket.

"I took the liberty," Dieter explained. "I remember how fond you were of French wines. I recalled our last dinner. Do you remember?"

Norah attempted to smile. "I remember. It was … quite lovely."

A smug look spread over Dieter's face. "Then let's not waste our time talking about any research grants. If Sutton has something, we'll continue, of course. But if not …"

His smile reminded Norah of the sidelong grin of a northern pike, just before it snatched at a fat minnow. She had grown up in Minnesota.

"I'm sure he is close. I'm sure of it," Norah said.

"And why, may I ask, are you so interested in Mr. Sutton and his funding? There are dozens of others with more promise."

Norah tried not to stammer. "Hays is a good man. He's an … an old friend."

Dieter leered at her, as if he imagined that she would offer him more than companionship at dinner to protect an "old friend."

KOPISCH PLATZ, HAMBURG, GERMANY—Hameed leaned back into the soft leather of the charcoal black Mercedes limousine, and the gentle hum of the car as it sped down the autobahn brought him a deep sense of peace and well-being.

He opened his palm against the leather seat and moved it in a small circle, feeling the supple thickness and reveling in the richness.

He opened his eyes as the car slowed. It headed onto a two-lane road cut into the forest. Sunlight splashed against the car as it moved under a graceful canopy of trees.

They slowed again and Hameed heard the sound of gravel under the tires, a thick, welcoming crunch.

He waited for the driver to open the door. He stepped out into the cool air—so different from Quadare. The air was still. From the dark green beyond he heard the trill of a bird. With deliberate steps he walked toward the Kopisch Platz, a small, very exclusive inn nestled in a deep forest on the outskirts of Hamburg.

As he approached the door, it swung open.

"Good morning, sir."

Hameed didn't turn his head to note which servant or doorman spoke.

"Would you like to freshen up?"

Everyone spoke with the lightest of German accents—as if the speakers came from nowhere specific.

He glanced into the sitting room. He could see the faint glow of the fireplace around the corner. A squat bottle and two glasses sat on the butler's table.

"Is he here?" Hameed asked.

There was a moment of silence, as if none of the servants were sure who should answer. Finally, a thin man with a long, drawn face spoke.

"Yes, sir. He is. He is in the library. I believe he has taken a phone call."

The words were spoken with great care and precision.

"Then I will wait for him in the drawing room," Hameed said.

He stood by the fire and stared at the dancing flames. Hameed loved fires and wished Quadare had more cold nights to justify the luxury of a hardwood blaze.

He walked over and gently touched the open bottle on the table. The vessel looked as if it were hand-blown. He read the label and let himself smile. It was port—very old and expensive.

"Ahh, Hameed, how good of you to visit."

Hameed turned and accepted a firm handshake from his host.

"You will join me, won't you? I found this bottle at an auction in Paris. It cries out to be consumed. I would say that it has waited long enough."

Hameed didn't say a word. He took the glass and let the aroma fill his senses. The port smelled as rich as the Mercedes.

"And how is our friend Fadhil? Has he divined any new plans? He is fond of divinations, is he not?"

It was now that Hameed allowed himself a low chuckle, a small shared laugh between the two men.

"He is," Hameed said with purposeful evenness.

"That is why I like you, Hameed. You don't rely on the fog of mysticism or the mumbling-jumbling of some odd faith beseeching the great unknown to guide you."

"Thank you," he said softly.

The two men sat near the fire on a fat leather couch the color of calf's blood.

Hameed counted five minutes of silence before his host spoke.

"I have heard things, Hameed."

He waited a full minute.

"About relics being stolen. About a curse. What can you tell me about such matters?"

Hameed tried his best not to appear shocked. He had been certain no one knew of his inquiries and his trip to Iran and the valley of Aga Bin Sarthe, looking for details, seeking out what the foreign archaeologists had discovered. He was certain such news had no interest to his friends in Germany. He was certain he had been most discrete.

"I have heard no news of such a theft," Hameed said softly.

"Perhaps I have been misinformed," the older man said with deliberate slowness.

Hameed instantly regretted his words, his chest now tight with fear. He knew that the old man knew everything.

"Yes … I do recall one item. I recall Fadhil mentioning a tomb being ransacked. Perhaps that is the same incident?" Hameed tried not to stammer.

His host smoothed the crease in his fine wool trousers.

"My friend, if a tomb has been raided and a curse is involved, I think I should know of these things. Regardless of how foolish or childish one considers curses to be. There is great power in image, and an ancient curse has a powerful image indeed."

Hameed lowered his head.

"After all," the older man continued, "resources do flow into Quadare. Resources that suddenly might find other outlets. Information is a child of those resources."

Hameed nodded. He had fully heard and understood the threat. Information is money.

"Sir, I have been told that the tomb carried the legend of a curse. I have learned who desecrated the grave. I will keep a close eye on this situation. One of our friends from Quadare is a student at that man's university. I have instructed him to wait."

Hameed looked up.

"Waiting—a most delicate and destructive weapon," said his host. He laughed and added, "A curse serves no purpose unless there is penalty. Hameed, you must tell me everything. You must never hold back." His words were no more than a whisper, a harsh, metallic whisper. And then the older man slapped his hand on Hameed's knee.

"That is why I asked you to come. You are a man of vision. You are a man I can trust."

His host stood and looked at his watch. It was a platinum Rolex, horribly expensive and very understated.

"You will be here for dinner?"

Hameed nodded. His host knew he had no other business.

"The Huber/Loss board is meeting this afternoon. I should be back by eight. Please wait for me. You and I have other matters to discuss."

He stood, walked out of the room, and left Hameed alone by the heat of the fire.

SHADYSIDE, PENNSYLVANIA—"That'll be fourteen dollars, please."

Hays pulled out a ten and a crumpled five dollar bill from his pocket and handed them in a wad to the pizza delivery man, who didn't smile or say thanks, but simply turned around and bounded down the steps.

"Keep the change," Hays called out after him.

He shouldered the door closed and headed to the kitchen, turning on the television and flipping open the cardboard box. He picked up a slice of pizza and began to chew on it, silent and nearly oblivious of the yammering television show.

Hays ate half the pizza without tasting a single bite.

He stumbled to the bedroom, sat on the unmade bed, and pulled on a pair of shoes. He grabbed a black sweatshirt from the stack.

He headed toward the front door and downstairs, then slipped his hands in his pockets and began to walk.

There was the slight nudge of summer in the air, as if the cooling of spring was reluctant to be overtaken by summer. Hays walked without direction, only stopping when darkness fell and he realized he was not sure where he was.

At the end of the block was a newsstand. A pink neon sign flashed on and off: "Coffee—Fresh When We Make It."

He couldn't help but smile, and he headed there.

He ordered a cup, took a seat by the window facing the street, and stared out.

Despite his attempts not to think about it, every few moments the skull—the evil, grinning, golden skull—would invade his thoughts like a specter.

Last Monday, he and Duffy dragged eighteen animal cages into the main lab. There were eighteen rats not used in any of the Huber/Loss testing. They were backups and expendable.

Tom surprised Hays by visiting the lab that day, looking gaunt and hollow, rattling on about additional tests and discoveries and going back to Iran. His almost manic behavior had made the three of them anxious, although none of them said a word.

By Thursday, the eighteen new rats were settled in the isolation chambers. Duffy and Roberta were busy with other tasks and Hays spent the afternoon with the skull.

Not the skull specifically, but what he had found inside it. At first, the white powder had made him nervous, thinking it might have been some biological component. He prepared a dozen microscope slides and quickly came to the calming conclusion that the powder was simply talc or chalk, perhaps combined with powdered spices. Under his microscope, he noted a uniform dispersion of ingredients.

Biology was never that neat. If it had been bacteria, he would have seen irregularities. The white powder was inert and harmless, he had concluded.

But what was most unsettling, what was most troubling and bizarre, had to do with the two mice that had been entombed in the skull.

There had been an elegant row of stitches on the underside of each creature, from the neck to the tail. Hays knew enough of medicine to recognize the skill of the seamstress who had sutured the flesh together. Archaeological treasure or not, Hays carefully snipped the threads.

Using two sets of tweezers, he pulled the dried flesh apart, exposing the cavity to light for the first time in perhaps centuries.

What he saw caught his breath.

Inside each mouse was a small cylinder fitting neatly into the rib cage and abdomen. The shiny black object was not much bigger than a child's little finger. When Hays carefully withdrew them he saw that each had a gold plug stopped into one end. Cut into that plug was a engraving of a skull—like the skull that held these things for so many years.

Inside the dark glass vial, preserved in some manner of viscous liquid, was the heart and lungs and stomach of the poor creature—floating, disembodied. They had been sealed in that vial for hundreds and hundreds of years.

He carefully set the black vial in a small specimen tray. He placed a lid on top. He stepped out of the gloves and back into the lab. Only then did he take a deep breath.

He tried not to think about what he had found.

And now, sipping on a cup of coffee, a thought came running to him as if it were waving its arms and shouting for his attention.

What if some manner of disease was sealed in there? Could it be a virus— or a strain of a virus? Could they have sealed it that way because they knew those disembodied organs were toxic? Would the ancients have known how to do that?

He rubbed his eyes.

Why would they do this? Why?

He knew the ancients had no idea such a thing as a virus existed. But that is what was in there—he was suddenly sure of it.

He swirled the last of his coffee in the cup, now cold, and tried his best to resist the fear that came from the leering of the gold skull.

KOPISCH PLATZ, HAMBURG, GERMANY—The fire danced softly. A silver knife snicked against delicate china.

"Tell me what you know about viruses, Hameed."

Hameed looked up from his braised lamb chop.

"Sir?"

"Viruses. What do you know about them?"

Hameed waited a long moment.

"They make one sick. Some of them do. They are hard to treat."

The older man smiled.

"Did you know that viruses are neither alive nor dead? Did you know that? They remain in limbo between life and death. No one can say for certain if they truly are alive—or when they are truly dead. I find that dance between the two worlds of life and death fascinating.

"Viruses are parasitical in a way—dependent on a host for life. They can lie dormant within you—or any host—until the perfect conditions for life are provided. They lie in wait until all conditions are just right."

Hameed took another bite of meat and said nothing.

"We can learn much from viruses. Patience, Hameed, for one. Stealth. And when the conditions are right, a virus can be lethal."

The older man reached for his glass.

"Patience is the key, my friend Hameed. One needs to wait for the exact, right moment to rise up. Don't you agree?"

Hameed nodded thoughtfully, then brought his knife back to his plate. A thin trickle of blood escaped from his lamb chop as he sawed through the delicate flesh.

6

PITTSBURGH, PENNSYLVANIA—"You scared me," Duffy called out
when he opened the door to the lab. "What are you doing here? You're never
early."

Sitting at his desk, staring at the door, Hays nodded in agreement.
Duffy was the more punctual of the two—but often by only a few minutes.

"I know. But I have to show you something—something in the isolation chamber. Something I should have told you about at the very
beginning."

He nodded toward the dark end of the lab. The red exit sign glowed
like an ember in a cave.

"What? Did all the rats keel over and die? Are you hiding a dead body
in there? What?"

Hays walked to the door. He unlocked both deadbolts, pulled the small
stool to the window, and sat down. He snapped on the lights to the magnification lenses and slipped his hands into the rubber gloves. Picking up a
metal tray he slid away the lid, and with a pair of forceps, held up the now-
empty mouse carcass.

"This was inside," he said

Duffy stared hard and shrugged. "It was inside. So?"

"Someone put its heart and stomach in this vial and sewed it back up,"
Hays said, explaining the obvious.

"I see what you're showing me ... but what is it that you want me to say?
That the people who did this are weird? I'll grant you that—they were weird."

"Duffy, don't you see? This is important. It has to be. Remember that
study on the Ebola virus? It spreads from animals to humans. The first person to die had some contact with an animal—a chimp, or maybe a mouse.
I believe that may be what has happened here. Why else would they have
gone to all this trouble to seal it so securely? Tom mentioned something
about a curse. Maybe this was an ancient curse."

At that moment the door to the isolation section swung open.

"A curse? Who's cursed?"

Both men jumped as Roberta walked in.

"You have given me heart palpitations." Duffy fanned at his face with his hand, playing that he was on the verge of fainting. "I believe I will need mouth-to-mouth resuscitation in order to survive this shock to my delicate system."

Roberta laughed. "Then Mr. Sutton will need to help you. Unfortunately, my CPR accreditation has expired."

Duffy's face crinkled downward. He gritted his teeth. "Well, then … it's a miracle. I have made a remarkable and immediate recovery."

"So what about a curse?" she asked as she leaned against the countertop.

Hays repeated what he had found inside the golden skull.

"So Hays thinks we have a container full of the plague," Duffy said. "An ancient curse of some sort. But what he doesn't say is that it simply couldn't happen. Like anything alive will survive for a few thousand years."

Roberta looked to Hays. "Could it? Could a virus or bacteria live that long?"

Duffy snorted. "Of course not."

There was silence for a moment.

"Could it?" Duffy added softly, almost apologetically.

It was Hays' turn to shrug. "I don't know. I wouldn't have thought so. But last night I couldn't sleep, so I did some Web surfing. I found a report from the British Museum about this archaeologist fellow, Judson Helms, who brought back a sorcerer's rattle—probably a thousand years old—from a site in the Andes Mountains in South America. He cut it up, and three days later he died. This was back in the seventies. Only thirty-something years ago and I don't think research was as good or thorough then as it is today. There was a link to that story from another researcher who claimed that was the first recorded case of the Ebola virus."

"But that virus is only in Africa, isn't it?" Roberta asked.

"It is as far as I'm aware. Most people don't even know the extent of Ebola's natural reservoir."

"Natural reservoir?" she asked.

"That's the home geography of a virus. The virus we're using on the rats over there," Duffy said, pointing to the other end of the lab, "is from a small island in the Caribbean. So far, that's the only place it has been found."

Hays nodded, then continued. "But the curious thing about that case in England is that two weeks after Helms died—in nineteen seventy-five—one of the members of Helms' expedition traveled to Africa. Three weeks later he died under mysterious circumstances. And the first record of Ebola in medical literature was nineteen seventy-six—only three months after that second fellow died. So the natural reservoir for Ebola may have been—or still is—South America. But did the archaeologists accidentally transmit the pathogen to Africa? The people at CDC are still debating it, I guess."

The three of them grew quiet and stared at the small metal trays, one holding a dead mouse and the other a small glass vial. A beam of light seemed to focus on the vial and light its interior—almost as if it were glowing and pulsing from the inside.

"Does everything that gets dug up on these trips always get tested?" Roberta asked Hays. "I mean, do researchers test all the Egyptian mummies when they find them? Are they worried about finding some disease in them?"

Hays shrugged. "I don't think so. Tom never mentioned it. But museums probably should be worried—at least with items like this. I don't think bacteria could last this long. They need food, and there isn't a lot of food here. And most bacteria need air. But a virus—well, since it's neither alive nor dead, maybe it could. It might just be in here waiting for conditions to be right to start replicating itself again."

There was another moment of somber quiet. Duffy dug out a bill from his pocket.

"Does anyone want coffee? A donut? All this talk of viruses and curses has me hungry."

Roberta looked ready to punch him again. Then she softened. "A bagel. With cream cheese. A lot of it. And jelly. A lot of that, too."

Duffy nodded. "On a diet, right?" he said as he left the room just inches ahead of Roberta's right arm.

The morning slipped past quickly. Duffy and Hays hurried through the day's routine. There were one hundred rats to feed and one hundred cages to clean and one hundred subjects to be analyzed; their work didn't stop simply because of an ancient mystery—or a purported ancient mystery.

Roberta wouldn't claim a great depth of medical expertise—and viruses were not her strong field in her medical knowledge—but what she could see offered little encouragement. Both the test and the placebo animals maintained much the same weight and appearance. *If there's a discovery in the data, it's well hidden*, she thought as she tapped in the long rows of figures.

Hays and Duffy stepped into the office, shedding lab coats as they walked. "Lunchtime," Duffy called out.

Roberta had brought a bagged lunch with her but thought she could easily be talked out of eating it if one of the two should offer an alternative.

"I'll be late getting back," Duffy explained as he reached for his jacket. "There is this little matter of a few parking tickets. I'm hoping that I get assigned to a female judge. I think she would be much more sympathetic."

Hays slipped his wallet out of the top desk drawer. "And how many tickets is it this time?"

Duffy grinned. "Only thirty."

Hays shook his head. "Incorrigible Lebanese," he murmured.

"I heard that!" Duffy called back as he sprinted down the hallway.

Hays grabbed his coat. "Roberta, would you want to have lunch with me?"

She smiled. "I don't want to intrude."

"I was just heading to the Original. I have a weakness for their chili dogs."

Standing up quickly, Roberta grabbed her purse. "I love a man who loves the Big O and their chili dogs. Let's go before the line gets too long."

In less than fifteen minutes, they had their food and a small table to one side of the jostling, busy eatery. Roberta chose a double order of fries and a diet Coke.

Hays was impressed. He had never seen a woman—or a man, for that matter—eat an entire double order. They were greasy, hot, salted, and delicious—and a double portion was nearly the size of a regulation basketball.

She picked up a ketchup bottle and emptied it onto a plate. "I guess I can get more if I need it," she said, swiping five fries at a time through the condiment.

Hays felt dainty in her wake.

Halfway through the order, Hays realized that Roberta would indeed consume the whole pile and was even more impressed with her than before.

"So," Roberta said as she neared the bottom of the basket of fries, "just how do you test for a virus? Bacteria, I know—I audited a few courses with Professor Feldman."

"Feldman? More than one class? Really? You must be a glutton for punishment."

Roberta took a sip from her diet Coke. "He's not so bad—as long as you sit downwind from him."

Nodding, Hays wiped his hands, pulling a handful of napkins from the chrome dispenser on the table.

"Well, testing for bacteria is easy in comparison. You culture them and in a few days you know. But for viruses … I would start off with an antigen-capture, enzyme-linked immunosorbent assay, then a polymerase chain reaction, and maybe a virus isolation. If it looks like the animal catches something, then we can test for IgM and IgC antibodies—and if it dies, we test using immunohistochemistry or virus isolation or PCR."

Roberta picked up another five fries, dipped them, and chewed thoughtfully. "Sounds complicated."

Hays shrugged. "When you start trying to unlock everything that goes on in an infected subject, the complexities are mind-boggling. When a virus enters a host cell, it inserts its genetic material into the host, and it literally takes over the host's functions. So the infected cell produces lots of viral protein and genetic stuff instead of what it's supposed to produce. It's funny that we talk about genetic engineering as a new science—but that's what viruses have been doing since the dawn of time. In fact, I've read that some think the dinosaurs were killed off by a virus."

"And you truly think a virus could last for centuries?"

Hays shrugged again. "Like I said, a virus is not alive—and it's not dead. It's sort of like a robot waiting for the right orders. Then it starts replicating itself. So as long as the stuff in that vial in the lab hasn't been diluted or compromised over the centuries, there's a chance a virus could still be active. Especially since it has been in some sort of liquid all this time. I imagine that if it had dried out, nothing would still be alive. But kept wet … maybe."

He leaned back in his chair. "That's if a virus was there to begin with."

"And you think it was?" Roberta asked.

Hays scrunched his eyes closed for a moment. "I don't know. Even the most educated people back then—the sorcerers and magicians and the like—had no idea something like a virus existed, of course. But I'm sure they knew about diseases. I read once when an army back then laid siege to a town or castle, they would use a catapult to toss over the carcasses of cows that had died from some illness. They knew the rotting flesh of the cow would spread disease. So maybe—just maybe—the people who made that skull knew enough about disease to do what they did. Maybe there was a disease that mice spread, and this was their way of warning us."

Roberta grabbed the last two fries. "We should walk back. I'm stuffed and I need some exercise."

The walk back to the lab took them past the student center on campus.

"Would you look at that," Hays said. "There's no line at Starbucks. That never happens. Must be an omen. You want a latte or something? My treat."

Roberta nodded. "A double tall latte. With whole milk."

Hays smiled. He was even more impressed. Even though a latte was not considered a steelworker's drink, Hays had never encountered a woman who took it with double the espresso. Normally the women he encountered ordered something half-decaf with a lot of fruity flavors and nonfat milk.

"Make that two of them. Sounds like a good drink to counteract the effects of the Big O."

They walked slowly along Fifth Avenue, sipping their drinks. At the center of the main campus lay an ornate jewel of a building, the French Gothic Heinz Chapel, built by the ketchup baron. He motioned to Roberta to stop a moment. A ring of benches surrounded the front portico of the chapel. They sat and sipped their coffee.

"One of my favorite places in the city," Hays said.

Roberta nodded. Despite having grown up within five miles of this chapel, she had never once been inside.

"Looks like a great place for a wedding," Roberta said.

"That's exactly what Norah said."

"Norah?" Roberta asked. Hays knew that she knew. Duffy wouldn't let such a story remain untold for long.

"Norah. That's the woman in the photographs on my desk."

"Photographs?" Roberta said.

"Taped to my typewriter shelf."

"Typewriter shelf?"

Hays waited a moment, then smiled. "Now I can tell you're lying. You've seen them, I'm sure. And I'm sure Duffy told you all about her."

A slight blush reddened Roberta's cheeks. "Well ... he did mention her once, I think."

Hays turned to look at his assistant. He could see the question in her eyes. He could almost hear it being formed.

"You want to know why we broke up, right? Isn't that what women want to know. Beautiful woman, semi-attractive man ..."

Roberta smiled. "Duffy said that you would say that. And he said that I should let the falsehood pass unchallenged."

"At least Duffy is predictable. Okay. Beautiful woman. Average man. What went wrong? How did he do her wrong? Right?"

She shrugged. "Something like that."

Hays sighed and put his coffee cup on the bench. He leaned forward, and folded his hands between his knees.

"You ever see an old movie called *Tender Mercies?* Robert Duvall was in it. I forget the woman who played opposite him. It was sort of like that."

"The one where he played a country-western singer—or ex-singer?"

Hays nodded. "The character was a drunk who had hit rock-bottom—but he found God and had his life given back to him."

Roberta turned to face him. "You were a drunk country-western singer?"

Hays laughed. "No, not exactly ... and I'm not telling you which one I wasn't."

She tilted her head back and laughed. The sound was both musical and powerful.

"No, it was nothing like that. But the movie showed a man adrift and lost—until he encountered God. That's sort of what happened to me. And it happened while Norah and I were engaged."

"And then you just left her?"

"No. But I did find God. And that was important. I wanted to share that with her—but she didn't want to hear anything about it. When I brought the subject up, she would just turn away."

It was obvious to Hays that Roberta did not know what sort of question or observation might follow his confession. He imagined that she had gown uncomfortable. He stood up, stretched, and tossed his empty coffee cup into a trash container.

"Well, we should be heading back. I don't want to let Duffy get back first. He would never let either of us hear the end of it."

7

SECURITY HEADQUARTERS, QUADARE CITY, QUADARE—
Thick dust weighted the fan, and the motor groaned as the blades wobbled
slowly. Fadhil glared up at the ceiling. "The fan should be cleaned," he
shouted. "The blades are filthy."

A young man in the room cowered, but didn't move.

"Did you hear me?"

The man didn't look up, but nodded.

"Go!" Fadhil shouted.

The young man scurried away without saying a word, his loose shoes
flapping on the tile like two hands slapping in the darkness.

Fadhil shook his head. He knew nothing would be done. He knew the
young man would later swear he spoke to a dozen people about this problem, who claimed it would be taken care of in short order. Fadhil knew that
it might be weeks until the fan was cleaned. It might be never.

Such was the way of the Quadare.

Fadhil didn't like this office, nor did he like the building. It was a hulking mass of concrete with tiny windows—a gift from the Soviets—and
designed with all the style and grace of a prison. Any sound—all sounds—
echoed in the building, like ghosts moaning and creeping up a cold stairwell.
While in his office on the fifth and top floor, Fadhil would swear he could
hear footsteps and conversations emanating in whispers from the first floor.

He picked the phone up from its cradle. It took several tries before he
heard a dial tone. He opened a small pad on his desk and ran his finger
down the list of names, written in both pen and pencil in a closed, claus-
trophobic scrawl.

He looked closer at the number, then slowly rotated the phone dial.

"I'm in my office. I want you to be here this afternoon. Make whatever
preparations you need to make." Fadhil listened for a moment. He nodded
to the phone and the empty office. "Yes. And bring the book."

He waited a moment. "The book from Jerusalem." He sighed again. "Yes. The Bible. The one you brought the last time. I'm interested to see what it might portend."

He hung up the phone. Then he shouted at the closed door. "Bring me some tea." He had to shout twice until the callow young man shouted back through the closed door that he would see to his request immediately.

PITTSBURGH, PENNSYLVANIA—"So how much longer do we let the rats stay in here before we start testing? A week? Two weeks?"

Duffy and Hays were in the west isolation chamber—the one with the skull. The new batch of rats had been quartered in there for the past week. If one of the animals had picked up some sort of bug or illness during the transfer, they wanted to see manifestations of it before starting a testing schedule.

Hays shrugged. "A few days. We only have a handful of subjects, and I don't want to risk any of this using a sick rat."

Duffy scooped a measure of rat chow and poured it into one of the feeding bins. "I know you've been doing a lot of reading on this. You still think a virus might be in those vials?"

Hays shrugged again. "It might. I haven't found much research at all on the longevity of a specific virus. I know that strains of viruses have been around for centuries—but no one has studied how long a specific virus remains virulent. If they are frozen—like at the CDC labs or army labs—I imagine decades can pass and the virus remains potent. But our sample wasn't frozen."

A rat launched himself at the cage door, and Duffy responded by rapping the wire bars with the plastic measuring cup.

"There are some references to long-dormant viruses being awakened—a lot of anecdotal evidence, but also some hard research," Hays continued. "You've heard about the curse of the mummy, haven't you?"

"I take it you don't mean the recent movies?" Duffy replied.

"No, this was back in the twenties. A fellow named Howard Carter had been digging in Egypt for years. In nineteen twenty-two he stumbled onto the burial tomb of King Tutankhamen. Above the door was an inscription that read, 'Death comes on wings to anyone who enters the tomb of a pharaoh' or something to that effect."

"So what happened?" Duffy said, casting a quick glance over to the golden skull, still covered with the dark-blue velvet cloth. "Not that I'm nervous or anything."

"Well, according to newspaper reports at the time, of the thirty-five people who were present when the tomb was opened, twenty-one of them died within a few years. Some died almost immediately."

Duffy stepped away from the glass window. "Really? That's the truth?"

"Depends on which source you read. A few claimed the curse was really a deadly form of mold or bacteria that was released when the sarcophagus was opened."

Duffy retreated another step. "I'm not sure I'm glad you told me this."

Hays offered a short laugh in reply. "You're afraid? All of a sudden?"

"I don't know. Knowing that skull is there, staring at me, gives me the … shivers. Shivers is the right word?"

"That's the right word," Hays confirmed. "Or the willies. Or the creeps. Heebie-jeebies, maybe."

"Enough. I get it." Duffy turned back to make sure it hadn't moved. He took a deep breath. "So was it a virus? From the mummy? What do you think?"

"I don't think so. People died quicker back then. The deaths could have been from malaria or cholera or bad water. It wasn't a curse, for sure. It could have been black mold."

Duffy looked deep in thought then he snapped his fingers and grinned broadly. "We could test for a virus with an electron microscope, couldn't we?"

"Sure," Hays said. "Maybe not for a positive identification, but it would help. At least eliminate some possibilities. But aren't you forgetting something?"

"What?"

"We don't have an electron microscope."

"The physics lab has one."

"So?"

"I know the woman who does the scheduling. A lovely young woman from Baltimore, I believe."

Hays brightened for a moment, marveling at his friend's wide circle of "close, personal friends." "But could we use it without leaving a record? Do we have to sign something? Do they have to know what we're looking at? If the university gets wind of what's up, somebody will start asking questions. And I don't want to get Tom into more trouble."

Duffy smiled. "No one will know we were there. It may take a little convincing, but Beverly will not refuse my offer. She has never refused me in the past."

"You've used the electron microscope before?"

Duffy laughed. "Not exactly."

"You're incorrigible."

Duffy stepped out of the isolation room and called back over his shoulder cheerfully. "At least I'm not lying to the university and the federal government."

Hays stood still for a long moment, trying to think of a reply, and found no words that could mitigate the truth of his friend's assessment

Hays and Duffy made their way through the bowels of the physics building. They were on the second sublevel basement, and with every step down the temperature seemed to increase by several degrees. The lighting was dim, the walls a turgid green, and the aroma peculiar to sunless academic corridors. Walking through the guts of a physics lab gave evidence that the science was not genteel in the least. There were loud bangings and shrieks of metal against metal. There was a constant hiss, as if the entire structure was a gigantic teakettle at a near-boil.

"Is it always this loud?" Hays asked.

Duffy shrugged. "I've never been here during the day. After hours, you know? But it was pretty loud then as well."

Hays held his grin in check, though it was hard. "Does she know we're coming?"

"She knows I'm coming."

Duffy tapped on the glass of a double door. The paint on the door, an institutional gunmetal gray, was chipped in a hundred places and the doorframe battered and bent in a dozen more, as if large and cumbersome equipment had frequently been jammed against it.

Duffy spoke softly. "They added an accelerator of some sort a few months ago. A semitruck pulled up, filled with cartons and cases of the latest equipment.

"And we struggle for every dime in our department."

A young man came to the door. Without opening it, he called out, "What? What business you have? What it is you want?"

Duffy's smile never left his face, though Hays knew he was perturbed. "Why can't they learn proper English?" he often complained. "I learned English when I came here. They should, too."

"Listen," Duffy replied evenly, looking down at the young man's name tag, "—Ayman. We need to see Beverly. Beverly, the young lady who handles the schedule for the electron microscope. She knows I'm coming."

Ayman shrugged and turned away.

"Is he going to get her?" Hays asked.

"I suppose. You would never know though, would you? People like him give us Middle Easterners a bad name," Duffy said calmly.

Ayman had recognized both men the moment they walked up to the door. Roberta had shown him a recent picture she'd taken with them. His halting English was a practiced act. People expected much less of one—and often told more than one needed to know—if they thought a foreigner didn't understand.

He led the two men to Beverly, then went back to his desk and dialed a familiar number. "Yes, it is me, my sweet one." He didn't smile as he talked. "I'm missing you. Would you do me the great pleasure of dining with me again this evening?"

He frowned. "Then tomorrow?"

He nodded. "I will pick you up at seven, my sweet Roberta."

"Do you know how to do all this?" Duffy asked as he began to assemble the materials on the lab bench.

"Piece of cake," Hays said. "I did it a couple of times when I was a grad student. But I'm still glad Beverly lent us that book on sample preparation. It's been awhile."

He flipped open the three-ring binder that had "don't remove from the physics lab" written in red marker on both sides.

"Okay," Hays said. "We need to incubate the sample—from the brain tissue first—in a Vero cell. It says here the school's equipment works best if the sample is fixed in glutaraldehyde."

Duffy nodded as if he understood. Hays was pretty sure he didn't. "Then we dehydrate it for a few days. We put the sample in an Epon resin bath, then section it. Those slices are put on a copper grid."

He brought the binder a bit closer to his face.

"About time for glasses, don't you think?" Duffy said.

"Nonsense," Hays snapped. "I can see fine. Those physics geeks just print too small."

He held his finger on a section of type.

"We stain that sample with uranyl acetate and lead citrate. The only way you can see this stuff is to negative stain. The stain blocks the rest of the sample from light and outlines the virus—if there is any—and forces the stain into any viral cavities."

Duffy nodded again. "Sounds simple enough. Can we do that here? Can we do any of it here?"

"We can do everything up to the thin slicing," Hays replied. "That we'll have to take back to the physics lab. They have a laser slicing unit that works real slick. And you're going to have to treat Beverly well for the next few weeks. I hope she doesn't try to charge us the thousand dollars an hour it costs to use the microscope."

Duffy smiled. "If I do my job, she'll be paying us to use it."

Roberta nestled against Ayman's chest, feeling wonderfully protected and safe. He had driven the Mercedes convertible through the tunnel heading toward the airport and navigated up the winding streets of Mount Washington, finally coming to a stop in the parking lot of the Duquesne Incline. The spot was well-known to many. The entire city of Pittsburgh lay below them, framed by the three rivers that coursed through it. The lights sparkled and danced. A long string of barges, laden with coal and lit fore and aft with green and red lights, slowly made its way along the languid Monongahela.

"It is not Quadare," Ayman said, "but it has its own charm, does it not?"

Roberta nodded. She felt satisfied and content. Ayman had treated her to a lovely and expensive dinner at one of the better restaurants on Mount Washington. He made her laugh as he told her of his childhood in Quadare.

And more than that, she thought to herself, here was a man who listened to her, who inquired about her feelings and how her week had gone. She told him of the intense activity in the lab—doing contract work for Huber/Loss as well as getting the process ready to do samples for the electron microscope.

"Why would they need that?" Ayman asked. "The virus they work with is well-known. It has been imaged dozens of times. Do they think they will find something new?"

Ayman listened politely, as if he didn't already know the answer.

"It's not that virus Hays is looking for. Its what he thinks might be a virus from that horrid gold skull. He keeps saying it must be a virus. Or at least he hopes it's a virus. It would be a real professional achievement to find something new and undiscovered."

"What will he do if that happens?"

Roberta shrugged. "I don't know," she said after a moment. "He's never talked about that. But it is exciting, being part of all this."

Ayman smiled down at her. "No, sweet Roberta, what is exciting is being here with you."

She nestled closer. He put his hand under her chin, lifted her face to his, and drew closer.

She closed her eyes just in time to miss the calculated smile wash across his face.

8

PITTSBURGH, PENNSYLVANIA—The late afternoon sun lit the campus with a warm, inviting glow. Hays stared out through the narrow gaps in the window blinds. He had been staring for nearly half an hour and would have been hard pressed to recall anything he had seen.

It was Friday afternoon. To Hays, it appeared that only a few people in the building truly worked a five-day week. He was alone in the lab; both of his coworkers had departed within an hour of lunch. He was lenient with Duffy and Roberta since they often stopped in on Saturdays, tending to the animals and finishing reports.

He sat up straight when he heard the ping of an incoming e-mail on his computer. Bending closer to the screen, he saw it was a note from Beverly in the physics department. He quickly opened the e-mail, his heart beating faster. The note was terse.

> *Images stored on SMS/Physics lab server. URL: 10.197.43.2*
> *User name HHS. Password 1234.*
> *Tell Duffy he owes me. Big time.*
> *B.*

Hays quickly pulled the keyboard closer, selected the school's Intranet network and typed in the URL. A screen opened up welcoming him to the SMS Electron Microscope Imaging Center. He scrolled down and entered his user name and password.

PLEASE WAIT.

Hays drummed his fingers on the table. The image was large and would take a few minutes to load. When the first file opened, all Hays could do was sit, slack-jawed, staring at the screen in dumbfounded amazement. If anyone else were in the lab, they would have said he looked frightened.

"So you are sure now? It's a virus, right?"

Duffy stood behind Hays. He was dressed in a black jogging suit. His sneakers were as white as they had been when he bought them two months prior.

"It's a virus. You can tell by the construction. See that large bit there—that's the head. Then there's the tail—that longish cylinder with an end plate there. Those wispy white streaks are the tail fibers. And I have never once seen a virus with as many tail fibers as this one."

Hays clicked to another view. It was the same virus from a top angle. He and Duffy had spent three hours with the microscope and taken nearly fifty images. Out of that fifty, four were clear images. That was a very good percentage of usable visual information. The spidery, feathery tail fibers seemed to wave ominously from the computer screen.

Hays cycled through the remaining images.

"So what do we do now? Call the Centers for Disease Control?" Duffy asked, his voice edgy.

Hays had spent hours debating what he should do. He knew the CDC would follow the exact same protocol as what he planned to do.

"No. We can start the same sort of test they would do. I looked on their Web site. They clearly outline their normal, standard-operating-procedure approach. We can do what they do—and we'll be able to do it faster as well. After all, this sample has been sitting around in the dark for a few thousand years. There's no way the virus is still virulent. It's dead and we'll prove it quickly."

"No CDC?" It was obvious Duffy was surprised. Hays was a man who followed the rules. This course of action was definitely not following the rules.

"If we call them, you know Jack Douglas will get involved."

Duffy looked pained. "That pompous jerk who was here last semester?"

"The same. I'm sure we would fall under his initial jurisdiction."

Duffy scowled. "Are all their agents like him?"

"All the ones that I know," Hays said, not adding that he only knew one agent—Jack Douglas.

"Then by all means—don't call them," Duffy urged. "I didn't like that guy. No one did."

Hays nodded. "To tell you the truth, I would be stunned if the virus were capable of reproducing. It's too old. I'm sure of it. And if by some rare chance, some rare alignment of the heavens causes the virus to have remained potent, then we call the CDC—regardless of whether or not Tom gets investigated."

Duffy nodded. "Let's get started," he said calmly. "Will we start with injections? Or should we use inhalations or material delivered via suspension?"

Hays scratched his cheek. "We'll try all three. I don't want to waste time waiting for results."

"We have enough of a sample?"

Hays pointed back to the isolation room. "We'll start with what's left of the brain matter from the first vial. That should probably give us more than enough parts per million for a decent trial."

"For all the rats?"

Hays nodded. "All the extra ones. This is no time for caution." He rose and walked toward the darkened room. "I'll set up the equipment—we can start first thing Monday."

Duffy followed him. "I'll give you a hand." He turned and began to gather sterilized tubes for the centrifuge.

QUADARE CITY, QUADARE—Hameed knocked once, didn't wait for an answer, opened the door and walked into the room with slow, yet deliberate steps.

Salim Fadhil looked up, his eyes perturbed and a scowl on his lips.

"Is there no one in the outer office?" he snapped. "Where is that imbecile?"

Hameed gave only the barest recognition of his superior's question, a very slight shrug of the shoulders and an even subtler downturn of the corners of his mouth. It was the gesture of acknowledgement when what was being acknowledged bore no consequence.

Hameed slowed and stopped five feet from the polished surface of Fadhil's vast desk. He looked directly at Fadhil, neither smiling nor frowning.

After another long pause, he spoke. "I bring greetings from our friends in Germany."

Fadhil brightened. "Greetings? And—?"

Hameed reached into the breast pocket of his Western-styled jacket and extracted a thin envelope. On the corner was a delicate green and black engraving of an eagle and globe. Hameed stepped forward slightly and leaned forward, placing the envelope on the slick surface, and slid it gently. It moved toward Fadhil making an almost imperceptible fluttery sound.

"He also sends his support," Hameed said evenly. He knew how many zeroes the check contained.

Fadhil placed his hand over the check and drew it closer to him. He pulled a small dagger from a drawer on the right side of the desk and slit the envelope open with a swift flick of his wrist.

He peered inside. He looked back to Hameed with an expansive grin.

"Our friend is most generous. I praise Allah for his goodness and provision."

Hameed nodded and narrowed his eyes. He thought of waiting for some manner of thanks, some acknowledgement—even though he was certain none would follow. Without Hameed there would be no generous German benefactor. Without Hameed, there would be no source to fund Fadhil's "friends" around the world. Without Hameed, Fadhil would be reduced to the status of a small-town policeman, given to hysterical rants about the injustices to his people. Without Hameed, revenge would be have to be left to the gods, rather than to Fadhil.

Hameed turned his shoulders as if to go. His feet didn't yet move. "If there is nothing else—" he said, as if an afterthought.

Fadhil raised his hand as if to dismiss him, then paused. "Hameed, may I ask you a personal question?"

Hameed turned back to face Fadhil directly. He waited.

"I'm grateful for our German friend's assistance to our country and our cause. But in all the time I have known of him, I have never once asked why he would choose to favor us so." Fadhil slid the check into the top drawer of his desk. "Has he ever said why?" Fadhil leaned back in his chair.

"His mother was from Quadare," Hameed said in a cool whisper.

Fadhil sat bolt upright. "From Quadare? From here? Are you certain?"

He waited a long moment, then spoke softly. "His mother was a beautiful woman. During the last Great War she traveled—or was taken—to Germany. There were many German soldiers in our country then. Some left with Quadare women as wives or mistresses."

"She was in Germany, a small town near the Rhine, when the Americans swept through. I'm told they took her to their camp. Such captivity is the way of war and such behavior is the way of soldiers. Americans are not as pure as they claim."

"His mother? Taken like a common harlot?"

Hameed allowed himself the smallest shrug as if to say, *Believe me or not, this is the truth.*

"Our German friend simply smiles when he mentions revenge on those who had wronged his mother and his family."

Fadhil thought for a moment, then said, "His taste for revenge is long-standing."

Hameed allowed himself to smile back. "You must remember that he is half Quadarese. Vengeance is sweetest when flavored with time."

PITTSBURGH, PENNSYLVANIA—"It's only been a week. I never would have expected this. I simply … I don't know what to think. I mean … only seven days." Hays spoke quickly, gesturing as if he were being pursued and only had a moment to divulge the information.

Duffy leaned against the glass of the isolation booth, flipping up pages on a clip chart.

The lab was empty except for the two men. Roberta had gone home after lunch. Hays almost insisted she leave, saying that she had worked so hard this week, working on both their projects. In reality Hays simply wanted to discuss his fears with Duffy, hoping perhaps that he might have overlooked something. He didn't want Roberta to overhear his concerns.

Hays picked up a second clip chart and thumb quickly through the pages.

"We've cross-checked the food?" Duffy asked.

Hays nodded. "I sent three blind samples to Murray in microbiology. He said he ran the gamut—all were identical. Nothing toxic. Nothing unusual."

Duffy stepped toward the window and stared at the twelve cages. "No biological contamination? No rat form of Legionnaires' disease?"

Hays shook his head. "I've looked. We've checked everything. I had the bedding checked. All came back normal, negative, nothing out of the ordinary."

Duffy tossed the clip chart to the cluttered countertop. It spun around and chinked against the glass wall. Several rats jumped at the noise.

"Then … it has to be viral, doesn't it?"

Duffy stared at Hays for a heartbeat, then at the rats. There was an unmistakable hint of sorrow in his eyes.

"I think so," Hays said softly. He felt like cursing but would not. He hadn't cursed since that day on his knees before God and he was not about to start now—no matter how desolate he felt. "I really didn't think we would find anything. I really didn't think anything would happen."

Duffy placed his hand on his friend's shoulder. "I know. But it is better that we found it here rather than having the sample opened up in some museum by a clumsy curator. Tom could have opened the vial up by accident. He could have broken it smuggling the skull into the country. Think of that. If it wasn't for us, whatever is affecting these rats could have affected the whole archaeology department." Duffy smiled. "Not that anyone would miss them."

Hays tried not to laugh but couldn't resist. "So, what are the primary symptoms thus far?"

Hays walked to the glass and tapped it, hoping to elicit some response from his specimens. In the past he would vigorously have scolded visitors for tapping on the glass. It was obvious that he wanted to make sure the animals were still responsive. He wanted to reassure himself.

And even though several of the rats turned to the noise, he felt unsure and unsettled—and more than a little panicked.

"It's been a week. They continue to eat. Food consumption is normal. Composition of stools is almost normal—but the weight of the stools is increasing. The samples contain mostly undigested material. As a result, their body weights are decreasing. Water consumption is higher than normal and the output is very high, as if very little water is actually being absorbed. I see evidence of lethargy and pelt flaccidity."

Duffy sighed and rubbed his hands over his chin. "They're eating—and losing weight."

"Close to 10 percent in a week. It would be like me losing twenty pounds a week."

The fluorescent lights flickered overhead. One bulb simply snapped to dark. Neither man looked up or even noticed.

"How is that happening?" Duffy asked, not expecting an answer.

Hays shrugged.

"We're going to have to open one of them up. You know that, don't you, Hays? We have to take a look at the gut."

Hays nodded and added in a soft whisper, "They're starving to death or dying of thirst—with all the food and water they want right in front of them."

Duffy waited a moment. He tried to smile. "The death part—you can't very well put a positive spin on '100 percent lethal,' can you?"

For a second Hays was angry at his friend's flippant remark. But then he smiled, and let himself enjoy laughter for the first time in days.

Laughter would become an even rarer commodity in the ensuing days.

Roberta edged up to the glass wall of the isolation room. She walked slowly. The room was relatively soundproof and several times over the last few weeks, she had come up quickly, tapped the glass making both Hays and Duffy jump, clutching at their hearts. They may have overacted, but she knew their surprise was real.

Both men were hunched over, close to the interior glass partition, their hands and forearms inserted into the rubber isolation gloves that were mounted in rubber grommets in the thick, double-pane window. She saw the flinty reflection of polished steel and the small, opened pelt of a laboratory rat stretched out on the polished metal tray. Roberta had audited enough medical courses to realize what was happening.

For a test to be valid, the time had to be right. Holding an animal in a test for a single week was simply not enough time.

Something must have gone wrong.

And for Hays to sacrifice one animal out of twelve—it must have gone very wrong.

Both men leaned close to the glass. Hays murmured to Duffy, who nodded, pointed with the tip of the scalpel, and replied. The masks they wore, as well as the glass walls, muffled their voices.

They are wearing masks—full-face respirators—all the while their patient is locked behind a thickness of isolation glass.

She waved her hand slowly. Duffy turned and she could tell he smiled at her from behind his mask. Hays looked up as well, appearing nervous.

"Did one of them die?" she called out, hoping they could hear her.

Duffy called back, but all she heard was a muffled garble. He slipped one hand out of the permanent gloves and held up a single finger.

She sighed, pulled up a chair, and watched as they continued. They had assembled the rat's internal organs around the animal and were now working on the stomach. Roberta had done enough lab work to know the inner workings of lab animals. With a practiced stroke, Hays sliced through the small stomach. Duffy used his blade to spread the incision open. Duffy swung the magnifying glass close to the animal. Roberta heard them talking and prob-ing. For nearly ten minutes they picked and sliced and lifted and looked. Then they grew silent, both simply staring at the small, dissected organ.

Hays spoke. Roberta thought she heard him say, "That's it, then."

She saw Duffy nod. Both men stepped away from their gloves and walked toward the back room. She knew they would remove their masks there—in the small room equipped with a powerful fan to draw any loose contaminants away from them as they shed the masks and lab coats.

Roberta felt sorry for the dead rat. It looked violated, spread open and emptied, its inner organs fanned out in a casual circle around the creature.

Duffy came out first, his hair wet in dark ringlets about his forehead. Hays' thinner blond hair was set in spikes. Both were silent. Then Hays spoke. "I thought I told you to go home. What are you doing back here?"

She held up the small black bag. "Makeup," she replied. "Don't leave home without it."

There was a haunted, troubled look in Hays' eyes.

"What happened? Did one of the rats die? And why the masks?" she asked.

"Just a precaution," Hays responded, running his hands through his wet hair. "None of them died, but we knew we had to take one of them—based on what was happening."

Roberta stared in at the cages. "No reason for the weight loss?" she asked. "I mean ... anyone looking at them can see they're losing weight—and fast."

Duffy shrugged. "We think the virus attacked the lining of the stomach."

Hays slumped into a rickety office chair. "It looks like the Ebola virus. That virus starts on the lipid rafts—little fat platforms that float over the membranes of human cells. That gives them a gateway into the cell and they start replicating. I think that's what's happening here."

Roberta hadn't known Hays long, but she was surprised at the fear she could see in his eyes.

"And I think this virus settles in the stomach. We looked at everything else and it seemed normal. Except for the stomach."

Duffy leaned against the counter. To Roberta, both men appeared anxious and concerned. Duffy exhaled loudly. "It looks like the rat grew a leather pouch inside its stomach—a hard, almost shell-like growth. No wonder the rats are starving."

A hundred questions swirled through Roberta's thoughts. And she asked the one that first came to mind. "It's still alive then, isn't it?"

Hays nodded. "No other explanation."

She took a shallow breath.

"Is it contagious?" Roberta asked. "Is that why you were wearing masks?"

Duffy looked at Hays and Hays stared blankly at Roberta.

All he could do was shrug. "I don't know if humans are at risk or not. But we can't take any chances."

Roberta looked into Hays' eyes one more time, then stepped backward and away from the eviscerated rat and the horrible golden skull.

9

PITTSBURGH, PENNSYLVANIA—Hays looked at his watch—half past three in the afternoon on Wednesday.

Duffy was weighing the lab rats involved in the Huber/Loss tests. Roberta had left at noon, telling them she had to drive a friend of the family to the airport.

Hays found himself walking back and forth the length of the lab, too distracted to concentrate. Since last Wednesday, after first seeing the leathery interior of test animal number eight, Hays had found it hard to concentrate, hard to focus, hard to hold his thoughts in a linear manner.

Hays had waited to contact Tom. He wanted to be sure of what he had found. He and Duffy sent the stomach to Reese Chunder, a friend in the pathology department. Reese claimed his exam required four days; he had to freeze the organ in order to thinly slice it, thus getting the best microscopic view. And Reese told them that he never worked on weekends. Hays fumed but had no other choice. He knew Reese would be discreet. He couldn't say the same for anyone else in pathology.

The pathologist posted his report via e-mail Tuesday evening. It was the first e-mail Hays read on Wednesday morning.

And within minutes, Hays was hurrying to the archaeology department and Tom's office. Over the course of the morning, he had left a dozen voice mails for Tom.

None had been answered.

The archaeology department, housed on the third floor of a nondescript brick building on the southern edge of campus, smelled of wet canvas and dust.

The department secretary, her nose red and swollen as if she had a cold, said she hadn't seen Mr. Stough since the middle of the previous week; that he had called in sick beginning last Thursday, but that he'd called her several times for messages.

"He called Tuesday afternoon—yesterday afternoon."

"So he retrieved his voice mails?" Hays asked.

The secretary looked back with a blank expression and sneezed. When she recovered, she replied, sniffing, "He should have. But I don't know. Did you try to call him?"

Instead of leaving another message, Hays returned to his office and looked up Tom's home address in the faculty handbook. He was surprised to learn Tom lived no more than five blocks from his own apartment, just across the border between Shadyside and East Liberty.

And by four o'clock, Hays stood in front of Tom's apartment building. He hurried through the double glass doors and into the vestibule and scanned the list of tenants.

1006C. STOUGH.

He pressed the bell. There was no response. He pressed again, longer this time.

He closed his eyes. *Lord, please help me. I don't know what to do … but I think Tom is in trouble.*

The elevator bell chimed from the other side of the lobby security door. A resident stepped out, pulled by two tiny, golden-colored dogs, their nails skittering and chattering on the polished tile. Hays stepped closer and took the door, holding it open.

"Thanks," the man said. "I hate these dogs, but they keep my wife company."

"I know what you mean," Hays said as he stepped into the lobby and inside the elevator. He tapped at the button for the tenth floor.

At first, Hays knocked politely at the door to 1006C. He pressed his ear to the door. He thought he might have heard the television, loud at first, then softer.

He knocked harder. He tried to peer in through the small security peephole.

He almost shouted, "Tom. I know you're in there. I heard the television. Open the door. I found something—something you should know about."

He listened and heard nothing now, nothing but white silence.

He pounded on the door, four, five times. "Tom. Open up. It's Hays. Please."

He bent to listen. He heard a muted shuffle-shuffle-shuffle. He stepped back. There was the sound of a deadbolt being turned, then the sound of a chain being unclasped. The doorknob turned and the door opened—slowly. The apartment was dark, the blinds drawn, the lights off.

The hall was lit with an amber glow. As the door opened, Hays felt a glowing ember of terror in his gut.

Did he catch the virus? Did he somehow manage to catch it by opening the tomb?

Standing in the shadows, holding the door with both hands, stood Tom. He leaned into the door, his forehead almost resting on the door edge.

"Don't get too close. I think I have the flu."

Hays breathed an audible sigh of relief. "The flu? Are you sure? Nothing else?"

Tom retreated into the dim interior. "No. Nothing else. I've had the flu before and this is what it felt like." Tom sniffed loudly and dragged his sleeve under his nose. He was clad in ill-fitting sweats and socks that puddled around his ankles.

But as he walked, Hays noticed a more pronounced angular jut to his bones. He could see the turn of his wrist and the pronouncement of his shoulder blades. His jawbone looked hard and tight.

Tom flopped onto the couch. A television murmured from the corner—CNN—and the floor was littered with used tissues and empty cans of diet ginger ale.

"I'd offer you something, but I don't think you'd take me up on it," Tom rasped, then sniffed loudly again.

Hays didn't sit. He felt as if an army of germs and bacteria were marching toward his feet, ready to mount an offensive.

"We found a virus ... in the vial in the golden skull," he said.

He waited. Tom looked up, a haze of interest breaking through his cloudy eyes.

"We sort of borrowed the school's electron microscope," Hays added.

Tom laughed and his chest was caught up in a loud, rolling, and rheumy cough. "Did your rats die?"

"A few of them. The virus attacks the lining of the stomach. Starves them to death."

Tom grimaced. "Not a very pleasant bug, is it?"

"No."

Tom took a deep wheezing breath.

"I need to call the CDC. This is big, Tom. And it could be very dangerous. Especially if it were to get loose."

Tom struggled to rise from his prone position. "You can't do that, Hays. You promised. If you go to the CDC, you'll have to tell them where the bug came from. I know all about you and your Bible and all that moral religious mumbo-jumbo. You're not going to lie to the CDC for me, are you?"

Hays shook his head no.

"Then I'm dead. If they find out about the virus, they'll find out that I stole the artifacts. And if they find out about that, then I can kiss my tenure good-bye. I can't have that, Hays. You can't do that to me. I'll be back leading museum tours at seven dollars an hour."

"Tom, if I can't call the CDC with the truth—then you have to think of some other way. I'll keep this as our secret for another few days or so. But after that—I have to call the CDC. If I don't … well, I couldn't live with myself. This is too big and too dangerous."

Tom fell back against the couch. His arms looked rail thin and Hays could see the cords of muscle in his neck. The muscles strained and tensed, as if holding his head erect was a great effort.

"Call me tomorrow, Tom. Please. Think of some way to protect yourself. I can do that much for you."

Tom managed a weak smile. "Thanks. I'll think of something."

Hays was about to turn and walk away, but stopped. "Tom, you should go to a doctor. You sound really sick."

Tom waved him off. "It's just a flu. Seems that half the people in my department have come down with it."

"And you're eating well? Getting enough liquids."

"I've eaten enough broth and crackers to fill a bathtub," he said with a wheeze. "It's just the flu. I'll be fine."

"You need me to get you anything?"

"No. The grocery downstairs delivers. I'm fine."

Hays nodded. "I'll call you tomorrow. If you need something, let me know, okay? And answer your phone."

Tom nodded. "Do me a favor. Toss me my cell phone. It's on the desk over there."

Hays retrieved the phone and tossed it. "I'll call tomorrow," he said.

And as he closed the door behind him, he wondered where the nearest bathroom was. He felt an overwhelming compulsion to wash his hands—and take a shower. But he would have to wait until he got home to do that.

QUADARE CITY, QUADARE—Ayman had never once been summoned back to his home country for a meeting. The e-mail was labeled urgent. Airline tickets were waiting. A car and driver had met him at the airport in Quadare City and deposited him in front of the soulless concrete building and given an office number. "He is expecting you," the driver had said.

Ayman tapped twice at the door. He was both nervous and excited. Seldom was a follower called to return home midway between an assignment. He adjusted his shirt and wiped the tops of his shoes on the backside of his trousers. Wincing, he knew he should have stopped to have them shined before this appearance. But he'd had so little time. The flight had been late in arriving—no doubt caused by the air traffic controllers in New York. He had been told they routinely delayed flights to his country and others in the region. He had been told the controllers were mostly Zionist supporters.

He tapped lightly at the outside door again. He waited.

From inside the office he heard a bellowing.

"Is there no one out there? Where is that useless son of a she-dog? Come in, then."

Ayman eased the door open and stepped into the room, almost moving sideways, attempting to be as obsequious as possible.

"Who are you?" The small man behind the desk leaned forward and waited. "Well?"

Ayman looked about, now more nervous than ever. The air was still and hot and he felt a trickle of sweat form in the middle of his back.

"Ayman, sir," he said, intimidated. "Ayman Qal Atwah."

"Ayman?"

Ayman nodded. "From America."

Fadhil sighed deeply, his patience obviously thin. "America? America is a large place. From where in America?"

"Pittsburgh, sir."

Fadhil squinted at him. "And who called you? Why are you here?"

The young man's face grew flushed. The trickle of sweat had become a wetness on his arms and stomach and face. "Uhhh, sir ... I was told that you did, sir."

Fadhil looked both agitated and surprised. "I called you? I don't believe I'm in the habit of calling—"

Just then the interior door swung open again. Hameed quickly stepped inside, walked to Ayman, and extended his hand.

Fadhil sputtered. "Is there no one at the desk? Is he hiding again? If he were not the cousin of my cousin I would have him caned."

Hameed ignored the rant and embraced Ayman in the traditional Quadare manner. "It is good that you could come."

Ayman appeared to take his first deep breath since his arrival. "Thank you sir. You are … Hameed?"

"Yes, I called for you. I have heard of your information and didn't think it wise to trust such information to phones or computers. Certain matters must be handled face-to-face. After all, that is the Quadare way, is it not?"

Ayman brightened and nodded in smiling agreement. "Yes, sir. Thank you, sir."

Fadhil half stood. "Please—what is all this about? I dislike not being told of the workings—"

Hameed didn't look in Fadhil's direction and cut him off in mid-sentence. "This is the young man from the University of Pittsburgh. He has information concerning the skull that was stolen from Iran some time ago."

Fadhil brightened like a child with a new toy. "Ahh, yes. And this young man knows about this matter—how, exactly? Was he with this infidel American in Iran?"

"Ayman is employed at the same university as the American. He has seen the skull. And he knows what they have found within that golden skull."

Fadhil jumped up from his chair, his face shining with excitement. "Yes. Of course. The curse. It has been foretold. You have news of this curse."

Ayman took a step backwards in surprise.

Hameed took his arm and said softly, almost whispering in his ear. "Please. In your own words. Tell us what you have discovered."

Ayman cleared his throat and spoke for ten minutes, describing how he had come to learn of the discovery and his good fortune in having met Sutton's new female assistant. Fadhil grew visibly excited as Ayman told of his relationship with Roberta.

"Women are so much bolder in America," Ayman explained. Hameed could barely contain his disgust at Fadhil's prurient interest.

Ayman spoke of seeing the skull, with Roberta allowing him access to the lab. He spoke of the virus symptoms visibly manifested in the lab animals.

"The animals quickly grew emaciated. Roberta claimed the virus attacks the lining of the stomach. The animals eat but starve."

Fadhil nearly jumped when he spoke those words. "The book. Where is that book?" he shouted. "Hameed. Where have you hidden that book?"

Hameed couldn't help himself. "It is where you placed it—in the safe behind the map," he sneered.

Fadhil ran to the east wall, lifted the framed map from its hanger, and let it fall to the ground. Hameed winced, hearing the glass crack. Fadhil hadn't locked the safe and he swung the door open. He grabbed the book and ran to his desk, flipping the pages.

"Where is that? Where is it?" Fadhil said, his words frantic with excitement. "Yes. Yes. Here it is. As was predicted!" he shouted, dancing about.

"The shaman let the desert wind turn the pages. He called upon the spirit of the desert and all those who have gone on to glory to breathe upon this book and show me the way. And they did. They opened the book to this page. Then the wind stopped."

He pointed. There were two rust-colored splatters on the page. "And then with the blood of a sacrifice, he asked the gods to show us the future. And they did. Read what it says, Hameed. Read it to us again. The words between the blood."

Hameed drew closer. He was sure Fadhil could read—but not very well.

"It is from their Bible—and from the book called Micah. '*Thou shalt eat, but not be satisfied; and thy casting down shall be in the midst of thee; and thou shalt take hold, but shalt not deliver; and that which thou deliverest will I give up to the sword.*'"

Fadhil danced and beamed, clapping his hands as a joyous child might before opening a birthday gift. "They will starve even with food on their table. And nothing they have will save them—it will all be put to the sword. And we, Hameed, we are that sword."

Fadhil collapsed onto his chair, almost careening backwards. His face glistered with a sheen of sweat and hunger.

"And you now know what to do? When you return to America, you must follow my instructions exactly. You must be extremely discreet in all your actions."

Ayman nodded.

"Now go to the house of your mother. Celebrate tonight. Spare no expense."

The young man smiled. "I will not fail you."

"My prayers will be following you," Hameed said.

He watched Ayman climb into the taxi. He nodded as it drove away. Then he took the satellite phone from his breast pocket and dialed a number starting with sixty-nine—the international area code for Frankfurt, Germany.

PITTSBURGH, PENNSYLVANIA—"Number sixteen died last night," Duffy said, the moment Hays entered the lab.

Hays never felt more like cursing, but instead muttered "Rats. And how do the last two look?"

Duffy brightened. "Actually, they look fine. It appears this virus does not have a 100 percent morbidity rate after all. And both animals were injected. It means that some animals have a built-in immunity."

Hays tossed his backpack onto his desk. "Thank heaven for small favors," he said.

Duffy closed the lab book and laid his pen on the table. "We need to call the CDC."

Hays didn't look his friend in the face. "I know. We will. But when we do, Tom is out. The university won't keep him. And with this on his record, he can forget about being hired anywhere." Hays sighed, leaned against the wall, and continued. "I thought that once I became a believer, all the hard questions would become easy."

He and Duffy talked often about Hays' faith. Duffy had been his friend before he found God, and was still his friend now—even if he didn't share the same beliefs.

Hays replied, his face tight, "What happens when you're faced with two equally hard choices? I call the CDC and Tom is fired and will never work again in his field. I don't call the CDC and maybe everyone on earth is at risk from this new virus."

Duffy didn't wait long before replying. "Seems pretty obvious to me."

Hays stared at his feet. "After reducing it to such a simple equation, it seems pretty obvious to me as well."

"Then we call them?

Hays took a long breath. "We'll call them—first thing tomorrow morning."

Duffy nodded, satisfied that the two of them would no longer bear the burden of keeping the horrible virus a secret. He flipped open his lab reporting book and began to write.

The day passed quickly. Their work for Huber/Loss had taken a new promising turn, and the change in testing parameters meant longer hours and more rigorous examination of the intermediate results.

Both men felt happy to be lost in productive work again—work that was neither secret nor dangerous. It was nearly nine o'clock when they finished the complete weight and caloric intake analysis for the one hundred test animals.

Hays stretched and let his back snap and crack.

"Don't do that around me," Duffy chided. "It sounds disgusting."

Hays laughed. "For a man who knows how to break someone's neck silently, a few bone cracks shouldn't be too hard to take."

"That was a long time ago, my friend. One gets out of practice breaking necks pretty quickly."

Hays smiled. Neither man had actually been involved in real-life, one-to-one, mortal combat. Yet it was a skill both possessed.

"You want to stop for dinner?" Hays asked. "The Original is still open."

"No, not tonight. I think I'll just head home. I rode my bike to work."

"I could take you and the bike home. I drove."

"No thanks. I need the exercise."

Duffy enjoyed riding, even in the city. He became less visible to drivers at night, but the traffic was usually lighter, so the tensions balanced themselves out.

He turned the corner at Bigelow and sped up to build momentum for the long uphill climb. Pittsburgh was a series of painful uphill climbs and exhilarating downhills. He envied Hays; if he lived where his friend did, it would be a half block up the hill, then all downhill to home.

From the small mirror on his handlebars, Duffy caught sight of headlights. He pursed his lips. He had seen the same headlights three blocks back. The car, an older model silver Mercedes, had sped past him. Now it was behind him again. The car had a diesel engine, with the signature rattling cough.

The hairs on the back of his neck stood up. It was an old but familiar feeling. Not since his days in the Rangers had he felt the same.

He turned two blocks early and headed in the general direction of Hays' apartment.

The silver Mercedes went straight.

He breathed a sigh of relief. Then he turned back north, up Summerlea, heading eventually to Bigelow. He stopped at a red light. In his mirror he saw the headlights.

It was the silver Mercedes.

Again.

10

PITTSBURGH, PENNSYLVANIA—The shadowy silver Mercedes had to be the same car Duffy had seen three times on his ride home that night. With a jolt he realized he was being followed.

What he didn't know was by whom and for what reason.

Duffy was not a man easily intimidated or scared, and this situation proved no exception. If the people in the car following him meant to do him harm, they could have easily shot him in the street by now or run him off the road. Apparently his followers were only interested in tracking his whereabouts.

He turned his bike left and then left again.

The driver of the silver Mercedes was good, and Duffy saw, from the corners of his vision, that the car was still following him—a block or two away, but it was there.

He rode up to the older, somewhat ramshackle Victorian house on a quiet street in Shadyside. He parked his bike, locked the wheels with his chain, and locked that chain to a light pole. He maintained an even step, and tapped lightly at the door at the second floor landing. After a moment, it swung open.

"Duffy? What—"

Duffy turned his back to the street and placed his finger on his lips. He stepped in and Hays stepped aside, shutting the door after him.

Duffy didn't speak, but walked into the bathroom, flushed the toilet, and turned the water on.

He leaned close to his friend. "I've been followed. A silver Mercedes with three, maybe four men in it. They haven't tried anything, and I don't think they will. There is another Mercedes—an old blue sedan—parked at the end of your block. Does it belong here?"

Hays shook his head no and whispered his reply. "I've never seen an old Mercedes in the neighborhood—but that doesn't mean it doesn't belong."

"There are three men inside that car—all slouched down. I saw the tops of their heads when a car passed. I'm sure they are watching this building. Someone is watching both of us."

"The virus?"

"Yes, the virus."

"But why? I don't understand—"

"Of course you do. People—or terrorists—steal anthrax, and that stuff makes a lousy weapon. This virus—your virus—you know how lethal it is, and how much more lethal it probably could be."

Duffy turned the water off. If a listening device was in place, running water for too long was a dead giveaway that the pursued knew about the pursuit. He stepped into the hall. In a normal voice, he asked, "Are you going to offer me a drink or not? We could order a pizza."

Hays nodded. He understood what Duffy was doing. "Get a Coke from the fridge. I'm not hungry. But you could call if you want."

He leaned in close to Duffy. He whispered softly. "Who knows about this? Who would be following you?"

"Us, my friend. Who is following us?"

Hays managed a grim, sardonic smile. "But who knows about the virus?"

Duffy opened the refrigerator and rattled a bottle out and unscrewed the cap. He leaned in closer to Hays. "We know. Roberta knows. Beverly knows at least something about it … that we're studying it, anyhow. And then there's Reese. And their assistants. That Middle Eastern guy at the physics lab. Maybe a dozen people. But maybe only you and I know how deadly it is.

"You know what we have to do, don't you?" Duffy whispered.

Hays nodded. His eyes narrowed. It was the look Duffy remembered seeing during their training as Army Rangers—what seemed like a lifetime ago.

"I'll stay here for a while longer. Is there a game on?" Duffy whispered.

"I have ESPN. There's always a game on."

"Then we need to turn on the television. And you need to get ready."

Hays nodded. Duffy walked into the kitchen, snapped the television on, and switched to ESPN.

With soft steps Hays walked to his closet in the guest bedroom. Without turning on any lights, he reached in toward the back. He pulled out a single piece jumpsuit—all black, with a dozen pockets.

He took a deep breath. *I hope it still fits.*

It hadn't taken long. Hays had dressed and now stood at the ready. A black watch cap was pulled low around his face. He stuffed a gray Pitt sweatshirt under the jumpsuit and a baseball cap in one of the pockets. Once he got a few blocks from home, he'd need the look of a normal fellow on a normal evening stroll. It would be unwise to stroll up Liberty Avenue looking like a cat burglar. He walked out into the kitchen. Duffy nodded silently and mouthed the question, "Are you ready?"

Hays nodded. He leaned in to whisper one last word. "You need to go home and act like everything is normal. I can handle it from here."

Duffy gave him the signal that he understood.

"I think I'll head home," Duffy said in a loud voice. "I'm on my bike— and if I'm fast, I can catch the last quarter from my place."

"Okay, then. I'll see you tomorrow."

Duffy took his time to open the front door, called out another farewell, adjusted his jacket, and then closed the door loudly. As he did that, Hays slipped out of his kitchen window, which overlooked the roof of the back porch below. A large cottonwood tree shielded the sloping roof from the street. He carefully lowered the window behind him and crawled to the edge of the roof.

He crouched at the end of the roof, and jumped, aiming for a dense patch of garden. The soil would be soft enough to break his fall and the foliage thick enough to hide him. He prayed his landlady wouldn't be sitting on the porch.

He landed with a soft harrumph and rolled to his knees. He destroyed a rose bush in his fall and a few thorns dug into his thigh. He would some- how find a way to replace the rose bush tomorrow—or blame it on the neighbor's dog.

Hays made it to the alley and crossed the narrow way in the shadows of the garage. Rather than head down the alley, which would have exposed him at either end, he headed straight past the house on the other side of it. He kept low and ran fast past the neighbor's garage, rear yard, and house. He crossed three more blocks in much the same manner.

A block away from Liberty, he pulled his sweatshirt out of his jumpsuit and pulled it over his head. He added the baseball cap and pulled it low over his face. He knew he looked no different now than a thousand other campus regulars.

He looked over his shoulder, stepped to the curb quickly, and hailed the first cab that passed.

"University Towers," he said.

The towers stood a block east of his office building. If he was being watched at home, he was certain his office was facing the same scrutiny.

Roberta kicked off her shoes and ran to answer the phone. She pulled her earring off and held the receiver close. "Hello?"

"Ahh, my sweet Roberta. I have found you at home. May Allah be praised."

"Ayman?"

"Of course, my sweet. I have missed you."

Her checks blushed pink. "You called from Quadare? That is so sweet of you. I never expected you to call."

A buzz of static filled the line.

"Hello? Hello?"

"Yes, sweet Roberta, I hear you."

There was a crackle and hiss.

"You're breaking up, Ayman."

A whoosh of silence filled her ear.

"Roberta, I'm calling to tell you I'm returning home tomorrow."

"Tomorrow? But you have only been there two days."

She listened closely through the static and heard Ayman say something about a reduced fare and an empty seat and his mother needing to travel on his ticket.

"That's wonderful, Ayman. I miss you."

A shrill burst of static erupted. Then she heard him clearly.

"And what will you do tonight? Stay in? Or dine out without me? I'm missing you so."

She wrinkled her nose. It was such a curious question. But Ayman often asked curious questions.

"Linda is taking me to Mazeroski's. She said she wanted Polish food. You remember Linda, don't you?"

"I remember her, yes. Just don't meet any of her boyfriends. That I will not like at all."

She giggled. He was jealous. "Of course not. Just me and Linda. I'll be back by nine."

"That is so very good. I miss you, my sweet American girl."

Roberta sighed.

Then the line went dead. She held the phone to her ear for another few moments, hoping he would come back on. A busy signal replaced the silence, then a dial tone.

He cares about me. He really, really does. He is so unlike my father.

Roberta wondered why the thought of her father came to mind. She closed her eyes remembering how her father towered over her and her mother, his fists raised in anger. She remembered his shouts that neither Roberta nor his worthless wife were of any value. She stopped and with as much force as she could muster, attempted to banish that hot, shaming sense of powerlessness and inferiority that welled up from deep within her.

After dinner Roberta stood at her front door. She reached into her purse and felt for her keys. She scowled. She reached in deeper, then lifted out her billfold. She shook the purse hoping to hear the jangle of keys and key chain.

There was no metallic sound at all.

That's odd. I'm sure I put them in here when I left.

She felt around the bottom of the purse one last time.

Didn't I put them in here? I couldn't have lost them at the restaurant. I never took them out of my purse.

She dropped the purse to the ground, then stood on the old milk box, tiptoed, and stretched to reach the top of the window frame. She tapped at the flat wood with her fingers. Finally, she felt the irregular edge of her secret key.

She stepped down, picked up her purse, unlocked the door, slipped inside, and snapped on the lights.

"Now where is that keychain hiding?"

Hays waited until the cab faded into the night. He didn't walk toward the front door of the University Towers, but instead, walked to the north side of the building.

Because it housed only faculty offices, there were no security guards at this location. The north side of the building was a windowless slab of concrete, and the sidewalk was as dark as the darkest area of campus.

Hays walked quickly and stopped midway along the building. He knelt down in front of a metal window well grating. He grabbed it and gave it a slight pull. It was still loose.

Hays stared into the darkness and neither saw nor heard anyone. He hefted the grate to the side and slipped down into the utility well. He pulled the grate overtop him and snugged it into place. It was all over in less than five seconds. Bending down, he took cover in the blackest shadow in the dark utility well. A cobweb tickled at his nose. He didn't move, but just listened. There were no sounds save the rumble of traffic along Forbes Avenue two blocks away. Hays waited another minute, then moved to the small, square, metal-framed window in the interior of the well. He ran his fingers around the frame. There were no handholds. He reached inside the large pocket on the thigh of his jumpsuit and extracted a flat metal bar. He wedged it against the frame.

Dear Lord, he prayed, *let this be as it was—unlocked.*

He shouldered the bar, and the window rasped open with a squeal. He held it open with his shoulder and peered inside.

The hallway was bathed in a soft red glow from an emergency exit sign. He saw no movement.

Hays slid feet first into the opening, holding the window up with his head. He lowered himself along the wall, his feet scrabbling for a firm purchase. His sneaker dug into a small cleft. He looked down—only four feet to the floor. He pulled his head in and lowered the window until it was almost to his fingers. Then he jumped backwards lightly. The window banged shut, louder than he had expected. He tensed and waited in the far shadows. He heard nothing.

To his left the service corridor led to the west, traveling under Arch Street and connecting the two buildings in a common run of utilities and piping. The building directly opposite the University Towers was the Medical Arts Building—and Hays' laboratory.

From another pocket he extracted a small flashlight. He flashed it along the corridor, then snapped it off. The floor and aisle were clear. He could keep one hand on the wall and walk—even in complete darkness. He worried that the flashlight might draw attention to himself, and he couldn't risk that.

Two years ago, when he had set up his lab, he, with the school, was forced to petition the city for sewage rights—all according to the city zoning regulations. Since he was dealing in diseases and viruses, the city had been justly concerned that someone might flush mistakes down the drain. If a hazardous incident did occur, the city wanted to know where the sewer lines drained and the location of all the tapped catch basins—the large holding tanks for sewage were standard for all medical laboratories as well as being mandated by city zoning regulations. Three building engineers, five city workers, one of the original architects of the building, three maintenance workers, and Hays had spent three days tracing sewer lines and locating catch basins.

The service corridors of most of the university buildings were interconnected; a man with a blueprint might travel from one end of the campus to another and never once see the sun. At the end of their daylong search, the group had come to the very spot in the building that Hays entered tonight.

The university's maintenance supervisor had spotted the unlocked service door and had blustered about security and incompetence of union labor. He'd sputtered at one of his assistants, a union member according to his lapel pin, to make note of it to be repaired. Hays remembered catching the fellow rolling his eyes, as if saying, "Who died and made you the boss of me?"

Some six months later, Hays had brought Duffy down to the same spot. Duffy needed to know the location of the catch basins as well. Hays had checked the access panel and sure enough, it remained unsecured.

"You never know when being aware of the location of this might come in handy," Hays had said.

Duffy slowly pedaled his bike home, all the while keeping an eye on the silver Mercedes following him. He'd taken a long time to unbolt his bike from the locks and ready himself to ride. In all that time the blue Mercedes down the block never moved. He was certain Hays had managed to slip out of his apartment undetected.

From the small bathroom window of his apartment, Duffy looked out over the busy street.

The silver Mercedes sat in a pool of light from the streetlight—nearly a half a block away. Duffy could see curls of smoke from the driver's side window and the glowing ember of a cigarette.

The sub-basement hallways of the Medical Arts Building intersected. Each of the three corridors was lit with the same unearthly red glow from the exit signs reflecting off the institutional beige walls. Hays spotted his flashlight beam at the door to his left: "Service/Medical Arts."

He tried the doorknob. The doorknob turned easily.

He hurried up the seven flights of stairs. The service stairwell in the Medical Arts Building opened into a small vestibule, with two doors on the west wall and two doors on the east. Hays stepped to the door marked No. 708. He pulled out a ring of keys and fumbled through them. One key fit the lock and he turned it silently.

Hays entered his lab through a door on the opposite side of the isolation chambers. Since the chambers had been installed two years ago, no one had ever used this door.

He unlocked a second inner door and hurried past the isolation rooms. He entered the main lab and carefully looked out one of the narrow slit windows. The university squad car idled in its normal spot across the street in the corner of the main parking lot. No hint of movement or extra security measures was evident.

Hays went first to his computer. He tapped in his access code. He needed to download his records and reports, even though the handwritten records were more complete and up to date.

The screen flickered. "Access Denied."

Hays never felt more like cursing than at this moment.

He typed the number in again. "Access Denied. UnivDataCom Network Down for Service."

Hays could only stare at the screen in angry disbelief. Then he shut his eyes tight. He remembered the e-mail announcing that the computer system would be off-line tonight—something about adding new file servers.

Hays smacked his hand on the side of the computer. "Blast it," he uttered softly.

There came a soft echo—from the hallway—of footsteps.

Hays sat bolt upright. *Does the security guard make rounds? Does this building even still have a roaming night security guard?*

Whoever it was out in the hall, they made no attempt to soften their steps. Hays heard the soft murmur of voices, though he couldn't make out a single distinct word. *There are three of them … maybe four.*

The outside hallway was partially lit. Hays saw a shadowy form stop just outside his door. Whoever was outside stood silhouetted against the frosted glass.

Hays could see one man gesture to another, and someone spoke. The words were not in English. The first shadow turned and gestured to a companion.

It was then that Hays moved—and moved quickly.

Shadowed against the glass was the unmistakable outline of an Uzi machine gun. Hays had used that weapon while in the Rangers and was perfectly acquainted with its deadly effectiveness. It was especially deadly at short range. A short burst of bullets would easily tear a man in two.

He blinked. Criminals loved the weapon—it was easy to use, relatively accurate, cheap, and easy to dismantle and hide under a coat.

Hays heard the jangling sound of a key ring. Someone laughed. It was a guttural laugh. A leering laugh followed.

Hays sucked in a breath of air, stood, and ran toward the isolation room. As he entered the chamber's door, he could see from the corner of his eye the main lab door swing open. He saw a glint of light from the black gunmetal barrel and the silhouette of three men.

He had only a second or two to act.

Four minutes later and two blocks from the University Towers, Hays stopped and gasped for air. He dropped two quarters in the pay phone outside the 7-Eleven store on Forbes Avenue.

He waited for a moment then dialed the number for the campus security office, hoping he would sound less frantic if he weren't panting into the phone.

"I saw some suspicious people on the seventh floor of the Medical Arts Building. There may have been three of them, and they were trying to open all the doors in the hall. They may have had guns."

He hung up, took another deep breath. He knew the campus police had jurisdiction on all campus matters but also knew that this situation may be more than they were trained for.

He dropped another two quarters into the phone and dialed 911 for the city police. He said exactly the same thing to them as he did to the campus security. From what Hays had gathered, neither organization trusted each other—but he felt better involving them both. If someone was carrying an Uzi in plain view, they might be tempted to use it. He did not want anyone's life on his conscience.

In the morning Hays could express great surprise and shock, and pretend that he knew nothing about an anonymous call. He knew that both the police and campus security could respond in minutes—leaving the intruders little time to do damage.

After all, the skull and the one vial were locked in a secure cabinet on the other side of the lab, hidden behind a false front and a stack of old magazines. The second vial was locked in the small but sturdy security safe tucked away beneath Hays' desk. The safe was usually empty, until these last few weeks.

Only Hays knew the combination to his safe. The isolation chamber was locked, and the deadbolt was sturdy. It would be impossible to break through without making a mess and a loud racket. And once inside, the intruders would find the interior door to the animal cages was locked as well.

Given all these situations, conditions, safeguards, and serendipities— even though Hays was certain that the intruders carried sophisticated tools and insider knowledge—they would need at least an hour to find the secrets that lay hidden in his lab.

He breathed a sigh of relief. There was not much else he could have done.

And as he walked the dark streets, he felt a guilty twinge. All of this had started with a lie. A lie told for a friend was no less a lie.

Tomorrow I will settle all this. I'll call the CDC in the morning, and even if Tom gets fired, I'll not risk my honor and truthfulness for him or anyone else— at least not any longer.

Twenty minutes later Hays stood alone on a darkened street on the far southern edge of Shadyside. He looked up to the second story windows. A blue light flickered from the front room.

The stairs creaked with great familiarity as he climbed the steps and faced the green door on the second floor. There was a small silver rectangular nameplate on the door with elegant engraving. Hays could just make out the letters in the pale moonlight: Norah Neale.

He took another deep breath. And then he tapped at the door. He waited, then called out, "Norah? It's me. Hays. Don't be alarmed. I need a favor."

Hays heard shuffling behind the door. He was certain Norah was peering at him through the peephole. He stepped back so she could see him more clearly in the reflected light of the streetlamp on the corner. "See? It's me. Hays."

The door opened only the length of the inside security chain. "Hays? What are you doing here? It's almost midnight."

Hays nodded. "I know."

"What do you want?" Norah asked. Her voice was wary but warm.

Hays offered what he hoped was a reassuring smile. "Do you like animals?"

Ten minutes later Hays was sitting in Norah's kitchen. Norah had her gray robe tightly belted at the waist and pulled up high under her chin.

"I still don't understand," she said, casting a glance to the corner of the room. "And I don't like rats."

Hays held his hands out, fingers spread, palms down, as if trying to calm the situation. Hays had brought with him two white rats. Norah stepped back when he lifted the Velcro flaps on his breast pockets and the two small creatures shyly emerged. Their pink noses twitched and they blinked their eyes nervously under the bright kitchen lights.

"I know you don't," Hays said as he adjusted the screen over Norah's terrarium—the expensive terrarium that he had bought her as a gift years ago. He placed a book on each end of the protective screen that lay across the open top. The two rats paid no attention to him, but instead concentrated on the small pile of Ritz crackers he tossed in with them.

"Please, Hays—tell me what's really going on. How long am I supposed to keep these rats here? You know my landlord says no pets."

"These aren't pets. And you'll only have to keep them for a day or two—at most. And about explaining all this … I don't think I can tell you any more than I already have."

Norah narrowed her eyes. "I can tell when you're lying, Hays. We were together a long time, remember?"

Hays lowered his head as if in defeat. "I'm not lying. Really. I just can't keep these rats in my lab. It's sort of complicated."

"And it has nothing to do with the Huber/Loss tests?"

Hays shook his head. "Nothing at all."

"And they're not contagious?"

"Not in the least."

Hays told himself that was a true statement. After all, the pair of rats had either been injected with the virus or consumed it. And now, weeks later, they were absolutely healthy, showing no signs of any illness. Hays was a scientist—and he knew viruses. If an active virus entered a patient, that patient would quickly show symptoms. These two rats showed no symptoms. They had immunity. Hays was sure of that.

From an immune patient, a vaccine might be developed.

Hays knew he had no choice. He had to believe in this. He could not take the rats home. He couldn't leave them in the lab. He had no choice.

And on his walk home, he convinced himself that the remotest of risks, the ten-million-to-one sort of risk would have to be worth it. It would simply have to be.

Hays closed his eyes for a moment. *These two rats were exposed to the virus and are still amazingly healthy,* he thought to himself. *They must have antibodies in their blood and are immune to the effects of the virus. I've seen it before. If they're not sick now—they never will be. And if they are immune, a vaccine could be developed. These two rats are very, very precious.*

Norah allowed herself a wary smile. "This is just like you, Hays. Some oddball scheme that makes no sense. And you came to me for help. Should I be pleased that you came to me first?"

"I—I don't know. I guess."

She smiled. "I have always known you were a man of strong convictions."

"I am."

She reached out and placed her hand on his. She squeezed it tight. "And if it takes two rats to get us talking again, then so be it."

"Thank you, Norah. Thank you for being such a good friend."

She smiled, leaned forward, and kissed Hays lightly on his lips. "You're welcome," she said.

Hays barely slept that night. The blue Mercedes remained parked in the middle of the next block, forcing him to shimmy up the cottonwood tree and climb back into his apartment through the unlatched kitchen window.

At six in the morning, he was dressed and ready to head to work. The blue Mercedes was still there. He thought it best to wait until his normal time of departure, so he spent another forty-five minutes in nervous agony.

When his watch showed 6:45 a.m., he grabbed his backpack and bounded down the stairs. Walking briskly, he took the sidewalk opposite the blue Mercedes. As he passed, he glanced in their direction. There were three men inside, two asleep in the back, and one, the driver, slouched behind the wheel. One looked to be Filipino, and the other two could have been from anywhere—almost any country in the Middle East, or even Greece or Italy.

The driver didn't even look up as Hays passed. But once he got to the corner of the block, Hays turned, as subtly as he could, and watched the car slowly pull away from the curb and head off in the opposite direction.

Duffy was already in the office. Hays stopped short of the door, then entered. He looked in two places. Both the safe under the desk and the hidden cabinet at the end of the lab were open and empty. Books and papers were strewn all over the floor.

"What happened?"

Duffy turned, a pained look in his eyes.

He picked up the phone and punched in four numbers.

"Listen to this. It was recorded by the voice mail system." The university's voice mail system was designed in-house and chock-full of odd quirks—such as unexpectedly recording incoming calls.

Hays stared at the disarray, slack-jawed, and listened. The first voice was professional and dispassionate.

"Hello, this is campus security. Officer Williamson. We just received a call about a disturbance in your building. Who am I speaking to?"

There was a moment's pause.

"This is Duffy Quahaar." The voice was heavily accented.

"And who are you?" Williamson asked.

"I'm assistant to Mr. Hays Sutton. I'm here for work. Late hours. Tough boss."

Hays stared at Duffy. Both men were incredulous. There was the sound of paper being shuffled.

"Well, that checks out. Mr. Quahaar, have you seen anyone? Out in the hall? People that shouldn't be there?"

"No. No one is here. Only me. Should I ask the night watchman?"

There was laughter on the line. "Night watchman? You don't work late very often, do you? Your building hasn't had a night watchman for the past eight months. Budget cutbacks, remember?"

The second voice laughed. "Budget, yes. I remember."

"We had a report of men with machine guns," the security officer said, clearly not believing the report was true.

"I was out in the hall with … with pipes … for an experiment. Perhaps they saw me with pipes?"

"It could have been, Mr. Quahaar. And you are sure that you have seen no one? No one at all? Our information said they were on your floor."

"No, no one at all."

"Well, then, if everything is under control, I'll let you get back to work."

"Good then. Thank you. All is under control. I have seen no one. If so, I will call your number."

"Thanks Mr. Quahaar. You do that."

"Sir, I will. Good night." Then the line went dead.

Hays stared at Duffy. "Did they get everything?"

Duffy hesitated, looked around again, and nodded. "I think so. The skull is gone. The second vial is gone. All the dead rats are gone. The two live rats are gone."

Hays held up his palm. "No. They're not. I have them. The two rats were all I managed to take."

Duffy took a deep breath. "Then thank God for small favors."

QUADARE CITY, QUADARE—A storm of static clattered and charged through the phone. "… have got all … may Allah be praised … we have everything … we have found everything …" And then the line went silent and dead.

Fadhil threw the phone to the side. Slowly, he grinned, then tilted his head back in a rolling boil of laughter.

11

PITTSBURGH, PENNSYLVANIA—"We need to call the FBI," Duffy said as he nudged a molecular biology book that was lying on the floor. Hays stood in the door, almost unwilling to enter.

"I did," Hays said. "As soon as I saw what happened. With what is missing, I knew I had to. The FBI is very polite and very professional. I told them about the missing virus. He asked if the police are involved. I said I didn't know—and he put me on hold and in a minute came back and said they were—and that they were coming in this morning to interview us. The FBI guy said that the local police would start the process—not me. And he was certain that in this case, if what I was saying was true, the police would call them in immediately."

Duffy knelt down at Hays' desk. He pushed at the door of the safe with a pencil. "They took everything."

Hays took a deep breath. "Don't touch anything just yet."

Duffy stood up and stepped back. Several notebooks appeared to be missing. A flurry of loose papers was scattered on the floor. The door to the isolation chamber was open as well as the inner door to the cages. Obviously, someone had keys to every lock—or had been trained at lock-picking.

"What do we tell them is missing?" Duffy asked.

Hays lowered his head and massaged his temples with his right hand.

"We have to tell them everything."

Hays pulled Roberta's chair from her desk and sat down wearily. His shoulders sagged.

"Duffy, you know as well as I do that this wasn't done by some dumb criminal looking for a VCR to pawn for crack money."

Duffy nodded in agreement and said, "Last night—those people following us are all part of this, aren't they?"

Hays looked up. His lost stare betrayed him. "They must be. Why else would we be followed? Someone must have told someone else or someone

103

overheard one of us talking. And it's heard by someone who shouldn't be hearing it."

"I'm not that well connected any more," Duffy replied, "but I suppose I could have found someone willing to pay top dollar for your virus. I could have called an uncle in Lebanon. He would have called a few people—and pretty soon I would have been filthy rich, living on some island in the Caribbean."

Hays smiled.

"Your virus could be that valuable, couldn't it?" Duffy continued.

Hays whispered, "Yes, I think it could be."

"So what do we tell the police?"

Hays sighed. "The truth, I guess. And if we tell them everything, then Tom is implicated in the theft, both of us are implicated in covering it up, and everyone associated with this is involved in a modern-day plague—and letting it loose. We can't tell them about the skull without telling them about the virus—and vice versa."

Duffy exhaled broadly. "Yep—those are the two choices that I see as well," he said, hoisting himself up onto a counter.

He walked to a cabinet midway down the lab, opened the door with a pencil, and extracted a cotton towel. He returned to the desk, and was about to cover the receiver with the cloth to preserve fingerprints. Instead of pretending he was with the CSI, he pulled the cell phone off his belt and punched in the number for campus security.

The three campus security officers were first to arrive and spent an hour in the lab, measuring, taking pictures, creating an inventory, and recording depositions from Hays, Duffy, and Roberta when she arrived.

Four uniformed officers of the city police force arrived a few moments later. "So there was a skull? A human skull?" asked Richard King, a detective for the Pittsburgh police. It appeared that he was the ranking officer—all the other police and security officers milled about quietly in the background as he and Hays spoke.

"No it wasn't a human skull—but a gold one. It was hollow and it had … some dead animals—mice—inside."

Detective King scribbled a note in a very small note pad he kept in his breast shirt pocket. "And where did this skull come from, Mr. Sutton?"

Duffy glanced at Hays. It was obvious that he paused a long moment before responding. "It was sent to us. From a ... researcher in Iran who I had met at a conference a few years ago. He knew I had isolation equipment and wanted me to look inside the skull."

King wrote a few words. "And his name was?"

Duffy spoke up quickly. "Mossel Sadim—from the University of Iran."

Hays did his best not to thank his friend for stepping in with an Arabic-sounding name. They both knew the truth was not being told—but in that instant, Hays wanted to extend Tom one last bit of protection.

The detective tapped his pencil on his tiny notebook. "So ... what makes the skull ... or what's inside of it so important? I mean, other than it being gold and all?"

Hays took a deep breath, and slowly, carefully, attempted to recreate the series of events that lead up to this morning. He did not claim that the virus discovered was a new plague, but insisted that it was dangerous. When he recounted the effects of the virus on the rats, every officer in the room, stood up straighter, tried their best not to touch or lean on anything else, and paid very close attention to the rest of the interview.

Hays brought the story up to the present moment.

"And can you tell me what's missing from the lab? Have you had time to review ... any inventory?" The detective had been sitting up, rigid, as if he did not want to take up any more space in the lab than was necessary.

"The skull is gone, of course. As well as all the contents inside. All the dead rats are missing. Our notebooks are gone."

"What about the cages where the rats were kept?" King asked.

"All of them had been sterilized ... completely cleaned. We use radiation. All except two."

"And they are where?"

"They were taken as well. The people who did this took a carton of bio-hazard bags. They must have gathered up all the material in them."

King nodded. "It makes sense. Nobody wants to open a biohazard bag. You would be surprised what sort of loot you can hide that way."

The detective flipped through the pages of his notebook, stopping every two or three pages to add a word or two. When he came to the end, he looked hard at Hays. "Mr. Sutton, you have presented us a problem. I'm not sure I like problems."

Hays wondered if he should offer an apology—but for what, he did not know.

"You see, Mr. Sutton," the detective continued, "anyone can see that a burglary has taken place here. And I would be a fool to say that even a vague hint of a biological threat is something that we would think trivial. In this era of making weapons out of innocents, we policemen must be ever vigilant."

Surprised at King's sudden literate improvement, Hays felt guilty at thinking he should have asked for a more senior detective.

"At first, I considered having our Hazmat team come in and do a sweep of the lab. But it sounds as if you were careful and precise—like any good scientist. And it appears that our burglars were careful and precise—and very, very thorough. They left nothing behind for us to examine. There are no prints—as expected—except yours. There are no witnesses—other than that anonymous call to campus security and to our police. Your campus security called this office and were told that all was well. And a team of our city police officers searched the building a few minutes thereafter—outside of our official jurisdiction—but we in the Pittsburgh Police Department are careful. The officers found nothing amiss. All doors were locked. No people wandering about. This office was snug and quiet. No criminal activity noted at all."

Hays wanted to protest, wanted to say something in the face of the detective's powerful logic, but was stopped by his raised palm.

"We do get any number of prank police calls every year—and not surprisingly, a number of them originate from this very university. Yet we took our jobs seriously, we investigated, we found nothing."

King made a small show of folding his notebook and slipping it into his pocket. "Now I am in the position of seeing evidence of a burglary, but having nothing—and I mean nothing—to investigate. No physical evidence left. No suspects. No suspected suspects. Nothing. And I ask myself—what do I do next? Call in the CDC? Call in the FBI? I am afraid, Mr. Sutton, that short of finding one of these dead rats tossed in a trash bin, we have very, very little to go on. I am sure that our friends in Washington and Atlanta would agree with my assessment."

Hays moved his mouth, as if attempting to jump-start a sentence—but no words came.

"So, Mr. Sutton, do you see my predicament?"

Hays snapped his fingers. "Why didn't I think of this earlier? Of course I have proof. The images from the EMS."

"EMS?" King asked.

"The physics lab—their electron microscope. We have six images stored in their files." Hays hurried over to his computer terminal. He entered his user name and password. The screen went blank for a moment.

A box popped up: "File not found."

Hays turned to Duffy. "We did call the folder H&D, didn't we?"

Duffy nodded as he typed it in again. Detective King took his notebook out of his short pocket, and opened it to a blank page.

"File not found? What do they mean, 'File not found'?"

Duffy dialed a number on the phone. "Beverly, its Duffy. I need a favor. We need are those images we took on the EMS. We tried to access them, but the computer keeps telling us that the file isn't found. Can you help?"

Duffy listened for a long moment. "But we never gave any order to delete. Why would we do that?"

He turned back to Hays, his face mirroring the bleak concern of his words. "But we never authorized the deletion. We didn't. There must be a way you can recover them, isn't there?"

He waited. "Are you sure?" He sighed deeply. "Okay. Thanks for your help."

Duffy hung up the phone. "The images are gone. Two days ago, she got an e-mail from you—your address was on it. She said the e-mail had your access code and password. It said you had copied the images to a separate hard drive and she could delete them. And she deleted them. It happens all the time, she said. Not much room on the servers for the physics lab—so people are always copying and deleting. She thought that's what you had done. So they're gone—for good."

Hays slumped further into his chair and closed his eyes.

King slowly closed his notebook and slipped it carefully back into the breast pocket of his shirt, and then placed his pencil there, point up.

A steady stream of the curious stopped by Hays' lab that morning to commiserate with him and Duffy. A few guests mentioned that since their Huber/Loss research work wasn't disturbed, they shouldn't be too distraught.

Neither Hays nor Duffy made mention of the virus that they thought they had discovered.

Roberta remained quiet during all of the visits, busying herself with straightening up the lab and doing some of the routine reporting that the Huber/Loss project guidelines required.

"This seems to have bothered her a lot," Duffy whispered to Hays mid-morning.

"She's a woman. This is a violation of security—her comfort. I think this sort of thing is harder on women,"

Duffy nodded, but arched his eyebrow in response. "Awfully quiet, is all. More quiet than I would have imagined."

Norah stopped by just before lunch. "I just heard. I was at a meeting across campus. I'm so sorry for you," she said.

"It's okay, Norah. Really," Hays said calmly. "No one was harmed. We lost a few things, but nothing that can't be replaced."

"You've called the police, haven't you? Do I need to notify Huber/Loss?"

Hays shook his head. He quickly filled her in on what had transpired, not once letting his eyes move from her, while her hands gripped his tightly.

"What can I do, Hays? Is there anything I can do to help?"

Hays smiled. "No. Not that I can think of."

"Well, then, let me take you to lunch," she said brightly, adjusting the blue scarf around her neck. It set off her dark eyes to great advantage. "I'm not sure if that's what etiquette requires—an after-burglary luncheon. But I want to do something. Please say yes."

He felt her squeeze his hands as she asked. From the corner of his eyes, he saw Roberta watching as she did.

"Why don't you all come with us?" Norah asked, obviously hoping no one would take her up on the offer.

Hays looked to Roberta, then to Duffy. Both were saying no with their eyes, even though he was sure Roberta would have loved to tag along. They both claimed other obligations.

"Then just the two of us, Hays. Just like old times."

Hays swallowed, then nodded.

"I'll be back in a minute," Norah said. "I have to get my purse and powder my nose."

Hays stood watching her walk away, taking efficient, quick steps, her hips swaying slightly, her hair swinging. He didn't turn back around, not wanting to see Duffy's and Roberta's expressions.

Roberta waited for a moment, tapping her fingernails on the desktop. She heard Duffy clattering behind her, stacking and unstacking notebooks in the proper chronological order.

Without turning to him, she said, "He still loves her, doesn't he?"

Duffy grunted, "Maybe."

"She still loves him, doesn't she?"

"Absolutely," he replied.

"Then why don't they get back together?"

Duffy stepped over to her desk and sat down facing her, pulling his lab coat over his legs. "You talked to him about this, didn't you?"

She shrugged. "He talked. I listened. It didn't make all that much sense."

"To me either. To outsiders, all of this belief stuff just sounds odd, doesn't it?"

Roberta agreed. "It does."

"So, do you want to go to lunch?"

Roberta smiled at him, then shook her head no.

"I have a few errands to run. But thanks, Duffy. Maybe next time."

"Okay, next time," he replied and noticed a curious look of regret on her face as she turned from him, the same look that seemed to have haunted her all morning. She almost looked ... guilty. Duffy quickly dismissed the idea.

After lunch Hays called the Pittsburgh regional office of the CDC. Hays knew the senior agent—Jack Douglas—having met him during a virology conference at the university last semester.

Back at Hays' lab, Hays told Douglas the same story that he had told Detective King, but this time included a great deal more medical terminology. The CDC agent did not take notes but clicked on a small tape recorder. After speaking for nearly twenty minutes, Hays came to the events of the morning and stopped.

The agent snapped off the recorder. "No evidence, right?"

"No."

"Can they scrub the physics lab's file server? Can they recover the data?"

Duffy spoke up. "We thought of that, too. I called back and was told that server went down that day, losing everyone's data. It was fried. No hope for any recovery."

"Well, now, that is too bad. I would have liked to have seen what you described," Douglas said calmly as if he encountered strange and terrifying new viruses every week. "But I just do not see how I can get the CDC involved in an agency way. There isn't anything to investigate now, is there?"

Hays had to nod his head.

"I can keep my ears open to see if anything hinky pops up—some odd discovery or whatnot. But aside from that, I'm not sure what else I can promise."

Hays did not want to agree with him, but had no choice. What would he expect the agent to do? Investigate a phantom virus that had no evidence, no real presence?

"Listen," Hays said, his words soft, "what would happen if you had a lab animal that had been exposed—but did not exhibit any symptoms? You could test that animal, couldn't you?"

Douglas did not look amused. "You don't have any other lab animals, exposed or otherwise."

"But if I did …?"

Agent Douglas stood as he answered. "Once a virus is dead, they are nigh on impossible to find—especially if a body's antibodies have gone and altered it. Maybe you could find a trace. It would take a lot of luck and months with an electron microscope. I have never heard of it being done. Maybe … if you were lucky … and if you had a few hundred animals with immunity. You'd have to do a lot of dissecting. And you would need an electron microscope in your basement."

The agent opened the lab door. "Well, then. If something else turns up, don't be afraid to give me a call. But as to what you have now—there really is nothing the CDC can do. I'm sorry."

He pulled the door shut after him.

Roberta looked at Duffy, and Duffy stared at Hays.

Hays lowered his eyes. "I guess the only thing left to do is pray."

Duffy couldn't even smile. "That's something you're going to have to do by yourself, my friend," he said. "I don't think Roberta or I carry much weight in that category."

QUADARE CITY, QUADARE—Fadhil stood on his balcony and gazed at the setting sun. At dusk the labyrinth of streets and narrow alleys took on a burnished look, the red tile roofs glowing like embers, the dusty clay walls mirroring the gold of the sun.

To Fadhil it was the most magical time of day, when the promise of his ancestors—now a thousand years past—seemed most real. He was a child when he heard the legends of Quadare, how once it was a great nation, feared by all who heard the name. Soldiers from Quadare, even though small in number, commanded respect from armies ten times their size and larger. Such was the tale of their ferociousness in battle and their heroism when faced with death.

Quadare City glowed and glistened beneath Fadhil's feet. From the east he heard, on the desert wind, the call to prayer. He was not a devout man. Fadhil left that to others. He was more concerned with practical matters, with raising the Eagle of the Desert, the fierce Quadare bird of prey, to its rightful position in the world arena.

He was close. He could taste victory. Even the seers and sorcerers claimed that Fadhil would once again lead this proud nation to victory.

Fadhil turned back to the dark room. "Where is my tea?" he shouted.

There was no sound save silence and the wailing chant of prayers at dusk.

From the darkness came a chirping sound. Fadhil realized he was alone and there was no one to answer the phone. He hurried in, bending at the waist. He couldn't see well, and twice in the last week rushing in the darkened room, he had bashed his toes into the furniture.

He thought the little toe on his left foot was broken, but had decided to wait to seek medical help. He would travel to Germany next week. He could deal with the throbbing pain until then.

"Yes. What is it?" he said into the phone.

Fadhil listened intently. From outside there came the wafting of the final prayer.

"It is? You are sure? Wondrous, wondrous news."

He hung up the phone, smiled broadly and almost without realizing it, he began to dance about the room in great leaps of joy. He danced and laughed and shouted, until he ran his sandaled foot hard against the leg of a table in the corner, and both he and the table collapsed in a great clatter, Fadhil cursing and clutching at his wounded toes in the growing darkness.

12

PITTSBURGH, PENNSYLVANIA—Roberta gathered her purse to her chest. She looked at her watch for a third time in five minutes.

"The wall clock says five p.m. Is that the right time? My watch says five minutes till."

Hays and Duffy had spent the afternoon slumping about the lab, doing only what was absolutely necessary to maintain the schedule with their Huber/Loss testing regime.

Without turning in his chair, Hays waved to her.

"Please. Take off, Roberta. We haven't accomplished anything all afternoon. Five minutes—give or take—won't make any difference."

Her hand on the doorknob, she turned back.

"Are you sure? I can stay and help—or something."

"I'm sure. Go home. Please."

She saw in his eyes an emptiness, as if he were a young child facing the loss of a treasured pet.

"It will all look better tomorrow," she said. "I'm sure of it."

She stepped out into the hall and her smile immediately vanished. She had tried to call Ayman all day, but all she got was an impersonal automatic recording.

"Do you think it will be a better day tomorrow?" Duffy asked as he slouched into his chair, tipping it back to near horizontal.

Hays didn't respond. He closed his eyes, trying to think of what he might have done differently.

Without evidence, all he had were words. The intruders were good, very good. They had taken the skull and everything that had been inside it. They had taken just the notebooks that related to the new virus. They had found and taken the second vial. They had taken the two cages of rats Hays had managed to rescue. They had taken the ten zip-seal bags, each containing the frozen body of a dead rat. They had taken everything that had come into contact with the rats.

It must have required an hour or more to gather up all the material—and a cart or two to carry it all to … wherever it was they took it.

Blast it. Why didn't I stay around to make sure the police came? Why just a phone call? I'm so stupid.

He blinked his eyes. He realized Duffy had spoken.

"What?"

"I said I know you're beating yourself for what happened."

Hays rubbed his eyes. "So what do we do? Call the FBI again?"

Duffy shook his head. "I thought about that, too. But what could we tell them that we didn't tell the CDC and the police? Do you really think they would pay attention to you?"

"Maybe," he said, then a moment later, with a resigned air, he softly added, "but then again, probably not."

Both men wore defeated looks.

"So what do we do? Pray the burglars are inept and that nothing bad happens?"

Duffy opened his palms to the sky.

"Listen, Hays. True, we found a virus. But we don't know if it will be easy to replicate—or even if it will harm a human. It might not. Remember that test last year—when we lost all those rats—and we caught a virus? Nothing more than a sniffle or two. It may not be anything at all. This virus kills rats most efficiently—but we have no evidence that it migrates to humans. It may not migrate easily—or at all."

Hays sighed again. "I hope you're right. I pray that you're right." His mouth tightened. "Are you sure we can't do something? Follow them? You have contacts over there? I mean, we're pretty sure these guys were from the Middle East, right?"

Duffy scowled back, but in a good-natured way.

"You know what I heard? That some of the terrorist cells in the Far East are using Middle East agents to throw people off."

"Really?"

Duffy threw a towel at him.

"You are too trusting, my friend. I just made that up. But the Middle East is not a small place. They might have been from there. But they might have been from anywhere in the world. India, the Philippines, Turkmenistan—any of those other 'stans.' I know what you want to do, Hays—but I don't think that just the two of us will manage to do anything productive."

"So we wait? That's all?"

Duffy shrugged. "It's all we can do. And we make sure those two rats of yours stay alive. Just in case."

"Ayman," she said a bit nervously, "the lab where I work was broken into yesterday."

He looked up from the couch, a wide, satisfied smile on his face.

"Yes, you told me. It's a terrible thing—the crime in America. No one feels safe. In Quadare, there is not such a thing as crime like this. If it happened, we would cut the offender's hands off. A very effective deterrent, let me say."

She snuggled close to him. He draped his arm over her bare shoulder.

"You don't know anything about it, do you?"

Ayman stiffened.

"About what? You accuse me of knowing of this crime?"

She sat up quickly. "No, no, it's not that."

He stood up and glared down at her.

"You did. You accuse me of robbing from your precious lab."

"No. Not you."

Without warning, he pulled his right hand close to his body and then uncoiled it, like a hose under great pressure. The back of his hand caught Roberta full on the cheek. Her teeth scraped across the back of his hand, drawing blood. She tumbled backwards against the couch, her hand flying to her face. The flesh inside her mouth had been cut as well, and she tasted a warm, wet saltiness.

"You cut my hand!" he shouted, and struck her again, with his left hand this time. Roberta cowered in the corner of the couch, hiding her face behind her palms and forearms.

"No, no, Ayman," she said between sobs, "I'm sorry. I shouldn't have said that. I'm sorry. Please, forgive me." She saw her father again, almost alive again in her thoughts as he stormed about shouting that she and her worthless mother were both stupid tramps and always would be. Ayman's words were the same words of her father—horrifying and yet, in a twisted way, oddly comforting.

Ayman stomped out of the room, muttering in his native tongue.

Roberta tried to stand and follow him, but a wave of dizziness forced her back to the couch.

I've done it again, she wept silently. *I've said something stupid and I'm going to drive him away. I won't let him go—he really loves me and I've done something stupid.*

She forced herself to her feet and stumbled after Ayman, calling out, "I'm sorry. It was my fault. Please come back. Please, Ayman, please."

Hays and Duffy continued to do their funded work, though to both of them the results seemed meaningless.

That night Hays had fallen asleep praying and when he woke, he had felt no better and no more directed or protected than the night before.

In the morning Roberta sounded groggy when she called, explaining that she wouldn't be in.

"I hope it's nothing serious," he said, praying that she hadn't contracted something from the lab—some form of the new virus.

As she spoke, beads of nervous sweat formed on his forehead and cheeks. "No, Hays. Don't worry. It's not the virus. It's just ... well, it's just a woman thing."

"Okay," he replied, feeling uncomfortable. "I hope you feel better soon."

What made it even more uncomfortable was that he had to repeat the news to Duffy, who had expressed the same concern as Hays.

"Well ... at least it's not the virus," he said.

Late that afternoon someone tapped on the door to the lab. A short, dark shadow framed the other side of the frosted glass.

Both men looked up, surprised. Visitors didn't knock; they simply entered and stated their business.

Hays opened the door to find a white-faced Norah. In her left hand she held a crumpled envelope.

"Norah, what is it?" Hays said, taking her free hand and pulling her into the lab. He ushered her to the nearest chair. "What happened?"

Hays felt worried. He wondered if she might have heard gossip about the virus and become frightened. She bit her lip and looked down. Duffy came over with water in a paper cup.

"It's this," she said, holding out the envelope, her hand trembling slightly.

"What is it?"

Hays recognized the black and green Huber/Loss logo on the corner of the envelope.

"It came by special courier just ten minutes ago," Norah said. "Huber/Loss wrote it yesterday."

Hays gently took the envelope and pulled the letter out. Even without reading it, he could tell from the brevity—a single paragraph—that it contained bad news.

> *Huber/Loss regrets to inform you that as of this date, all funding for the Sutton Virus Analogue Test and Trials will be terminated. Please send all data and notebooks to corporate headquarters at your earliest convenience. Any live specimens may be disposed of as you see fit. Your funding director will arrange for a transfer of all other physical inventory belonging to Huber/Loss.*

"No explanation?" Hays asked.

Norah shook her head. "You'll be all right. You'll find work."

It appeared that she wanted to hug them both but did not. Instead, she gave them a sympathetic smile and quickly left the lab, her heels clicking sharply in the hall.

"Well, my friend," Duffy said after some moments of silence, "it appears that we are behind one giant eight ball this week."

Hays nodded. There wasn't much he could say that would make the situation better, more understandable. He wanted to believe in God's hand on his life, but couldn't understand how any of this could be construed as God's handiwork.

"We should call Roberta," he said. "We shouldn't let her come in tomorrow thinking nothing is wrong."

Duffy nodded. "I can call her if you like."

Hays shook his head no.

"It's my job. But before I do, I'll call Norah. There is a secretarial opening on her staff. Maybe she could offer the position to Roberta. I'm sure she's qualified, and it's not a bidding position, so Norah can give it to whomever she wants."

"That would be nice. I feel worse for her than I do for myself. She just started and all."

Both men fell silent. They walked to opposite ends of the lab. Both seemed to stare off at some distant image.

Minutes later, Duffy broke the silence. "Hays, we have to do something."

"What?"

"I don't know ... but something."

Hays fell asleep, finally, after midnight. He'd tried to shake his worried thoughts, but they kept spiraling, drawing tighter and tighter circles. He found it hard to concentrate on anything.

From the nearly empty refrigerator, he'd pulled out two pieces of leftover pizza. He wasn't sure just how leftover they were. He ate them without tasting, stared at the television, and then paced around the apartment. He stopped and started, looking at the picture of his parents. He held it up to the light. Tightness formed in his throat. He picked up the photo of himself and Duffy and Norah.

He paced back and forth. Then he heard the bell in the great tower of the Presbyterian church toll twelve times.

Without changing, he fell into his bed and stared at the ceiling. He wasn't aware of sleep overtaking him.

He awoke to hear a furious pounding on his door. He looked about, a little lost and confused. He jumped up, trying to focus his eyes.

The banging grew louder.

He unsnapped the lock and the door chain and pulled the door open.

Standing in front of it were two uniformed police officers.

"You Hays Sutton?"

Hays nodded. "I am."

"You work over at Pitt?"

"I do."

"You know a fellow by the name of Tom Stough?"

"I do."

Hays answered the questions evenly until they mentioned Tom's name. All manner of images ran through his head. Maybe the customs officials had finally caught up with Tom.

"Excuse me, but what's this about? It's past midnight."

The larger of the two officers held out a single sheet of notebook paper in his hand—a hand masked with a protective glove.

"You have any idea of why Mr. Stough might write this?"

The officer held the paper up to the light. The writing was done in pencil, in a looped, nearly childish scrawl.

"call Hays Sutton. emergency. he knows."

"Where did you get this? Is Tom all right?"

The second officer took a half step forward. He wore sunglasses despite the darkness. Hays couldn't read his tight expression behind them. "Mr. Stough wrote the note, sir."

There was a crawling, prickly sensation forming inside Hays' stomach. He felt the pizza roil within. "Where did you get the note?" Hays asked, his voice a whisper.

"We took the note out of his hand."

"What?"

"Oh, sorry. Is he a friend of yours?"

"Well ... sort of a friend. We both work at the university. At Pitt. He's in the archaeology department."

The officer turned to his partner. The officer in the rear simply shrugged.

"I hate to be the one to bring bad news, Mr. Sutton, but Tom Stough died. We had to pry this letter out of his hand."

13

PITTSBURGH, PENNSYLVANIA—The officers didn't step farther into the apartment, nor did they retreat.

"You think of any reason Mr. Stough might have written you this note?"

"No. I can't think of a reason he might have written that," Hays said, hoping his words were spoken at an even keel. "Not any reason at all. I'm sure."

"You're not going to leave town anytime soon, are you, Mr. Sutton?" It was the taller and more somber of the two officers who spoke. He hadn't phrased a question, but issued a subtle but unmistakable demand. "You'll be where we can reach you?"

Hays nodded, too quickly, he imagined, and both officers appeared as if they were making detailed mental notes on his exact actions and responses.

"No. I'm not planning any trips. I don't travel often. I don't think … I mean … I have no reason to go anywhere."

"Well, then," the tall officer said softly. It sounded like the words of a parent spoken to a sleepy child. "Then you wouldn't mind coming down to the station tomorrow? We know it's late and you need time to … collect your thoughts. If you would, come in sometime tomorrow and ask for Detective Lytwak. He'll be expecting you."

The tall officer held out a creased business card. Hays took it and carefully looked at it. He had seen this manner of exchange a thousand times in movies and television shows, when the policeman handed out a card to a reluctant or guilty witness. He had always wondered what those cards looked like.

It was a simple business card with a police shield in the middle. A few names and telephones numbers were listed.

"Anytime tomorrow. That would be convenient for you, wouldn't it?"

Hays nodded as he tucked the card into his breast pocket. He then became acutely aware of how deranged and rumpled he looked—as if he had fallen asleep in what he was wearing, which is just what had happened.

"Sure," Hays said, knowing he sounded much too positive. "I'll be there. I don't have a tight schedule anymore. I mean … I'll be there tomorrow."

"Thank you, Mr. Sutton, for cooperating with us. That's appreciated."

As they began to turn to leave, a thought jumped into Hays' awareness.

"When did Tom—Mr. Stough—die? Tonight?"

The taller officer slowly looked at the shorter officer—as if he could see the expression behind the sunglasses. Then he turned back to Hays and peered at him. The porch light cast dark shadows under his eyes, making them look like black, expressionless pools.

"Why do you ask?"

"Just curious, I guess. I need to find out when visitation is and all that."

The tall officer turned his face to profile. He had a tight jaw line.

"He must have passed on a few days ago. The super at the building was concerned at the pile of uncollected mail and let himself in. May have been dead a few days longer. Hard to tell."

Hays' heart began to thump wildly. He was sure the policemen could hear it.

"That long ago?"

"Yeah. It took awhile to find you. Your friend didn't exactly leave great records. It took some time to find out where he worked."

"Curious thing, though," the tall officer continued. "The apartment was a shambles. Not from intruders, but the guy was a pig, looked like to me, anyhow. We didn't find anything much in the place—except for the guy's will. That's right on the top of his desk. Curious, isn't it?"

Hays croaked, "Do you know what funeral home he's at?"

What if he's contagious? Good God. Don't let this happen.

The officer tapped at his nightstick.

"No funeral home that I know of. We sent the body to the morgue. I imagine they did an autopsy on him."

Oh God, no. An autopsy means they opened him up—and that means … oh my God … I don't know what that means.

Hays pulled himself upright. He held his face blank.

"Well, thank you, officers. I'll be at the station tomorrow."

The tall officer tapped at the bill of his hat with a forefinger.

"See that you are. And thanks."

Hays shut the door, his heart palpitating wildly. By the time he splashed cold water on his face and changed his clothes, the beating had slowed to a furious pounding. He prayed that by the time he reached his destination, his heart rate might slip back to normal, whatever normal might be these days.

It was because of Duffy that Hays knew where to go and what to do next—at least in a general sense. One night, several years ago, Duffy wanted to impress Hays and Norah and took them to the city morgue. Duffy was a friend of the coroner, and the fellow gave the three of them a comprehensive tour.

Hays remembered the surprised and shocked look on Norah's face as the coroner rolled out a body from the cooler racks and whipped off the covering shroud. The coroner had given a detailed and graphic lesson in the fine art of the autopsy. Hays had found it fascinating. All the while, Duffy had beamed at showing his friends a dark corner of the city neither had ever seen before.

Hays knew enough of the coroner's office to be frightened. If the body had been fully autopsied, he wasn't certain what he might do to contain any possible contamination—if indeed it was the virus that killed Tom—but he knew he had to try.

If the virus is what killed him—then everyone who came into contact with the body might be exposed. The two policemen, the ambulance drivers, the morgue attendants, the pathologist, the coroner—the list could include dozens of people. And in a few days, it could include thousands.

The streets were deserted as Hays raced through Oakland, the actual home of the University of Pittsburgh, then on through the poverty-torn Hill District and down into Pittsburgh proper.

All the way, Hays prayed as he had never prayed before. He parked his car in a deserted lot across from the castlelike City and County Building—a gothic fortress of a building with thick walls and narrow slashes for windows. Hays ran around the side of the building and ducked into a doorway lit by a single bulb in a wire cage and pushed the door open.

The lights were dim; the smell of formaldehyde filled the air, along with the biting scent of astringent and antiseptic. The wide corridor was dark and empty. To one side lay the three autopsy rooms, dark and silently ominous.

The other side housed the coolers and holding chambers. He stood still for a moment, trying to remember where the offices were. He heard muted and hollow sounds of talking and scraping, and a distorted buzz of laughter.

He could see pools of light from beyond. He stopped at the first office. Dr. CYRIL CRENCH. The office was dark.

It was the next office that he was searching for—Dr. DAVID WEAVER.

He heard the phone ring, then stop. Somebody was there. Hays tapped at the door.

The coroner's office was a twenty-four-hour facility, as it was in most large cities. Bodies were found at all hours, and often police needed a quick and late-night review on the state of death. If it was foul play, the sooner they began their investigations, the more leads they found.

"What?" A voice bellowed, annoyed, from behind the door. "If you have a body, ring over to services. They do the tagging, not me."

Hays cleared his throat. "Its Hays Sutton. I'm a friend of Duffy's. Do you remember me?"

The door swung open. Dave Weaver stood framed by the light, a cigar clenched in his teeth. "Duffy, I remember. You, not so much."

Hays tried to reconstruct his visit. It was only after he described Norah that the coroner recalled him.

"Yeah. I remember now. She was a looker, right?"

Hays nodded.

"So ..." Dave asked, leaning against the door, barring his entry.

"I know I have no right, really, to ask a favor from you."

"That's right. You don't. Duffy, maybe, but you I don't know."

"Then I'm asking for Duffy's favor."

Dave gave a crooked smile. "Hey, ask away. I can tell you if it's too big a favor. And it's not like I'm all that busy."

Hays had rehearsed the next line during his frantic trip. He wanted it to sound normal, natural, and not at all desperate.

"I have a friend who died a day or two ago and the body was sent here ... and no one is telling me the cause of death. And I want to know. And I know the official report won't be out for weeks. He was ... well, he was a real good friend."

Dave unclenched the cigar and rolled it to the other side of his mouth. He looked into Hays' eyes and then offered an all but imperceptible nod. "And you're here at two in the morning?"

"I figured this would be the least 'official' time you had."

"What's the name? Of the goner, I mean. Sorry, the deceased. I mean … you said a friend and all. Working here makes one a bit calloused to death, you know?"

"No problem. I understand. His name was Tom Stough. Came in late yesterday."

Scratching at his jaw, Dave grabbed a clipboard and flipped through a thick batch of papers.

"A skinny guy—a skinny white guy? With red hair?"

"That's him."

"I remember him. Looked like he was anorexic or something. You don't see that in middle-aged white men that often."

"You think it was anorexia?"

Dave shrugged. "Don't know."

"You have an autopsy report on him?"

Hays felt overwhelmed, almost as if swallowed by a wave of fear. He had no idea of what to hope for—or what to pray for. He couldn't imagine a scenario developing that might be benign.

"Yeah, I have one. The prelim is here." Dave flipped another page. "No. I take that back. It's all here. The prelim was all we did."

"Prelim?"

Dave tucked the clipboard under his arm. "Yeah. Preliminary autopsy. We may cut a little here and there—a quick down and dirty. For this one— well, we didn't even do that."

"You didn't?"

"No. We took one look and knew it was a massive coronary. The heart just exploded. You can tell by the way the blood pools. A textbook case of a heart attack."

Hays felt a small current of relief. They hadn't cut the body yet. Maybe there was something he might do to prevent the autopsy from happening.

"When is the full autopsy scheduled?"

"No full autopsy scheduled. Our favorite pathologist, Dr. Crench, is on a golfing vacation in North Carolina. Not due back for a week. He doesn't like it when he gets back to a morgue full of bodies. So we just process the usual cases. And your friend … well, he was pretty usual. No sense in bothering the pathologist with a usual case."

"Then …" Hays wasn't sure what to ask next. "Then … where's the body?"

He flipped back to the clipboard. "Hmmm. Now that may be a tad unusual."

"What?"

"They burned it."

"Burned it?"

"Cremated. Sent off to the Tri-County Mortuary and Crematorium in Ambridge. Funny thing—the police brought a copy of his will with him. Claimed it was sitting next to the body. The will called for an immediate cremation—something to do with the fellow's religion or something. That ring a bell to you?"

Hays ignored the question. "Tri-County? In Ambridge?"

"Yeah. They're fast."

They burned it. If it was contagious, it is gone.

"Well, then. Thanks."

Dave pulled the cigar out of his mouth and spit into the hallway. "Hey … sorry. I know you said he was a friend and all. I just get so used to seeing bodies that sometimes none of it registers. I know everyone has a story and all that." The doctor looked away. "Sorry for your loss," he said, in a smaller, kinder voice.

"Thanks."

And with that, Dave turned his back, walked toward the inner door, and let the outer door of the office slowly close.

Hays stood outside the dark doorway to the morgue for a long time, drawing in great gulps of air. He didn't feel relief, exactly, but he no longer felt that clinging, jangling sensation, the foot-trembling mixture of terror and dread. Tom had arrived dead—wrapped in a body bag. There were no open wounds, no festering. No one set a scalpel to the flesh. What happened was terrible—but it offered no scenario for a serious case of disease transmission.

And that is what Hays had prayed for.

Thank you, Lord, for your protection. Thank you for protecting me from my own sin and my own stupidity. Thank you—and please forgive me. Please forgive me.

14

QUADARE CITY, QUADARE—"You have been injured?" Hameed asked. "Should we call for medical assistance?"

Fadhil waved his hand angrily. "Some fool placed a table in the wrong location. It was days ago. I believe I may have broken a toe. But it will heal."

Hameed nodded. "As all wounds do, eventually."

"You have a report? I believe you mentioned that the trials are going well."

Fadhil was seated behind his desk with his left foot elevated on it. He was wearing slippers, and he had cut out a hole for his small toe. Threads unraveled around the swollen digit, making it appear that a small wreath circled his toe.

"Yes. The trials are going very well. Dr. Salim Haj stated that he was shocked at the virulence of the new virus. Without any modifications or alterations, the test animals succumbed to the virus quickly. The doctor said it took his breath away, such was its ferocity. He said that it does not appear to easily jump species. He used dogs, I believe, in tests, and it was not as pathogenic. But with slight modifications it should be as effective on other species as it is on rats. So I instructed him to make sure that all was safely quarantined and to begin at once to construct a new facility with any and all safeguards that are needed."

Fadhil appeared crestfallen. "But this is a delay. How long? I'm not happy with any manner of delay in this research."

"Yes, sir. I realize that," Hameed said. "But if we are to safeguard our citizens, as well as our leadership, we must construct the new facility. Dr. Haj says all samples will be stored in a secure area until then. But he emphasized that he couldn't guarantee the safety of anyone with his current facility. It simply must be upgraded to the level of a Western medical lab, he says."

Hameed knew the comparison would irritate Fadhil.

Wincing, Fadhil lowered his left leg to the floor. "I don't want a delay. If a few deaths are the result, so be it."

An owl cried in the darkness. Hameed looked out over the balcony. A gibbous moon seemed to float over Quadare harbor, reflecting itself in the languid, oily waters.

"Sir, I understand. But in order to properly replicate the virus, the doctor requires more sophisticated equipment than currently exists in Quadare. We must wait. I do understand your impatience—but this waiting is a necessary evil."

Fadhil walked to the open balcony. "I'm not happy. I have set plans in motion. We must not be delayed."

"Only a few more weeks," Hameed insisted. "Perhaps a month."

Hameed knew that the time would be longer. After all, delay was the Quadare way. It would be weeks and months until the new isolation lab was finished and the trials concluded.

I would rather tell him in increments. It is more amusing to watch him rant in installments.

As Fadhil turned from his view of the city, his left foot bounced against the edge of the open balcony door. He fell to his knees, howling to the dim light of the moon, clutching at his foot, tossing his defaced slipper onto the street below.

PITTSBURGH, PENNSYLVANIA—Roberta slid her chair closer to her desk. She took her compact and looked once again at her reflection. She smiled, turned her head to the left and the right and tried to see if anyone might discern the bruise she'd hidden under a skillful application of concealer cream and foundation.

She snapped the compact shut.

Perfectly normal, she assessed, and returned to her keyboard, glancing first at the figures on the screen, then down at the handwritten list on her desk.

Following the termination of the Huber/Loss funding for Hays' work, Norah had graciously offered her at least six months additional work filling in for her assistant, who was home on maternity leave.

It was Roberta's second week on the job. The tasks may have been routine and unchallenging, but she was grateful for the work.

"Want to get lunch? My treat today," Norah said. Then she reached into her purse, opened her billfold, and added, "as long as the tab for the two of us doesn't add up to more than fourteen dollars."

Roberta laughed. "Payday can't come soon enough, can it? I would love lunch, and I even have "—she reached into her pocket—"another three dollars and change. That should be enough for the two of us."

Fifteen minutes later they were in a back booth at Marzelli's, ordering a plate of baked mostaccioli and a salad to split between them.

The food came, and while they ate, conversation slowed.

"So, have you seen Hays recently?" Norah said, attempting to sound nonchalant.

"I did. I didn't expect to—but I did. I saw them both—Duffy, too."

"And where? I mean how?" She lowered her eyes. "How are they?"

"I think they're fine," Roberta said. "I was down at the Fish House in Market Square with a friend last night. Hays and Duffy were sitting at the bar. Hays had his usual diet Coke in front of him and one of the giant fish sandwiches."

"And how did Hays look?"

Roberta put her fork down. "He looked fine."

"Really?"

"Well, I think he's both a little depressed and a little nervous. They were working on some odd stuff before the burglary. They said it could have been dangerous."

"But no one is doing any follow-up investigation, are they?" Norah asked. "If the police or the CDC thought something dangerous was happening, they'd be investigating."

Roberta shrugged and speared another forkful of pasta. She chewed slowly. "Hays said that you still have two of his rats. Is that true?"

Norah laughed. "He told you about that?"

"You know men—they talk about such odd things at odd times."

Norah nodded. "He did give me two rats to take care of. He called three weeks ago and said he was trying to find another home for them. But then he never called back. So I'm stuck with these two rats in my terrarium. He knows I am not that fond of rats. But I don't want to bother him about it. I know he has other things on his mind. It seems like the more a man has to say, the fewer words he uses. I don't understand them."

Roberta poked the last few pieces of pasta on her plate. "I know. Men don't like words—they just like action."

They two women remained silent.

"I have an envelope to give Hays," Norah said, picking up her purse, almost patting it for reassurance. "Do you think I should mail it to him? Or call and have him pick it up at the office?"

Roberta considered. "Why not drop it off at his place? You only live a few blocks away, don't you?"

Norah brightened. "I think I will. That's a good idea. He'll be easier to talk to there than at the office." Then she blushed a little. "If he wants to talk, that is." She picked up her napkin. "You know how mysterious men are."

Roberta nodded.

Norah felt her heart beat faster than normal as she climbed the steps to Hays' apartment. She debated before she actually pressed the bell. She heard the metallic ringing sound. She waited. There was no noise from within. She pressed the bell again, a longer ring. Still no response.

What had felt like a good afternoon quickly dissolved into a dark and somber one. She waited a bit longer, ringing the bell twice more—just in case. Then she scowled and took out a pen from her purse. On the manila envelope she wrote: *The people who cleaned your lab found this—under counters and equipment, I guess. Some of it might be important.*

She stared at the door. Then she wrote: *Call me. We can talk about your rats.*

And then she added a little smiling face at the end and signed her name.

The pair walked slowly along Forbes Avenue, ignoring the steady stream of buses and cars that sped past. They stopped at the red light on Liberty.

"You're coming over, aren't you?" Hays asked.

"Sure," Duffy replied. "I have nothing else to do. And you still have cable, right?"

Hays laughed. "For at least the next month."

"And then you start stealing it from your landlady?"

Hays nodded, and just for a moment Duffy considered that he might be serious.

As Hays unlatched the lock, he saw the corner of the manila envelope under the door. He swung the door open and picked it up.

"Eviction notice?" Duffy asked and made his way to the refrigerator.

"No. It's from Norah. Says that this is stuff they found in the lab after we left."

"Really? I thought we cleaned everything out."

Hays reached into the refrigerator. There was one diet Coke left.

"Well, friend, there is clean and then there is clean."

He spilled the envelope's contents onto the kitchen table. At the top of the pile were the dozen photographs that had been taped to his typewriter shelf at his desk. He had forgotten about them. On the top of the photos was the picture of himself with Norah and Duffy. He picked it up and gazed at it for a moment. "She was so pretty."

Duffy took the snapshot. "Still is, you fool. And who's that handsome guy with her? Not you—I mean the other guy. The really handsome one. The one who looks like me. Well, I'll be. That *is* me. The handsome one."

Hays snatched the picture away, clicked the photos into a neat pile and set them aside.

He began to sort through the small stack of papers. Some were pages of notebooks that must have slipped under cabinets or behind shelves. There were a few printed e-mails, a few pages from reports—but none of it was of a personal nature. In a sense, all of it belonged to Huber/Loss, and none of it had any value to Hays or Duffy.

Hays sighed as he sorted through. "Seems a big part of our life has been reduced to a small pile of worthless paper."

Duffy leaned back in the kitchen chair. It creaked loudly. "Your life, friend, not mine. I still have value and worth—don't I?"

Duffy let a frown overtake his face. "Please tell me I have *worth*," he cried like a bad actor. "*Please* say I still have some value. Please, please, *please*."

Laughing, Hays pushed him away. He could always count on Duffy to bring a moment of lightness to any situation.

Suddenly Duffy stopped and sat bolt upright. He reached into the pile and snatched out a standard, business-sized envelope.

"What's this?" he said, his voice growing serious. "Is this yours? Do you recognize it?"

The envelope bore the stylish—and always familiar—eagle and globe logo of Huber/Loss.

The address was scrawled in Arabic script.

"I've never seen this before," Hays said. "Have you?"

Duffy shook his head. "No. That is not my handwriting. And I don't write in Arabic anymore. Where did this come from?"

"Norah said on her note that the cleaning crew found all of this. It must have been behind or under something. Can you read it?"

Duffy held it closer to his face. He wouldn't admit that he needed glasses—any more than Hays would.

"Whoever it is has terrible handwriting, just terrible. Almost childish. My Arabic is rusty, but this looks like an address in Lebanon."

"What?"

"Not all that far from my parents. Near to the docks, I think. And these two words are *cat* or *animal*. Doesn't make any sense."

Hays held the envelope in his hand.

"The burglars, right? The ones that made off with the virus. They dropped this, didn't they?" Duffy said.

Hays thought for a moment. "No other answer, is there? We need to call the FBI—or the CDC on this."

A few seconds ticked by. "I'll call in the morning," he added, hoping someone would offer a quick and painless solution to his rising panic.

Hays sat in the large chair in his living room. He'd spent the night in the chair watching the moon arc across the sky. He spent the dawn watching the sun edge away the darkness.

After the break-in at his lab, he had berated himself for being foolish and shortsighted. He had agonized over his choices. But now, after Tom's death, after realizing this virus possessed great potential for evil, his self-recriminations had turned to fear. Hays had known fear before. As an Army Ranger, he faced it on a regular basis. But those were expected fears—like parachuting from a plane in darkness. He recalled pitching forward into a black abyss, hearing the wind scream past his ears.

Back then Hays and the rest of his unit made fatalistic jokes about their chances. Behind their joking was a grim truth—the parachute opened or it didn't. You survived the jump or you didn't. Results were clean-cut and precise.

At the moment when the body began to fall through space, a part of the brain would scream out, "No. No. No." But a trained soldier could ignore those screams and hurtle himself into the welcoming blackness, his eyes wide open. If you were going to die, you'd soon know it. If the parachute didn't open, there would be no jerking back into safety. Instead, it would be a fast and furious plummeting toward oblivion.

Hays remembered how his heart had raced. And now, sitting in the comfort and quiet of his living room, watching the darkness draw back from the city, Hays felt his heart once again beating in terror.

What he had discovered was not just a minor threat. In his deepest awareness, he realized that the virus might mean a new strain of terror—if it jumped to humans. There would be no vaccine, no safety. If it fell into the wrong hands, the virus could mean death to literally millions of people.

And as such thoughts became truth to Hays, he began to tremble and sweat, and his heart began to hurt.

He had to do something.

Duffy's call brought him out of his reverie late that morning. "Did you call the FBI?"

Hays nodded into the phone. "I did."

"So what did the FBI say?"

Hays sighed loudly. "That nothing had changed. I spoke to the same agent that I called the first time. Apparently the Pittsburgh Police kept him in the loop. I told the FBI agent everything about the Huber/Loss envelope and the address in Lebanon."

"And?"

"And they said nothing had changed. A scribbled address in Lebanon is not cause for alarm, I guess. He said I should send it to him. They would test it for prints"

Hays slumped in the chair. He took one last drink of coffee. "Duffy," he said, his tone weary, "we have to do something. We really have to do something. I could all but guarantee that the FBI won't find a thing on this paper."

A moment passed.

"We have to go to Lebanon, Duffy. We have to do something. We have an address and maybe a name—and perhaps with help from your family back there, we can find out who is behind all this. We have to do something, Duffy, and I think this is where God wants us to start."

"I don't know about God, Hays," he said. "But you do. You're right—why else would we have this clue? Norah could have just tossed that stuff. She didn't. The cleaning crew could have tossed it. They didn't. Why on earth the burglars dropped it is too much of a coincidence to ignore. We do have to do something. Maybe what you hear your God telling you is right. Maybe we should to go to Lebanon."

Hays reluctantly nodded his head. "I think we have to go. Since no one else will, we do. We may not have more than a week or two to get ready."

"And the police will be done with you then?"

"I'm sure they will," Hays said as if assuring himself. "If not, well, no … they will be. At least they had better be."

15

PITTSBURGH, PENNSYLVANIA—"If we go to Lebanon," Duffy said as he stood in line at the Original.

"When we go," Hays corrected him. "We are going. We are. When we go. Soon. You're getting nervous, aren't you?" Hays asked.

Duffy managed to get a corner of the chili dog in his mouth without spilling any on his shirt—an accomplishment, considering the size of the chili dog.

"I am," he said between chews. "So tell me—just how did we get put in this situation where *we* have to go. The FBI or CIA should be planning what we're considering. Not us. Not a couple of amateurs."

Hays punched him lightly on the shoulder. "Careful who you call an amateur. I'll have you know I've read every James Bond book ever published."

Duffy opened hands. "Beware of the lily that calls itself a cedar."

"Lebanese saying?"

Duffy nodded.

"And it means …?"

Duffy shrugged. "I'm not sure. My grandfather used to say it all the time. I think it may have made more sense in the original Lebanese language."

Hays opened a notebook he had brought with him. He flipped open the cover. He'd filled two pages with his tight, controlled printing.

"Should have been an architect," Duffy said as he glanced at the page. "Every letter looks the same every time you write it. It's the handwriting of an obsessive-compulsive, if you ask me."

"And this from a man who throws his change away because he doesn't like the way it makes his pants look."

Duffy feigned taking offense. "I give the change away. And it's not just the look—it's the noise. I can't stand clanking like a cow with a pocket full of nickels."

"Passport?"

"I have it. Checked it last night," Duffy said. "It's good for three more years."

"Same here. I think we both renewed for that trip to the conference in England. Visa?"

Duffy put down his empty milkshake container and leaned in close to the table. Without turning his head, he peered both left and right as if the CIA were in the habit of surveillance at the Original Hot Dog Stand.

"I have a third cousin at the Lebanese embassy in Washington. Actually, I think he's a fourth cousin. He's on my mother's side of the family. Her aunt's sister's in-laws from the marriage of two cousins back in the twenties. It was Uncle Fehlet and Aunt Bara—he was a shoemaker, one of the best, they said. They had twelve children, all of which survived into adulthood."

Hays waited patiently. Duffy had an amazing recall of every nuance of his genealogy—cousins, second and third cousins, shirttail relatives. Even the genealogy of long-time neighbors was as familiar to him as the roster and batting averages of the 1973 Pirates were to Hays.

"Anyhow—to make a long story short—I called him last night, after Norah started this whole thing by finding the envelope. By the way, did you call and thank her for that? You should, you know."

Hays felt a familiar constriction between his shoulder blades. It was the same tightness he felt when his mother would force him to write thank-you notes back in grade school. Duffy understood family and social obligations with greater clarity than Hays ever could hope to.

"I haven't—yet," Hays said quickly, hoping to avoid one of Duffy's stares. "I'll call her this afternoon. I promise."

Duffy lowered his voice. "Is she still taking care of the rats? Are they still alive?"

"She is. And they are fine."

Duffy grew serious. "Listen—just because you broke her heart and now she might make you uncomfortable is no reason not to be civil and polite. Call her. Now."

"I will. I promise."

"And get those rats someplace else."

Hays leaned closer this time and whispered. "I don't want to. I think I've seen that same blue Mercedes in the neighborhood again. If I take the rats out, they might be there, and they might see me. And if they see me take them out of her apartment, wouldn't she be at risk? It's a sure way to get her implicated in all this—and I don't want that to happen."

Duffy rubbed at his chin. "You're probably right. That makes me uncomfortable—agreeing with you, that is—but I don't want to get her hurt either."

Both men sat still, lost in thought. After a moment, he spoke up.

"So what about the visas? Can your cousin—or your fourth cousin—get them for us?"

"No."

"No? Why? I thought you Lebanese stuck together."

"We do. And he has." Duffy looked to the left and right again, making sure there were no new suspicious people in the restaurant.

"He said we shouldn't apply. Lebanon is one of those places that certain people notice. They have to let the U.S. State Department know who's applying for visas."

"They do? That's against privacy laws, isn't it?"

"It's not a law. But if certain people want to receive certain financial considerations and aid—then certain people cooperate."

"Couldn't your cousin keep us off the list of ... cooperation?"

"He said he couldn't. He's just a low-level civil servant—and in Lebanon, that's pretty low. He said if we applied the U.S. government would know right away and that with our recent calls to the FBI and CDC, our names would probably be highlighted by someone's yellow marker. He said—my cousin, that is—that given the current geopolitical climate—he doesn't recommend applying for an official visa."

Hays appeared crestfallen. "Then what do we do? How do we go now?"

Duffy tapped the side of his nose, like a bad spy in a bad spy movie. He mouthed one word: "Italy."

Hays felt as though his vision had improved, as if he could see the world with greater clarity and understanding. After weeks of despair and feelings of hopelessness, he felt infused with a sense of purpose—that he and Duffy actually might be able to do something about the terror they might have unleashed.

Hays wasn't sure what they could do, but it felt good to be moving forward, heading toward some goal, engaging in some kind of positive action. Over lunch Duffy had explained that rather than seek a visa to

Lebanon, they should instead travel to Italy, which required no visa, no government notifications. From Rome, he explained, it was a short train ride to the eastern coast. From there, a short voyage to Lebanon.

"There have been fishermen in our family for two hundred years," Duffy said. "There are many secluded beaches on the Adriatic Sea. A night on the water—and the next morning we can be having Turkish coffee in Lebanon."

"Better to pack as a tourist," Duffy said. "What we need, my family in Lebanon can get."

"Anything we need?"

Duffy offered a wry, knowing smile. "Anything you might need—and then some."

"Like what?" Hays pressed.

"Like you don't really want to know," Duffy said, "We'll just leave it at that. Just pack as a tourist. It will be all we need to take, I swear."

Hays got lightheaded thinking about the ramifications of their intended trip. Besides a grand sense of unreality, he struggled with the illegality of his intended course of action.

He had called Norah's office after lunch. He was told that she was working at home that day. He knew her well enough to recognize she wouldn't claim such a thing unless it was true. He debated over visiting her, then decided making a phone call would be easier and safer.

Obviously, Norah was surprised and pleased at the sound of Hays' voice.

"I want to thank you again for dropping that envelope off. I really appreciated it."

"It was no problem at all. I wish that you had been there. It would have been nice to talk to you in person."

"So the rats—they're okay? They're eating okay and doing fine?"

"Yes, Hays. They're fine. I went out and bought them a new cage. They were chewing up the terrarium—so I had to do something. And they are fine. They eat like horses—for rats, I mean. I have to send them away to camp with my aunt in Homestead next week. I'm going to a conference in Orlando—and then I'm taking another week's vacation. I think it's a state law that if you go to Orlando you have to visit Disney World. Or did you tell me that?"

Hays was both surprised and concerned.

"Your aunt—does she know anything about animals?"

"My aunt Harriet? She's the vet, remember? She knows about animals."

"I had forgotten about her. How is she?"

"Aunt Harriet? She's fine. She's asked about you from time to time. I'm the only family she has, so she takes quite an interest in my life—such as it is.

"She said she missed seeing you," Norah said, then added softly, "I've missed seeing you. You know that, don't you? I miss talking to you. I miss being with you," she said.

"I know … but, you know … I'm not …" His words were a shorthand form of confession.

"I know, Hays," she said. "I know."

He could tell by the timbre of her voice that she was near tears. "You know how I feel, what I believe. We've talked about it. For hours. You said you understood."

She nodded. "I guess I do."

"Unless we can both believe that same thing …" Hays continued, his voice trailing off. "You know about my faith, my Christian beliefs, Norah. You do. I talked enough about it. You have all the books I gave you. Have you read them?"

"Some of them. Sort of."

"I can't change my decision. It simply has to be this way. I'm leaving the country next week. Myself and Duffy. We have some very important … business to attend to. It's about a job—an unfinished job. You have to promise to take care of those rats. I'm mailing you a letter. I want you to keep it safe, just in case. It's important. Promise me you'll do that."

"I—I promise. But in case of what?"

"Well … just in case. That's all. Being on airplanes and all that. Just promise me that you'll take of the rats."

"I promise, Hays."

"And promise me you'll read the books I gave you. When I get back, we can talk. Promise me you'll read them."

"Oh, I will," she said.

"Good-bye, Norah," he said.

"Good-bye, Hays. I promise—I'll read the books, and I'll take care of the rats."

"You're in a good mood," Roberta said as Norah breezed into the office and twirled about with a grin on her face. She was carrying an armful of spring flowers with her.

"I am. My flowers are beginning to bloom, and I'm happy," she said, and opened up the closet, pulling out two vases.

"Flowers don't merit this much happiness," Roberta said. "Not unless they come with something else."

Norah hiked herself up onto Roberta's desk with a grin. "He called last night," she whispered.

"Who?"

"Hays, of course. He said he wanted to thank me for getting all the papers from his lab to him."

Norah placed the flowers in the vases, arranging them carefully.

"Are you two, like, seeing each other again?" Roberta asked.

"Hays? Well, no. Not now. Maybe. But later. He said he would call later. Hays said something about him and Duffy traveling to Europe—some business to take care of—in Italy, I think he said. He did have a good research grant two years ago with the University of Bologna. He may go there to see if they have other research to conduct. Maybe they'll go visit Duffy's family in Lebanon. He didn't say that exactly, but those countries are pretty close to each other."

Roberta asked, "Did he say anything else? Like personal stuff?"

"Some. A little. What I do remember is that he said we were going to talk when he comes back. And when a man says he wants to talk, you know that he wants more than talk. He wants a relationship. It's just the opposite of what a woman means when she says 'we have to talk.'"

"It is?"

Norah smiled knowingly. "It is. He still loves me. "

"He does? He said that?"

"Not exactly, but I am sure that he does. I can tell."

And with that she spun around again, smiling, and headed into her office, humming.

Roberta sat silent for a moment. She looked up at the photo on her desk and felt swallowed up by Ayman's dark and smoldering eyes.

She tried to smile, but couldn't.

16

QUADARE CITY, QUADARE—"And what of our good doctor?" Fadhil asked Hameed as he stirred his tea. "I have not heard any news in the past few weeks. I want to be sure he is not simply taking our money and doing nothing."

"Our doctor is on schedule. His equipment has arrived in advance of our expectations. You must thank our friends at Huber/Loss for expediting the orders in such a judicious manner."

Fadhil slurped at the tea.

The man is a pig, Hameed thought, trying to hide his disgust.

"And you say he has continued to work, even without the equipment?"

Hameed seldom sat for these meetings, choosing instead to stand in front of Fadhil's desk and stare down at the man. Tonight was no different. Fadhil offered, to near the point of insulted insistence, a seat on the nearby sofa. But Hameed resisted every offer, knowing that Fadhil viewed his refusal as rudeness.

"Yes," he said, collecting his thoughts. "He has translated the notes that were provided him. He believes that once the isolation equipment is in place, he will be able to duplicate the American's findings quickly. And then proceed to testing it on other species."

"And the curse?" Fadhil whispered as he carefully placed his teacup on the saucer. "He will validate the ancient curse?"

Hameed waited. *There is no curse, you evil fool. It is simply an ancient disease.*

"Yes."

"Ahh, such a delicious blessing. And when that happens …"

Fadhil stood up and for a moment. Hameed feared he might come around his desk and attempt to embrace him. Instead he walked to the balcony and gestured at the tired and dusty city.

"When that happens, then Quadare will no longer be ignored and pushed about. No, my dear friend Hameed, then we will be the tiger in the garden."

PITTSBURGH, PENNSYLVANIA—Three piles of clothing lay almost haphazardly on Hays' bed. At its foot was a large, black duffel bag. He had purchased it last year at Wal-Mart and was thrilled at the cheap price and sturdy construction.

"Who would steal a Wal-Mart bag?" he laughed when Duffy chided him for his purchase. "It's bigger than your Louis Vuitton bag, and if it gets torn, I won't cry—unlike you."

Hays disliked packing. He told himself—and others—that he was a light packer. He claimed he only took the essentials on any trip, but agonized over his pretrip winnowing process. It wasn't that he cared what he wore—he just wanted to have the item he wanted to wear when the time came.

There was a pile of T-shirts, a pile of slacks and jeans, socks, sweaters, underwear, shoes, boots, coats, books, toiletries, magazines, snack foods, camera gear, headphones and portable CD player, CDs, a DVD player—plus another pile of things he would like to take, but had already discarded, with a second pile of sweatshirts and shorts and a small selection of camping gear.

He sighed and tossed in two sport coats into the take-along pile. He hesitated, then took two ties and tossed them in as well.

He realized that he would need three large bags to accommodate his wish list.

The bell from his front door sounded and he gratefully retreated from the guestroom and hurried to the door.

"Roberta," he exclaimed. "What are you doing here?"

"And welcome to you, too," she laughed.

Hays' cheeks reddened. "I mean, it's nice to see you. What brings you to the neighborhood?"

She dropped her purse by the door, a gesture Hays interpreted as her meaning to stay awhile.

"Norah and I are going to dinner. And I'm early. And I wanted to see you before you left."

Hays appeared a little flustered. Women had never made a habit of just "dropping by" his place.

"And I wanted to make sure to thank you once again for getting me my job. Norah is nice to work for."

"You were more than qualified," he said. "And yes, she's a nice person."

There was an odd few seconds of silence.

"Would you like some coffee?" he asked.

Roberta nodded quickly. "Coffee would be great."

Roberta coiled into the kitchen chair in a manner Hays had never seen. Norah always seemed to perch on any stool or chair. Roberta, a much taller woman, could wrap her legs about a chair and still have body left over.

"Cream? Sugar?"

"Just black."

Hays busied himself with the coffee. Alone, he usually resorted to instant, but for company, he took whole beans and ground them.

"Are you packing? Norah said you were leaving soon. I didn't interrupt you, did I?"

"I hate packing. So I'm glad for the diversion."

"Where are you going? Vacation? Job interview?"

"Well, both actually," he replied. He hoped that he had gotten better at telling falsehoods, and at the same time he felt dismay that he mostly likely had gotten better. "Duffy and I are going to Rome and then to Bologna. We've done work for them before. We're going to … a conference on microbiology and hope to press the flesh, make a few contacts—that sort of thing."

He poured out two coffees. Roberta sipped loudly.

"Sounds like fun, almost." She put down her cup. "You know, Norah said you might head to Lebanon—to visit Duffy's family."

Hays shook his head no, but there was enough surprise in his face that Roberta noticed. Respond too quickly and the guess is all but accurate.

"Not this trip," he explained. "Duffy's parents are … going to be away. No sense in visiting."

"I did really want to thank you again, Hays," Roberta continued, apparently accepting his explanation. "For the job with Norah and all. You really didn't know me all that well. Without your intervention Norah would have hired someone else."

"It was nothing," he said as he stirred cream and sugar into his coffee. "And she probably would have hired you regardless."

They were both silent for a moment. There came an echo of applause and laughter—the landlady downstairs didn't hear well and watched game shows with the volume way up.

Hays grinned when he heard "I'd like to buy a vowel."

Roberta laughed as well. She looked into Hays' eyes.

"Do you still love her?"

For a moment, Hays was not sure of whom Roberta spoke.

"Norah, I mean. I didn't mean to confuse you. Norah. She talks about you, you know."

"Yes. I know. I mean, I kind of thought she might."

"Do you then?"

"I … in a way. Yes. I do. It's hard to explain."

Roberta tapped the rim of her cup with a polished nail. "This faith thing of yours is pretty hard to understand. Norah is a sweet person. I don't see why you shouldn't be together. So she doesn't believe what you believe—can't you both be tolerant? Doesn't God like people to be tolerant?"

Now Hays stood. "He does—in a way. But if I make a vow to be with a woman for the rest of my life, I want to be able to share what's most important to me with her. Two become one in marriage. I don't want her to simply 'tolerate' what I believe. I loved Norah too much to compromise myself—or her."

Roberta nodded as if she understood. Hays sensed that she did understand but didn't agree with him. She looked at her watch. "Well, thanks for the coffee."

He followed her to the door. She surprised him by turning and embracing him, a sense of urgency in her grasp.

"You take care of yourself, Hays." She leaned in and kissed him delicately on the cheek.

"I will," he replied, overwhelmed at her action.

"I know you still love her," she whispered. "And love will find a way."

And with those words, she slipped out the door and hurried down the steps. She didn't look back. Hays watched until she turned on the street and disappeared from view.

Roberta hurried down the street. As Hays had talked about his faith and the simplicity of his beliefs, she had begun to grow anxious. She figured that some people are destined to find peace—and others are destined to search and seek all their lives.

She wondered if she should tell Ayman of this discussion. Then again, she thought, it might make him angry that she was in the company of another man with no one else present. Almost without thinking, she touched at her left arm. She winced as her fingers grazed the blue and black welt there.

I don't want to make him angry, she thought as she stepped onto the street. *There's no reason to aggravate him further.*

She sighed.

But perhaps he will be interested in knowing that Hays is heading to Rome. He seemed so concerned when I spoke of Hays the last time. And he was so nice afterwards.

She began to smile.

Yes, maybe I will tell him about Hays. But I will leave out that I went to his home uninvited. I'll say that I bumped into him on the street. That will be fine. That won't make him angry with me.

In Norah's front room sat an immense bookcase, filled mostly with fashion and travel magazines. On the top shelf, which she could only access with a chair or ladder, was a stack of books, all apparently unread. She grabbed at the top two.

They were the books Hays had brought her. She had tried to read them on several occasions, but never got past the first few pages.

While waiting for Roberta, she curled up in the chair by the bay window. She flipped open one of the books and immediately cracked the spine. Hays nearly shouted the first time she did this in his presence. But she was alone now and could do as she pleased. She didn't like books that snapped shut when you dropped them.

She tried to concentrate on the words. But after only a few minutes she felt as if she were swimming in a pool of gelatin. The individual words all made sense, but when strung together, they seemed to float—just out of reach.

She breathed deeply, then let the book drop to the side of the chair and then picked up a recent magazine from the stack on the table. She thumbed through the pages slowly, folding down corners when she saw some fashion she liked and might try to find later.

Hays returned to the bedroom and began ruthlessly paring down the piles. He reduced his must-take clothes to three pairs of slacks, three shirts, three T-shirts, one sport coat, one sweatshirt, one pair of swimming trunks, one pair of sneakers, one pair of sandals, socks and underwear—plus, a kit bag for his razor and toiletries, three books, and his BlackBerry.

He slipped everything inside the bag. It fit with some room to spare.

He picked up a thin Bible; his Army Ranger training manual; and a thick, comprehensive, and recent touring guidebook to the Middle East.

"And I'll have what I'm wearing on the flight—plus what I can squeeze into my carry-on."

He whistled as he replaced all the discarded clothing into drawers and shelves. Yet he knew that before their flight to Rome, he would unpack once more, just to make sure of his selections.

17

ROME, ITALY—Duffy grinned as the taxi driver sped through the narrow streets at what seemed to be breakneck and foolhardy speeds, using the horn more often than the brakes.

"Don't you love this—the Italian way—*la dolce vita,*" Duffy crowed, his elbow out the window, a wide grin on his face.

Hays thought he'd kept his eyes shut more than he'd had them open during the ride from the Leonardo da Vinci Airport, somehow thinking that if he didn't see the possibility of a crash, it wouldn't happen.

"No," Hays replied. "I'd prefer not to die just yet."

"You worry too much," Duffy laughed, as the driver slammed both feet on the brakes, the taxi sliding and bumping along the ancient cobblestones. "This cab had the fewest dents of any at the airport. He must be a good driver."

Hays held on to the doorframe as the vehicle lurched to the right, narrowly avoiding a tour bus. "The thing I don't understand is that they get paid for the amount of time the ride takes, as well. Wouldn't they make more money if they drove slower?"

The driver, who apparently spoke English, turned full round in his seat, almost facing the rear, while still careening down the narrow street, narrowly missing a few Vespa motor scooters.

"The car suffers if driven too slowly. You must treat them like a woman—you must be hard and in control."

He turned around just in time to veer to the right, avoiding a parked mini-truck.

By the time they reached their hotel, Hays was sweating—and not just from the warm Italian air. He had booked them at the InterItalia Hotel, a moderate establishment catering to businessmen with limited expense accounts. Their room on the fourth and top floor was small, but clean and modestly comfortable, and it had a nice view of the piazza below.

"It's just for a few nights," Hays said as he noticed Duffy's sour expression.

"That's good—because I wouldn't stay here long. Life is too short for bad hotel rooms."

"Your relatives do know we are coming?" Hays asked.

Duffy nodded. "I sent e-mails to those who need to know. When we get to Venice, I will call them. And a few days after that, we will be at my home. They know the coast there very well. I have detailed instructions as to the exact location where we will meet them. 'The death of the moon,' they said. The fifteenth. We will have time for some Roman and Venetian pleasure until they arrive." Duffy paused a moment, then asked softly. "You called Norah before we left, right? You thanked her?"

Hays nodded. "I did."

"How was she?"

"She was fine. We talked."

Duffy waited for more details, then scowled when none were forthcoming.

QUADARE CITY, QUADARE—Dr. Salim Haj stepped into his office, and when he saw Fadhil sitting on his sofa and Hameed standing off to one side, he began to wring his hands, offering them both a wide and obviously frightened smile, showing too many teeth, bowing without reason.

"You honor me," the doctor said, almost too soft to be heard. "To come to my humble offices like this, unannounced and unexpected. It is too great an honor."

Fadhil appeared to enjoy the man's obsequious groveling and his visible discomfort. Hameed simply looked perturbed.

The doctor's office was in a less-than-savory part of the city. As they drove there, Fadhil remarked that if he were a good doctor, why would he practice on the low class? Hameed explained most doctors wouldn't be as close-mouthed as Dr. Haj. Hameed had entrusted him with several other "opportunities to serve" and had never once heard of a secret leaving his office. "University doctors with fancy offices simply wouldn't serve us well," Hameed concluded.

The doctor noticed Fadhil staring at the floor—noticing, he was sure, the cracked and peeling vinyl tile and the chips of paint in the corner.

"Please, sirs," he said. "I know these furnishing are modest, but a doctor in Quadare never earns as much as the corrupt doctors in the West earn.

They receive free medicines from drug companies and free education from their governments. It is not so in Quadare, and so much is the pity."

Fadhil held his hand up to stop the doctor's lament. "We are not here to inspect your office, doctor. I'm hear to learn of your progress with our ..." Fadhil said, hesitating and instantly regretted that he hadn't coined a code name for the investigation. He loved code names and secrets. "We want to hear of your progress on the—the Micah virus."

Fadhil grinned expansively, pleased with the name he had just created for the research. "We have decided to call it the Micah virus."

"Micah virus?" the doctor asked, confused. "Oh. Oh yes, the virus. From the skull. Yes, yes. If it is a virus. It could be a prion, however."

"Prion?" Fadhil asked, crossing his legs and sliding backwards on the sofa.

"Yes, yes. Prions. Like a virus, but not a true virus. Once I get the isolation equipment fully operational, I can begin testing. With rats it is lethal. With dogs, less so. But the notes—well, from the notes, I think I know what needs to be done. I am now testing my first theory."

As he spoke, the doctor stood further upright. He began to gesture. He thrust his jaw out as he spoke, poking at the air with his fingers extended in an arc.

"Are prions a disease?" Fadhil asked.

"Well, yes—and then no. Prions are agents that don't have a nucleic acid genome. No virus—but a simple protein alone causes the infectious agent."

"But what is a prion? I have never once heard that term," Fadhil asked.

"A prion. Well, a prion is a small proteinaceous infectious particle that resists inactivation by procedures that modify nucleic acids. I tell you, when it was discovered that proteins alone can transmit an infectious disease, it was a considerable surprise to the medical community—even here in Quadare."

"But what is it?" Hameed was displeased. He wanted the virus to be a virus. That was simple and understandable.

"Prion diseases are called spongiform encephalopathies because when a person or animal dies, their brain is riddled with large holes—like Swiss cheese, actually. Mad cow disease—like in England—was caused by prions. It's called bovine spongiform encephalopathy."

"Prions? But that is just with livestock," Fadhil said, his tone rising. "I don't care about livestock. Do these prions affect people?"

The doctor waited a long moment to reply, as if considering why Fadhil wanted to know if it affected people as well as animals.

Hameed coughed, cleared his throat, and stared icily at the doctor.

The doctor blinked and continued. "It does—they do—or it does affect humans. There's the Creutzfeldt-Jakob disease, the Gerstmann-Straussler-Scheinker syndrome, kuru—but that's just among cannibals—and the Alpers syndrome."

"And the Micah virus is like them?"

"Perhaps. Perhaps it is simply a deadly virus. I will know for certain by week's end. I am sure of that."

"You will have a sample by then?"

The doctor nodded. "Unless it is a prion. A prion is harder to duplicate. With prions, patients lose motor control. They fall into dementia, then quickly into a paralyzed state in which muscles and organs simply cease functioning. Then they die. Very quick and very painful. Imagine—just the muscles around the lungs dying—or the left side of the heart. It is as if the prion targets a certain part of the body, at the exclusion of all others—and apparently at random as well. Truly a spectacular disease."

The doctor drew a deep breath and allowed his hands to fall to his side.

"And these prions, they can be isolated?" Fadhil asked.

The doctor shrugged and scratched at his chin. "Perhaps. If it is prions—two weeks. If it is a virus, in two days."

"If it is a virus, can it be delivered in anonymous manner?"

The doctor's face grew solemn. "Anonymous? Do you mean weaponized?"

"An ugly word, but yes," Fadhil replied.

Dr. Haj didn't hesitate. "Yes. Prions will be more difficult. But it can be done as well. Yes to viruses. Yes to both. But the effect depends on species. We will need to fully test. In a few days I will know much more."

Fadhil drew his hands together over his stomach and sighed. "Let us pray that the prophecy will be completed. And pray that I will be used to fulfill that prophecy. May it please Allah."

Later that day, sitting in his car in a parking lot of the country's only Western-style supermarket, Hameed called the doctor on a secure phone.

"I need enough of a sample to test, doctor." His words were cold.

"I am not sure I have enough. I … have not completed testing. I do not think … for safety's sake—"

Hameed cut the doctor off. "Listen, you are not paid to think. You will prepare a large sample of this virus. I will pick this sample up this evening. Please pack it well."

Hameed did not allow the doctor to respond, but simply broke the connection.

He will do as I request—or he will face the penalty.

He waited a moment, then dialed a second number from memory.

"Yes?"

"This is Hameed."

The accent was almost neutral, but if you listened carefully, there was a hint of the Teutonic about it, just a hint of the clipped and precise Bavarian-accented English. "Yes?"

Hameed recognized the signs of business. He would keep the conversation to a minimum. "The doctor sees great promise."

"And you?"

"I'm sure the discovery will be able to be put to good use."

"How long?"

"The doctor told Fadhil a few months until everything is tested fully. But I can send a sample on tonight's courier plane."

There was a pause and a crackle of static. "You have done excellent work, Hameed."

Hameed smiled at the disembodied voice on the cell phone. "Thank you, sir. But there is one more thing."

"Yes."

"It is time for a change."

"Change?"

"In leadership. There is decadence involved. Corruption. Depravity. It should not be this way."

"And?"

"I'm suggesting we consider a new direction. A bold leader. Someone unaffected by the desires of the flesh."

"You?"

"Yes."

There was a long, hesitant pause at the other end. "I will consider it."

"Thank you."

And with that, the line went dead.

Hameed drew a deep breath and realized he was sweating profusely, his heart pounding wildly. He let himself smile.

"He didn't refuse my request. It is within my grasp."

He sucked in another deep breath and gripped the steering wheel to calm the shaking of his hands.

PITTSBURGH, PENNSYLVANIA—Ayman stretched out on the sofa, placing his feet on the coffee table. Roberta never liked guests doing this, but she didn't want to upset him by reminding him.

She returned to the living room carrying the two glasses filled with soda. "Here you are," she said sweetly.

He smiled up at her, took the drink, and returned to staring at the television. He had a fascination with American baseball, even though he didn't fully understand the game. He would quiz her on the rules, and she tried her best to answer them, even though some of the rules mystified her as well. He was not happy when she couldn't answer him.

He grunted his thanks.

"You know I was talking to Norah the other day," she said.

He didn't respond in any way.

"She's my boss, remember?"

He nodded.

"And she used to date Hays Sutton. You remember Hays, don't you? Of course you do. I used to work for him."

Ayman turned to her, suddenly interested. "Yes, I remember. What about this Hays?"

"Oh, nothing really."

She took a sip of her drink. She had splashed a little vodka into the soda, just to take the edge off the day. He would never know, she told herself. She took another sip and felt the warmth.

"Then why talk of him?" His words grew hard.

She smiled at him sweetly, hoping to defuse or deflect his rising anger. "Well, just to make conversation."

There was a pause while the baseball game droned on in the background.

"And she said that she is taking care of his rats while he is gone."

Ayman blinked, then sat up straighter.

"Rats? Gone? What are you talking about?"

Roberta felt her stomach tighten. It was the tone of his voice, the sound of premonition.

"Oh, nothing. Just chatter. That's all."

He put his drink on the side table, spilling some. She would have to wipe that up before it left a ring. He grabbed her arm, tightly. Her eyes never left his even though his grip tightened.

"What rats?"

She felt her breath come faster. "The night they broke into his lab. Norah said that he got there just in time to rescue two rats. She said he said that was all he managed to get. She said he brought the two rats to her so she could take care of them. He said he was heading to Rome or someplace in Italy, so she had to help him out. She still loves him even though he broke off their engagement. She says he still loves her as well, but I'm not so sure."

Ayman was now sitting sideways on the sofa facing her. "What about the rats?" His voice was loud, almost a shriek.

"He took two rats from the lab. Just before the burglary."

Roberta felt herself form the words. She knew what the words meant. She knew, in the back of her mind, that the words would affect, enrage Ayman. And yet she said them. Her breath was shallow, her heart racing.

"He took two rats. Why have you not told me this before now," he bellowed, his words falling into a thicker accent as the volume increased.

"I only heard about this three days ago. It's not like I had—"

And as she spoke, he coiled his right arm and backhanded her across her cheek. Her head snapped back to the sofa. She felt a warm numbness on her lip.

"Three days. You knew three days ago."

As his knuckles creased her check, Roberta felt transported back to her childhood, her father exploding in an unexpected rage, shouting at her worthlessness and her stupidity. Her mother was once his target, and now that she was gone, Roberta was.

And curiously, she knew that she deserved it. It was what she had always known, what he had always told her—even as a little girl—that she was stupid and worthless and would amount to nothing.

Ayman slapped her again, this time with an open palm on the other side of her face. This blow she anticipated and managed to bend in time to deflect much of the sting. She knew she had stupidly made him angry. She knew he had every right to be angry because she was worthless.

"Does this Norah still have the rats?"

"Maybe. I don't know. She didn't say."

He slapped again, and then reached to the neck of her blouse and tore at the fabric. She knew what would happen next. She knew it was just what she deserved.

"Who has them?" he shouted as he stood above her.

"I don't know. She didn't say."

He struck her again, not as hard as before.

"You stupid woman. Why did you withhold this from me?"

She shrugged. "She has an aunt. In Homestead. She's a vet. Maybe she took them there."

He raised his hand. She narrowed her eyes in anticipation of the pain.

He stared at her, anger and disgust on his face. "You are worse than a goat," he hissed, then began to undo his belt buckle.

She closed her eyes. She knew what was coming now. She felt his hands, and she let herself be maneuvered to his pleasing. She felt a sense of calm as he stormed over her.

After all, it was only what she deserved.

EMBASSY SUITES RESORT, ORLANDO, FLORIDA—Norah never enjoyed these seminars, despite being held in exotic locations.

"The only reason they hold them in Orlando," she told Roberta before she left, "is because if they were held in Des Moines, no one—and I mean no one—would go."

Roberta had laughed and urged her to have a good time, to skip the afternoon sessions and sit by the pool and work on a tan.

And Norah did exactly that. The warm sun felt good. She selected a lounge chair on the far side of the pool, well away from the children's pool. She reached into her bag—she had tubes of sunscreen, several pairs of sunglasses, a hat, and three books. Two books she had purchased at the Pittsburgh airport bookstore—both promising nonstop thrills and guaranteeing a long, sleepless night for the reader.

She wasn't sure why she'd picked those two books, but their covers were intriguing.

The third book was one Hays had given her many months ago. Before she left, she'd gone through all of them once again and had selected the one that appeared least intimidating. It was also the thinnest.

She read a half-dozen pages and actually understood what the author wrote—an unusual result with any of the books Hays gave her.

A shadow passed over her face. She looked up. A thin woman with white hair and a bathing suit that was at least thirty years old sat down, leaving one empty lounge chair between them. The older woman smiled.

All the chairs are empty and she sits here? Norah thought, a little perturbed.

"Hello," the stranger said. "Isn't it a lovely day?"

Norah forced a smile and nodded. "It is very nice. The sun feels so good."

"Oh doesn't it, though. I'm from Seattle, and it seems we never get enough sun there. The folks down here are just spoiled, I bet."

Norah smiled. "But they have bugs the size of Volkswagens. To get something nice, you have to give something."

The older lady laughed. "I'm Sophia Gust. And I'm here escaping my grandchildren. They kidnapped my husband and took him to Universal for an afternoon of roller coasters. Not my cup of tea, so I will bake here by the pool."

"And I'm Norah. I'm escaping a boring lecture on nonprofit gift accounting procedures. Not my cup of tea, either."

Sophia leaned back and pulled a book from her bag. Norah stared for a moment. It was the same book she was reading. Sophia noticed her stare, then caught a glimpse of the book in her hands.

"Well, I'll be. It *is* a small world, or something like that," she said with a smile. "I guess you're a Christian too, then."

At that, Norah felt unsettled and nervous. She bit her lip and tried to formulate an answer.

Sophia must have noticed her discomfort. "Or not," she added gaily. "Don't worry. I won't quiz you. But it was the wrong thing to say."

"Oh, it's okay," Norah replied. "My … boyfriend gave me this book. He said I need to read it. He's a Christian."

Nodding like only a grandmother can nod, Sophia replied, "It's a wonderful book. I reread it every few years. One thing it helps me do is listen—and hear the voice of God."

"Really? You hear God?"

Sophia smiled. "Sometimes. Not always in a loud voice. Not always in words. But I hear him. Then again, I'm always asking him questions, so it stands to reason. If he is answering people, one of them might as well be me."

"He really talks to you?"

"He does," she replied.

Neither woman spoke and after a few minutes, the older woman busied herself with a magazine and Norah returned to her book, although the words seemed to float and dance on the page. Warmed by the sun, she let her eyes close, and woke with a start. She glanced at her watch. She had napped for forty-five minutes.

The old woman sat up and turned to her.

She spoke in a confidential whisper. "You know, Norah, it was almost like I was supposed to sit here today. Normally I sit real close to the snack bar. But today I felt that I should be over here."

"Why?"

Norah didn't know why she asked the question, but she did.

Sophia looked like she was thinking hard. "You know, I think I'm supposed to tell you something."

"Really?"

"Yes," the older woman replied. "I'm supposed to tell you that you're supposed to listen."

"Listen? To what?"

Sophia shrugged. "I don't rightly know. Just listen, I guess. You'll hear what you need to hear. Listen. That's what I've been impressed to tell you."

Just then a young girl, no more than eleven, with freckles and sun-bleached blonde hair came running up to them.

"Nina," Sophia called out. "What are you doing here? You're supposed to be at Universal."

The little girl grinned. "We were. Until Bucky threw up all over Grandpa and himself. I told him that they stank too bad to stay. So me and Glissy decided to go to the pool while Grandpa and Bucky took a shower and burned their clothes."

"Is Bucky—Benjamin—all right?"

Nina nodded. "He's okay. He snuck the whole can of macadamia nuts from the mini-bar when we got back.

"Heavens. They're seven dollars a can."

Nina shrugged.

Sophia slipped her book back in her bag. "Well, Norah, I think this is good-bye for now. Keep reading. And listen. Listen good and you'll hear what you need to hear."

Norah watched the older woman walk after her granddaughter, who bounced in front of her more careful steps like a rabbit in front of a turtle.

Norah woke with a start. She blinked her eyes and sat up. For a long moment, she wasn't really aware of where she was or what was happening. She put her hand over her heart and felt its wild pulsing.

It was so real.

It must have been a dream, she decided.

It was only a dream. It felt real, but it was only a dream.

She heard the words ringing in her ears. She never remembered dreams, even only seconds after she woke up. But today she heard the words.

She had fallen asleep by the pool. The sun was just about to slip behind the building. The words still echoed in her head.

Then she recalled what Sophia had said. *Listen good and you'll hear what you need to hear.*

She blinked again, then sat up. She dropped her book into the bag. She stood up, slipped on her sandals, threw her cover-up over her shoulders, and began to walk toward the building. By the time she was halfway there, she was running, her sandals making loud flapping noises with each step.

HOMESTEAD, PENNSYLVANIA—"Harriet Neale. May I help you?"

She was wondering who might be calling her on her cell phone during office hours.

Harriet was a full-sized woman, with thick arms and legs and a substantial figure. The phone looked small in her hands. Her brown hair was tied up into a large bun at the back of her head. Her lab coat was dragged down with notepads and stethoscope.

She listened intently for a moment.

"Calm down, Norah. The rats are fine. I'm fine."

Her face tightened in concentration. She nodded every few seconds and offered a grunted affirmation. After five minutes she sighed and said, "Okay. You're right about that. It does sound crazy."

She listened again for another minute.

"Okay, Norah. You haven't been drinking, have you?"

She actually held the phone away from her ear. "I'm kidding, Norah. If a spinster aunt can't kid her favorite niece, who can she kid?"

She listened again. "Okay. It doesn't make any sense. You're right. Dreams can sometimes seem very real. And it sounds like you had a doozy. But if it makes you feel better, I'll do it."

She paused. "Yes, right now. I've just locked the office. I can get the rats over to Dr. Matt's in five minutes. That okay? Can I tell him what this is all about?"

She listened, then sighed. "Okay then, I won't. But when you get home, you have a lot of explaining to do. You'll be home in a week, right? Good. And remember that I'll be gone for my fishing trip to Canada then. No cell phones—so don't try and track me down, okay?"

She smiled. "And I love you, too."

She clicked off the phone, slipped it back into her pocket. She went into a small room filled with an assortment of cages. The two rats Norah had given her stood on their rear legs, their noses sniffing greedily at the air. Harriet seldom entered the room without giving them some sort of snack. She was a sucker for begging.

She reached into her pocket and split a small dog biscuit. The rats took it eagerly and began to nibble away.

Harriet reached over and took each cage by the handle. She kicked open the back door of the office, knowing the dogs in the boarding kennel would start barking furiously. She hoped the racket wouldn't disturb the two rats.

In five minutes she had delivered them to a fellow vet, in practice just a few blocks away. Because of the late hour, Dr. Matt was gone of course, but the rats were accepted by the young technician without comment or interest.

"I'll call Dr. Matt in the morning to explain," Harriet said.

The young man shrugged and muttered, "Whatever."

Harriet stood for a moment, decried the state of manners among the young, and then headed back to her office.

PITTSBURGH, PENNSYLVANIA—As Ayman unlocked his car, he banged the back of his hand on the rearview mirror. He cursed as the knuckles throbbed.

He started the car and jammed it into gear and tore away from the street with a great squeal. He drove fast and carefully. He pulled to a stop several blocks away. He turned off the car and unlocked the glove box. He pulled out a velvet bag.

There was the flash of metal and a rattle. He extracted five stocky bullets and loaded them carefully into the chamber of the pistol. He checked the safety and slipped the gun under his belt. He grinned, enjoying the feeling of the cold metal.

He held up a page torn from the phone directory. He folded it twice, then once again.

Holding it up to the light from the street lamp, he ran his finger down the column until he came to one name: Harriet Neale, DVM/Office: 516 E. Kaufman/Residence: 518 E. Kaufman.

He smiled broadly, switched on the car, and sped off into the night.

The next day, a short news item appeared in the *Pittsburgh Tribune-Review:*

LOCAL VET SHOT DURING BURGLARY

Homestead veterinarian Dr. Harriet Neale was shot last night in an apparent robbery at her office on East Kaufman Street. She stated to police that she had returned to her office after dark when confronted by an unknown assailant. The assailant fired several shots. Dr. Neale was struck in the neck and chest. She is listed in serious but stable condition.

Police stated they have no suspects in the case. Several veterinary offices have been broken into over the past several months in Armstrong County, presumably in an effort to obtain illegal drugs. Animal tranquilizers are often ground into a powder and resold as a cheap substitute for heroin. Police were unable to determine at this time if any drugs were missing.

Harriet lay in her hospital bed, running over the previous night's events in her mind through the haze of the painkillers she'd been administered. She briefly considered calling her niece, but not wanting Norah to feel compelled to return early from her conference, she decided to wait until Norah's return. She'd heard of other vets' offices being robbed, and there was nothing to indicate this incident was any different.

18

SAINT MARK'S SQUARE, VENICE, ITALY—The flock of pigeons took off in a fluttery whir, wheeling and turning about the piazza in one great feathered mass.

"What did you do?" Duffy asked. "I walked through this piazza yesterday and the pigeons milled about, calm as cows. You come by and they take off in a panic. Do you think they can sense that you kill small animals for fun and profit?"

Hays, not in the mood for lighthearted banter, simply grunted. He stopped at a newsstand and bought a *USA Today*, a copy of the *International Herald Tribune*, and a day-old *New York Times*.

"You're like a dog at a hydrant, Hays," Duffy continued. "You can't pass a newsstand without stopping."

Hays continued to ignore him.

Duffy appeared to be energized by the picturesque city, with its near-stifling humidity, canals, and scent of intrigue. He chatted in cheery, broken Italian with gondoliers, waiters, and shopkeepers. He seemed to want to stop at every sidewalk café for cappuccino and biscotti, and he began before lunch planning where to have dinner.

Hays and Duffy sat at Café Florian facing the square. Music played as tourists fed the pigeons. Hays began to read through his papers, starting with *USA Today* and concluding with the *New York Times*. Duffy was about to comment on his precise reading order, but he had already done so every morning since they'd left the United States nearly a week ago.

They had walked from their small *pensione* several blocks and bridges away. Venice was a crowded city, and very expensive, but they had managed, after a diligent hunt, to find a not-truly-expensive, quaint bed and breakfast with a partially obstructed view of the Grand Canal. Hays had argued against selecting Venice as the jumping-off point, but Duffy had dismissed his reservations.

"There is a small town south of Venice—Chioggia. And south of that small town is a beach the locals call the Devil's Landing. It is well-known by those who, shall I say, circumnavigate the government's import and export taxes."

Hays had argued that they should stay there, then, near that beach. "Chioggia has hostels. I looked it up on the Internet in Rome," he told Duffy.

"My friend, we are closer to my world now than yours," Duffy had explained. "A tourist in Venice—no one notices. Look—the city is crawling with them. We disappear here—nameless and faceless. A tourist in Chioggia—especially two male tourists traveling together, one of them extremely handsome—well, that may get tongues wagging. We don't want that. One never knows who is listening. In Chioggia there are many keen ears—of that I'm certain."

Hays had reluctantly agreed, knowing they were paying ten times as much for a modest hotel in Venice than they would pay in Chioggia—or anyplace else in Italy, for that matter.

Duffy had just signaled to the waiter that he would like a third cappuccino. Hays returned to his newspaper, not having finished his first coffee.

"You Italians have a way with coffee and milk," Duffy said in Italian to the waiter, who feigned amusement over his awkward pronunciation.

At that moment Hays gasped. He held the newspaper rigid in his hands. After a short moment, he sat up straight. He slapped at the newsprint.

"Look, Duffy, it's started. It's already started."

Duffy looked around, wondering what had started without his notice.

Hays slapped the paper open. He folded it again in half and pointed to a one-column article, buried near the middle of the paper.

Duffy took it, and trying not to squint, read the few paragraphs.

UNKNOWN DISEASE ANNIHILATES ISLAND VILLAGE
Reuters, Pemba Island

"Where is Pemba Island?" Duffy asked.

"Just off the coast of Tanzania. By Zanzibar. It used to be part of German East Africa," Hays answered. Geography was one of his hobbies.

Duffy read:

Officials are mystified by a disease that appears to have killed every inhabitant of the small village of Chake-chake on the tropical island of Pemba, just off the coast of Tanzania.

"Every inhabitant of the village, approximately 500 people, was found dead or dying," said Dr. Rudolph Glosser. "We have done tests and so far we have ruled out Ebola or its variants. We are leaning to suspect the community water supply. It may have been contaminated in some manner. There has been some mining in the area in recent years."

Officials theorize that the isolated community may have been suffering from the malady for some time prior to the discovery. Chake-chake has no telephone service, nor regular supply deliveries. A reporter on the scene stated there was sufficient food in the village and that the bodies showed no signs of obvious trauma.

Reports are that the bodies had been burned to prevent any further spread of possible infection.

Glosser, an infectious disease specialist with the Trans-Africa Medical Group, was in Tanzania when the first reports of the mass death were received. The Trans-Africa Medical Group provides medical assistance through East Africa and is funded by the German pharmaceutical firm Huber/Loss.

Duffy lowered the newspaper. His shocked features must have matched Hays'.

"Huber/Loss is involved in this, aren't they?" Duffy said. It was a declaration, not a question.

"I'm sure they are. I didn't want to believe it at first. But somehow, they are. They keep showing up where they shouldn't be. Maybe they are just funding the wrong people."

"Would they do that?" Duffy asked.

"I wouldn't have thought so. But it all points in their direction."

"Do we go to Germany, then?" Duffy asked.

Hays shook his head, as if he had already considered the idea and discarded it. "No. There would be no trail to Germany. Besides, the virus isn't there. It's in the Middle East, somewhere. They would never be so foolish to put their home country at risk. No, the virus is not there. We start in the Middle East first."

"They've started it, haven't they? They used the virus already." Duffy spoke without emotion, yet the words were edged with an acknowledgement of an unspeakable terror that had been tested—and now awaited further trials.

Hays stared off into the endless, pellucid Italian sky for a long time. His words were measured, burnished quiet, solid as steel.

"We have to get them, Duffy. We have to stop this from going any further."

Hays and Duffy sat at the small table at Café Florian for close to an hour after reading the news report about the African village. They sat in silence, hardly seeing the flood of tourists swarming past them.

Hays finally summoned up the energy to fold up his newspapers. "We have to move fast, Duffy. We need to leave now."

It was obvious Duffy wanted to agree, but couldn't. "The moon, my friend. It all waits on the moon. You know that. We only have another day to wait."

A "fishing" boat had been dispatched from Lebanon a few days earlier. The small vessel was scheduled to pick them up just south of Chioggia. The "fishermen" wanted a moonless night for their task. No one could have persuaded them to take a greater risk by coming early. The vessel was already at sea, making stops, pickups, and deliveries in less secure ports with much more lax security.

"Italy—no one goes there anymore. Except the immigrant smugglers, and even those people don't take unneeded risks," the owner of the fishing boat had explained when he spoke to Duffy. "The Italians have patrol boats now, not like in the old days. They like to shoot things. It is dangerous for men like me to be in Italian waters. We must wait for the death of the moon. There is no way to come before the fifteenth. No way at all."

"Do you really think this is the virus you found?" Duffy asked as they crossed a small footbridge.

"If it wasn't Huber/Loss, if it wasn't an isolated village, if they hadn't burned the bodies, if there hadn't been reports of ample food, if there hadn't been any signs of trauma—there are too many ifs and coincidences for it to be anything else. Can you think of anything else?"

Duffy shook his head no. "We both know how virulent the virus was.

We know how quickly it impacted the test animals. Within days we saw results. It was fast. A clever high school biology teacher could have begun to accumulate the virus in sufficient quantities for just such an experiment in a day, maybe two days. There's no rocket science involved in this."

"Delivering the virus is another matter," he added. "We saw that delivery in a water solution was every bit as effective as inoculation. Apparently it does migrate to humans. The African officials will blame it on a contaminated well. In a week or two, as long as it doesn't happen again, everyone will forget about this and any poor people who died. And if Huber/Loss is behind it, there's no way they'll risk another test. They've found out that it works."

Hays stopped, took a deep breath. "It has to be the virus from the skull. It has to be. A weapon is no good unless you test it. I think whoever took the virus from us has now tested it. We may not have much time left. Will we be able to find them, Duffy? Your connections in Lebanon—can they help us find them?"

Duffy waited, then shrugged. He wasn't a man given to uncertainty. The small movement of his shoulders disquieted Hays to no end.

"I'm hoping they can help. My family is connected throughout the Middle East. But the Middle East is not a small place, my friend. It is a big area, and there are more tribes and cliques and factions and sects than anyone imagines. If we are lucky, perhaps. If we are good, all the better. Very lucky and very good, even better. And perhaps," Duffy added quietly, "perhaps if your God favors us with his assistance. Perhaps that favor is what we need most."

"I've been asking for his help all along," Hays said. "If he isn't on our side, we have no hope."

"Is he on our side, Hays? Is your God on our side?"

Hays looked away. He looked out to the water of the Grand Canal and blue sky beyond the window of the sitting room. He had been doing little else than praying since they left the United States. He prayed all the time, more than he had ever prayed in his life. And yet he didn't feel any answer, any sense that their mission met with God's favor. He prayed and asked and beseeched and did all the spiritual things that he knew to do—yet he felt no assurance in his soul. There was no obvious answer from the heavens. God hadn't descended to earth in the guise of a flaming bush. Nor had he sent any angels, as far as Hays could determine, to offer guidance or assistance.

Hays looked back to Duffy and saw in his eyes a glimmer of childlike expectancy, an almost innocent yearning for someone to be in control and have an answer. It was a yearning unlike any Hays had ever seen. Duffy was as desperate as he was—desperate to have someone on their side.

"Yes," Hays said firmly, "I know God will be with us."

Duffy smiled. "Then that is all the reassurance I need right now. Your God is on our side."

Hays looked down at his feet. *I said that God will be with us. I didn't say he was on our side.*

He hoped he wasn't misleading his friend.

ITALIAN COAST, ADRIATIC SEA—Hays waded out into the surf, following Duffy into the waist-high waves toward a small red lamp the size of a man's hand on the bow of the boat. He hoisted his duffel bag onto the boat and clambered on board. The vessel nearly capsized as he did.

When he and Duffy arranged themselves on deck in the deep darkness and felt the wind gather as the captain turned back toward the sea, Hays spoke.

"This will get us to Lebanon? I would be afraid taking this small of a boat across the Monongahela River back home."

He was sure that Duffy was as worried as he, but the darkness hid all visible signs of fear.

"The captain has been doing this since I was a little boy. As did his father before him. We descended from the Phoenicians, who were magical sailors and navigators. We will get to Lebanon, my friend. Be sure of that."

Hays found no comfort hearing the loud, coughing chug of the ancient diesel engine that seemed to invite whatever sea patrol was out there to investigate. In a few minutes the lights of Venice and Chioggia had vanished from the horizon behind them. Now only dark remained—and the glow of the captain's cigarette. It illuminated his lined, leathery face like a coal lit under his chin. His eyes were only half-open, as if he were riding a late commuter train home, bored and tired and uninterested.

Duffy pulled his windbreaker closer about his throat. The air had gone chilly, filled with salt and fear.

"And, my friend, your God will see to it that we make it home. He has promised, right?"

Hays didn't hesitate to answer, as if reassuring himself as well. "He has, Duffy. That he has."

MEDITERRANEAN SEA, SOUTH OF THE GREEK ISLANDS—A spray of seawater awoke Hays. The sky remained dark, save for a sliver of purple at the eastern horizon of the Mediterranean marking the beginning of the day. The boat dipped into the crest of a wave and the spray arced up, the drops catching the faint purple of the sunrise.

Hays found himself lost in a familiar debate. *If I had only listened to that small voice and called the CDC when I first opened the skull, none of this would be happening now. If I had thought rationally, there would have been no hesitation—friend or no friend. Tom Stough might have lost his job, but he also might not be dead.* He had thought he was doing the right thing. He had thought he was protecting a friend. But he had protected no one. In fact, he had put thousands, maybe millions at risk—all because he thought he was smart enough and clever enough to handle any situation that might come up.

He reviewed in his mind, for the thousandth time, his options. Every police and security agency had been informed. But the crushing reality was that there was no evidence. Hays and Duffy both saw the results—but how many lunatic scientists does the CDC and the FBI deal with daily? Yes, he could have pestered and cajoled them—and perhaps someone might have believed him, given enough time. But what would Hays have had them do?

Hays sighed at this sudden surge of reality. He knew all this weeks ago. It took great energy to keep from dwelling on it. And he suddenly felt fatigued—more tired than he had been in years.

And now, in addition to weariness, Hays felt great remorse. And there was little he could do to atone for it—other than undertaking the journey he was now on.

Hays looked to the eastern horizon. A faint slip of the sun cut through the thin scud of clouds.

God, I will do what you want—but I desperately need your help and your protection and guidance. This evil has to be stopped. I pray that this is an evil Duffy and I can stop. Help us. Please. Help us.

The boat dug into a bigger swell and a handful of water splashed aboard, washing over Hays' head, fully waking him. He wiped his palm over his face and eyes. The air chilled his skin. He wondered if it was some sort of sign. After a long moment he decided it probably was not.

19

QUADARE CITY, QUADARE—Fadhil couldn't recall a time when he felt more alive, more in tune with the gods—when the very colors of the sky seemed to grow more intense, more vivid. He stepped out on to his small balcony and took a deep breath. The air was hot, nearly fetid, but it was no matter. Fadhil wanted to draw energy from the heat, let it fill his lungs and encompass him like a blanket.

He remained outside for only a moment, then hurried back into the dark air-conditioned office. He wiped at the sweat that had already formed on his forehead. His shirt stuck to his back, and he wedged his shoulders back and forth, feeling the cloying sensation of fabric clammy with sweat.

He glanced at the remote thermometer on his desk that produced a digital readout of the temperature in both Fahrenheit and centigrade. He always thought the Western style made the heat sound more impressive.

"One hundred and one," he whispered, as if saying it aloud would make it hotter.

He wiped his fingers on his shirt, leaving a small streak over his heart. He picked up the hard copy of the e-mail one more time. A corner was already damp from his fingerprints.

> *Your report was most astonishing. It appears that your predic-*
> *tion has come to fruition. Please accept my congratulations.*

The e-mail was not signed. It had come from an address that Fadhil assumed originated in Germany. But then again, Fadhil was not astute in the ways of electronic messaging. It might have been relayed a number of times before it landed at Fadhil's office.

He heard the timid tapping of his assistant.

"What?" Fadhil shouted. "Come in or stay out, but announce yourself, you son of a goat-herder."

The door edged open, as if moved by spirits. Fadhil could see only the crown of his assistant's head, peaking past the door. "The doctor, sir?"

Fadhil scowled, then brightened. "Oh, yes. Send him in—at once."

Fadhil had almost forgotten that he'd sent for the doctor. They had spoken on the phone after Fadhil watched the news on CNN. But he wanted a more personal report, more details.

"My good Doctor Haj. I trust that you received my thanks."

The doctor nearly bowed. "Yes, indeed. It was most generous."

Fadhil knew a few extra Quadare dollars might boost the doctor's morale, and perhaps his loyalty as well.

"Good. You must tell me more about the test. You must tell me of the effectiveness of the Micah virus."

The doctor took a deep breath. He began to speak in dense medical terms, Fadhil nodding and smiling as if he understood it. At the point when he grew bored, he stopped the doctor by raising his hand.

"All of this to say that the test was very successful?"

The doctor swallowed. He paused. "Yes. It was very successful."

"Is there any danger of the virus spreading from that location?"

The doctor looked at his palms and didn't raise his eyes as he spoke. "From the report, it was said that the virus was placed in the one community well. When the test was complete, the well was fired."

"Fired?"

"A mixture of explosives that produce intense heat. I am sure that the virus was eradicated."

Fadhil leaned back and placed his hands on his stomach as if he'd eaten a full meal. "And you will be able to duplicate this event? You are working to that end?"

The doctor hesitated.

"Well? Can you?"

"Yes. Perhaps. Not immediately. Not safely. Repeating will be difficult."

Fadhil didn't say a word, but pursed his lips.

The doctor stuttered and continued. "On a small scale, we, if Allah wills it, might be able to repeat the experiment. But one must take into account the variables—that the village was isolated, that it was so unsophisticated, that it had but a single water source. That made dispersion observable and controllable. But such conditions are not easy to replicate. We have to determine optimum motility levels, and we are yet uncertain of the host's vitality. A virus is complicated. A great concern is managing containment so it does not attack the people who have set the trap. This is unlike a weapon. A virus has no gun sights, no way to aim. Unfortunately the person who was our agent to the village was also among the dead."

It was obvious Fadhil shared few, if any, of the doctor's worries. The doctor wiped his forehead. Despite the drone of the air-conditioning, the room grew warmer. He continued. "I'm told that two rats survived the original testing."

Fadhil shrugged. "I'm told that also. Why would that matter? Does it have any bearing on your work?"

Color returned to the doctor's face. "If we could examine those animals ... we have not been able to duplicate a nonfatal exposure in rats. The virus, as I can see, has so far proven to be 100 percent efficient. That makes what we have dangerous to everyone who comes near. If we had access to those specimens, we might find a way to formulate some treatment or inoculation. Otherwise, we must use the extreme caution. A false move and hundreds or thousands could be at risk."

Fadhil grinned. "So many at risk. The great Satan would be at peril, would he not?"

The doctor, after a moment, nodded. "As we might be as well, sir. That is, without those two lab animals—without their immunity."

Fadhil flipped his hand through the air as if batting at a fly. The safety of hundreds and thousands was of no great concern to him now.

The day of the Micah virus—and the Micah Judgment—was at hand. If Quadare was the anvil, Fadhil was the hammer.

He couldn't help but grin broadly.

LEBANON COAST—Hays was surprised at how cold the water felt. The waters of the Adriatic Sea on the Italian coast had seemed much warmer. He and Duffy took their leave from the boat fifty yards from shore.

The captain gestured toward the beach.

Duffy offered a few words in reply, then slipped into the water, holding his canvas duffle over his head.

Hays jumped with a gasp. "I'm freezing. I thought the Mediterranean climate was supposed to be warm," he said.

Duffy grinned back at his friend. "Welcome to the land of surprises, where things are never what they seem to be."

The beach was deserted as they sloshed out of the surf. To their right Hays could see a glow. "Is that Beirut?"

Duffy looked to the south, past the small dunes and sea grass bending in the early morning breeze. "No, we are much farther north. North of Byblos—the oldest city in the world. Just a few clicks south of Messaylha."

Duffy sat down and unlaced his shoes, removed his wet socks and wrung them out.

"This is a deserted strip of beach. Except for the smugglers."

Hays still held his duffle bag as if expecting to need to sprint to safety. "Now where?"

Duffy looked up. "Now we sit and wait. Our ride will be here soon enough."

"Our ride?"

Duffy pointed over his shoulder.

"The bus service starts at six a.m. Having a ride waiting—that could be dangerous to both. We will pretend to be vagabonds—professional travelers. If the bus keeps its schedule, we will have our breakfast in Beirut. And you will meet my family. So I suggest you try to dry your socks. A man with wet shoes is welcome in no home."

Hays waited, but knew he had to ask. "Old Lebanese saying?"

Duffy grinned as Hays took the bait. "No, but it is what my mother would say."

Hays set his duffle down, and slowly, reluctantly, undid his shoes and socks, wrung them out, and waited for the sun.

BEIRUT, LEBANON—Hays imagined if he took one more morsel of food, he would literally explode. He couldn't remember ever eating as much as he had just consumed.

Duffy's family slipped in and out in a steady stream. Duffy would hug and kiss and shake hands and introduce Hays as his best American friend. Hays repeated the few words in Arabic that he knew: *sukran, taba yawmuka, yus iduni t-a arruf ilayka* ("thank you," "hello," "glad to meet you").

Many of Duffy's family members spoke at least a smattering of English. Yet for most of that first morning, much of Hays' response was limited to smiling and chewing and smiling some more.

Duffy hadn't been home in almost five years, so it was cause for celebration—a celebration not tempered by the unorthodoxy of his arrival. It seemed to Hays as though everyone knew how they slipped into the country and no one seemed all that surprised.

"Lebanese are wonderful at keeping secrets," Duffy told Hays. "Keeping the peace is another matter. That's probably why this city has been destroyed and rebuilt seven times. But a secret—that is a sacred trust. No one will ask and no one will tell further than what needs to be told."

Somewhere near noon, Hays held up his hands in surrender. Duffy's mother took his capitulation with a smile. She chattered a moment, then Duffy groaned as he translated.

"She wants to know what you would like for dinner."

After Hays had agreed that roast lamb stuffed with rice and vegetables, with chicken kabobs and a dozen salads and appetizers, would be fine for dinner, he and Duffy were allowed to leave the Quahaar home.

Duffy's family lived in the Ashrafieh neighborhood of Beirut, a cluster of narrow winding streets and some beautiful old residences. The family's modest home was old and had escaped unscathed when civil war tore the country apart a few decades prior. If the Quahaars were wealthy and influential, however, they didn't flaunt it. Duffy explained that was the way of the Lebanese, who believe only the gauche display their wealth with pride. Those who truly held power and prestige seldom made public note of their status. Hays concluded that Duffy's family might be much more powerful and connected than their modest settings indicated.

As they left, Duffy's grandfather grasped Hays by the shoulder and whispered to him, "Whatever it is you seek, you must let us help. What it is you and my grandson are looking for, you will let us help you find that thing."

At least that is what Hays thought he said. It came out a bit more garbled than that, a thick blending of Arabic, French, and English. He thumped Hays on the chest as a point of exclamation. "*Hada laka. Atamanna laka najahan bahiran.*"

Duffy translated the words. "My grandfather says that all of the family is at our service, and he blesses us with great success on our journey."

Hays and Duffy strolled down the street, accompanied by two male cousins, both in their early twenties, and both dressed in what Hays identified as Donald Trump casual. Their destination was a small shop that featured an Internet café a short walk beyond the Corniche, Beirut's seaside promenade.

In the store, selling stacks of the forty daily Lebanese newspapers, Coca-Cola, and *narghile*—flavored tobacco the Lebanese used in their hookahs—the two men were drawn farther into the dimmer recesses of the store, through a beaded curtain—another prop from a bad espionage movie, Hays thought—and on into a back room with a small table. The room, no bigger than a closet, smelled of strong espresso and inexpensive cologne.

A thick-necked man who hadn't shaved in several days nodded to them. Duffy turned to Hays and said softly, "This is Sadek. He is called the *allama*—the teacher. Sometimes they call him the *sikkiyn*—the knife."

"Why the knife?" Hays asked.

"I have never asked. You have the envelope with you?"

Hays carried a photocopy of the envelope. Hays handed it to the man, who didn't raise his hand to take it. Hays gently placed it on the table and slid the note toward him.

The man sniffed once, then leaned close to the table. He remained silent for a moment, then looked up and sniffed again, and spoke in thick French-accented English.

"The man who writes this, he is from Quadare. Maybe he lives in Lebanon, but he is from Quadare."

Hays looked to the stranger, then to Duffy, then back. "How can you be sure?"

Sadek flexed his neck in a deliberate manner. The pops and cracks sounded as loud as gunshots.

"I'm sure."

"Why?" Hays asked again, colder, harder.

Sadek grunted and jabbed at the note with his forefinger. "See here—in the first line of the address—he writes *hayawan qitta*. That means, literally, 'cat animal.' Only in Quadare have I heard that phrase. It refers to the ancient lions that used to roam the desert. They use those words to mean the lions of the desert. Nowhere else will you hear that phrase. The person who wrote this is from Quadare."

"Are you sure?" Hays asked. It was obvious that Sadek was not a man accustomed to being questioned.

Sadek held up his palms. "My friend, I'm sure."

No one spoke for a long minute.

Sadek tapped at the envelope once. "You must be careful. When the Quadarese have said those words—'for the lion of the desert'—they most often then repeat the phrase *dam manisr.*"

Hays saw Duffy tense.

"It means blood will be broken. Not shed. But broken. It means total annihilation. The Quadarese may be delusional—but they are vengeful. You must be careful."

Sadek slid the envelope back toward Hays. He slipped it into his pocket. "We will be careful."

"See that you are. Duffy now owes me a favor, and I expect him to be alive in order to repay."

And with that Sadek erupted into a coughing fit of laughing, or a laughing fit of coughing. The hacking noise followed them as they made their exit back into the crowds on the street.

PITTSBURGH, PENNSYLVANIA—Ayman paced, his steps hypnotically repetitive. Roberta sat on the couch in his small apartment and tried not to move, nor watch him.

She had heard the news about Norah's aunt, the veterinarian, and grew anxious and silent. She stopped herself from considering that he had anything to do with the robbery and the shooting. She told herself he was a good man. She believed that. She tried her best to believe that.

Ayman stopped and scowled at her. She tried her best not to cringe.

He flipped open his cell phone and punched in a long series of numbers. He listened, then slapped the phone closed. He said something in his native tongue, and Roberta was quite sure it was a string of curses and invective. His eyes danced a certain way when he cursed—as if he thought his words might be causing someone actual pain.

He went closer to the window and tried the number again.

Again he cursed, then glowered at Roberta.

"Why did you not tell me about this Hays and Duffy before? They are in Italy for a week and I know nothing about it. Why?"

Ayman words were edged in metal, sharp metal.

Roberta had answered him before.

"I did mention it before. Didn't I? I think I told you." Her words grew more frantic. "I—I didn't think it was of any interest to anyone. I would have mentioned it to you again. Norah hardly mentioned it to me. I didn't think—"

He slapped at the air in her direction. "You are a stupid woman. Sometimes I wonder why I have bothered with you."

Roberta hung her head. She wondered the same—why a handsome, virile man such as Ayman would bother with her. She could understand his anger. If she had just mentioned the news about Hays, everything would have been better. Ayman wouldn't be upset with her. Ayman would be holding her in his strong arms. It would all be perfect if it hadn't been for her failures. She needed to think more clearly. That was what he needed—a woman who could support him and give him what he needed.

He turned away from her and punched the numbers again into his cell phone. He spoke rapidly, then listened. He spoke again—for several minutes. He glared at Roberta as he continued to speak. *He must be talking about me now*, she thought.

He listened for a long time, nodding.

He spoke once more, for several minutes, listened, then snapped the phone shut.

He carefully placed the phone on the counter. He walked over to the sofa and sat next to Roberta. He took her hands in his.

"You say this Norah will return in three days?"

Roberta thought for a moment, then told herself that she must tell the truth. *If I tell the truth, Ayman will be pleased. Just tell the truth.*

"Yes. She will be back early Sunday morning."

Ayman smiled. Then he drew her hands closer to his chest.

"We will wait for her together, you and I. You will not call her. We will wait. Three days. Not a long time. Not so long at all."

Roberta felt the pressure on her hands and felt him lean toward her.

She had no option but to let herself be lowered onto the sofa.

"Not so long at all."

20

QUADARE CITY, QUADARE—The cool air flowing over his face from the car air conditioner, Hameed listened patiently to Ayman on his phone.

Hameed at once grew concerned when Ayman mentioned Hays and Duffy. He had investigated their backgrounds some weeks prior—and when he'd discovered their Army Ranger training, he had become, not anxious, exactly, but not exactly calm either.

Hameed was close to his goal—closer than he had ever been. He could taste the power and the authority. He wouldn't allow these two third-rate researchers to block his path. Italy was too close.

"Does either of these men have a wife or girlfriend?"

Ayman had answered that Duffy had no single woman—that he had scores of them. Hameed smiled at hearing of Western women and their propensity for finding Arab men irresistible.

"Hays," Ayman said, "did have such a woman—to whom he was once engaged to be married."

"Ayman, listen to me carefully," Hameed instructed, "That woman is a person of interest. Do you know what that means?"

Ayman knew what it meant.

"A person of interest, Ayman. And I know that as a soldier in the noble army of the just cause of Quadare, you will not disappoint me or your native land."

Hameed could nearly see the young man beam proudly through the phone. Selecting a simple soldier for such an undertaking was indeed a high honor. And if he succeeded, he would be celebrated in song and poetry.

Ayman reassured Hameed that he wouldn't fail.

"A person of interest, Ayman."

Hameed clicked his phone closed and allowed himself a moment of smug pride. He had handled the situation well. In case this Hays and Duffy grew troublesome, he now would have a deterrent.

Hameed slipped down into the leather seat and smiled.

BEIRUT, LEBANON—Hays could hardly see through the thick *narghile* smoke of the café, tinted blue by the dozen computer screens set about the perimeter of the room.

"Do they have a nonsmoking section?" he asked, pretending to gasp.

"This is the nonsmoking section," Duffy responded with a grin.

Duffy led Hays and the two cousins to a table near the back. A slight, very intense young man, a half-smoked cigarette dangling from his lip, greeted them with a nonchalant nod, his eyes half-lidded shut.

"Duffy—long time, my friend."

"Years," Duffy said. "I see you're doing well."

"Caught the right wave. Computers. Internet. Who knew?"

Duffy leaned over to Hays. "This is Yass. We went to school together. Now he owns this place and a dozen more all over Beirut."

"It's a living," Yass said in perfectly nuanced English. "Your family, are they well?"

Duffy nodded. "They asked about you."

"Give my regards."

"I will."

Yass snubbed out his cigarette in an already overflowing ashtray, then took another from the pack and lit it. "You have a question for me?"

Hays took out the envelope that had been found in their lab after the burglary—the envelope with the Huber/Loss logo on it. "Does this address mean anything to you?"

Yass studied the writing. "No. But I have friends who can check for you. Official records—and unofficial records—if you like. I know little about computers, can you believe it? But I know friends who know everything about them. Let me ask."

Hays' face reflected his disappointment.

Yass coughed and the ash on his cigarette tumbled onto the keyboard. He bent over and blew it away. "Come back tonight. We will know more tonight."

Hays was almost in a coma from the lamb and chicken and other dishes numerous enough to make the dining-room table groan in protest. He was glad they had made their evening appointment. It gave them both reason to escape before the third and fourth deserts were brought out.

"Your mother," Hays said as they neared the Internet café, "could be classified as a dangerous weapon."

Duffy agreed. "It's how she shows love. And at least she's a good cook. What would happen if she weren't?"

The café had become smokier, were such a thing possible. Yass greeted them both warmly and offered them coffee. Hays accepted, Duffy demurred.

The coffee, thick as honey, surprised Hays. He stole a glance around at other tables and saw no creams or sugars. He took that to mean it was to be drunk as is, black and strong. It was definitely strong. Hays resigned himself to spending the next two nights awake in reaction to its potency.

He spoke first. "Did you have any luck?"

A look of pain swept over Duffy's face. Hays suddenly became aware that this direct sort of question would be thought improper by Lebanese standards.

Yass must have noticed the exchange. "It is all right, my friend. I have enough American customers that I know how they think. Always the direct route. Always in your face, as they say. There is no offense. I almost see their common affectation as charming." He motioned them to come closer.

"The address is a shabby apartment block in the Hamra neighborhood, south of the American University. Mostly guest workers. I'm told that many Quadarese live there."

Hays waited with great expectation, leaning in closer to Yass. Yass said nothing more, then grinned. "You Americans want everything all at once, do you not? Patience is not one of your country's virtues."

He stopped and slowly lit a cigarette.

"We could find little about this address. But the words here at the top—*hayawan qitta*—those words we found interesting. Someone remembered a fellow saying those exact words in this café several weeks ago—maybe a month. He cannot recall if this person calls them to someone, or names himself those words. But nevertheless, we will take a walk to this apartment block tonight. We will ask questions."

He exhaled a long draft of smoke. "Duffy, since you are asking for a favor, I'm assuming this is a serious matter. Otherwise, you wouldn't come to me, would you?"

The din of the café crowded and jostled, and Duffy nodded. "It is serious. And I do need answers."

Yass shrugged. "I imagined that was the case. It is difficult to forget as well as forgive—is it not, my friend?"

"It is indeed," Duffy replied.

A small cluster of young men gathered outside the café. Midnight had passed and traffic had slowed. The streets of Beirut never grew totally quiet, but the busy hum had subsided. Duffy's two cousins had changed from Donald Trump casual to outfits done all in black. Even the gold jewelry they had worn around their necks had been removed and the shiny watches replaced by ones with black straps and luminescent faces. Yass brought two friends with him as well, also dressed all in black, or nearly so.

Hays felt out of place in his khakis and blue golf shirt.

"We should walk," Yass said. "It is only ten minutes from here. I wouldn't park my Mercedes in that neighborhood. Too many petty thieves."

The streets grew narrower. A thin sliver of moon hung over the water and did little to help light their steps. Hays heard ratlike scuffling as they passed the dark, narrow alleyways.

Yass stopped them. He pointed across the street. "It's that building— that's the address on the envelope."

Hays couldn't see much detail. The building was nondescript: pale brick, three stories high, a cluster of television antennas and satellite dishes on the roof, silhouetted by the scant moonlight. A few windows glowed with dim illumination.

They crossed the street and entered the cramped vestibule. A tattered row of buzzers lined the left wall. Yass ran his fingers down the list of names, and stopped.

"The 'Lion of the Desert' lives in three rear. Let's go."

One of Yass's friends bent over at the door, pulled a small wire out of his pocket, and within five seconds had the door open. Everyone except Duffy's cousins entered the room, the cousins remaining outside, flanking the door.

Yass motioned to the window, and the shade was pulled down.

Hays was expecting squalor or a jumble of possessions, but the room had an aesthetic, monklike look. There was a single bed in the corner covered by white sheets and a thin brown blanket. Next to it stood a nightstand with a small lamp and three or four newspapers. Duffy picked one up.

"The *Voice of Quadare*. Three weeks old."

On the far wall was a wooden bookcase filled to overflowing. One of Yass's associates pulled a few volumes out. "Medical books. Textbooks."

He paged through a well-worn book. "He is not a guest worker," he said. "He's a medical student."

He held up a sheet of paper. "His third year at Université Libanaise. Not the best medical school."

Hays wasn't sure what he had expected—a shambling room filled with terrorist literature, perhaps. The ingredients to make bombs, possibly—but not the neat, orderly abode of a medical student.

Duffy was at the small desk and opened the drawers. They were neat and organized. "His student ID."

He passed it to Hays.

Hafez Sadi.

Hays stared at the small picture. He doubted, even after studying the photo, if he would be able to pick the man out of a lineup. Hafez appeared to be normal in every way.

One of Yass's friends sat on the bed and took out his laptop, and waited for a moment. "We have a hot spot nearby. Give me a minute to log on. I'm in his university e-mail account. I figured his password was 'Lion of the Desert.' Not very original—or safe. Anyone here read French?"

Hays opened the small refrigerator. It held a few bottles of water. There was a hotplate by the sink. A few clean dishes had been stacked on the drain board. "I can," Hays said and sat down on the bed.

There was only one incoming e-mail listed under the account of Hafez Sadi—a confirmation from Air France for flight reservations to Quadare and on to Tanzania.

"He sent one e-mail—but not from here—this one originated from a Web mail server in Africa.

The e-mail opened up. The message was short and chilling.

100 percent inoculation. 100 percent success.

"Where was it sent?" Hays asked.

"Just an address. Could be anyone, anywhere. One address in the chain … is in Germany. I know because I use the same server, but this e-mail could be bounced all over the world. Impossible to track."

21

BEIRUT, LEBANON—Smoke swirled about the café. The overhead lights drilled shafts of illumination through the haze. In the back of the room, one might not know if it were daylight or the middle of the night. Hays stretched out in the booth as Duffy went to fetch coffees.

"See if they can make American coffee. Weak American coffee. I don't want another jolt to my system," Hays called out. He rubbed his face, hoping to clear his head and his thoughts.

Yass and Duffy returned with a tray filled with cups and a plate of small desserts. "No Lebanese drinks coffee naked," Yass said. "You must have a sweet with it."

Hays picked up a small triangle of crispy dough. He could feel the sugar and honey before he tasted it.

The three of them drank and ate silently.

Hays finished his coffee. He slid the empty cup to the center of the table and took a deep breath. "We have to get to Quadare."

Yass and Duffy stared at him calmly. Neither appeared the least bit surprised.

Yass first looked about, making sure there were no listening ears in the vicinity.

"It would be a simple matter if you were tourists. You're not tourists. You have no visas, and to visit Quadare, one needs a visa."

Duffy nodded. "We knew that before we left the states. We thought it wouldn't be prudent to announce ourselves so obviously, in any country—especially Quadare."

"Smart," Yass agreed. "If the people who broke into your lab were Quadarese agents, then your names are on their list. You would never get a visa. And if you did, you would be watched from the moment you set foot on Quadare soil."

Duffy and Hays had told Yass as much about the break-in and the virus as they felt comfortable. They didn't relate the whole story. Yass affirmed their suspicions that Quadare had earned a reputation of placing shadowy operatives all over the world—waiting for the moment when they might be of use. Flush with oil money, agents provided an inexpensive offensive weapon—if need be.

"Travel will not be easy. You could take a boat," Yass said, "but that would take days and days. You would have to go through the Suez Canal. Does your family have any big pleasure craft?"

"No," Duffy said.

Yass smiled. "A fishing boat—or a smuggler's boat—would never make it through the canal without arousing a lot of attention. The Egyptians would spot you a mile away. Especially since you have no business in the gulf. No, a boat would be out of the question."

Duffy drummed on the table with his fingers. He always did when he was working on a problem. "We can go overland."

Yass narrowed his eyes. "Through Iraq? Or Israel?"

"Israel is much too well protected," Duffy said. "It must be Iraq. And then through Iran. Down to Bushehr. I have a cousin on my mother's side who manages a marina there. We could charter a boat. We could make the crossing in less than a night."

Hays waited. He looked at Yass to judge if Duffy's plan might be workable.

"Iraq? In these times?" Yass asked.

"When the pot boils over," Duffy said calmly, "the cook is easily distracted."

Yass nodded as if he understood the sentiment.

"The Americans bring heavy security. But the Americans don't patrol every mile. My grandfather still has dealings with the Kurds and the Shiites. There are people there who owe him favors," Duffy said. "He has offered his help."

"What languages do you speak?" Yass asked Hays.

"I'm fluent in German, passable in Russian, and a little less so in French."

Yass appeared impressed. "Most Americans know only one language—and even then, their English is not so good."

Hays looked to Duffy, whose face seemed set, intent. Yass appeared deep in concentration.

"Yes," Duffy said again. "We will go overland. It is our only way."

QUADARE CITY, QUADARE—Fadhil was screaming. He slapped at the desk. "They have been spotted in Beirut. You promised that those two third-rate researchers would never become an issue. You guaranteed it."

Hameed didn't speak.

Fadhil's breath came in angry spurts, like a bull, ready for a charge.

Hameed held his smile. When a bull charges, the matador's cape conceals the glistening, deadly blade. And so it was today.

He waited, counting to twenty, silently.

"I assumed that they wouldn't interfere," he said, never once raising his voice much above a whisper. "It is unlike Americans to worry about consequences of dangerous research. They conduct such criminal activities every day all over the world and never give a thought to people they might poison. However, we must remember that one of these men is Lebanese. I believe it is because of his strength of character—the Arab sense of character—that they have embarked on their mission of interference. If it was only the American—well, they would never have left their home."

Fadhil threw himself back into his chair. He miscalculated and almost tipped over, grabbing at the armrests, his legs flailing into the air.

"Tell me again what you know," Fadhil said, spitting his words out with venom.

"The two Americans broke into the apartment of our operative in Beirut—the one who took the virus to Africa. We have not heard from him in weeks and now believe he died in that experiment. A man in Beirut, the manager of the building where his apartment was located, called—and asked to be compensated for the lost rent as well as requesting a reward for the information about the two Americans—although he did nothing to stop them from entering in the first place."

Fadhil cursed again, loudly.

"Our operatives are told to leave their places clean at all times," he continued, "but the manager said that he found our operative's student ID card there after the Americans visited. I don't know what they might have found."

Fadhil glowered. "Imbecile. Now what are you going to do? These amateurs can't expect to come here and disrupt things, can they? What if they contact their embassy? Or worse yet, CNN? This is a terrible bungle, Hameed, a terrible bungle."

Fadhil glared at the man. Hameed stood without moving, taking great comfort in his matador-with-the-hidden-sword analogy.

Some day I will plunge the blade into your neck, you vile little man, and I will dance in your blood.

Hameed counted to twenty again. "Don't worry. I have purchased the necessary insurance."

"Insurance? What do you mean, insurance?"

Hameed's grin couldn't be held back. "This American has a fiancée—a very attractive young woman who works at the school they call the University of Pittsburgh—as did both these researchers. I have instructed our operative who was stationed there to bring this woman for a visit to Quadare."

Fadhil looked up and unclenched his fists. "A visit?"

"Fadhil," he said, finally playing all his cards, "there is no way these two amateurs could do anything to harm us. There is simply no way. James Bond existed only in the pages of a book."

Fadhil's grimace turned to a smile. He had a complete collection of first printings of all the James Bond spy novels.

"True. No man could be that skilled."

Hameed continued laying out his plan. "But let us assume the worst and that they somehow manage to threaten us and our research. If that were to occur, we hold the ace of all cards—his fiancée. Americans will never do anything that endangers a loved one. That is why they love bombing from airplanes—like in Bosnia. They won't ever get involved on a personal level. Too much risk. The American will stop, and that will stop both of them. The woman will be our protection."

Fadhil appeared to slowly comprehend. His smile grew until it filled his face and the gold crown on his lower jaw glistened in the afternoon light.

"This woman—you are bringing her here? To Quadare?"

"Yes."

Fadhil smiled. "And you say that she is attractive?"

Hameed nodded. "I have seen a picture. Very attractive."

Fadhil leaned back in his chair. "When she arrives, I would like her brought in to see me," he said, allowing the words to slowly form in his mouth, as if savoring them.

Hameed knew what he intended—and replied promptly. "I will bring her to you—if time permits."

Hameed took his leave, knowing that he'd played the game with expert precision.

PITTSBURGH INTERNATIONAL AIRPORT—Norah hated flying. She hated cramped airplanes with dry air, people sneezing and coughing and too many strong, cloying cologne scents. If she had had the time, she would have driven to Florida.

At long last she felt the jolt of the tires on tarmac and the slow, sweeping turn toward the passenger terminal. When the door finally opened, she surged forward, willing the passengers in front to disembark quickly. When she finally entered the terminal, she drew a deep breath.

She gathered her carry-on bag under her arm and headed toward baggage claim. The last two days, nearing sunburn, she had retreated to a lounge chair isolated by the shade and had read the book Hays kept insisting she read.

The book puzzled Norah, yet for some reason she kept at it, and now was only a few pages shy of finishing it. While the book answered a few of her questions, it produced a whole litany of new ones.

Her bag clattered down the motorized ramp, the pink bow making it a snap to identify. She checked the nametag regardless. She pulled out the handle, set her carry-on on top, and headed out of the airport toward the parking lot. She had left her car in the long-term lot, which was well lit and patrolled, offsetting any concern about safety. *What could go wrong?* she thought as she headed into the night.

BEIRUT, LEBANON—Duffy explained their itinerary. "A truck will pick us up in Beirut. We will be hidden behind the cargo, and further hidden behind a small false wall at the front of the cargo area. The driver will carry a handful of American fifty-dollar bills. Any border guards will inspect a box or two, make a great show of being thorough, take their bribes, and we will drive on—the whole way across Iraq, not stopping until we reach the Iranian border."

"How did you do all this? It has been only a few hours since we decided," Hays said.

Duffy shrugged as only a Lebanese could shrug. "A bull looks fast when it is close," he said. "My father said that to me and whatever it means, it means. The work is done, my friend. We will leave tomorrow at dark."

Hays realized that without Duffy's help, without the help of his family, they could have done nothing. "Is traveling at night wise?" he asked. "I read the newspapers. I've read stories of bandits attacking truck convoys. They say travel anywhere in Iraq is dangerous."

"Because of the bandits?" Duffy asked.

"Sure," Hays replied, his words edging toward nervous.

"Well," Duffy responded lightly, "when the bandits drive your truck, the risk drops dramatically."

And with that Duffy held his hand up, palm out, giving Hays the clear signal that it would do no good to discuss this matter further.

"And today, my friend, we will use your unsullied American credit card to purchase a few items that we will need on our journey."

Hays waited a moment, then asked, "Bandits now take American Express?"

Duffy laughed. "Bandits have always taken American Express, my friend. Always."

PITTSBURGH INTERNATIONAL AIRPORT—Had Norah been warned, she might have paid closer attention to her surroundings. True, she'd parked toward the far end of the long-term parking area, but her car wasn't totally isolated. Every corner of the lot was well lit. There were signs indicating the premises were under twenty-four-hour watch.

The airport relied on a private security firm to patrol the farther reaches of the airport grounds. Many security workers were recent immigrants—happy to get the minimum wage—and a large contingent on duty at the airport were recent arrivals from a small Middle-Eastern country called Quadare.

BEIRUT, LEBANON—Hays and Duffy entered the small, modern office building. Their destination was a few blocks off the fishing docks. Modern tankers and freighters unloaded off the large piers farther south.

The air had an antiseptic smell, at least at first. Hays sniffed, trying not to be obvious. Then he recognized the odor. It was packing grease, the material used to prevent weapons from rusting in storage.

Hays, without needing to ask, knew this place dealt in military weaponry.

The two men stood in a bare waiting room, with no windows, no chairs, no desk. A very artificial plastic plant leaned against the far wall. A blank door opened and Duffy was warmly greeted by a thin man in gold rim glasses who looked more like an accountant than arms dealer. "It is a long time, Duffy. Your family is well?"

"They are, Masjed. And yours?"

"My daughter is a freshman at Bryn Mawr," he said, beaming.

Duffy stepped back and placed his hand over his heart. "Rellat? In college? That cannot be true. She cannot be old enough."

"It is true, Duffy. We get old so quickly."

Duffy asked, "Do you have everything on our list?"

Masjed offered a knowing grin. "For such a loyal friend, we have scoured the city for all your requests. You will not be disappointed."

He then leaned close to Duffy so his mouth was only inches from his ear. "You have brought payment?"

Hays had heard and pulled out his card.

Masjed looked at the name imprinted on it. "Mr. Sutton, you will be billed from a Swiss company that manufactures watches. At no time will Beirut appear on your records. Of course, there will be a small upcharge for this little service."

Hays was in no position to bargain.

Masjed left the room for under a minute. He returned, gave Hays his card, extended his hand to Duffy first, then to Hays.

"It was pleasant to see you again, Duffy. Give your family my greetings."

"And likewise, sir. Tell Rellat that I will be waiting for her to return."

Masjed laughed. "If it were only that easy these days, Duffy. Young women, especially those who travel to America, have minds of their own. Not like when I was young. She writes e-mail to her mother that she thinks I do not see. She tells her mother of boys she has met. Boys that are not from Lebanon. Can you believe such impertinence?"

Duffy shrugged. "The way of the world."

Masjed almost bowed. "I will pass on your respects."

And Duffy led Hays out of the building and back onto the street.

Hays felt a little bewildered. "Where are our purchases?"

Duffy motioned to the car. "In the trunk."

"But it was locked," Hays protested.

Duffy stared at him as if buying a cache of weapons, ammunition, and ordnance with a credit card and having them deposited into a locked car trunk was the most natural thing to happen. "As you notice," he said as he slipped into the driver's seat, "*was* is a word in the past tense, is it not?"

Hays sighed. "It is indeed. Or was."

PITTSBURGH INTERNATIONAL AIRPORT—Had Norah been observant, she might have noticed the white van parked at the end of the row of cars. But she was distracted as her suitcase bumped awkwardly off the curb. She didn't see the figure in the front seat, leaning far back into the shadows of the van.

She looked at her ticket once again and made sure that she was in the right row. She stood on tiptoe and peered into the distance. Her car, parked directly under a light pole, was easy to spot. It had two plastic roses tied to the antenna with pink yarn. She rolled her bag down to the end of the row. Traffic was light—closer to nonexistent, actually. Norah guessed that not many flights arrived at this time on a Thursday night.

She stopped by her car and leaned the bag upright. She stood on tiptoe again, hoping it hadn't rained and tightened the knots on the yarn, and attempted to untie the plastic roses.

So intent was she on her task that she didn't hear the van slowly pull to a stop next to her, blocking her from view of the rest of the lot and from being seen from any passing security patrol.

The door of the white van snapped open, and Norah felt herself lifted in the air, an arm grabbing her across her arms and chest. Another hand slapped a length of duct tape across her mouth, holding back her initial surprised scream. She felt herself thrown roughly to the floor of the van. Another strip of tape was yanked across her eyes, shutting out whatever light there might have been. She felt her suitcase tossed in the van, and it bounced off her shoulder. The door slammed shut. At least two pair of hands held her tight, keeping her pinned to the floor, preventing her from kicking or thrashing about.

The van slowly exited the airport and turned east.

22

SERO, IRAN—It hadn't been an easy transit. Iraq might be in the process of rebuilding, but Hays claimed no one could prove it by the quality of their roads. He and Duffy were bounced, banged, vibrated, and jostled for hours. The truck stopped at the Iraq/Lebanon border for no more than five minutes. They heard the tailgate open, felt an influx of fresh air, then silence. Hays could smell cigarette smoke and heard the coarse laughter of men.

Within minutes their journey resumed and didn't stop until many hours later.

When it did stop, Hays nudged Duffy, who had somehow fallen asleep.

Duffy leaned against the wall, cupping his ear. He nodded, then whispered back, "We're in Turkey."

"Turkey? We weren't supposed to be in Turkey. We didn't stop at any border, did we? I would have noticed if we had stopped."

Duffy listened intently. "This area is all Kurds. Our drivers are Kurds. The man who owns this truck is a Kurd. Blood endures. Politics does not. Borders are only lines on maps in some areas. Turkey, Iran, Iraq—it's all land belonging to the Kurds."

The tailgate swung open. There was the sound of boxes being moved. The false wall was canted to the side.

Duffy called out in Arabic and was answered. He listened and then interpreted for Hays.

"We are at the Turkish border just north of a small town in Iran called Sero. The driver says the town has nothing to recommend it—save that this is a very easy place to cross the border."

Both men shouldered their heavy packs and jumped from the truck. Their trip through Iraq had been rapid. Dawn had just begun.

One of the drivers chattered on for a long bit, Duffy nodding all the while and staring out over the eastern horizon. The sharp ridges of mountains were outlined by the first flinty light of dawn, while the rest of the world remained colorless. A brook on their left bubbled, and a flock of birds twittered then took flight in a rush of feathers. The road was empty of traffic. The truck engine pinged loudly as it cooled, clicking in the chill of the morning.

Duffy nodded one last time. He passed on a small handful of bills to the driver, and Hays heard the words "thanks" and "blessings" repeated often.

The drivers climbed back into their truck, started the engine, and backed away. In a moment, all that could be seen were the small red taillights disappearing into the western darkness.

"He said we must hurry," Duffy explained. "The border guards will be replaced at nine this morning. There are Kurds there now—and our friends have insisted that they will be momentarily blinded as we pass. Just on the other side of the border we can find a cab to take us to Orumiyeh—about forty-five minutes due east. We can find breakfast there. And once there, we need to look up an old friend."

With that, Duffy started marching east along the gravel edge of the road. He smelled the scent of a wood fire and the heady smell of Turkish coffee. Hays hitched up his heavy pack, adjusting the straps, and followed, walking briskly into the early morning sun.

With every step Hays took, from his pack came a thick metallic tapping sound of cold metal striking cold metal.

PITTSBURGH, PENNSYLVANIA—Norah was no longer held against the floor. Whoever had pinned her shoulders down had pawed at her as his grip relaxed. Norah wanted to scream and to kick, but did nothing. Struggle would have done no good. She lay on her back, hands now bound in front of her with some sort of plastic cord, her feet bound in the same manner. She had heard voices muttering in a language she didn't recognize.

She tried to keep track of left and right turns and the time between them. She'd seen a television show about that once, where the kidnap victim had been able to recreate the kidnap route using the time between turns and their direction.

After only a few minutes though, Norah lost track. She had no idea which direction they were traveling. Norah guessed that more than an hour had passed. Her left arm felt swollen, bruised.

She tried a hundred ways to imagine a scenario where this abduction might be explained. And Hays and his rats provided the only plausible solution.

Norah wasn't wealthy, and no one could expect money in exchange for her safety. If her abductors were interested in rape or murder, those would, no doubt, have already transpired. She knew women were taken by force to work in brothels and the like, but she couldn't imagine women snatched off the grounds of the Pittsburgh Airport for that purpose.

She felt the van make several sharp, bumpy turns. She heard the sound of wheels on gravel, and the van slowed to a stop.

The tape over her eyes was ripped away. The tape over her mouth muffled her scream. Her eyes fluttered, trying to adjust to the dark.

"Listen," growled a voice, "you will remain still."

Her eyes darted about and counted three men, or three figures, each dressed in black, each face covered by a black, pullover mask. She could see their eyes, narrow and dark. She nodded.

"Do you feel this?"

There was a sharp pinch in between her ribs. She nodded.

"This is a knife. I'm removing the tape from your mouth. If you scream, you will die. Do you understand?"

She nodded.

A hand reached out, roughly grabbed at the edge of the tape, and tore it off her face. She winced in pain but didn't cry out this time.

"I'm now cutting the ties from your hands and your feet. You will try nothing. The knife is still ready."

Norah managed to whisper, "Okay."

She was pulled into an upright position, then yanked to her knees. She felt the prick of the metal again against her side, almost hard enough to draw blood. Someone behind wrapped an arm around her neck and drew her close to his body. She allowed herself to be pulled, offering no resistance.

"You will walk now as if you are not terrified of me. You will not try to escape. If you do, you will die," the voice said, and the point of the blade pressed sharply into her side.

"I understand," she said, trying to keep the fear from her voice.

The door of the van rolled open. One figure, clad in black, jumped out and motioned for Norah to follow. She climbed down to the ground, her knees shaking, her breath coming in fast gulps. The man who had given her instructions jumped behind her and jabbed her once again with the blade.

"Just follow. And no noise."

Norah looked around her as she obeyed the men. The van was parked by the side of an empty two-lane road, at the bottom of a small dip. She hurried to keep up as they scurried down a small gully, weeds and grass to her knees. In a few seconds they were all virtually hidden from sight of any passing car. She could see a red glow behind and in front of her, just over the crest of a small hill.

"Hurry. No talking."

The three of them—the figure in front of her and the man behind her—reached the crest of the hill. Norah stood for a moment, staring, until she was shoved forward, almost tumbling down the small slope.

In front of her lay a small airport. Norah thought she recognized it as the Latrobe Airport—a small regional facility fifty miles east of Pittsburgh. She had seen it often—it was only a few miles from where the Steelers had their training camp—which she had not missed in twelve years. Beyond the airport, over a mile away, was a busy highway. She could see the red warning lights on the approach to the runway. To the right more than a thousand yards away, was a terminal and several hangars and a small tower with a radar dish turning lazy circles. A few steps in front of them stood a tall chain-link fence with razor wire looped as a defense on top.

The first man simply pressed against a section of chain link and it parted open. Norah was shoved through the gap. Forty yards in front of them sat a small jet plane. It bore no identifying markings on it, save a series of nondescript letters and numbers on the tail.

As they approached, a gangway opened and Norah was roughly pushed up the few stairs. Neither man followed her. The gangway closed immediately after her.

The cabin was dark, and a voice behind her barked out that she must sit and fasten the seatbelt at once.

Norah slipped into an open seat.

The jet's engines began to whine, and within a moment, the plane taxied to the north and gained speed. With a shudder the aircraft seemed to leap into the air and climb into the dark night sky.

QUADARE CITY, QUADARE—Hameed snapped on the light. The cell phone warbled again.

Hameed also refused to change the ring tone to anything other than the standard electronic chirp. There would be no music or odd sounds on his phone. The camel-headed Fadhil had installed some sort of cartoon music on his phone, infuriating Hameed every time it rang in his presence.

He wiped his face awake.

"Yes, Hameed here."

He listened for a moment.

"You have her? Wonderful. She is in transit?"

He smiled.

"Then we will have our cargo by tomorrow evening. I commend you on your fine operation."

His insurance policy would be delivered tomorrow evening. In spite of Fadhil's request, he wouldn't bring her to him. There would be no sense in damaging her value just to satisfy the son of a pig's carnal appetites.

No, he would keep her safely hidden somewhere else.

Fadhil could be informed in due time. And if he did discover her presence early, Hameed would tell him that the time was not right—it was the woman's time, he would say. His smile grew broader. He knew how much Fadhil hated subjects like that. Hameed would have to amplify the situation to an uncomfortable degree.

There was, fortunately, some news that he would take great relish in delivering.

ORUMIYEH, IRAN—Duffy and Hays sat perched on small metal chairs huddled against a masonry wall along the main route through Orumiyeh, just off Qods Square. The city had a Turkish air about it; the colors of the fabrics and the people didn't appear typically Persian. Hays and Duffy bought baked potatoes wrapped in crumbly bread and urfa kebabs with yogurt sauce from street vendors. The food, wrapped in newspaper, steamed in the early morning chill. No one seemed to give either Hays or Duffy a second look, as if men carrying cumbersome backpacks were the norm.

"We do look a little like backpackers," Duffy said. "Though for traveling hippies, we may be a bit long in the tooth."

A vendor came by offering orange juice, fresh squeezed from local produce. The drink was sweet and warm, and Hays said he had never tasted juice as good. As he drank, he looked about at the hustle of pedestrians and the growing traffic around the square.

"If I checked my BlackBerry, would anyone be suspicious?" Hays asked.

Duffy looked about as well.

"Go ahead. As long as you don't scream out in English, you'll be fine. The Arab way is to not intrude. Not like in America. They may eye you a bit, but no one will stop. And besides, this city is a crossroads of sorts up here. People are used to seeing strangers."

Hays switched the device on and punched in his account. A list of e-mails popped up a moment later.

"Spam. Spam. Spam. Spam. Class reunion news. Cheap prescriptions. Refinance my mortgage. So much for the filtering system at Pitt."

He typed in another address.

"I never get bothered with junk like this at my personal address." He stopped staring at the tiny screen and looked up. "You gave Yass my e-mail address, right?"

Duffy nodded.

Hays tapped at the small buttons and waited.

He began to read:

> Trust that all has gone well. Last night a stranger came in the café, asking questions about the two of you. He asked about an American who travels with an Arab. No one said anything. Later we discovered that the man was from Quadare. Not positive, but he might have been on the government payroll. Be careful. If they know you were here, they might know you are on your way there.

Duffy stuffed the last morsels in his mouth. He looked at his watch. "We have one stop to make and then we will be on our way."

The two men stood and shouldered their packs, and Duffy led the way down Khayyam, onto Kasshani Street, and then to Bakeri Avenue. Hays was just beginning to sweat in the rapidly warming air when Duffy stopped in front of a low, squat building the color of dust and tapped on the side door.

"Where are we?"

Duffy pointed upwards. "I'm surprised you didn't notice."

Hays looked up, and at the top of the building rested a small steeple, and on top of the small steeple, the brass cross glinting in the morning sun.

"Is this a church?"

Duffy pulled off his pack and set it at his feet. "Of all the people I know,

I would have guaranteed *you* would have been able to spot a church at a thousand paces."

"But this is Iran," Hays tried to explain. "Muslims and Imams and all that."

Duffy shook his head. "You Americans are religious jingoists, aren't you?"

"I'm not, but—" Hays was obviously confused.

From deep within the church came a call.

"This town is the most Christian of all towns in Iran. English missionaries all but overran the place back in the nineteenth century and converted most of the citizens. Afterwards there were wars and slaughters of believers and the usual litany of religious bigotry, but there is still a strong Christian presence here."

The door swung open and a man no taller than five feet, with a fringe of hair exploding around his head like a halo, blinked with surprise at the light and his visitors.

"Come in, you must come in," he said hurrying them through the door. Had Hays closed his eyes outside and then reopened them inside, he could have sworn he had been magically transported back to a small church in rural Pennsylvania. The chairs looked the same, the pulpit the same, the wooden frame holding a Bible verse and the piano the same. Even the speckled and veined linoleum floor was the same. The paint on the walls was the same pale ochre tint. The smell—of musty old books and wool—was also the same. The only difference was the Bible verse and the banner behind the pulpit written in Farsi, not English.

"Mr. Dufhara Quahaar, as I live and breath. You must pass on my blessings and best wishes to your saintly mother and father. How I miss them. How I loved having them in my home all those years ago. And you were just a toddler then. You are all grown—and it is remarkable that I have not aged a moment since that day."

Duffy offered a hint of a bow.

"Pastor Azadi Jamshid, I bring you the blessings of my family and greetings from all. You are part of our history, sir, and will always be blessed."

Hays had never heard Duffy use such terms, and with such reverence.

Duffy noticed his astonishment, explained. "When I was a toddler and Beirut was being blown apart by war, Pastor Jamshid offered our entire family sanctuary," he told Hays. "He was a pastor at a Christian church, and despite death threats and violence against himself, allowed us to stay with him. It is because of him that I'm alive. He is a devout and noble man."

Duffy appeared to be close to tears.

Azadi swept his hand through the air. "It is a trifling. After all, I only did what my Lord would have asked me to do. And for that simple act, I have been continually blessed, my friend. You have returned to see me after all these years and will be able to take my blessings back with you to your family. It is a perfect world, is it not?"

Azadi put his hand on Hays' shoulder and tilted his head.

"I sense that you, too, believe. Am I correct? It would be so nice if young Dufhara here had a positive influence on his life. You are then a follower?"

Hays nodded. "I am, sir."

"Then we must all share in breakfast," Azadi chirped. "I know you have already eaten some. I could smell the kebabs and potatoes on you. I don't see as well as I once did, but I smell keenly. If you are not hungry, I will share coffee with you. Come, come into my humble home."

Norah closed her eyes, hoping this had all been just a terrible dream and that if she waited long enough, she would awaken and would find herself warm and cozy in her own bed. She waited a long time and opened her eyes. Nothing had changed. She was still in an aircraft, still climbing, still flying through the dark.

She had been afraid to look about, afraid one of her abductors would think she was trying to escape and would do something harsh and painful to her. She turned her head slightly. The seat across from her was empty. There was movement behind her and a man stood, crouched over and walked toward the front of the aircraft. She heard him speak to another, the words soft, hard to hear.

The man returned, stopped by the seat on the other side, one row up. She could see the end of a plastic tie, the sort used to wrap wires, wobbling slightly above the seat. The man reached down with some sort of cutter and snapped it apart. Two hands rose and flexed, as if they had been bound for some time. He reached down and pulled his hand away sharply.

Norah heard the sound of tape being wrenched from skin and the sharp intake of breath.

"You will be quiet. You will try nothing. You understand?"

"I understand," was the whispered reply.

The man glowered at Norah as he passed. The cabin lights hadn't been illuminated, but there was an unearthly glow from the galley in the back. The figure in the seat in front of Norah turned around. Norah could see the features clearly.

"Roberta," Norah mouthed silently, dumbfounded.

"I'm so sorry, Norah," Roberta called out softly. "I'm so, so sorry. I didn't think something like this would ever happen."

From behind the man ran up the aisle and with the back of his hand swung at Roberta. Norah could see that he caught her full on the cheek, and her head snapped to the side.

"Both of you. Silent. There will be not another spoken word. Understand?"

Norah could only nod as she listened to Roberta's hushed crying and helplessly watched her shoulders shake with the tremor of her tears.

23

QUADARE CITY, QUADARE—Fadhil felt happy and content—a rare occurrence these days. His breakfast had been hot and the tea sweetened just right. Most days he imagined that his assistant placed his food in the freezer before bringing it to him. And for some reason, the sand-brained peasant couldn't come to grips with adding three sugars to his tea. It usually tasted of five—or even worse—six sugars.

Fadhil hadn't been able to devise any set of instructions that would make his meals more consistently palatable. But today, the food was served at the right temperature, and the tea contained the correct sweetness, and for that Fadhil was thankful.

Besides the wonderful breakfast, Fadhil was looking forward to his tour of the new scientific facility, now almost complete, that would be used to finish the work of Dr. Haj. He had phoned the doctor some days earlier and requested an update and a tour. The doctor always sounded nervous, anxious, and Fadhil was heartened to hear that it had nothing to do with the construction schedule.

This morning Fadhil picked up the phone and waited. Some days a dial tone was issued promptly. Some days a dial tone never arrived. He waited nearly a minute, then slammed the phone down and shouted for his assistant. "Come in here at once."

The door opened an inch.

"Yes, sir?" came the disembodied voice from the outer office.

Fadhil shook his head in disgust. "Call my driver. Now."

There came a moment of silence. "And what should I tell your driver, sir?"

Fadhil sighed in resignation. "That I need a ride."

The door didn't shut.

"What?" Fadhil said, exasperated.

"Sir, to where?"

"Where, what?"

After a pause, "Where to your driver, sir. Does he know where to go?"

Fadhil picked up the stapler and threw it at the door, nicking it deeply once again. "Just call my driver. Have him meet me in front of this building in five minutes. Thick-headed son of a sow."

The door slowly edged shut.

And what had started out as a wonderful morning now became a much more normal and ordinary, horrible day.

CHURCH OF ALL BELIEVERS, ORUMIYEH, IRAN—The kitchen was the size of a compact car. Duffy and Hays left their packs outside, in the sanctuary, just under the painting of Jesus floating heavenward. Azadi bustled about, standing on tiptoe to reach the coffee on the bottom shelf, leaning into a half-size refrigerator for milk, setting the sugar and honey on a silver tray just so, placing a plate of chocolate squares on the table.

Hays felt like a giant in the man's presence. He leaned into the wall to make himself as unobtrusive as possible.

Azadi poured steaming water into a pot, stirred it once, and sat down with a flourish.

"It is so good to see you, my old friend Dufhara."

"They all call me Duffy, now," Duffy explained.

"Duffy is a good almost-American name. Duffy. I like that. It goes well with you."

Azadi turned to Hays.

"And you must be, of course, Mr. Hays Sutton. I expected someone much more scientific-looking. You, well, you look like an athlete. A quarterback. Is that how they call the man with the ball? In your crazy American football?"

"Yes," Hays replied. "That man is called a quarterback—but I don't think I much resemble the type."

Azadi laughed. "You Americans should take compliments with more grace. Had you said that to me, I would have nodded in agreement. If you don't, then you are disagreeing with the host. And that will never do, will it?"

"I try to teach him how to act in a civilized manner," Duffy said, "but you see what I have to work with."

Azadi clapped his hands. "It is so good to see you. And I'm honored to offer what assistance I may on your journey."

Hays shook his head, perplexed and amazed once again. How Duffy had managed to line up so much support in a matter of days was mind-boggling.

"We are honored to be here, Pastor Jamshid," Duffy replied.

"Allow me to ask a personal query—for I know your time is limited. Tell me, how are your wonderful mother and father?"

Duffy spoke for several minutes. Hays learned more of Duffy's family and their history and current activities than he'd learned in all the years he and Duffy had been friends.

Azadi leaned forward, as if gathering every morsel of news and holding it close.

"I'm grateful, Duffy, for such a report. And now, for the reason you have visited me this wonderful day." Azadi handed Duffy a manila envelope wrapped tight with two intersecting rubber bands.

"I have forced myself not to hold you here longer, though I wish you could stay for a week. And Hays, how I wish you could stay for a church service, to share worship with us. The children would be so delighted to meet you. I wish … but that cannot be. Not today. I know that." He took a deep breath. "These are the documents I told your grandfather I could procure. And I have." The little man had stopped smiling.

Duffy carefully unwrapped the envelope and slid the contents out on the table. There were tickets and official-appearing papers, with official-appearing stamps and embossing. Hays picked up one page.

"This is an Iranian visa for travel," he said, incredulous. "It has my name and picture on it."

The little man nodded gravely.

"But on one matter, one request, I must offer my most humble and sincere apologies. You will be forced to travel south to Bushehr on public transport. There was no other reliable means to make that journey. You could drive yourself, but a rental car is too soon noticed. Even private cars of Iranians are stopped and searched quite often and for no apparent reason. It is a curious thing that the buses, seldom, if ever, are stopped and searched. I suspect the police think that those wanting to evade them will never step foot on a bus. It will be the safest way."

"How—?" Hays asked. "You are a pastor—I mean—"

Azadi held up his hand. "I understand your quandary. I have been in such tightnesses before. Life is not always clean, nor pleasant, nor done exactly by the book of rules. In Iran, maybe in America as well, one must sometimes consider the lesser of the two evils. Back when Dufhara was a little boy, I lied every day to protect my friends in Beirut. God understands. I know he didn't consider such things a sin. Think of Rahab in the Old Testament, who did the same. And to protect a child? It is no sin. I was called to do so. God is not waiting in the shadows so he may jump out and punish us by surprise. He sees a much bigger picture than we do. Dufhara's grandfather said this was an emergency, and I responded as I did all those years ago."

Duffy carefully folded the papers. "I'm so thankful."

"I'm honored to offer my meager assistance. I have lived in this town for nearly three decades now. Even pastors have friends who have friends."

Hays took the pages and slipped them into his breast pocket.

"There will be a bus at Qod Square departing to the south in fifteen minutes. So you must hurry."

The two friends gathered their backpacks and headed to the door.

Azadi embraced both of them fiercely.

"There is one more thing, Mr. Hays Sutton. Since I have learned of your visit, now for three days duration, I have had the same dream. I don't know what it means, yet I know I must tell you."

Azadi closed his eyes and held Hays' forearm.

"In my dream there are two boats. There is a large boat. There is a small boat. I don't know why, but each night, I have forced you into the small boat. God has forced me to make you climb into the small boat."

His eyes snapped open.

"If on your journey you employ a boat, you must promise me to take the smaller craft of the two—regardless," Azadi shouted.

Hays was taken aback by the shout.

"You must promise. The small boat."

Hays put his hand on the little man's shoulder.

"I promise. If we find ourselves in a situation like that, we will take the small boat."

Azadi appeared to breathe a great sigh of relief.

"Now, my friends, you must go or you will miss your bus. I will pray for you without ceasing until I hear from you again."

Azadi hugged them both, and they set off.

QUADARE CITY, QUADARE—Hameed reached into his pocket and removed a page torn out of an electronics catalog.

"If you were aware that a certain man employed this sort of communication device—" Hameed began.

"You mean, like a BlackBerry?" Shova Sharif replied, cutting him off midsentence.

Hameed waited, to control his response. "Yes. If that is what you call it."

"It's what everyone calls it."

Sharif was a guest worker in Quadare. He had grown up in Karachi, Pakistan, and had left there midway through his senior year at university. He studied computer programming and discovered that the things he learned in his first year had already been made obsolete.

"You want one? They're totally cool. Keep in touch from anywhere to anywhere. North Pole, South Pole, as long as you're near a wi-fi hotspot—or if you have a satellite uplink, which would be so cool—you can reach out and touch someone."

Hameed hated the fellow's flippant insolence. He would have terminated him long ago, but everyone agreed he was the most skillful computer expert in the security agency.

"No," he replied, realizing it was much too loud.

Sharif shrugged and turned back to his computer screen and began typing rapidly. "I'm in the middle of this crunching. Just thought of something. Hang on a sec, would you?"

Hameed coiled his fist and wanted, with every fiber of his body, to thrash this young person soundly. He wondered if they taught manners in Pakistan.

"Okeydokey. So you want a BlackBerry. There's that guy on the Square of the Revolution—or is that on the Boulevard of the Martyrs—no, the square. Anyhow, I don't know where he gets them, but they are always way below manufacturer's suggested—if you know what I mean."

Hameed shouted this time, intentionally.

"Shut up. I don't want one. I have a question about them."

If Sharif had been frightened or worried, he didn't exhibit any symptoms. He offered a casual shrug. "Okay."

"Look, I believe a person we are interested in carries one of these devices," Hameed explained. "We have his e-mail addresses and phone number. What I want to know is, if we send him a message, can we determine where the device is located that receives the message?"

Sharif shook his head. "I don't think so. They've been using Triple DES encryption—a two-way authenticated environment. Keys are in the PDA and in the server firewall. In transit you can't touch it. Behind the firewall you can't touch it."

Hameed had no idea of what the young man was saying.

"So, your answer is no?"

Sharif offered a pained look. "If I had a team of crackers and a long time, maybe. But by then, they'd change the coding. So—no. No way, really."

The disappointment showed on Hameed's face.

Sharif was not a stupid man. He knew the power this nondescript person wielded.

"Is this person around here? The one you're interested in. I mean, like in the area?"

Hameed glared at the Pakistani. "Why? Does it make a difference?"

"Maybe."

Hameed really disliked this Pakistani hooligan. "Maybe? Can you find him?"

Sharif screwed up his face. "Listen, it's like this. I have friends who spend a lot of time wardriving."

Hameed hated to be forced to ask questions about things he knew nothing about.

"And what is wardriving?" he asked, resigned to the necessity.

"They cruise around with a laptop or PDA—with wireless networking—and they scan for LANs and open networks. All it takes is software, the right chipset—stuff like Linksys or ApSniff or Prism-2 powered NICs. If you're good and sort of jazz up the software a notch or two, you can clock any wireless network in a big area—then you can tech out its name, operating channels, security settings, and even the location—if you've got GPS."

Hameed still had no idea what the young man was talking about.

"All I'm saying is that if you know this guy's e-mail or phone number, we could start wardriving—or trolling—and see if that name or number pops up. Kind of like a scavenger hunt. No guarantees, but I've had it work before."

Finally, Hameed began to understand.

"How big of an area?"

"Individually, not all that big. But I've got friends all over Quadare."

"Any farther than that?"

Sharif seemed to grow a little uncomfortable.

"Going outside Quadare is illegal."

Hameed stared at him.

"How big a net can you cast?"

"If I offer a few dollars? Through all of Iraq, most of Iran, some of Israel, all of Cairo, some of Saudi Arabia. Pretty much all over."

"How many dollars?"

"Dollars?"

"You said dollars—as a reward. How many?" Hameed was on ground he now understood well—the cost of a man and the price of loyalty.

Sharif gulped. "Maybe—maybe five hundred?"

Hameed snorted in reply as if he had found the number too inconsequential to be believed.

"Offer five thousand. I want this man found."

Sharif swallowed then smiled. "We'll find him for sure."

As Hameed left the computer room, he was certain Sharif would offer his odd computer friends five hundred dollars and pocket the rest. But even at that lower number, Hameed knew it would be enough.

For a fraction of that, a man could be made to disappear. For that much more, a man should be able to be made to appear.

The plane carrying Hameed's insurance was scheduled to land after dark. Hameed thought it best that no one be in attendance, other than the most essential personnel.

His cell phone warbled. He waited for three rings. No one should appear too anxious.

"Yes?"

"I think we found your guy. Your BlackBerry guy. There was a download this morning in Iran, in Orumiyeh. My friend didn't copy the e-mail address, but he swears it was the same."

Iran? They are coming through Iran?

"Wonderful. But that is more than twelve hours old. You must keep looking. I want to know where he is now. Keep looking. Send your little friend in Iran a thousand for the information. And raise the reward for finding them to ten thousand."

"Yes, sir," Sharif answered with a snap.

It is wonderful what money will buy, Hameed chuckled. *Insurance, respect.*

Hameed hung up and then dialed a number. He waited a minute until the line became secure.

"Orumiyeh. In Iran. They were there this morning. See if you can track them."

He snapped the phone shut and stared out the windshield.

Through the darkness the small plane descended quickly. From Latrobe, the sleek Gulfstream had flown to Orlando first, then to the Azores. At both stops the plane had taken on fuel. Neither passenger had been permitted to debark from the plan—especially since it was undertaking a diplomatic assignment. From the Azores it was an easy flight to Quadare.

The engines whined to a stop. The gangway door flipped open. A tall, Nordic-looking man stepped out and walked with authority to the gate.

"Hameed Qaws?"

"Yes."

"May I see identification?"

Hameed seethed but didn't say a word. *How dare these foreigners ask me for identification?*

Hameed withdrew his passport from his breast pocket. The man from the plane opened and examined it carefully, then had the temerity to stare at Hameed, verifying that his person and his picture matched.

The man handed the passport back to Hameed, then signaled to the plane. Two women stepped down the gangway, taking tentative steps, as if they hadn't walked in quite some time.

Even in the dark, with only the glare of a sodium vapor light for illumination, Hameed felt his pulse quicken. Both women were attractive, in a brash American way.

He steeled his initial desire, forcing that powerful emotion to be held in check. He knew he would enjoy what was to come next. He would enjoy it immensely.

"Take them to citadel. Feed them. Let them sleep. They will need their rest," Hameed said, his words as near to loving as he had ever uttered.

24

QUADARE CITY, QUADARE—In Quadare City, scores of buildings lay as fallow fields—concrete hulks, some with roofs, some without, all abandoned midconstruction.

A building boom was to accompany the regime's privatization of the oil fields. The boom never materialized. Money flowed, attracting funds from banks and investors, but all too soon the money for Quadare dried up and was diverted into other, more greedy hands and pockets. So buildings remained empty and jagged.

As a result, Hameed had his pick of very safe, very clandestine, and very private spots to conduct whatever business needed to be conducted out of the public view.

He drove up to the shell of what should have been a new twenty-story hotel. This project had come close to completion. Windows and doors had been installed, and some of the public rooms had been nearly ready—and now lay empty.

Hameed slammed the car door shut. The building stood by itself, well away from any neighborhood. In the open portico a white van sat—the only other car in the vicinity.

The front door of the forlorn hotel opened with a shrill twisting sound. Hameed thought it an appropriate sound—a shriek of the dead. The tapping of his hard heels echoed in the darkened hallway. He walked farther into the center of the building. A few lights remained unbroken.

He entered rooms that had been designed to be corporate offices. Rich wood paneling had been installed, dark and burled, but the floor had been littered with scraps of building materials, plastic cups, and food wrappers. He stepped through one door, then another, until he reached the interior offices.

He smiled. His equipment had been assembled: restraints, a tape recorder, a cardboard box of his favorite tools. He nodded to the two men standing in the shadows. Without a word they slipped out of the room, as if on a mission.

Hameed sat down on an expensive leather chair, crossed his legs, adjusted his cuffs, and closed his eyes, imagining what would soon transpire.

The only illumination came through a rusted air vent at the top of the wall, creating a slanted ladder of light and dark.

Roberta had hardly stopped crying, claiming this whole mess was entirely her fault, that she had never imagined that Ayman would do such a thing to her, that she had no idea that Norah would ever be at risk. She kept repeating that it was all her fault, over and over, until, whimpering, she had at last fallen asleep.

Norah slept only a few hours and awoke with a start. She heard the key turn in the lock and stood quickly, wanting to be ready for whatever might occur.

A guard shoved a tray inside the room with the toe of his boot.

"Bathroom after," he barked and slammed the door. Roberta, curled on the other thin mattress pad in the far corner, sat up with a start, surprised awake by the noise.

"I think it's breakfast," Norah said softly.

"I don't think I can eat," Roberta said, each word sounding as if it caused pain.

"Nonsense," Norah replied. "You have to eat. You have to. None of this was your fault. You didn't do it. Other people did."

Norah sat down by the tray. It held two bottles of water, a stack of some type of flatbread, and a plate piled with what she thought might be hummus.

She dipped a corner of the bread and tasted. It was hummus, thick and garlicky. It was the first food she had eaten in many hours and it tasted very, very good.

"Roberta, come on now. You must eat this with me. Please. It's made of chickpeas. It's good."

Slowly, Roberta made her way toward the tray. Her right eye was swollen and the skin blackened where she had been struck.

"Does it hurt?" Norah asked.

"A little. If I only hadn't tried to talk, it never would have happened. It's all my fault."

Norah took Roberta's hand.

"Look at me. This is not your fault. None of this is. None of it. Do you understand?"

Roberta nodded meekly, as if she was used to acquiescing.

The two of them ate in silence.

Norah knew that neither she nor Roberta had done anything to warrant being kidnapped. Like polishing a stone by hand, she turned the problem over and over again in her thoughts. And every thought started and ended with Hays.

Roberta nibbled at some bread, but broke down in tears as she attempted to open the bottle of water.

Norah nudged closer and placed her arm around her.

"It's okay, Roberta. Don't cry. Really, don't cry. It will all turn out fine in the end."

Roberta shook her head and blubbered. "No, it won't. We're going to die, and it's all my fault."

In the back of Norah's mind the possibility of death rattled about. She didn't want to consider death as a possibility, but now that Roberta had voiced it, she acknowledged it as reality. They might die. Anyone who would go to all this trouble to kidnap them, use a private jet to transport them, have bodyguards and private prisons, might well see their lives as expendable.

Norah stiffened. Then another thought came flooding into her mind. *Something about being in the shadow of death. What were the words? "I will fear no evil, for you are with me."*

It was something she had read in that book she had taken to Florida. The book Hays had insisted she read.

Norah almost laughed. Florida and sitting in the sun by the pool seemed to have occurred to another person, in another lifetime, decades and decades ago.

It was in his book—about not fearing—but only if we knew God. Was that it? If we knew who God was … yes, something like that … then we wouldn't have fear because he would be with us. God would be there. That's what that chapter was talking about. That God would be with us in times of despair.

Norah brightened as the thought took hold, expanding in her consciousness, unexpectedly rippling and growing in power. She leaned down to Roberta. "Roberta, honey, please stop crying. We may not have much time."

Roberta sat up and wiped at her face.

"Listen, before I came here I read one of Hays' religion books. And it said if we believe in God, we shouldn't have any reason to be frightened. I think maybe that's why I'm not scared. Now I see what that means—not because we're in trouble—but because God promised. That's what Hays was always talking about—the promises of God."

Roberta looked like she wanted to agree. "If I say I believe too, will he get us out of here?"

Norah wanted so much to say yes. "I don't know. I don't think so. It may not work that way. But in that book, it talked about one part of the Bible that said something like, 'even when I'm walking through the shadow of valley of death, I won't be afraid, because God is close beside.'"

Norah felt an unfolding in her chest, as if something were being born. She so wanted to pass this sudden, unexpected comfort to Roberta, who was so very near the edge.

"We don't have to be afraid, Roberta. God will be with us. Do you understand, Roberta? You don't have to be afraid. Not if you have God."

Her words were interrupted by the turning of the key and a gruff voice shouting out, "You. Up. Come." Norah stood, smoothing her blouse, pushing the hair from her face, and straightening her shoulders.

IRAN—The bus jostled and bumped its way south through a rural and starkly beautiful landscape that, if Hays had been asked, he would have said looked much like rural Kansas.

Hays looked at the map. The sun was close to the western horizon. Duffy glanced down at the map, then looked outside.

"We're near Dezful, maybe a few clicks outside of Shush."

Hays traced the route with his finger. "Almost four hundred miles. We've made good time."

"The roads were empty. The driver didn't pay attention to the speed limit," Duffy replied.

"Do we stay with the bus?"

Duffy shook his head. "No. There's a terminal south of Dezful. We should be able to find a hotel there."

A few miles distant, off to the west, the lights of Shush softly glowed. The bus began to slow. Hays looked out into the aisle and toward the front.

"Oh, God, no," he whispered.

"What?"

"It's a roadblock."

Duffy stood up, his hands tightly gripping the seat back in front of him, his knuckles white. He could feel the adrenaline begin to pump furiously. He could feel his heart tighten, and his hands grow clammy, his breath fast and shallow.

"I thought they never stopped buses," Hays managed to whisper.

"Until now, I guess. We need to do something."

Hays turned to his friend, surprised, and now very, very alarmed. "The papers we have—they'll work—right? Safe transit passes."

"I think they look authentic. Maybe the police will buy it. Maybe they won't. You don't look like the typical tourist. Neither do I."

The bus driver shifted down a gear and began to slow.

"If they ask to look through our backpacks, we're done."

Hays felt his heart beat even faster. He knew the weapons and explosives would land them in jail in a heartbeat. Not just in Iran, but in any country. They would be branded as terrorists or mercenaries and locked up for a very long time.

"We could jump from the rear door," Hays suggested.

"They would shoot first and maybe ask questions later," Duffy whispered back through clenched teeth.

"What do we do?" Hays asked, his words tumbling out in a frantic jumble. "We have to do something." He stood, then sat, then stood again, grasping the strap on his backpack, looking over his shoulder at the rear door, trying to determine how long it would take him to remove the 9mm Glock pistol from the interior of his backpack.

Sweat formed in big drops on his forehead. He felt the moisture pool on his back.

"What do we do?"

Duffy had his hand on the strap of his backpack as well, fumbling to unsnap a section, going for a weapon. Hays began to do the same. An armed confrontation might be futile, but they had no choice. They couldn't allow themselves to be stopped.

Hays recalled in that tiny instant how this feeling was much like the panicky sensations that occurred on Ranger missions. The possibility of a fight, of death, or having to cause death, filled a man's chest with cement.

Just then, as the bus shuddered to a complete stop, a woman sitting behind them stood, walked two steps forward, put her hand on Hay's hand, and pulled it away from the backpack.

She leaned in close and whispered in his ear.

"Don't worry, my brother. Stay in Shush tonight and continue your journey on the morrow. All will be well."

Hays stared up at her face, but she turned away and ran toward the front of the bus. She hurried down the steps, hit the gravel on the side of the road, and sprinted away from the police, in the opposite direction the bus had been going. Two of the police quickly gave chase, hands on pistols, and all but tackled her just behind the bus. She screamed loud and flailed her arms, appearing to be crazed with escaping. As she did so, a small glint caught Hays' eyes. It was her necklace, highlighted in the dying sun.

It's a cross. It's a cross.

Hays saw her face, but only for a moment. It was not the face of a mad-woman, but composed and almost serene. He saw her eyes—quiet and peaceful eyes.

Two other police came and helped restrain her, pulling her back toward their cars, shouting, gesturing wildly, pointing in one direction, then another. A hat was knocked to the ground. One officer tumbled to his knees, grimacing as the gravel tore his carefully pressed trousers. Another one tried to grab the woman's arms and legs and appeared to merely flail at the air. In another moment, with the woman thrown into the back seat of the police car, they tore away, gravel spitting from the tires, a storm of dust clouding the air.

No one on the bus spoke, all dazed by what they had witnessed. Talking began again as a low buzz, and grew more excited.

Duffy listened, then translated.

"Everyone on the bus said she was alone. No one was with her. No one remembered seeing her get on."

On the opposite side of the road, one police car remained, with its single driver standing at its side. Hays saw him look at his watch, then to the darkening sky. He shrugged at the bus driver, then waved them on. The bus started with a lurch and rumbled off again.

Half a mile later, Hays and Duffy clambered to the front and asked to be let off at Shush. Without saying a word, they made their way down the empty avenue of the quiet town and found a small hotel overlooking a narrow canal. One large room was still available.

Only after they sat on their beds, safe, did either of them break their silence.

"Was your gun loaded?" Hays asked.

"No. I don't like traveling with loaded weapons."

"If it had been loaded, would you have used it?"

"I don't know. Would you have?"

Hays waited a long minute.

"Yes. I think I would have. If it had been loaded. It has to be done. We both agreed. There's no other choice—and no second chances. We have to do this."

Duffy drew in a deep breath.

"That's the way I have it figured as well. Yes. I would have used the pistol. But if I did, I think we both would have been killed."

Hays waited to respond.

"I think she was an angel."

"Who?"

"That woman on the bus. I think she was an angel sent to protect us."

"An angel? Are you serious?"

"I am," Hays said. "How else could you explain it?"

Duffy bit as his lip. "Maybe she was a smuggler. Maybe she was wanted by the police as well."

"No," Hays said firmly. "Why would she say 'all will be well?' How did she know? How did she know what we were going to do? Duffy—she had to be an angel. There's no other explanation."

Duffy didn't respond right away.

"Does God do that?"

"Do what?"

"Send angels like that? Does he do that a lot?"

Hays shrugged. "Maybe. Maybe more than we know. Maybe if people ask for them."

"Did you ask for them?"

Hays took a deep breath. "Not specifically. Maybe Azadi did. Maybe other people did."

"And God sent an angel, just like that?"

"I know it sounds insane, but what else could it have been?"

Duffy didn't answer for a long time.

"Maybe ... maybe you are right."

He reached over for his water bottle.

"Me believing in angels," Duffy muttered, not truly believing in the words he spoke. "This is as crazy an idea as—as us going to Quadare."

Hays could do nothing other than nod in agreement.

QUADARE CITY, QUADARE—Frustrated, Fadhil began tapping furiously at his computer. The little blinking thing had disappeared and no matter what combination of buttons he pressed or how hard and fast he pressed them, it wouldn't reappear.

He stared at the closed door of his office and sighed with great resignation.

"I need help in here," he shouted. He waited, hoping to hear some manner of rustling. But all was silent.

"I need help. The computer is broken. The Internet is broken."

Fadhil liked seeing what material possessions the decadent West was gorging itself on. And he liked to read the latest soccer news from England. This year, he believed that Arsenal stood the best chance for a championship.

"I said the computer is broken, you peasant. Get in here and fix it."

The door opened the barest of cracks.

"Sir?"

"The computer. It is broken. You must fix it."

Even though Fadhil had assumed this fellow to be nearly illiterate, he was pleasantly surprised that the man appeared to know the rudiments of computer technology.

"Sir," he mumbled and walked closer to the desk. He stopped in front.

"Come on. I'm not going to strike you tonight. Just fix this blasted thing."

Fadhil couldn't close the Web site he had been visiting—a very chic London men's shoe store. Fadhil needed new boots and he didn't want to search through the grubby local stores trying to find his size.

The servant looked at the screen. If he was surprised by the display of shoes, he made no mention of it. He picked up the mouse. Then he pushed the connection into the keyboard, snugging it tighter.

"There, sir. The cord was loose."

Fadhil pushed him from the computer.

"Good. Now fetch me a cup of tea. Four sugars this time. Can you remember four sugars?"

The servant nodded.

Fadhil didn't see the venomous look in the servant's eyes as he turned his back and walked to the outer door. He didn't see the tight smile of revenge color the man's face as the lock latched.

Roberta sat in a chair, her arms bound behind her, a set of handcuffs tight about her wrists. Her mouth was not gagged, nor was a blindfold placed on her eyes—though she wished both had been.

What she saw, what she anticipated, was more terrifying than she thought she could bear.

A smallish man, with a thin neck and small eyes that darted in one direction and then another like a weasel, stood in the farthest, darkest end of the room. In the middle of the room stood a lone table. Norah was brought in and roughly tossed on top of the table, face down. She didn't shout or struggle.

Roberta began to breath fast.

The two sturdy-looking men grabbed Norah's arms and shackled a set of cuffs to each wrist, then tightened the cuffs to opposing table legs.

The small man from the shadows walked up to Norah. He placed his hand at the bottom of her blouse and yanked it up. Her skin—from her waist to her shoulder blades—was bare.

Roberta wanted to scream, to thrash about, to distract them somehow, to trade places with Norah. After all, this was her fault. She should be the one being punished, not Norah.

The small man stared hard at Norah's bare back, and licked his lips in anticipation.

Roberta struggled with the handcuffs, but couldn't budge them.

He walked to the front of the table. He pulled out a small sheet of paper.

"Can you read this?" he asked, his words oily.

"Yes," she replied.

"I want you to read this into the tape recorder. I want to make sure our work is not disturbed. Do you understand?"

Norah nodded.

The small man took the tape recorder and placed it close to Norah's mouth.

She didn't speak.

"You can read this," the small man shouted. "Read it aloud."

Norah waited a moment, then answered. "No."

The small man with the weasel-like features calmly placed the paper on the floor, directly below her eyes, then stepped to a small cardboard box in the shadows. He came back to Norah's side. In his hand was a small cascade of leather straps. Even in the darkness Roberta could see a cold, metallic glistening at each end.

"I wonder why you Americans always want to be so noble and brave. I wonder why you think it is such an honor to protect those who don't need protecting. Why is it that you don't see your foolishness?"

And without a warning, he wheeled his arm around in a great circle. The straps met Norah's flesh with a sound like an angry, raw slap of thunder. Norah arched against her restraints, but didn't cry out.

Roberta had shut her eyes. When she opened them, she saw the twisting grin of the small man and the thick beads of sweat on his forehead that had formed, a few specks of the innocent's blood on his cheek.

She shut her eyes.

And she began to pray.

25

SHUSH, IRAN—Hays awoke well before dawn and slipped out the door of the small hotel.

The street was empty as he made his way to the canal, a half block to the east. Water ran briskly between the stone walls of the canal. The fresh smell reminded him of streams back home in Pennsylvania—the streams he had fished and played in. For a moment he found himself back in Luxor, back by the small creek that ran at the edge of the field behind his house. He remembered endless summer days, sitting with his feet in the crisp cool water, daydreaming of adventures and of the time he could leave his boring childhood home and the boring state of Pennsylvania and see the world in its unfettered glory.

From behind him came the call to morning prayers, warbling over a tinny loudspeaker, startling him back to reality.

This wasn't the sort of adventure he had ever hoped to engage in. Their mission was as near to futile as one could get—yet Hays had realized many days earlier that even if they failed, they had to act, they had to try. If they failed or died in the process, so be it. Their failure to act would be a splintered death every day for the rest of their lives.

He took a deep breath, clearing his thoughts. He pulled out his squat little BlackBerry from inside his coat and looked around. There were people in the street, but no one appeared to be paying him any attention. Shopkeepers rolled up their metal protective curtains, women in veils carried bags with bread, and traffic began to build slowly.

He tapped in his personal e-mail address. There were a few obvious spam attempts. Then he logged into his e-mail address from the university. He received updates on meetings he no longer attended, reminders of future meetings he wouldn't attend, calls for volunteers for the university charity he no longer contributed to.

But one e-mail near the end of a long list of soon-to-be-deleted e-mails caught his attention. The subject line read: "Urgent H. Sutton. Must Read. Horridly Vital."

He tapped at the keys with the small metal stylus.

The PDA seemed to hesitate, then lit up with a simple, terse message.

"Call 518-974-45-17-191. Urg. Messg from N. Neale."

Hays stared. It was a shock to see a familiar name. Norah never wrote e-mails, claiming she thought the process to be cold, impersonal.

At home Hays' BlackBerry doubled as a phone—a bulky one—but filled with features he hadn't fully utilized. American cell phones didn't generally work overseas—unless you knew who to talk to and how to customize the equipment. Duffy had friends who could customize virtually anything—and Hays now had a phone compatible with European and Middle Eastern standards.

His BlackBerry blinked cheerfully and indicated that there was a cell tower nearby and adequate coverage. He stared at the number, switched to the phone function, and carefully dialed it, hoping he didn't need a specific code to access the number—a standard feature in many Middle East countries.

He pressed "send," put the phone to his ear and waited, nervously scanning the street for anyone who looked out of the ordinary, who might be paying too much attention to an out-of-place tourist sitting by a canal in a small rural town in the middle of Iran.

The phone buzzed and chirped, indicating that it was seeking the number dialed.

The connection barked into life. No one answered. It was as if a recording began at the first snap of connection.

There was the sound of a slap, or what might have been a slap, then an anguished cry of pain. It was a woman's voice. In that split-second scream, Hays prayed that it wasn't Norah's—though it could have been. There was a hint of her voice in the brief cry. Someone shouted something in Farsi. Hays couldn't make out the words. Then another slap and another scream. Hays hurt down to his bones. He winced. Then came the same man's voice— again in Farsi. There was a moment of silence, then another slap and another scream. A woman's voice broke in a guttural wail.

Scuffling sounds followed, then the crackling of paper.

"Read this." The voice was harsh—a man, not speaking his native tongue.

"Hays. You have to go home. They'll kill her if you don't. Hays. You have to go home. Please." The urgency in Roberta's voice was gut-wrenching.

There came a sharp, rippling sound of flesh striking flesh.

Then the man spoke again.

"You go home now. If you do not, this woman, Norah, will be dead and will be on your hands. You go back to America. Now."

While the connection didn't end, a subtle hiss followed—like the hiss of a phone tape machine at the end of a message. Then a click, followed by a broken connection.

Hays stared out into the distance and didn't fully panic until he began the sprint back to his hotel.

QUADARE CITY, QUADARE—Norah was all but dumped, like so much trash, back into the same windowless room where they'd been kept before. She began to crawl toward the thin mattress, hoping the pain would end, trying not to move more than a few inches at a time, praying that if she moved her arm just a bit, the searing pain wouldn't begin again.

The door bounced open a second time, and Roberta was roughly tossed into the darkness. She stumbled and fell, only a few inches from Norah. Her eye was swollen, and tears streaked her face.

Roberta pulled herself up on her right elbow. She reached out and touched Norah's shoulder.

"I'm sorry, I'm so sorry," she sobbed.

Norah stopped crawling and turned her face. "Not ... your ... fault," she gasped through clenched teeth.

Roberta managed to sit. She pulled a thin mattress, the cleaner of the two, closer. She put her hands under Norah's shoulders and helped her lean up, nudging the mattress with her knee to get it under her. They worked in silence, tiny gasps of pain the only sounds coming from the two battered women.

Neither could say how long it took, but Norah eventually lay down on the pad, flat on her stomach. Roberta folded the other pad in half and laid it next to Norah for a pillow. Then she knelt beside her and gently lifted Norah's blouse. Her skin had been flayed nearly to the bone, the slashes deep and long and angry-looking. Roberta was afraid to do anything, knowing it would cause more pain.

There was an unopened bottle of water in the corner. Roberta tore off a long strip from her skirt and poured some of the water on it. She began to dab at Norah's back, trying to clean the wounds and remove the dried blood, hoping it might reduce the risk of infection. With every touch, Norah winced.

It took nearly an hour to complete the task. Roberta had attended enough premed classes to know Norah should have stitches for some of the wounds, have a more thorough cleaning, start a course in antibiotics—but none of that would likely occur.

She knew now, at this specific moment and without a doubt, that both she and Norah would die. If that man was willing to torture Norah just as a warning—then how long before he decided to be rid of them permanently?

She heard a faint whispering for water. A few drops remained. Norah swallowed and lowered her head to the mattress.

"I'm sorry, Norah. I'm so sorry."

Norah moved her right hand, as if trying to wave away her apology. Roberta remained silent. Hoping she wouldn't hurt her further, she put her hand on Norah's head and gently stroked her hair, as if calming a frightened kitten.

"It ... will be ... all right," Norah whispered. "Not ... afraid. You ..."

Roberta bent closer.

"Don't be ... afraid," Norah whispered, each word causing her pain. "God is ... here. I know it. Hays ... will come."

Roberta held her friend carefully without speaking. She knew Norah was wrong—they both would be dead before long. But if Norah wanted to hope that Hays was on the way and that God was watching out for them, Roberta would let her find solace in that delusion.

"He ... will ... come," Norah insisted faintly, and then closed her eyes.

Roberta was terrified that Norah had died, and until she saw the slight rise of her back from her tortured inhaling and exhaling, she didn't breathe either.

She wouldn't be able to survive alone.

SHUSH, IRAN—Hays took the stairs three at a time, slamming the door open and scaring Duffy enough to cause him to lunge for his backpack and the hidden cache of weapons.

"They've got Norah," Hays all but shouted.

Duffy hurried to close the door, grabbed his friend, and pulled him to a sitting position on the bed beside him. Ranger training had taught him a person can't be as frantic sitting down as standing up.

"Who has Norah? What do you mean? How?"

"*They* have her," Hays repeated, trying to keep his words soft, but failing.

"Who?"

Hays held the phone out to Duffy. "Dial this number."

Then he buried his head against his closed fists, pressing his eyelids against his knuckles, hoping to force the images from swimming before him. He could only imagine what agony Norah was enduring.

He could hear the faint noise from the phone as Duffy listened. He felt his anger and panic rise again.

Duffy snapped off the phone. There was a cold fury in his eyes.

"We have to go. She's in Quadare. That man—he spoke with a Quadare accent. There is no other possibility."

While Duffy dressed, Hays sat by his backpack. He removed the Austrian-made Glock 29. It was one of the smallest, least complicated, and most powerful pistols ever made. He slipped it into an inside coat pocket. He pulled out three ten-shot magazines, thought for a moment, pulled the gun out, loaded a magazine into the weapon, and slipped the extra two clips into his trouser pocket.

Duffy finished dressing and pulled on his boots.

"We need to go. Now," he said as he tightened the lacing.

Hays simply shouldered his backpack, then patted at his chest, feeling for the familiar outline nestling against his heart.

The bus rattled and bounced, and Hays and Duffy bumped shoulders. Sleep was impossible on this segment of their trip.

Hays took the window seat, figuring that if anyone asked questions, they would ask them of Duffy, who had the best chance of answering in the correct language.

So which is the greater evil? A man torturing an innocent woman—or me killing that man?

If Hays could find that man, there would be no doubt as to his actions.

As the bus bounced and rolled, Hays kept touching the Glock nestled safely against him.

This time, if pressed, he wouldn't think twice about using it against anyone who stood in their way.

26

QUADARE CITY, QUADARE—Fadhil paced his office, the worn leather of his slippers making a scuffing noise on the thick Oriental carpet. He had pulled off his imported boots immediately after he arrived, the tight arch causing his little toe to throb. He had carried his bedroom slippers from home in a brown paper bag, not wanting anyone to see.

He jabbed at the intercom button, hearing the device buzz in the outer office. There was no response. He waited, palms flat on the desk.

He could wait no longer and shouted as loud as he could. "Get in here, you donkey!"

The door slipped open.

"Why did you not answer that buzzer?" he demanded. "I have told you that the buzzer is always me. You answer the buzzer."

"Buzzer? There was no buzzer. I heard no buzzer, sir."

Fadhil knew he was lying and wanted to climb over the desk and throttle the man, but his toe hurt too much for him to attempt it. "Get Hameed in here."

The servant nodded and slowly edged his way outside and eased the door shut.

Fadhil resigned himself to a thirty-minute wait. Rather than stewing in poisonous silence, he instead pulled his computer closer and tapped at the keyboard.

His list of favorite Web sites came up in a blink. If he had to wait, he might as well be entertained, he told himself.

Nearly forty-five minutes passed before the door opened again. Hameed entered without permission, a behavior that had only recently begun, Fadhil had noted. It was a habit he didn't at all like.

"Those two Westerners—the infidels. The ones that your prisoner—that woman—is supposed to stop. I have heard that they are not stopping."

If Hameed was surprised by Fadhil's knowledge, he didn't show it.

"Not stopping? What do you mean?" he asked, his tone innocent.

Fadhil smirked. "You are not the only one who hears things. I'm told that they were in Lebanon and are now in Iran. You said that the woman would stop them."

Hameed was not a man given to squirming. He stood motionless, a slight twitch nibbling at his right eye.

"Well? Now they are closer. In Iran. They are obviously coming to Quadare. Or haven't your sources confirmed this latest report?" In Quadare there were no secrets to those who held money or power. Gossip, intrigue, scraps of news were bartered and sold, much like ration tickets. Fadhil built up a small cadre of informers, and sprinkled them throughout the city. He purchased some of the same informants that Hameed purchased, and their whispered information came quickly to the highest bidder. Fadhil was closer to power, and power was closer to the source of money.

Fadhil took some delight in tormenting Hameed. He knew after he was finished, Hameed would scurry out to wherever it was that he scurried in times like these and would beat some foolish informant senseless for breaching security.

It was a punishment Fadhil would happily let occur. When one man is beaten, many tremble.

"Sir," Hameed said, licking his lips for moisture, "they are only two men. The fact they are in Iran is no great achievement. They will never be able to cross the gulf and set foot on Quadare soil."

Fadhil stood up and winced. Standing on his inflamed toe was painful. He shuffled around to the front of the desk, drawing closer and closer to Hameed. Hameed wanted to step back, but he stood his ground.

Fadhil reached in the breast pocket of his shirt and extracted a crumpled piece of paper. He spoke softly, but his words were coiled and tight.

"You will prepare for their arrival—and take all means necessary."

Hameed was about to voice a polite objection but the angry glow of Fadhil's scowl stopped him.

"I have gone back to the infidel's holy book. I have read further. I was surprised to see that the curse changes quickly and another person is addressed. Do you know what this so-called holy book then says?"

Fadhil knew Hameed had no idea.

"Let me read it to you. The prophet Micah says, '*I should make thee a desolation, and the inhabitants thereof a hissing: therefore ye shall bear the reproach of my people.'* It is clearly a reference to those who treat this curse—this judgment—without proper respect. I will not be made fool of by any ancient curse."

He stared hard at Hameed, his nostrils flaring. "I will not let any of this happen to me. You do understand that, don't you? I will not be humiliated. I will not be brought to ruin. That cannot happen. It cannot."

Hameed remained still.

"I said," Fadhil shouted, spittle landing on Hameed's cheek, *"I will not let that happen."*

The next moment was a blur to both men. Fadhil saw an equivocation forming on Hameed's lips—some manner of excuse, some desultory dismissal of the threat, a soul-clenching simpering—and rather than hear a single word, without giving warning, Fadhil drew his backhand, and as hard and fast as he could, he struck Hameed across the cheek, splitting his lip, blood splattering on the dusty carpet. Hameed reeled backward from the blow and as he stumbled, his hand slapped at his waist, and his fingers tightened around the black metal of the Glock 19 holstered under his coat. He had it withdrawn and aimed at Fadhil's chest in the time it took to blink.

Both men stood, as if paralyzed for that moment, neither one giving an inch of power away.

The door to the outer office swung open, and the servant almost stumbled into the room, distracting both Hameed and Fadhil from their murderous rage.

Both combatants stepped back, their eyes fixed on each other, still flaming with a cold rage. Had they paid attention, they would have seen the gleeful smile pass quickly over the servant's face as he bowed and made his way back into the outer office, pulling the door closed behind him.

CDC HEADQUARTERS, ATLANTA, GEORGIA—"So what's the deal with this African dust-up? Our embassy contact seems to think it's the return of the plague."

Alan Symmers sat back in his swivel desk chair, reading over the tops of his glasses, moving his arms in and out, adjusting the telex at different lengths from his eyes to make out the small type.

Charles Hild lumbered to the windowsill and sat heavily, his sport coat ruffling the window blinds. "I dunno. Maybe our man just wants to come back home—you know, if you carp about something long and loud enough, they shuffle you around. Africa isn't exactly the top pick of the embassies."

Alan had been with the CDC for decades; Chuck was new, just out of graduate school and a recent participant in the FBI's six-month training in counter-terrorism. He was also a former Navy Seal, but one would never have assumed that from his demeanor and style.

Both men were part of the CDC's emergency response unit, determining which medical hot spot was worth investigating by sending a team to do more thorough fieldwork.

"So what's the deal?"

Chuck smashed his back harder against the blinds, a move that would drive Alan to distraction.

"Well, according to the Huber/Loss people, they were on the scene pretty quick. Fertilizer runoff is the probable cause."

"Fertilizer? What fertilizer is that deadly?"

Chuck shook his head. "Sorry. I mean pesticide. That's what they said it was. They were killing rats and mice with aluminum phosphide. The village was in sort of a bowl, geographically speaking—and when they use that pesticide, phosphine gas forms. That's what kills the varmints."

"And that's lethal to people?" Alan asked. He was not expert in pesticides.

Chuck nodded. "Yep. The gas is heavier than air, so it settles. That's why they use it in burrows. It always flows down. And it is deadly. If you're talking about people, then two thousand parts per million can kill an adult male in a few minutes. Huber/Loss said it was probably double or triple that amount—there were that many empty containers of the stuff around. Natives tend to use more of something than they need to."

"Any autopsy reports?"

Chuck rummaged in his pocket for a cookie, which he always carried with him. He began nibbling on a slightly bruised Oreo while he talked.

"They burned everything. The village was isolated. No refrigeration, you know what I mean? The gas causes pulmonary edema—plus vomiting, convulsions, paralysis. Not pleasant. I think they did the only decent thing by torching the place."

Alan wanted to get up and drag Chuck from the windowsill, but held his tongue.

"What about the pesticide? Any liability issues?"

"No. It came from some African company. I mean, I don't think anyone is going to sue—they're all dead, right? And it sure sounded like they

used the stuff in the wrong way. I know the States have laws protecting anyone who is just downright stupid, but I don't think Africa does."

Alan took a deep breath and focused on the cup of yellow pencils at the
edge of his desk.

"Okay, then. I'll telex the ambassador and settle his nerves."

Chuck grinned and slowly pushed himself upright. "You get a chance
to read that report from our agent in Pittsburgh? About that researcher who
claimed he found a new virus and someone stole it?"

Alan hadn't read it, but so wanted Chuck to be out of his office that he
nodded in reply. "Yes—what about it?"

Chuck stopped halfway to the door.

"Just wanted to know if you want me to ask around about it or something."

"No," Alan said, wanting to keep him going. "I'm sure it was nothing.
You can file it away. No action required."

Chuck shrugged, then smiled, reached into his pocket, and extracted
one more cookie. "Okeydokey. Anything you say."

Alan called out to his back, "And please close the door. I have some sensitive calls to make."

As soon as the door snapped shut, Alan hurried to the window to
readjust the flattened window-blind slats, sweeping the crumbs off the sill
into a small pile in his hand.

QUADARE CITY, QUADARE—Norah woke, her head feverish, sweat
soaking the thin mattress. She tried not to move, but she had to sit, had to
try to clear the spinning, violent motion she felt. She pushed herself to the
side and clenched her teeth. She couldn't contain the shriek of pain the
movement brought.

Roberta jerked awake and hurried to her side.

Norah had slept fitfully, moaning softly with each breath.

"It's okay," Roberta said and she tried to help Norah into a sitting
position.

"Is there any water?"

They had each been given a bowl of rice and a bottle of water the night
prior, and Roberta hadn't opened her water, wanting to save it for Norah.
She quickly grabbed it and snapped the seal open. Norah drank a small
mouthful, closing her eyes as if it pained her to swallow.

The two of them sat that way for a long time, Roberta holding Norah upright, Norah leaning her head against her friend's shoulder.

The door slid open. A woman walked in. She wasn't a guard. She was dressed in the traditional Middle Eastern manner, her face nearly obscured by a veil, her form wrapped in a flowing jilbab. She knelt at Norah's side.

"They have allowed me here for only a moment."

She carefully lifted off the makeshift bandages that Roberta had applied earlier. Norah winced. The woman opened a small valise and took out a small canister. She shook it and sprayed a fine mist directly onto Norah's slashed and broken skin. Norah reacted with a loud gasp, but after a few seconds, her shoulders relaxed, and she let her head drop forward.

"It is an antiseptic and a painkiller. I will leave it here. You must apply often. I have no antibiotics, but perhaps this will be enough. Here is a bottle of aspirin as well. It is not much. But it is all I have."

Roberta took the canister and the aspirin. "Thank you."

The woman snapped the small valise shut and stood. "The guard outside—I know his mother well. There are few secrets anywhere—especially in Quadare. The guard told his mother about two Western women, and his mother told me. I know of the man who brought you to Quadare. And I knew pain would follow that man, so I am here. The guard outside would never disobey his mother."

Norah looked up at the woman. "Thank you. Thank you so much."

"What are your names?" the woman asked.

"I'm Roberta and this is Norah," Roberta said softly.

"I will pray for you both, then, by name. I trust that you know the one true God."

Roberta blinked in surprise and Norah offered a weak smile. "I do … now."

The woman stepped to the door.

"Then you know he will protect you. I must go now. If I can return, I will. God will watch over you."

The door clanged shut.

And a thin sliver of hope returned.

BUSHEHR, IRAN—There was a hint of saltwater and oil in the air. The bus pulled to a wheezing stop. Hays jumped off, with Duffy a half-step behind, and set off at a jog toward the marina, only a dozen blocks to the south.

Hays could barely contain himself, could barely sit, could barely string coherent thoughts together. He wanted to charge in blindly, attacking and destroying—exactly what to destroy, he did not yet know. But he forced himself, with every bit of self-control he had, to be patient and carefully think through each situation. To fail would not only condemn himself and his friend, but Norah as well—and perhaps millions more. Waiting was the most cruel and horrible punishment Hays could imagine—and all he could do now was wait.

The image of Norah in danger grew more real and intense. That image drove both men, haunting their thoughts.

And now they were two blocks away from their transport to Quadare.

27

BUSHEHR, IRAN—Hays watched while Duffy entered a ramshackle building perched at the beginning of a rickety pier. The structure canted several degrees from plumb and was nearly hidden by mounds of gull droppings and dirt. Duffy introduced himself. If this was the right marina and the correct time, then the man standing behind the counter with folded arms and scowl was, in some fashion, a relative of Duffy's—a third cousin of a third cousin, perhaps, on his mother's side. Duffy's arms and hands traced elaborate diagrams in the air as he punctuated a very complicated lineage—even for a man with Duffy's experience at genealogy. A bright smile lit the man's face, and he hurried from around the counter and embraced Duffy with a fierceness that definitely seemed reserved for relatives.

Hays attempted to follow their discussion, and to his credit, understood a few phrases and words. He believed most of the conversation dealt with Duffy's family, then moved on to Lebanon, and finally to Duffy's journey to America. That's when the man behind the counter eyed Hays with a serious, concerned look.

All sense of the genial family host disappeared. The man's expression turned businesslike.

The discussion grew quietly intense, and Hays heard the Farsi word for money—followed quickly by the question, "American dollars?"

Duffy nodded.

The man pulled out his cell phone, tapped in a number, and spoke no more than ten seconds. He flipped the phone shut and grinned at Hays, showing three lower gold teeth. He spoke in English. "Tonight. Moonrise. You go. Quadare. Good pilot. Experienced."

Duffy bent to his friend and spoke barely above a whisper. "Count out three hundred dollars. Show him another three hundred in your wallet. And then show him your pistol. Make it seem like an accident, but make sure he sees it. To cross the gulf costs six hundred American dollars. I want to assure him that we have the rest of the money."

"But why the pistol?"

Duffy smiled. "I want to make sure the captain understands that they are supposed to gets us completely across—and not leave us halfway as shark food—without our wallets."

Hays did exactly as he was instructed. His Glock slipped out of his pocket, and Hays made a theatrical catch. He didn't smile as he slipped it back inside. Neither did the man behind the desk.

The hour between the payment and the moonrise seemed to Hays as the longest hour a man could ever spend.

The harbor grew dark and quiet, save the warning horn at the entrance and the thunderous humming rumble of tanker ships gliding out into the sea beyond.

Duffy explained that they would be met at moonrise at the end of the pier. They'd take one fast boat and would make the crossing in just over twelve hours. It would be morning by the time they reached the Quadare shores—and since Quadare had no navy, there would be no one to notice their arrival.

Duffy said his distant cousin behind the counter had claimed that no one sneaks into Quadare—there are too many people sneaking out to notice anyone coming in.

Hays looked at his watch. It was now a few minutes before ten. He heard the boat before he saw it, a velvety puttering sound of a hull creasing heavy water. The boat was almost upon them. Hays could see the lit cigarette of someone on board. Instead of one single boat, two crafts pulled up. No ropes were tossed; there was just a hard banging into the jutting pier posts.

"You," came a harsh whisper, "into the smaller boat. You will follow us. Little boat much faster."

Hays and Duffy clambered aboard. The boat wasn't much bigger than a large sofa, maybe a sofa and a loveseat—but no more than that.

The lead boat was bigger, with a flying bridge and a whip of antennas catching the moon, swaying with the swells of the bay.

Hays placed his pack in the bow and turned back to Duffy. "Faster? Do you think something this small will actually get us across the gulf?"

Duffy shrugged. "My family descended from a long line of goatherders, not fisherman. But given the circumstances, I think we're forced to depend on the honesty of a cousin of a cousin of a cousin. Do you think he would lie to us?"

"Remember—the pastor said to get into the smaller boat. Remember?"

The captain called out in a pleasant way and gestured into the night sky as he explained.

Duffy translated. "He says this small boat belongs to the sister of his brother-in-law … I think. He wants his nephew here or second nephew or maybe he's just some sort of business associate … to learn the ropes. A fast crossing at night can be dangerous, he says. He'll lead the way, but he wants his nephew, or whoever he is, to have the 'cargo' tonight. I think it's sort of like having an intern. He says this small boat is seaworthy, despite how it looks."

The lead boat turned into the waters of the harbor and with a shushing sound, headed south. The smaller boat, captained by a single young man who appeared to be no more than a teenager, spun about and followed.

Hays and Duffy sat toward the stern and watched the lights of Bushehr disappear into the northern horizon.

Soon, all that could be seen was the ghostly moon and a thousand mirrored reflections dancing on small waves around them.

Somewhere around 4:00 a.m., the small craft sidled alongside the larger lead boat. There was much shouting and gesturing, with arms waving in a wild fashion.

"They want us to take the lead," Duffy explained as he rubbed his eyes, clearing the sleep from them.

"Why?" Hays asked.

Duffy called out to the pilot, first in Farsi, which got no reply, then in Arabic. The young man answered, but only after a long moment of consideration.

"He says that we will offer a smaller target. There should be no gunboats out here—but sometimes the Iranians stray out of their waters.

Sometimes the Saudis do too. The second boat is what will show up on radar since it's so much bigger. We'll just keep going, he says."

Hays thought for a moment.

"Do you believe that?"

Duffy stared at his friend. "Not for a minute, but what choice do we have?"

Hays decided not to answer, thinking the real reason had to do with mines floating in the murky water.

He knew they had no choice, no choice at all.

QUADARE WATERS—More than an hour remained until dawn when over the boats' rumbling and watery sounds came a louder sound—a choppier, heavy sound.

Hays knew in an instant what it was. The look in Duffy's eyes told the same story.

Helicopters. Maybe just one, but a big one.

"We're in Quadare waters, aren't we?" shouted Hays.

Duffy shouted a translation to the pilot who simply nodded.

They scanned the sky. A helicopter never appeared from where its sound came. The night and the water do strange things to a man's perception. Hays debated unpacking his Uzi, but quickly dismissed the thought. The weapon had an intimidating rate of fire, but at long distances it wasn't exactly accurate. If the sound did come from a helicopter—a helicopter packed with weapons—both boats would soon be reduced to driftwood regardless of Hays' marksmanship.

From behind them a spotlight exploded its illumination on the ocean. A search lamp, as dazzling as the sun, began to sweep the waves. Small crests of seawater, lit from above, sparkled like fountains. The light swept in one direction and then another, like a magical broom sweeping the ocean, handled by a giant.

The young pilot of their small boat jammed the throttle full open. The boat lurched and jumped and shouldered into the surf with more vigor and noise.

From the corner of his eye, Hays saw Duffy make the same preparations he was making. He grabbed his backpack, tucked the straps in his left arm, and prepared to leap into the water if the beam from the lamp above caught them.

The giant illuminated eye swept back and forth and the helicopter's engine grew louder and louder, as if the aircraft were slowly descending, drawing closer to its prey. The larger boat lay less than a hundred yards behind the smaller craft. Hays could barely make out the crest of the larger boat's wake. On the ocean there was no place to hide.

Hays saw a glint from behind them. The pilot must have seen it, too, for he shouted something in Farsi.

The larger boat waited until the searchlight swung to the farthest point away in its arc, then nearly capsized attempting a very fast, 180-degree turn, back upon its own wake. If it could slip past the forward sweep of the light, they would be safe and headed for home.

The larger boat hit its own wake and bounced, veering to one side, then another, the white fiberglass hull flashing in the darkness. At the last second the light from above caught an edge of the larger boat as it retreated north. The light passed, then stopped and returned, sweeping in tighter and tighter circles until the larger boat was flush with illumination, sparkling, ablaze with light in the darkness.

Hays assumed an amplified, disembodied voice from the sky would call out for the craft's captain to identify himself, his boat, and his destination and cargo. They'd be ordered to return to whatever port the helicopter was based at. If that occurred, Hays imagined, they would soon suffer the same fate.

Instead of an order from a loudspeaker, there came a flash.

Hays ducked instinctively, as did Duffy. Almost instantly Hays recognized it for what it was—an air-to-surface missile fired at close range, with little chance of failure.

It was like shooting a rabbit in a phone booth with a shotgun.

The larger ship erupted into a huge, rolling cloud of fire and flame, explosion and rumbling, the percussive wave knocking Hays to the deck. Their pilot did fall, clutching at the tiller, causing the small craft to swing widely. In a heartbeat a rain of debris started falling around them—bits of wood and plastic and a wash of seawater and cloth and fabric—and wet bits of what might have been flesh. The sound of the explosion rolled past them like summer thunder.

No one could see for a moment, so bright was the explosion. Hays began blinking furiously, hoping to clear his vision. Through the mist and the smoke and the carnage, he watched as the light from the helicopter stayed on the wreckage for a long moment, then swept around in a lazy circle.

Then, nearly as suddenly as it came on, the light simply snapped off, and the world was plunged back into darkness.

No one spoke.

The little boat continued to plow through the turgid water, undetected, unmolested, unchallenged.

Perhaps five minutes passed in absolute, watery calm.

"Quadare. Now five hundred American. In cash."

The pilot suddenly sounded twice as old as his face looked. There were lines now where only smooth flesh had been before.

Hays felt twice as old as well, and instead of speaking, simply nodded in agreement. "Five hundred. Okay."

And no one spoke again until the faint glimmer of the Quadare coast-line began to glisten in the morning sun.

28

QUADARE CITY, QUADARE—In the faint hushing of the wind, the branches of the twin alders outside the doctor's window scrabbled and scratched at the glass. The doctor awoke, his nightshirt clammy with sweat. He knew he should trim the two trees, but so little grew in his neighborhood that cutting anything green verged on sacrilege.

He slipped out of bed, careful not to wake his wife. Haj had been recently given to waking at night with a startled gasp. Sleep would then elude him, and he would sit in the cramped living room of his small house, smoking, not moving in the darkness, staring out at the black street, listening for the creaks and groans of the structure as it flexed in the night chill. He would often creep into the room where his two daughters lay asleep to make sure a blanket covered each, and stare at them for long moments, memorizing their faces as they rested in their innocent slumber. Then he made sure the door to his daughters' room was fastened shut.

At the beginning of this horrible experiment, the doctor slept well, serene, uncaring. But as the days passed, the full weight of what he worked with became more apparent. He could no longer hide. His sleep became more fitful and sporadic, and he spent more time in the dark, only the burning end of his Marlboro cigarette visible. He would hold the ashtray in his right hand, the cigarette in his left, and nervously tap the ash every few seconds. Once it was burnt to the filter, he would light another one from the short end before he snubbed it out.

Then the process would be repeated until dawn interrupted.

It was the virus that so bedeviled his sleep.

Fadhil's evil virus—what he called the "Judgment of Micah." Only an infidel, Haj believed, would be so insensitive as to use a religion's holy book to name a deadly agent like this. Only an infidel would be so foolish as to tempt someone's God—anyone's God.

Initially, Haj had hoped what Fadhil had given him in those two vials had been a prion. Making a weapon out of a prion would be nearly impossible. Deadly by themselves, to be sure, prions were notoriously resistant to duplication and difficult to infect into others. You often had to eat or ingest them in sufficient quantities—and even then, transmission was not assured. Once you were infected, you could expect a truly hideous death.

But viruses ... well, Haj hated viruses. He especially hated this one. This virus was unlike any he had ever encountered. Two workers in his lab had been infected—the fools. They had disregarded his warnings and ignored safety procedures. They died quickly. Starvation is not quick, but this virus not only blocked nutrients from getting into the bloodstream it also prevented the absorption of water as well. A week and both were dead. Their bodies had been triple-bagged and burned.

Now Fadhil was insisting this horrible and dangerous virus be weaponized.

At the outset of his research, the doctor had taken Fadhil's rantings as the words of a lunatic. He knew biological weapons were fickle, hard to control and much harder to aim. A shift in the wind and the hunter becomes the hunted. Loading a virus into an artillery shell and lobbing it into a city had been tried in the past, but the process generally wasn't effective. The heat of the shell often killed the biological agent's potency. Plus, there was always the risk of a misfire and a release of that deadly agent onto "your" side of the battlefield. Generals hated biological weapons—what general liked a weapon that might kill his men first? But what the generals hated, madmen loved.

The Micah virus had proved amazingly resilient. He worried that it might even survive being dropped from a plane into a city's water supply. That fact would have been enough to keep Haj awake. But there was more.

This virus liked to reproduce. It grew quickly, regardless of the medium in which it was placed. Flesh, blood, and animal waste—it intensified in size in nearly anything and everything that could host life.

The doctor could kill it—but not once it entered a host's body—at least in some species. Rats were prime targets—as were humans, apparently. He had found no antibodies, no immunization, no treatment that would prevent the virus from spreading and growing and destroying the viability of its host body. He had sacrificed nearly three hundred rats so far, attempting to stop its explosive growth. They all died swiftly. They were all burnt in his lab's crematorium.

Fadhil had joked during his last visit over the ease of developing a new delivery system for this weapon. Life apparently meant little to him. Life apparently was no longer sacred.

"We could infect a man—a suicide bomber intent on finding paradise—put him on a plane, and have him drown himself in the water reservoir of New York City. That would allow the virus to spread to all of New York, would it not?" Fadhil had laughed.

The doctor could still hear the laughter—especially at night, when all was quiet. It was an evil laugh, a maniacal laugh that Haj felt echoed from hell.

"And I have no shortage of young men who seek paradise—plus a small stipend for their families as payment for their martyrdom," Fadhil had continued. "I could have America humbled in a week, could I not? I could have the world bowing down to me … and to Quadare."

And now, Haj neared the end of his research. He could no longer find any rest. He was perhaps only a week from finishing his tests. He was a week from finalizing the processes needed to manufacture the virus in large enough quantities—and to stabilize it for delivery.

He lit another cigarette and drew in deeply. His hand shook, the burning embers dancing in tight circles in the darkness. The smoldering tobacco traced a devil's head in the dark.

There was nothing he could do to stop this terrible plague from being unleashed upon the world. If he tried, those two small girls in the next room would be at peril. If he resisted, his family would be in peril. If he cooperated, the world might be at peril.

But simply saying no to Fadhil would be signing his family's death warrant.

And that was something he simply couldn't do. Ever.

Quadare City claimed it had no slums. But four blocks west of Haj's modest home, the streets grew narrow, and the houses and shops canted toward the street. The pavement disappeared, replaced by well-packed dirt and sand. Sewage gathered in fetid pools along the crumbling sidewalks, attended to by a buzz of flies.

Midway along one block of this area, just next to a ragged storefront offering a dusty assortment of tinned food and bottled drinks, a young woman locked a windowless door behind her, checking it twice, making sure the bolt held. Her mother remained asleep inside.

Maslis hoisted her small bag to her shoulder, hearing her small cache of coins jangle together. She figured she had enough to purchase breakfast—or ride a hot bus to her job.

It was early, and she decided to walk this morning. She would buy something from a sidewalk vendor when she came closer to the lab.

And walking would give her more time to pray.

In Quadare City she knew of a small handful of believers—believers in the God, Jehovah, and his son, Christ Jesus. Maybe there were more, but no one in Quadare could be seen with a Bible or a cross—that could bring a death sentence.

Three years ago a young woman from Korea—a guest worker in Quadare—had befriended Maslis. Her Farsi was spoken without an accent, and Maslis had been astounded—a woman with slanted eyes speaking her own language.

This foreigner had invited Maslis to her small apartment.

There was a Bible—in Farsi—on a table in the kitchen.

Maslis was no longer sure how it happened, or what she said, or how this foreigner explained the truths of the Bible. But she had believed in Jesus and he had entered her heart and changed her life.

The Korean girl had left a year ago, and had given the Bible to Maslis. She hid it under her mattress, reading it—devouring it—in secret, not allowing even her mother to know of her faith.

And this day, Maslis needed the time to pray. She was only an assistant—but she could tell what was happening. Every rat died. Two of her coworkers simply stopped appearing at work—and no one knew of their whereabouts. Those two shadowy men were visiting more often. Maslis saw their dead eyes and grew frightened.

She prayed as she walked. She prayed to her Jesus and asked, over and over, that he send an angel to stop the evil that they were working on in the lab.

Even poor Haj looked more and more anxious—the gray, hollow circles under his eyes growing deeper and deeper.

Whatever the need, God, please send your agent. He will know what to do. But you must hurry.

QUADARE COAST—The water was nearly up to their necks, and they stumbled and scratched for footing. The pilot of the boat would come no closer to shore, and as soon as Hays and Duffy splashed into the water, he turned the small boat into the swells and roared back toward Iran, back across the open water.

The shore in front of them lay barren—no homes, piers, or fancy waterfront mansions. There were just hillocks of sand peppered with tufts of sea grass, some hard-scrabble shrubs bending into the breeze, with a blue-green line of foothills stretching away from the sea.

"So, did your cousin sell you out?" Hays called out over the noise of the water. He had been unwilling to ask before now, thinking their young pilot might have understood a smattering of English.

"He might have," Duffy said grudgingly. "Money is persuasive."

They sloshed closer to shore. The water was warm and the waves were slight.

"And I'm not exactly his nearest living relative. But he had to sell out the captain, as well as us. Maybe he thought we would just be, you know, taken prisoner or put into custody. I don't think he could have anticipated what happened. And, you know, it just might have been a chance encounter."

"With air-to-surface missiles? I don't see that as a chance meeting," Hays replied.

"You might be right. But remember, to people in this area—well—family is sacred, but there are many things that are *more* sacred. Honor maybe. Revenge. Retaliation. Settling an old score. I don't know." Duffy didn't smile. "But life is viewed differently here. It's more fatalistic. You just have to accept it as it is."

Hays reached the edge of the surf, the sand already warming from the sun.

"I don't think it was random, but I can't worry about that now. If they think we're dead, then we're better off. More an element of surprise now," he said. "Where's the map?"

Duffy had always been better at maps and directions than Hays. He pulled the waterproof map from his pack. Hays flicked the switch on his GPS unit and quickly determined their exact longitude and latitude. Duffy placed a single dot on the map, on the coastline north of Quadare City.

"We're right where we asked to be," Duffy said as he marked the map. "We'll go that way. Our destination looks no more than twenty clicks away. There's not much of a road here—but it should be just over that small rise. We follow it right to the city."

Hays adjusted the straps on his pack and set out inland. The road lay a kilometer or so away from the sea.

"Wait," Duffy called out to his back. "We're not going to walk in wet clothes. We need to change. We're not just going to waltz into Quadare City in broad daylight, remember? We have a plan for this. You do remember our plan, right?"

Hays took a deep breath. "Right. I know. I'm jumping the gun. Sorry. I'm just—"

"I know. Norah. We'll find her. But first things first, okay? We follow the plan. That's really our only hope of doing this right."

"Okay."

CDC HEADQUARTERS, ATLANTA, GEORGIA—He straightened the file folders on his desk, making sure each was an even distance from each other and that all were canted at the same identical angle. It took him a few moments, then Alan Symmers smiled, satisfied.

It was always good to start the day with the proper order.

Then came the tapping. He would have been happier if no one bothered him during the day. His office would stay that much neater. But the interruptions came whether he liked it or not.

Chuck Hild shambled in, probably bringing a multitude of toast crumbs from his breakfast or Danish crumbs from his early morning snack. Alan wondered if the CDC would authorize him to purchase a small vacuum cleaner for his office. It would make cleaning so much more efficient.

Chuck's tie was already askew—a remarkable achievement after only sixty minutes of actual work.

He hunkered down on the windowsill, his shoulder misaligning the blinds in an aggravating fashion. He twisted his mouth in a curl, trying to dislodge a morsel of something from a back molar. He must have been successful, for he moved his jaws and smiled.

"Anyhow, you remember our agent from Pittsburgh? The one what's-his-face—Jack Douglas—the guy with the goofy crew cut? He sent in a report awhile back. You remember that, don't cha?"

Alan had no idea what Chuck was referring to. He got many such reports and summaries to track and didn't recall field reports based on their city of origin.

"No."

"Sure you do," Chuck insisted with a laugh. "I told you about it. Right here in this office. I remember that exactly. It was a real hot day and I was sweating a lot, and you had your office even warmer. You remember, right?"

Alan stared back at him, hoping his blank look might be interpreted as hostile and that Chuck would get the hint, make his story short and sweet and then leave.

"I bet you do. You're just not remembering it right, that's all. Anyhow, the agent in Pittsburgh, he sent in this report saying he didn't report something earlier, but was reporting it now because of a whole series of odd and weird things happening."

Alan folded his hands and sighed deeply, as a mother might sigh when dealing with a disobedient child's repeat offense.

"I don't recall the report. Do you have a file number?"

Chuck shrugged and slapped at his pockets. "I thought I wrote it down. Must have stuck it in one of these pockets."

Alan had visions of a week's worth of crumbs tumbling out onto the carpet.

"Never mind. Just tell me about it. I'll look it up later."

Chuck shrugged again, this time with a grin, and began his story. After a few minutes of preamble he got to the fulcrum of the report.

"So this research guy at the University of Pittsburgh says he discovered this old virus—and it makes people starve to death. But then a bunch of thieves broke into his lab and stole it. Took everything, he claimed. Well, you and I both know how odd researchers can get—too many chemical fumes, I think. Anyhow, our Pittsburgh agent thought it was nothing, but then a few weeks later, the researcher goes missing. Said he was going to Italy for a conference, but there wasn't any conference scheduled when he said it was. I guess that's no big deal in itself. But a couple of weeks later the woman who worked with him, she goes missing, along with this other lady that worked on the research grants. Nobody reported anything suspicious and they're both, like, single, so maybe they went off on some singles jaunt, but they left without telling anybody. Didn't request vacation time, so they've got a lot of folks concerned. Then, remember that report on the African village where everyone died? So our Pittsburgh agent calls and asks if we think any of this is related. Says he's getting odd vibes."

Alan wanted to lower his head and cradle it in his hands, but didn't.

"Vibes?"

"That's what he said. Odd vibes. 'Hinky.' I think he said 'hinky.' Anyhow, something like that."

"And that's how the CDC does its work now? We base our investigation on vibes? 'Hinky' vibes?"

Chuck shrugged. Shrugging seemed to be as much a part of him as breathing.

"I don't know. Probably not, right?"

Alan took a deep breath. "Do you think we need to explore this situation a bit further?"

"Maybe. I had what's-his-name in the computer lab—you know—the MIS guy with the big nose? Anyhow, I had him check our researcher's e-mail address. Seems he's no longer in Italy like he claimed he was going to be. The last trace was an e-mail received in Quadare. Couldn't break the code to read it, but it was sent from Lebanon to Quadare."

"Quadare?"

"Yeah, I never heard of it either. Some tiny little country on the Persian Gulf."

"So what's he doing there?"

Chuck shrugged again.

Alan reacted as if nails had been scraped repeatedly across a blackboard. "Do you want to investigate this?"

Chuck perked up. "Yeah. Sure. Can I go to Quadare? I've never been to Quadare before. I'm collecting passport stamps."

Alan might have agreed to anything just to get Chuck out of his office. "Yes, by all means, go to Quadare. And take what's-his—I mean Norman Williamson, the fellow from our MIS department, with you."

And as soon as the door closed shut, Alan began the memo to request funds for a vacuum cleaner. In the second paragraph he added that a HEPA filter would be necessary.

QUADARE CITY, QUADARE—"And you are saying the boat was completely destroyed?" Fadhil asked.

"Yes. It was reduced to rubble. A large air-to-surface missile. There was little left but an oil slick." Hameed felt sure of himself today.

"And you are sure the two of them were on that craft?" Fadhil had been heartened to hear the Americans were dead, but the curse kept echoing in his thoughts.

"I'm sure. Our agent in Iran claimed that he personally saw to it that they were the only ones on board."

"Did he see them get on the boat?"

Hameed waited a fraction of a moment longer than he should have. If he had known the answer, he would have responded immediately. But as it was, he waited that second, calculating his options, his possible answers, what might be said to cover the situation.

"Yes," Hameed said, louder than he needed to say it. "They boarded the craft. He saw them get on. Only the captain and one crew member were with them."

"All four perished?"

Hameed responded quickly this time. "Yes. All four. Unfortunate, but necessary. We had no time to board the craft. If a boat had approached, it would have given them time to jump overboard and make their way to shore. The helicopter was the only and the safest way to deal with them."

Fadhil tapped his desk with a yellowed fingernail. He didn't believe Hameed. He no longer fully trusted him. But he had no choice.

"Very well. You may go now."

Hameed turned and did his best not to show his angry sneer. He detested being dismissed by a man inferior to himself.

Norah sat up. She winced as she moved. Roberta heard the movement and also rose to a sitting position.

"What is it?" Roberta asked. "Is it the pain? Do you need more spray? There is still some left—we haven't used it all yet. Or an aspirin? We still have half the bottle."

Norah raised her hand.

"No. I'm fine. I—I just thought I heard something."

Roberta slid over toward the door and listened by the crack.

"No. Nothing here. What did it sound like?"

Norah shrugged, then winced. She wasn't yet able to predict what would hurt and what wouldn't. Shrugging hurt.

"I'm not sure. Maybe I dreamt it. Maybe I just thought I heard it."

"What was it?" Roberta asked again.

Norah slowly lowered herself back to the mat.

"I thought I heard his voice."

Roberta didn't have to ask whose voice.

"It sounded like Hays. It really did," Norah said, more to convince herself than Roberta.

BEIRUT, LEBANON—Yass sat in the far end of his café, hunched over a keyboard, the blue glow of the monitor reflecting off his glasses. He thought Duffy and his impatient American friend were lunatics when they had first arrived in Lebanon. No one flies halfway around the world on a hunch. Viruses and thieves and spies all seemed to be more in the stuff of the an espionage novel—not the stuff of real life.

But now, Yass was not sure anymore.

The Middle East was late in arriving at the computer revolution. But now that it had begun, its devotees were fierce and loyal. Yass knew scores of other computer aficionados from all over the region—from countries where e-mailing was almost unknown to countries where the Internet was illegal. In this group no one cared much for political or geographic boundaries. Information was the new king—and access for all was the new slogan.

Hays kept in touch with Yass as they traveled through Iraq, then Iran, catching uplinks on his BlackBerry where he could.

The last communication had been from a small port in southern Iran. Hays had written that they were waiting for their transport.

A warbled beep alerted Yass of an incoming e-mail.

It was very short.

"Can you check on the address of Quadare Refuse and Recycling?"

Yass smiled and tapped over to the Internet. In a few seconds he had the answer and sent it back to his traveling friends.

QUADARE COAST—Quadare posed the biggest piece of the puzzle of their outlandish plan. Quadare wasn't a country on anyone's pleasure-travel agenda. There was little natural beauty. There was little cultural significance. There were few tourist amenities.

There was only oil—and not much of that.

Duffy was the one who came up with their subterfuge.

In Quadare, as in most Middle Eastern countries, there were jobs no one wanted. Working in a slaughterhouse. Repairing toilets. Hard construction work.

It might have been an unwritten caste system or because of status. In Quadare City, even with its high unemployment, even under severe duress and economic dislocation, certain jobs remained unfilled. These jobs always went to the worst off and the poorest. In recent years they were filled by "guest workers."

Collecting garbage was one of those jobs no native Quadare aspired to—ever. Even the poorest of the poor wouldn't seek such a job. For some decades now, all the garbage men had been recruited from the ranks of visiting workers—Albanians, Slavs, Pakistani—men even more desperate than the poorest Quadarese.

Hays and Duffy collected their wet clothes and donned their coveralls. Their disguise was the standard Quadare Refuse and Recycling uniform.

They'd found the company's Web site on the Internet, and had duplicated its logo at an embroidery shop in Shadyside—"It's for a joke on a friend," they explained—and had stitched the patches onto a standard, one-piece coverall. The result was virtually indistinguishable from the real thing.

With Hays' knowledge of Russian, he might easily pass for a Slav guest worker. Duffy would play the part of a low-caste, light-skinned Pakistani.

They could pretend to be ignorant of the language. No one would give them a second look—or want to. Even the police, they imagined, would stay away from men who reeked of garbage.

The "garbage collectors" lightened their packs of all nonessentials. They loaded their Uzis with ammunition, tucked their Glock pistols into their thigh pockets, sheathed their knives, and began their walk toward Quadare City.

29

QUADARE CITY, QUADARE—Maslis spent the morning with her hands snugged into thick, yellow plastic gloves built into the far end of the containment chamber. Maslis recorded the number tattooed on the stomach of each rat, weighed the specimen carefully, then placed the rat into a separate tub. Once the second tub was filled, she slid it down the counter to a second set of gloves. At that station she would slit open the bellies of each animal, gently extract the stomach, and place it into a smaller vial. Each would have to be cut again and examined under magnification.

To autopsy the animal's gut meant someone had to don an anti-contamination suit and endure the long and careful process of thorough sterilization before entering the containment unit and then again upon exiting.

Maslis had worked in labs before, so there was no surprise in the tedious and painstaking nature of the job.

She tried not to think about what was transpiring and what they were testing. No one in the lab, outside Dr. Haj, had a clear idea of the scope of these experiments. All they knew was that they were testing some biological agent—that proved quite lethal.

In other labs, in every other animal-testing protocol, she always had live animals to measure. Even if the medicine or treatment were exceptionally potent, a few lab animals would survive. Then, to test the efficacy of whatever treatment was being investigated, she would grab their squirming bodies, and using a special set of shears, clip off the top third of their heads. Death would be instantaneous, and the bodies would be ready for further testing.

But in this lab—there were no worries of nipping, biting animals.

They were all dead.

Every last one of them wound up stiff and cold in its cage, nearly emaciated—a lump of bones covered with mangy patches of fur.

Maslis tried not to think about that.

She watched as Dr. Haj arrived, nervous and haggard. She saw him pace about his office, holding a clutch of papers in his hand, never once reading them, but simply pacing back and forth, smoking cigarette after cigarette.

A few minutes before Maslis was to hang up her white lab coat and return to her small home, she felt a nudge—no, it was more than a nudge, it was almost a command.

The aroma of Quadare City descended on Hays and Duffy well before they could actually see the city. A brace of refineries dotted the coast a few miles north of downtown, and the smell of burning waste filtered along the shoreline, mixing with the salt and the humidity and the smell of baking asphalt.

The smell coagulated in the dense heat.

The dirt road suddenly gave way to asphalt and snaked along in the heat, the black surface rippling with the afternoon sun. Each footstep made small sucking noises, the paved surface turning sticky and viscous from the heat.

Only two vehicles had passed them as they made their way along the coastal road. One was an ancient pickup truck, wheezing and coughing as it pushed north; the other was a late-model Mercedes that roared past without slowing. According to their plan they would take no rides, nor solicit rides. They sought to limit contact with Quadare citizens—at least until they were in the city.

"We should call a cab, you know that, don't you?" Duffy coughed.

Hays replied, "Only a few kilometers. Then we can find a place to rest and eat."

Duffy nodded and trudged along without complaint. His question caught Hays a bit off guard, not expecting a theological quiz this late into a very hot and tiring day.

"Hays, you would call yourself a true believer in your God, right?"

"I would."

"And you have studied your faith's holy words—your Bible."

"Studied, but not mastered."

Duffy wiped his forehead with his sleeve. "Well, much to my delight, your God seems to have watched over us so far."

"It seems that way," Hays replied.

"And yet, we know the virus is still out there. Some have already died. And we are fairly sure that it could get worse—much, much worse."

Hays nodded. He hoped Duffy wasn't simply reciting the truths they knew to make him feel guilty.

"You've told me how much your God loves people—how much he loves me—and how much he cares for this world that you say he has created."

"He does love you. He loves all of us."

Duffy took a deep breath despite the petroleum fumes.

"Then why has he allowed all this to happen? If we don't get very, very lucky, the whole world could be at risk. That thought keeps me from sleeping. It keeps me from thinking about anything happy and clean and pure anymore. I just keep thinking what the world will look like if we fail. I think about the millions of innocent people who are now at risk—who might be dead in a week."

Hays registered no surprise. It was a question that he had searched for an answer to as well.

"God didn't exactly allow this to happen," he said with certainty. "What it all comes down to is that it was essentially my fault this evil thing surfaced—or should I say, resurfaced. I guess I could blame it all on Tom— but he had no inkling of the evil he uncovered. I was stupid, too. Had I followed the rules, none of this would be happening. I let him talk me into committing the first of a whole string of sins."

Hays tried to see Duffy's reaction. But the sweat, sun, and haze made it difficult to determine if his friend was following his argument.

"So, I have to ask myself—what was God's role in all this? Was he in this at all?" Hays continued. "Or did God simply let me—or man in general— make some incredibly stupid decisions. We do have free will. We suffer the consequences of our foolish decisions. And it's times like this that proves it— unfortunately."

"But you said God loves us," Duffy said. "Why would he allow this to happen?"

Hays had never felt quite as hot and miserable as he did now.

"Duffy, God has been here forever—and there have been catastrophes and plagues throughout history. Did he allow them? Did he create them? Or did they happen because we live in a broken, sinful world? God's best intentions for a perfect world disappeared in the garden of Eden with Adam and Eve. The evil began there and continues."

Duffy stopped walking. He turned to Hays, his face sweaty and marked with fear and confusion.

"So it might happen? Evil might win?"

Hays stopped and faced his friend. "Evil might win this battle. It just might. Evil has won in the past and it will win in the future—until Jesus comes. Then it won't win. We are facing some very, very long odds here. I know God is merciful—but bad things do happen. Some very bad things."

"Like the Holocaust and the killing fields?"

"Man has always been horrible to other men," Hays said. "I'm praying that we can stop evil this time. I know we're doing the right thing now, but so far, God hasn't revealed any special insights or plans or secrets to me. But even despite the silence, I pray for his mercy. I pray for his power in this, because it may be just you and me against a huge, evil enemy we don't know and we can't see."

Duffy took another deep breath. "Thanks for cheering me up," he said. "And yet you say you have faith."

Hays squared his shoulders. "I do have faith. I have to try my best to right the wrong, the evil I helped unleash. If I—or if we—fail, well, God is still in control. He's still good. He will still love us. He will still protect us."

Duffy adjusted the straps on his pack and turned back toward the city.

"And you say our Eastern religions are hard to understand, Hays. If you only saw yourself from the other side."

And Hays let the remark go, for he had no reply he felt made sense.

Maslis returned her lab coat to her small locker. No one stayed in the building longer than absolutely necessary—except for Dr. Haj. Maslis adjusted the veil on her face. She didn't truly believe in the veil's necessity, but wore one because it was expected. Men like Dr. Haj would be uncomfortable seeing a woman full face.

She tapped and slipped into his office.

"Yes?" he snapped, then softened, his body curving behind his desk as if his angry tone had frightened him, too.

"I wanted—I wanted to tell you that I'm leaving, Dr. Haj," Maslis said softly. "I will see you in the morning."

He dismissed her with a slight flexing of his hand.

She didn't move, and he looked up slowly, almost as if he didn't want their eyes to meet. But they did.

Maslis took a step forward. She moved her mouth, and yet no words escaped.

"Yes? What is it?" The doctor's words weren't harsh.

"Doctor," Maslis felt the words in her soul before giving them voice—as if they were coming from some other place. "You will be protected."

She saw his body stiffen, his eyes widen.

"What? What did you say?"

She licked her lips. They were suddenly dry.

"You will be protected."

The words had come from somewhere else—not from her thoughts, to be sure.

"Protected?"

Maslis didn't move.

"You are afraid. You are afraid for your family."

"You are speaking like an insane woman," he said without conviction.

"I'm not. You are afraid. I have prayed to God, and he will protect you. He will provide a way out for you and your family. There is no need to spend your nights in worry. God has promised me that he will protect you."

"Allah has said that?"

Maslis pulled out the small silver cross that she wore around her neck, hidden from view. "No. The one true God—Jehovah—has promised that. His son, Jesus, will protect you. He will send some manner of deliverance."

And without waiting to be dismissed, Maslis stepped backwards, pulled the door behind her until the latch snapped shut. Then she turned and hurried out of the building and down the street. She didn't stop, nearly running, until her heart was pounding and sweat soaked the gauzy veil over her face.

THE FIELDS OF ASMARA, QUADARE CITY, QUADARE—The road led into an area of the city called Asmara Fields—filled with a rat's warren of narrow streets and buildings standing cheek to jowl, dust filling the air, nearly obscuring the fading sun. The slums oozed wide—low, squat—that stretched for kilometers, filling the narrow strip of land between the ocean and the small foothills, filling the air with the ripe, piquant odor of too many people in too small a space.

Hays and Duffy walked along what appeared to be one of the major streets, no wider than a two-lane path. The people they passed—huddled in doorways or leaning out windows—watched but paid no special attention to them.

The garbage collectors' uniforms were marked with dust and sweat, and no one would pay attention to them. Their backpacks were dirty and worn—just like the ones garbage collectors might come across in the trash of the more affluent.

Duffy stopped at a corner and cocked his head toward a building across the street.

"We can stay there tonight. The building at the corner—directly across from us," Duffy replied.

It was a two-story structure, the second story hulking over the sidewalk, drowning the walkway in hot shadows. The second story appeared to be nearing collapse, but no one seemed to notice, passers-by walking in those shadows without looking up. Most of the windows gaped open, the gauzy curtains hanging limp and lifeless in the evening's heat.

"How can you tell it's a hotel?" Hays asked, squinting at the ramshackle building. "It doesn't look any different from any other building."

Duffy stepped off the curb onto the packed dirt of the street.

"That small round sign—with an *H* in it," Duffy explained. "It marks it as a hotel, one the city has inspected."

Hays squinted and could barely make out the letter—nearly obscured by a thick patina of dust and dirt.

"In this part of town, I don't think we have the option of being fussy," Duffy said softly.

A blue haze hovered over the streets, the result of thousands of charcoal and wood fires cooking the evening meal. The Asmara neighborhood was the poorest in all of Quadare. Even the most diplomatic guidebooks urged tourists give the area a wide berth.

"No better place to hide than a place where even the police are reluctant to patrol," Duffy had explained when they made their plans.

Duffy hemmed and stumbled through his request for a room for the night, hoping his Pakistani accent was neither obvious nor amateurish.

The desk clerk hardly looked up. Duffy explained that they'd left their former residence because of an argument over rent. The clerk tapped his finger hard on the counter. Hays knew the tapping meant "pay in advance." Duffy quickly slipped a handful of the local currency toward the clerk and a key slid back across the counter. The clerk returned to the small, flickering television set. The show was *Baywatch*, dubbed into Farsi.

As they climbed the constricted staircase, Hays whispered, "Do you think we'll get a chocolate mint on our pillow?"

Duffy smiled.

"That depends on if there's a pillow, doesn't it?"

Only moments after Maslis left, a dusty, silver Mercedes pulled up to the nondescript building in the decaying neighborhood. Hameed exited the vehicle, peered at his reflection in the window, adjusted his sunglasses, and then entered the building.

He left his driver in the car, telling him to keep the engine running and the air-conditioning on full force. Hameed disliked sweat and, too often, as soon as he slammed the car door, the driver would open the windows, unused to chilly air in the middle of a Quadare summer and unwilling to take advantage of new technology.

Hameed used his key card on the sophisticated electronic lock and pushed the windowless door open, striding confidently toward the doctor's office. He didn't knock or announce himself.

"It is going well, I understand," he said with cool detachment.

Haj answered too quickly. "Yes, yes, all things are going well. Very well. No problems."

Hameed waited. He didn't like people who told him only what he wanted to hear. Haj appeared to be one of those people. He didn't like Haj at all.

"I understand you are close to—how does our friend Fadhil state it—weaponizing this virus?"

Haj blanched, but only a little. "We are close, very close. I have explained all this to Commissioner Fadhil. I have explained that using this sort of biological agent is a tricky business, most tricky indeed. We must not hurry this process. We must take all precautions."

The doctor began to list some of the tests still required, some of the medical precautions that needed to be implemented. Hameed's eyes glazed. He didn't like long explanations that didn't pertain to him.

After a few minutes of listening to a litany of arcane medical terminology, Hameed snapped off his sunglasses and twirled them in his hand.

"Impressive, I'm sure," he said with impatience, "but I don't care to hear any more excuses. You must finish this project as you stated you could, as you promised you would do so many weeks ago—and so many dollars ago, I might remind you," Hameed said with a backward glance. "None of this machinery came cheaply. You do know Quadare is a poor country and we cannot afford to spend money frivolously, do you not? You are aware of that fact, are you not?"

Haj began to sweat even more profusely. He didn't like Fadhil and his coarseness, but this man was another matter. Hameed frightened him very much, as a sharpened ax frightens a chicken with its neck on the stump. He had dreams about this man storming into his home, taking his daughters, violating his wife, then slaughtering them all.

"I will have it done as soon as possible. This all takes time. We must be careful. If we hurry, we run the risk of spreading this to our own citizens."

Hameed dismissed his concern with a limp wave of his hand.

"Is it always fatal? This virus, I mean. Does it always kill?"

Haj hesitated. He didn't want to tell this man the truth.

Hameed grinned, his teeth glistening with saliva. "Your hesitation has answered me. It is that deadly, then, is it not?"

The doctor's hands moved as if he were trying to construct a reply.

"What you are not saying—I will. You need a human subject. That is what you don't wish to voice, correct? You seek a participant in these trials. Is that what you mean to say?"

The doctor shook his head. "No. I don't … animal testing is all …"

Hameed placed his hands on the desk and leaned forward.

"You will have them. Two subjects. Two large test animals. Yes, that is what you need."

Beads of sweat formed in waves on the doctor's forehead. "No. Animals are enough. We can do what we need with animals."

Hameed left his handprints on the doctor's desk—two shiny smears of sweat.

"You will have them, Dr. Haj. I will bring them to you soon."

"But I don't—"

Hameed stopped at the door and turned back, glaring.

"And you will use them, won't you, Dr. Haj?" Just before slipping the door closed, Hameed whispered, "Say hello to your lovely wife and daughters. Such a sweet family."

Hameed pulled the door shut, the latch clicked, and the air conditioner whirred into life again, blowing a cold current across the doctor's desk.

Hays flipped open his small notebook. On one page were three names and addresses. Each address lay in Quadare City. Each man was a medical doctor who had experience with infectious diseases, virology, or toxicology.

Hays had met all three men. They'd been at various conferences and seminars that Hays had also attended. He supposed they were the only men in Quadare who might be able to deal with the complexities a deadly virus posed.

When they were planning this mission, Duffy had asked him if he were sure there could be no others.

"No, there couldn't," he'd responded. "Quadare doesn't have many doctors. They have fewer specialists. Those who focus on this sort of medicine and research are fewer still. I'm sure these are all of them. And if some foreign doctor has been recruited—these men will know. After all, it's a small country."

Sitting in their hotel room in the evening heat, with a single bare bulb dangling from a wire overhead, Duffy asked, "Who's first on the list?"

Hays shrugged. "The closest one."

"Good. But let's get some dinner first."

As they stood, Hay's BlackBerry buzzed in his pocket. He flipped it open.

It was an e-mail from Yass, back in Lebanon.

Hays,
　　A friend stumbled across this press release on the Internet. It's several months old. Maybe it will be useful.

Quadare City, Quadare.
　　Hoch International announces it has shipped a fully equipped isolation/decontamination unit to Quadare Health Officials. A Hoch spokesman claims the self-contained unit will be the largest and most sophisticated equipment of its type on the Arabian Peninsula. Quadare officials stated that this new

equipment will provide improved health care for the country's citizens and allow them to conduct more sensitive viral research. Leading the Quadare health team is world-renowned virologist Dr. Salim Haj.

Yass.

Duffy was reading over Hays' shoulder.

"Is he on our list?" he asked.

Hays nodded and snapped the unit closed. "He's the first name."

"Good. Probably should keep your BlackBerry hidden at dinner. Not too many garbage men have them."

30

QUADARE CITY, QUADARE—Duffy stumbled over his question about breakfast with the hotel's clerk, who apparently lived behind the desk. He was there when they checked in the previous evening and was still there this morning, wearing the same clothing. Duffy accented his Farsi as best he could, which sounded to Hays like a badly dubbed movie from Pakistan. Regardless, Duffy's mangled diction apparently was good enough—or bad enough—to fool the man.

Pointing and gesturing and leaning toward the window, the clerk identified a small restaurant at the far end of the next block. Duffy bowed and Hays offered a vague wave of his hand, calling out "thanks" in a very polite form of college-educated Russian.

The door to the cell swung open.

Norah looked up and reacted, almost by instinct.

It was the man who wielded the whip.

She pushed herself toward the far corner of the room. Roberta awoke and immediately stood, feet wide apart, placing herself between the man and Norah. She clenched her fists.

Hameed saw the gesture and for a moment toyed with the idea of batting this impudent, insolent woman across the face with the butt of his gun. His arm twitched in that direction.

Roberta stiffened.

Hameed saw her tension and relaxed his arm, letting it slowly drop to his side.

"There is no reason for you to be frightened," he said. His words were devoid of emotion.

He looked over at Norah, who had sidled into the corner.

"You have been fed today?"

Neither woman replied.

Hameed turned and shouted in angry Farsi. A guard scuttled in, eyes focused on the ground. Hameed continued shouting even though the man was only a few feet away.

"You will have a full breakfast this morning. You will eat well, a meal not enjoyed by many people in my poor country."

Hameed stood and rocked on his heels for a silent moment. Roberta hadn't budged, nor had Norah moved.

"You must no longer be frightened. You must resign yourselves—the two men who were coming for you, they are both dead. Their boat intruded into Quadare waters and had to be destroyed. Most unfortunate. We seek only to live in peace."

Hameed smiled at Norah's reaction. "I will send a physician to see to your wounds. You need to be in good health."

And with that, he left the room, slamming the door behind him.

And for a long moment, it remained silent.

Hameed waited just outside. When he heard one of the women begin to weep, he grinned with satisfaction and set off for his morning appointment with his barber.

The coded telex flittered into his in-basket. Hameed felt the scratching of small hairs in his collar and berated himself for not returning home for a shower after his cut. It was a short message, whatever it was, contained in five lines of letters and numbers, all gibberish.

Decoding messages took time and patience, both in short supply in Hameed's world. Instead he shouted for his assistant. He held he paper in the air and flapped it back and forth several times.

"Sir?" the assistant said, his words nervous, clipped.

Hameed rolled his eyes. "Translate this. Why do you think I'm holding it like this? If I must give you such small, minute instructions ..."

The assistant made a step forward, then caught himself. "But sir ... a coded message—"

"I have given you an order. Now do it," he shouted as he tossed the paper at him. It fluttered like a butterfly and settled delicately on the desktop.

The assistant picked it up with two fingers, touching it as if it might be contagious and holding it away from his body, and hurried from the office, the page flapping in the air.

Hameed glowered at him until the door shut. Then he relaxed, and turned back to the computer and logged on to the Internet, the blue glow illuminating his face, highlighting the bones in his cheeks, narrowing his nose to a point, and bringing a skull-like visage to his features.

Hays and Duffy sat together on stools by the window, nibbling at their breakfast, staring out at Quadare citizens walking on their way to jobs or school or shopping.

"Does anyone smile in this country?" Hays asked Duffy in a whisper.

Duffy shook his head. "I don't think they have much to smile about. It is not the Quadare way to show much emotion."

Hays took a bite from the sweetened flatbread and chewed.

"But everyone looks miserable."

"You know, they do, they really do," Duffy admitted. After a moment, he looked up. "Are you vibrating? Didn't you leave your BlackBerry in the room?"

Hays slapped at a pocket on his thigh. "Too much information on it."

Duffy hissed a warning. "Don't let anyone see it."

Hays hunched over and retrieved the unit, opened it up, and punched through a series of buttons. The vibration alerted him to an incoming e-mail. He waited.

He whispered as he read the message.

"It's from Yass. He says: *You must be careful. I have heard from a contact in Quadare that your e-mail address came to his attention. They are looking for you, my friends. You may be in danger if you leave your BlackBerry on.*"

Hays looked over at Duffy in disbelief.

"Turn it off," Duffy insisted. "Shut it down."

Hays fumbled as he powered it down.

"Can they do that? Can they trace this by looking for its signal?"

Duffy turned and looked behind. "I thought it was impossible. BlackBerry devices are supposed to have built in coding systems. But for money, people do the impossible."

"Your friends back home who set this up, could they have—?"

Duffy closed his eyes and shrugged. "Perhaps. Money over blood, my friend, money over blood."

Hameed's assistant tapped on the door—little mouse taps, little scratchings.

"Come in," Hameed shouted.

"Your telex, sir."

Hameed snatched it from his hand.

"Now, go."

He waited until the door latched shut to read the message. It was indeed brief.

> We are growing impatient. Many dollars have been spent on this project. Please inform me as to revised timetable. Report progress or potential, or I will be forced to find someone else who can deliver.

Hameed was at once both furious and terrified.

Furious at the incompetence of Haj and his time-wasting blatherings, and terrified that if he lost the support of Huber/Loss, Hameed would find himself freefalling into some inconsequential desk job in some inconsequential office, wielding no power. That was the most terrifying image of all. He crumpled the sheet and tossed it at the door. Hameed would pay a call on Haj to ensure his research was brought to a quick—and deadly—conclusion.

"It's not true," Norah said. "What he said about the boat being blown up. It wasn't Hays and Duffy."

Roberta sat next to her, both of them eating from a tray piled high with fruits, breads, and meat. It was the first normal meal they'd been given since their abduction.

"I hope you're right," she said.

"I know I am. I believe I would have known if they were dead. They're not. They're alive. They're coming, Roberta. I know that."

Roberta took a bite of a sweet, dense, honey-flavored bread.

"I know you believe it, Norah, but I don't see how they'd be able to get here. I mean—crossing borders and sneaking into countries. And even if they got here, what would they do once they did? It's two men against a whole country."

Norah didn't back down. "They're coming. I know it. I just know it."

Though the air in Fadhil's office had grown thick and pungent, he hadn't once opened the windows in the past fortnight. He wouldn't admit his fears to anyone, but with this virus being tested, he wanted no stray germ flittering into his private space. The Russian-built air-conditioning system worked, but not well, and never fully removed existing odors, stacking them instead one on top of another, so the air became a stew of combative fragrances.

Fadhil lit a stick of incense and fanned the smoke, hoping it would transform the air to something more breathable.

He cocked his head to one side. There came the faintest of tappings on his door.

Why doesn't the stupid goat just use the intercom? I have told him hundreds of times.

"What is it? What do you want?"

The door opened a few inches. A shaft of light burst into the room. Dust motes danced about, thick as sand in a desert sirocco.

"Sir," his assistant said softly, then waited. The waiting infuriated Fadhil. It always had, and he suspected the fool did it on purpose simply to annoy him.

"What is it?" Fadhil wheezed, exasperated.

The assistant sidled into the room and slowly closed the door behind him.

"Sir," he said as he shuffled two steps closer to the desk. Fadhil wouldn't prompt the man again. He would wait until this evening, if necessary, for his simple-minded assistant to gather his thoughts.

"Sir," the servant began again, "I have heard information that might …"

"Might what?" Fadhil said loudly, his growing anger obvious.

"Might be of interest to you."

Fadhil waited, then began drumming his fingers on the desk in an odd, out-of-rhythm manner. The assistant looked up. His eyes actually met Fadhil's eyes. He had seldom, if ever, looked directly at him, and Fadhil was unnerved by this sudden boldness. The small man straightened his back and squared his shoulders.

"The boat that was destroyed—it didn't carry the men you seek."

Silence filled the room. Fadhil blinked.

"What? Hameed—"

"They are in Quadare, sir. They have penetrated your defenses."

Fadhil's jaw moved silently, then he croaked out, "How do you know? Does Hameed know?"

"A satellite transmission has been intercepted. From Quadare. I know people who monitor such things for amusement. And as for Mr. Hameed, I think he knows as well."

Fadhil's stomach churned and twisted. His rage and terror were obvious.

The assistant bowed, and as he opened the door to exit, quietly said, "I thought, sir, it would be best to tell you, rather than leave you in the dark."

And with that, he closed the door behind him, leaving Fadhil alone in the darkness.

31

QUADARE CITY, QUADARE—After breakfast, Duffy and Hays began walking toward the center of town and the address of the first doctor on their list. The air began to warm to the point of being oppressive.

Normally the faster of the two, Hays this morning walked slower, as if his feet had suddenly gone leaden.

"Are you okay?" Duffy asked.

Hays shook his head. "It's nothing. It'll pass."

They continued on for another block until Hays reached out and placed his hand on the side of the building for support.

"What is it?" Duffy asked, concerned. "You don't look so well."

"I'm not sure. All of sudden, I feel terrible. Maybe it was the food."

"But we ate the same things. And I feel okay," Duffy replied.

Now leaning against the building, Hays wiped his forehead. His palm came away wet. His knees bent, as if he were close to fainting.

Duffy put his arm around his friend. He put his hand to his forehead.

"You *are* sick. Maybe it was the food. Let's hope it was—because that will pass in a few hours."

"No," Hays protested, trying to shrug off his friend. "We have to go on. We're too close."

Duffy held tight and turned him around. "No. You can hardly stand up. We'll go back to the room."

Another wave of nausea seemed to break over Hays, and he offered no further protest.

"But why would God let this happen? Why now?" he mumbled.

Duffy had no answer.

There was a knock, the door opened, and Hameed strolled into Fadhil's office, appearing as if he were on a Sunday jaunt in the park. He stopped midstride, obviously not expecting to see his superior standing.

Fadhil wasn't the catlike sort that liked to play with his prey, but rather, leapt doglike for the throat.

"You have misled me, Hameed. And I trusted you."

Fadhil didn't shout nor bellow as was his custom. His words were ice on a hot day.

"Misled you? Never. There must be some misunderstanding."

Fadhil stared hard.

"I was told they were dead." Fadhil allowed himself a tight grin of satisfaction. "I know the truth."

Hameed made an indistinct gesture with his hands. He struggled to deliver the correct response—to maintain his strength and admit to no failings.

Fadhil folded his arms over his chest.

"The two men—the ones from the Pittsburgh university—they are not dead. I'm told their e-mail has been located as originating inside of Quadare. You told me they were dead. They are not. You have lied to me. You cannot be trusted."

Hameed had little color in his face to begin with, and now what there was drained, leaving his skin nearly translucent. Fadhil wondered how long it would be until he groveled—or fought back.

"Sir, I had no idea. My staff said nothing of this. Nothing at all. Their boat was destroyed."

Fadhil felt gratified that Hameed groveled. Had he chosen another tack, Fadhil had his pistol in good repair and loaded with ammunition.

"I've been told otherwise," Fadhil said.

"It's not true, I swear on the graves of my ancestors. It is all lies. Perfidious, disloyal, treacherous underlings. Incompetent as well, sir," Hameed babbled. "Allow me to interrogate my staff. Let me discover who among them should have known."

Fadhil smiled, as a butcher might smile at a lamb. "Very well, interrogate your staff. Find the leak."

Hameed nodded, eager to avoid punishment.

"But you also must find those two men, Hameed. If they are in Quadare, they must be found."

"Yes, sir," Hameed replied quickly.

"And if you don't," Fadhil said with relish, "I will be forced to find someone who will."

"Yes, sir," came the immediate, automatic response.

Hameed nearly struck Fadhil's assistant, as the man appeared smug and condescending, taunting Hameed with his hostile silence and narrowed eyes. Hameed stormed out of the office, his face burning, his anger in full storm, fists clenched, nails nearly puncturing his palms. He slammed the door to his Mercedes, rattling the rearview mirror out of place. He muttered a string of invectives and curses.

How could that imbecile have found out? There must be a traitor on my staff. How could that happen? How could anyone think of betraying me?

He drove toward his office, then stopped and doubled back. An underling with loose lips didn't matter. He would take his time and purge the staff later. But now he had more pressing issues to attend to. He had more urgent business with Haj.

Hameed was a realist. He knew the doctor was under Fadhil's authority. But he also knew Fadhil had many other projects, all competing and clamoring for his attention.

If Hameed could stage a preemptive strike, gather the findings before Fadhil was aware of what had occurred, get the doctor and the samples back to Germany—then his mission would be accomplished. Fadhil would be out, and Hameed would be placed at the top of security—his rightful position. Information was power.

He flipped open his cell phone and dialed as he drove, veering close to a sidewalk as he did. "Get the women ready. I will need them soon."

He tossed the phone onto the seat next to him. He came to a jarring stop, folded down the visor mirror, inspected his hair, patting it into place, then exited the car, the lines on his face screwed tight.

Maslis heard the shouting and the muffled curses. Her chair, at the end of the long bench, was no more than a few feet from Dr. Haj's office. All the other research staff were at the far end of the room, almost out of earshot.

"You will have what I need ready by the end of the week."

Maslis didn't recognize the man who had bullied his way into the doctor's office, but she understood the terror and the threat in his voice.

"But—it is not stable. The virus is not ready to be replicated in large amounts. Until I'm certain of its power, I don't intend to risk the safety of my staff."

Maslis heard derisive laughter.

"You are not to be worried about risk. That is for me to be concerned with—not you."

"But we don't know enough. I'm not aware of any safe delivery process," Dr. Haj shouted back, clearly frightened.

Then she heard the slap, a sharp, angry crack.

"I will not have this. You have spent millions of dollars. It will be done within the next five days."

"But, it cannot be—"

Another slap. Maslis could tell the doctor had staggered, falling back against the closed blinds of his office.

"Five days," the stranger bellowed again. "You will have live test subjects tomorrow. And you will report to me the progress of this weapon, using those subjects as your test. Do you understand?"

There was silence, then another slap.

"Do you understand?"

"Yes," came the barely intelligible reply. "I understand."

Duffy all but dragged Hays the last few blocks back to their hotel, making several stops for Hays to empty his stomach. "It's food poisoning," Duffy said as he folded a wet cloth over Hays' forehead. "The body moves fast to get rid of what's offending it." Duffy propped up Hays' feet. "You feel like you're about to die?"

Hays mumbled an affirmative.

"Then that's all the more proof that it was the food. People say it's the closest thing to death without dying. But it should pass within a few hours."

Hays removed the wet cloth from his forehead. "We don't have time for this. Why would God have allowed this now?" He fell back against the pillow.

"You're asking *me* theological questions?" Duffy replied. "Listen, your God has already sent an angel to protect us. Maybe we need to stay hidden today."

Hays struggled to answer. "Maybe."

"And now I'm the one who sounds like he believes in God," Duffy said.

Hays offered a wan smile. "Maybe that's it. So you'll understand."

Duffy made no reply, but sat silent at the bedside of his friend, wondering if indeed God had made this part of his plan.

The windowless door banged open. Roberta and Norah had moved to the far corner after hearing the shouting and cursing from the room beyond.

It was the man with the face of a weasel.

Norah refused to cower and didn't avert her eyes.

"You will be ready to leave this place in the morning," Hameed commanded. "You will have new clothing brought to you. You must eat all the food that we bring you this evening."

Norah's eyes blazed with silent defiance.

"I will return tomorrow," he added.

No one spoke.

"Do you understand?"

Norah allowed herself the smallest of nods in reply.

The door clanged shut and the key was turned.

A moment passed, then Roberta asked in a whisper, "Do you think they are sending us home?"

"No."

"But why—why would they release us if it wasn't to send us home?"

Roberta was on the verge of tears.

Norah put her hand over Roberta's, bidding the trembling to stop.

"I'm not sure," she said. She wanted to add that unless Hays and Duffy showed up she didn't anticipate being alive the following evening, but she dared not voice her fears. There was no sense in upsetting Roberta any further.

"I'm sure everything will be fine," she said soothingly, hoping Roberta believed her. She wasn't sure she believed it herself.

Maslis waited an hour after the stranger had left and then tapped softly at the door to Dr. Haj's office.

She tapped louder, hearing no reply. Finally, she simply turned the handle and cracked open the door.

The doctor was sitting at his desk, his elbows on the surface, his head cradled in his hands.

"Dr. Haj? What is the matter?"

The doctor lifted his head as if awakening from a dream. His right eye was swollen, puffy and red. There was an angry red swatch on his left cheek as well.

"There is nothing wrong. You must go now. It is past time to leave tonight."

Maslis nodded, but didn't move.

All day she had felt stronger and stronger—more certain that she was to deliver yet one more message to this man.

"You are in trouble, Dr. Haj."

He looked at her blankly. "And if I am, what concern of it is yours?"

Maslis answered quickly, "You are a good man and I respect you. I would have concern for anyone caught in a web of sin."

"Sin? This is not sin. It is evil—and it is evil that I cannot control."

Maslis knew that the virus seemed to be malevolent at its core. The number of dead rats in the freezer grew every day. In fact, two new, larger freezers had been delivered just the day before. Rats normally didn't die so easily or so quickly—until now with this horrible sickness.

"It's not your problem to control sin," Maslis said quietly. "If there comes a time when you are lost and cannot control this evil, you must call on the name of Jesus to help you."

The doctor snorted. "What can that do? It is only a name. Is his name some sort of magical incantation? Do I expect it to work as a charm against evil? That simply will not happen."

"But—"

"No. There is nothing anyone can do. Not even your god, Jesus, will stop this. Not even he has such power."

Maslis waited a moment to reply, as if listening to an invisible voice.

"You will call on the name of Jesus tonight. You will have to call upon him to save your life. And that will be all the power you need. I'm telling you this because I have heard it from God. Call on the name of Jesus."

Without waiting for a reply, she turned and walked out of his office, her breath coming in short gasps.

Her hands were trembling.

She had indeed heard the voice of God.

All day Duffy sat in a rickety chair and watched both the street below and his friend on the bed next to him.

As evening came, all remained normal, as best as Duffy could ascertain. He saw nothing that seemed out of the ordinary. Had they been discovered, Duffy was sure police or security forces would have fanned out through this neighborhood looking for strangers. Enough people had seen and taken note of them that someone would have been bound to report them.

Hays slept fitfully. He was sick a few more times and racked with a terrible headache. That, Duffy concluded, was part and parcel of food poisoning. He wondered why he hadn't suffered the same fate.

Hays had lain still for some time now, his breathing normal, his sweating ceased. Duffy imagined the worst had passed and that he would now sleep.

He scrawled a short note and placed it under the water bottle where Hays was sure to see it if he awoke. He hurried down the steps. The same clerk was sitting behind the counter, focused on a small black-and-white television propped up against the window with paperback books. He didn't speak, but Duffy was certain that he noticed him leaving.

He could no longer sit without doing something. They had traveled too far and had come too close to detection too often to compromise their mission now.

Duffy had seen much death as a child—had claimed he was accustomed to it. But the potential the virus held for widespread annihilation was different. If a man with no restraint controlled this virus, entire countries might be at risk. If it were as virulent as it portended to be, then humankind itself might be at risk.

Duffy wasn't a medical man by training, but he knew enough of the virus to be terrified. He could hear the fear in Hays' voice and demeanor, and while he had done his best to remain calm he, too, was horrified. Nothing in his experience, short of an active poison, killed all that it came in contact with.

Duffy couldn't wait for Hays to recover. He had to act now, had to do something, had to move forward.

Navigation was an innate, native ability with Duffy, almost as if he had been born with a compass in his head. He counted the streets as he walked, aware that many of them lacked even a rudimentary street sign. Farther along, the houses grew larger. Some had fences or gates around a small withered patch of desert grass or flowers. Some streets were lit with garish neon signs glowing from inside store windows. There were more automobiles in this section of town—battered and dusty to be sure, but automobiles nonetheless.

Duffy found himself standing in front of the home of the first doctor on their list. The house was no more than modest. As a Lebanese native, he didn't make the Western assumption that every doctor was wealthy and prosperous. Duffy felt the hard metal of the Glock pistol tucked under his belt. He knew that Hays would not first resort to violent measures, but he himself might. If he had to hurt someone to save thousands of innocent people, he wouldn't think twice. If he found the doctor, and if the doctor resisted, Duffy knew he would be quick to force information from him—and even quicker now that Hays wasn't with him.

Maybe this is why Hays is ill tonight, he thought. *Maybe his God wants me to find out what we need to know—without Hays slowing me down.*

After a few moments in the dark, Duffy nodded to himself.

That must be why, he concluded.

32

QUADARE CITY, QUADARE—Duffy walked past the house several times. He could see lights and smell meat being cooked over an open flame, a pungent, sweet smell.

He checked his watch. It was nearing seven. He hoped the doctor would appear soon. He knew he couldn't linger on the street indefinitely. Duffy felt the adrenaline start to flow. His hands grew cool, almost clammy.

A man turned the corner. He carried a heavy briefcase, like a doctor's bag. He shambled, rather than walked, as if he was carrying a heavy load.

Duffy knew what he had to do. He walked quickly toward the doctor and at the last minute stepped into the middle of the sidewalk, squaring his shoulders and feet, bending his knees slightly. His hand slipped into the wide pocket of his trousers. "Dr. Haj?"

The man looked up, startled and obviously taken off guard. In the light of the street lamp, Duffy could see a flicker of fear in his eyes.

"Yes? What do you want? Do I know you?"

There was a hint of an English accent in the doctor's voice—as if he had received his training at a school in Great Britain.

Duffy moved quickly. His hand snapped out from his pocket, holding the Glock pistol. There was a stubby silencer screwed into the end of the barrel. Duffy held it close to his body, unwilling to wave it about in the open, unwilling to have the doctor turn brave and attempt to lunge at it.

"I don't have much money with me. I'm not a rich man."

Duffy gave a sideways nod. "Cross the street. Into the alley."

"You can have all my money," the doctor said, his voice starting to waver. He reached for his billfold in his back pocket. "Here, take my wallet. Just let me go home."

Duffy growled, "Just cross the street, my friend. Into the alley. We need to talk."

The pistol glinted in the evening light. Duffy's finger was on the trigger.

In that moment he was angrier than he had ever been. The fates brought this terrible evil into his life, disrupted his life, cost him his job, and placed his friends in great jeopardy. It was not fair.

Duffy hated that his life—and Hays'—was in a tragic spiral, and none of it was of their making. Duffy wanted to be back home in Pittsburgh, in his comfortable apartment with his long list of female acquaintances. He wanted to be safe and content and happy. He didn't want to be in a dark alley in Quadare, aiming a loaded pistol at another human.

And at that moment, he hated the doctor enough to do something Hays never would have done.

They walked silently into the deep shadows.

"That's far enough," he said, with real menace in his voice. He eased the safety off his pistol. He lowered the barrel, so that the shot would hit he doctor in the leg first. Painful—but not life-threatening.

"You are the Dr. Haj that attended a conference in Pittsburgh?"

The doctor's momentary silence bore witness to his confusion. "Conference? I ... perhaps ..."

"A conference on virology. You gave a paper on smallpox transmission."

After a pause, he answered quietly, "Yes. I was there."

"That means you're the expert on viruses."

Dr. Haj made a small, hesitant, futile gesture with his free hand.

"And that means you're working on the virus they found in the desert. In Iran. In that skull."

The doctor lowered his head and inhaled deeply, as if he had finally been caught by a relentless pursuer. His eyes locked on Duffy's, measuring the danger. In a few seconds, he blinked, shaken. It was obvious to both men that lying would be a very unsafe action.

"Yes."

Duffy's arms wavered as he brought the gun up and aimed it at the man's heart. He wanted to pull the trigger but knew he wouldn't. The doctor's death wouldn't stop the virus. But it was obvious that the doctor didn't know that.

"Jesus," the doctor said sharply, "I call on your name."

There was silence in the alley. In the distance, Duffy heard the rumble of a truck, then the sharper whine of a scooter. "What? What did you say?" he asked.

The doctor took a step back. A shaft of light illuminated his face, marked with fear, yet oddly at peace.

"What did you say?" It was a name Duffy would have felt quite certain he would never hear spoken in this godforsaken place.

"I was told that tonight when I was in danger, I was to call on the name of Jesus."

Duffy's surprise was obvious. "Jesus? Someone told you to call on Jesus and he would save you?"

The doctor didn't hesitate. "Yes. And … I think he will protect me," he said, then added softly, knowingly, "And I think you know that as well."

Duffy felt his breath come quickly and slowly lowered his gun until it was hidden by the shadows.

Hays sat bolt upright in bed. A premonition of something wrong had pulled him abruptly awake, as awake as he had ever been. He felt his forehead and took several deep breaths. The pain in his stomach had all but disappeared. He swung his legs to the floor. The dizziness had stopped. He reached for the water bottle, then saw the note.

I went to find the doctor. He will answer to me. It is the Arab way.

Hays stood up, reaching out to the wall. His legs seemed to be working again. He wavered—just a bit—but knew he had to move. He grabbed his shoes and slid them on, grabbed his pistol, grabbed the map. He hurried out the door.

The Arab way would consist of anything and everything.

And he couldn't let anything bad happen.

Norah's eyes opened wide. She had been sleeping sitting up, leaning against the wall. It was the most comfortable position for her—the skin on her back stretched and protested if she lay down.

Roberta slept peacefully on the thin mat beside her.

In the span of a few days and in the midst of this terrifying ordeal, she felt at peace—more peaceful than she had ever felt before. If she had only listened to what Hays had been saying. How blind she must have appeared. And how wonderful the inward change that occurred.

She gently placed her hand on Roberta's shoulder. She felt sad to think Roberta was alone in facing a dark and ominous future.

God, make yourself real to her. I don't know how, but you must. I know we don't have much time left … do we? It's okay. I don't mind. I don't.

Hays kept looking at the map, trying to find a street number, a name, anything that might give him an indication as to where he was. He stopped at a small food shop still open and asked in Russian, keeping to his disguise, for help in finding the doctor's address. The small man behind the counter chattered away, Hays not understanding any of it. Hays pointed to the map, to the street, then presented the man with his best, quizzical look.

The man took him outside, pointed on the map, pointed down the street, held two fingers up, then pointed to the right, then back to a new location on the map. Hays bowed, offered him thanks, and set off in that direction, almost at a jog, his pistol bouncing with every step.

EN ROUTE FROM ATLANTA, GEORGIA, TO THE MIDDLE EAST—Chuck Hild loved his job, and despite his back-country drawl and sometimes slovenly appearance, he took it very, very seriously.

But the greatest thing about being on the CDC emergency response team, he thought, was that he could hop aboard any commercial flight, bumping anyone and everyone if required—and avoid all the ticket lines—with no passport hassles.

Instead of a commercial flight this time, Chuck had landed passage on a diplomatic plane to Israel. The plane would serve as a backup to the ambassador's plane on his visit to the Middle East the following week. The crew would drop off the pair from the CDC in Quadare and then head back to Israel.

Hild and Norman Williamson, one of CDC's top computer experts, lounged in the first-class section. The plane was nearly empty, carrying only a few advanced staff members, most of them lost in endless briefings. Chuck's equipment was strapped into a row of seats behind him. Even the State Department kept their hands off of it.

It was a good flight. The attendants had little to occupy their time so they happily served Chuck four in-flight meals.

He consumed six desserts as well.

33

QUADARE CITY, QUADARE—Hays stirred up dust as he ran, and as he made his way farther into the neighborhood the houses appeared a little more substantial, indicating that their owners might be low-level government employees or midlevel managers at one of the government-run oil refineries.

"My Lord," Hays whispered to himself as he looked. "This street actually has a name written on it." He took off at a trot, the heft of the pistol clumping against his thigh with every step.

Some homes had numbers, some didn't. He was certain any doctor, trained to be precise in all matters, would place house numbers on his residence. Hays certainly would have.

He stopped, panting, at a modest home with fancy iron filigree work over the windows. The numbers matched. Hays looked up and down the street. He saw no one. He walked carefully toward the front door, unsure of what next step he should take.

The small cement landing was flanked by two pots of flowers, appearing near death in the desert dryness. From inside he heard a voice, then another, louder. It was Duffy's voice, speaking Farsi, booming.

Hays couldn't let Duffy do something that would be impossible to undo. He slipped the Glock pistol from his pocket and snapped the safety off. He stepped back, planted his left foot square, pulled back his right foot and kicked, with all his might, just to the side of the lock.

The door splintered open with a crash.

Hays jumped inside, his pistol at arm's length and faced a tableau of three very shocked people. He watched as Duffy rolled from his chair, drawing and aiming a pistol back at Hays. A balding, middle-aged Quadare man leaned over and engulfed a small woman in his arms, offering her what scant protection he could with a look of fierce defiance in his eyes.

Hays' eyes nicked back and forth. Duffy withdrew his weapon and slowly stood.

"The door was unlocked," he said. "You could have knocked."

Hays' arm slowly lowered as Duffy walked past him to close the front door as best he could. Despite the splintering, it remained closed.

"But I heard yelling," Hays explained. "I thought you might be on the verge of doing something … dangerous."

Hays stumbled over his words, trying to make some sense of the situation.

"Well, you could have gotten killed, my friend. Have you forgotten all your Ranger training? Never burst into a room until you know what lies in wait behind the door," Duffy scolded. "Now, put the pistol away and meet Dr. Haj and his wife. They are going to help us, my friend."

"But what was the shouting about?"

Duffy grinned, the tension past. "My culture expects a story—especially from a guest. I was explaining to Dr. Haj how we got here. I was being dramatic in the retelling—that's all."

Duffy pointed to Hays. "This is the man I was telling you about. The one who will destroy the virus."

Only then did Dr. Haj appear to uncoil. Still shaken, he nervously bowed slightly and extended his hand. "You will be the angel then," he said softly.

Duffy jumped in. "Don't hurry the story. Could my friend have some tea?"

"Of course, please sit down. We will get you tea."

The doctor instructed his wife in Farsi. She rose, never once taking her eyes from Hays. It was apparent that she wasn't as good as the rest at hiding her discomfort.

Hays slipped off his pack and sat at the table, hoping he wasn't committing another error in Arabic etiquette. He could hear the hiss of a kettle being filled and the snap of a gas heater being ignited.

Hays turned to the doctor with a lost look in his eyes, then back to Duffy. "Duffy, what in the world just happened here?"

Duffy grinned. "You will love this, Hays. It fits your guardian angel theory—or something like that. I was a few seconds away from shooting the good doctor in the leg to get him to cooperate. I might have actually killed him if he hadn't answered my questions quickly enough. But—but he called on Jesus. For protection. He called on Jesus to protect him from me. That's when I lowered my pistol, and he invited me inside."

Chuck Hild tapped the buttons of the phone in his room. Quadare didn't have many hotels, and even fewer good hotels, so the two-year-old Hilton was the only logical choice. Besides the embassy it was the only location with high-speed Internet access. And it had twenty-four-hour-a-day room service.

Chuck patiently listened to the ringing. After nearly two minutes, a sleepy voice answered. Chuck had the menu spread out on his lap. He barked off five items in quick succession.

"Plus a pot of real coffee. Hot. In a pot. With lots of cream and lots of sugar."

There was no reply. Chuck figured it was the Arabic way to remain silent.

"And make it quick," he said curtly. "I'm hungry."

And with that, he turned to the television and switched on CNN.

"I wonder if the Hawks won tonight," he said to no one in particular.

Hays sipped the soothing tea, sweetened with a healthy glob of honey, and felt his stomach gently uncoil from the tightness that had plagued it for the last few hours. He listened intently as the doctor's story unfolded.

Haj spoke at length, explaining how he had come to be in the desperate position he was now in.

"If I cease cooperating, if I express my horror at this situation, if I try to sabotage the experiment now, my family will be in jeopardy. Perhaps at the outset, I could have done something. But I was intrigued. Like any scientist, I wanted to see how this thing worked. But I have found out that it is pure evil. And I don't think I can stop it. It has taken on a life of its own."

His wife's eyes darted to the hallway behind her, to the doors shielding her two daughters. Hays could see terror poison the gentleness in her face.

"I know this virus might be deadly—even for my family. But if I stop now, then I have assured my family's death. I cannot risk my family," Haj said. "I could endure being fired and humiliated. That would be a minor sacrifice. But the barbarians in charge of this—they wouldn't hesitate to kill us all. Maybe even do worse. My daughters ... they are young and pretty ... and such attributes are dangerous when dealing with such animals."

The doctor's voice dropped low as if he didn't want his wife to hear.

"I have heard tales of fathers being forced to watch unspeakable acts. Then being forced to pull the trigger. This woman—the woman on my staff who told me to call on Jesus—she told me she has been praying to your Christian God. She has been praying that God would send an angel down to destroy this thing, this evil. She said she could see the terror in my eyes. I may be the only person who truly understands what calamity this virus could bring upon the world. The rest of my staff—they do a small part of a small job and don't know how horrible this thing really is."

He drew in a deep breath and wiped at his eyes.

"So this woman has been praying for an angel from God to come down and destroy this virus. She tells me she has been praying since the first day we stepped into that new laboratory. She prays all the time. And she said she expected to see an angel any moment."

The doctor looked hard into Hays' eyes. "Are you that angel?"

Hays closed his eyes.

Maybe I am. Maybe we are.

"Yes, I think I am," he said, his words quiet, rocklike in their conviction.

Norman Williamson began unpacking his gear, stored in a half-dozen silver aluminum traveling cases. Chuck had requested the full array of computer support, a coded security base to establish a Comsat uplink, complete wireless transmission, and enough computer processing power to crack through any e-mail coding system.

The CDC, by charter, had no authorization for security intrusions of any manner and had been instructed on several past occasions to allow the FBI or CIA to intercept suspicious computer chatter. But that process never worked.

Norman had called the FBI on a case several years ago. The agents had taken all the pertinent data and information and had promptly disappeared, never to return with a solution or an explanation.

No, it was much easier to simply track down suspicious e-mails and crack into suspect networks on your own. At least, that was the prevailing attitude of the CDC computer experts.

Norman smiled as he plugged in his laptop to the system. Not one of his supervisors had ever declared it as an official policy—but his budget for surveillance and snooping equipment was approved without a murmur.

"Now ... where did our friend Mr. Hays disappear to?" he said out loud.

He began tapping the coding parameters into his searching software, tunelessly humming a song he had heard in his earphones on the flight to Quadare.

Hays finished his tea and asked for a pad of paper.

"Where is your laboratory?"

"A few kilometers north of here. It is in the middle of a large area of abandoned buildings—some sort of industrial project that never materialized, I'm told."

Hays wrote on the pad: *No neighbors.*

"How big is your isolation unit?"

Hays had sketched the layout of the lab according to the doctor's description.

"It is maybe fifteen meters long and ten meters wide. In the center at the eastern end is the double isolation chamber."

Hays drew the rectangle and then pointed.

"The double chamber is here?"

The doctor nodded. He pointed at specific spots on the drawing, stating which piece of equipment was located where, the thickness of the walls, the location of the air scrubber units, the electrical supply sources, the sewage drains—everything that might be helpful to know.

Duffy and Hays and Haj gathered around the paper. The doctor's wife remained in the kitchen. Hays could hear the occasional rattle of pans and dishes.

"The outside chamber—is it prefab?"

"Prefab? That word I don't know."

"Prefabricated. Did it come in one piece or was it assembled on site?"

"The second unit came as one piece. It seems to be mostly stainless steel. The larger unit came in many panels and those sections have been welded together. The glass panels had already been installed. A team of German engineers and workers assembled it. They tested it very thoroughly."

Hays and Duffy stared at the drawing for a long time. "How long before you've completed all your tests?"

Dr. Haj lowered his head. "It is a question I hoped you wouldn't ask—nor a question that I want to answer."

Hays looked up, puzzled.

"Mr. Sutton, I'm done with all my testing. The work is finished. It has been finished for weeks."

"Do—does anyone—everyone—know this?"

"No. No one knows this. I have not told a soul, save you two, that the work is complete. This virus is real, gentlemen."

Hays knew he had to ask the next question. "And is it as deadly as we found—perhaps eighty percent fatal?"

The doctor lowered his head.

"How I wish that were true. But it is not. This evil is virtually 100 percent fatal on most species. I have never seen anything like this in my life. It kills quickly."

"One hundred percent?" Duffy asked. The pain and fear were obvious in his question.

"Yes. I have tested rats, dogs, monkeys, cats. The rate of death for rats and monkeys was 100 percent. At first, the virus simply prevented their stomachs from absorbing food. Then, perhaps a mutation occurred—and then it just prevented the absorption of water. Now it does not take weeks to kill—but days. How long can a man hold out without water? Six days? Maybe a few more if conditions are right? If this is unleashed, the world is at peril."

The men fell silent.

Haj looked up.

"How many more men do you have with you on your mission?"

Hays looked confused for a moment. "Other men?"

"Yes," the doctor answered. "This is a true danger. You must have brought other men—other soldiers—with you, did you not?"

Hays looked at Duffy, and Duffy looked at the doctor. "No. There are only the two of us."

It was obvious from the look he gave them that the doctor thought the odds impossible to beat.

34

QUADARE CITY, QUADARE—On the south side of Quadare City hulked a squat building, concrete gray, lit by a series of ill-canted bulbs, the outside wall topped with coils of razor wire. The building was unmarked, unnumbered, yet somehow gave mute testimony to what occurred inside. Pedestrians would cross to the opposite side of the street rather than walk close to the cold walls.

Inside, on the top floor in an interior cell, two women huddled together.

The cell door creaked open, and a wizened guard entered with two pots of tea and a battered tin tray piled high with food.

Norah watched as Roberta retrieved the tray. She wouldn't voice the thought in her head: that this looked every bit like a last meal for a condemned prisoner.

Roberta carefully divided the food onto two plates. A scent of lamb filled the small room, mixed with the pungent scent of garlic and rosemary.

Roberta let Norah offer a prayer for the food. "The food has gotten better," Roberta said. "Do you think they changed chefs?"

Norah smiled. "I don't know," she replied. "But it is better. Much better."

Norah leaned back against the wall. The medicine and ointment she had received had done their work. The wounds on her back had improved, and the searing pain she had felt with the slightest movement had dissipated. The new skin felt tight under the scabs, but the pain had slackened to a dull ache and nothing more.

They finished eating and Roberta poured the tea, now thick and strong, into two old, nicked cups. Steam rose in small circles above the cups. The women held their cups with both hands, as if drawing warmth from it. Roberta sipped and looked over at Norah. "Something is going to happen, isn't it?" she asked with apprehension in her voice.

"Roberta," Norah said softly, "why are you asking? Do you think anything worse can happen to us? Do you think they'll take our spa privileges away?"

Roberta stared back and then, almost against her will, began to laugh softly, a serious laugh that acknowledged the absurdity of her question.

"I do think something's up," Norah continued, glad she had made her friend laugh. "I thought maybe they would release us—but to whom? And where? To our embassy? And I had to ask myself—if they did that, wouldn't they know we'd tell our government the whole story? I'm sure no one would believe all of what we told them—but it would be enough to get some people investigating.

"I don't know much about international relations and embassies and political protocol and all that—but kidnapping and torture and imprisonment of American citizens for no reason would probably be embarrassing to a foreign government."

Roberta looked at her teacup and nodded. "That's kind of what I figured as well."

Neither spoke for a moment.

"So … this is sort of the end, then? They're being nice to us just before they—you know—do what they …" Roberta said. Then she started crying, just as softly as she had laughed. It wasn't a good idea to do anything loudly enough to attract the attention of a guard.

"Maybe," Norah said. "There's no sense in being hopeful in a hopeless situation. I think—well, I'm pretty sure—that our time here is close to the end. But that doesn't mean the end of hope. We still have God."

Norah heard Roberta's sharp intake of breath. Neither had really broached this subject before, yet each of them knew that the other had thought about little else these last several days.

"It's okay, Roberta," Norah said. "I'm sure we're now simply an irritant to them. You and I know we're here because of what Hays and Duffy discovered. Somehow that sickness must have been brought here, and maybe Hays and Duffy are coming to try to take it back. I know Hays. I know him better than I've known any man. If there's a right to be wronged, he will be the one to attempt it. And he knows his way around difficult situations. He had his fair share of adventures in the army. He could stop these people."

Roberta looked up, a hopeful look in her eyes. "If he's near, then maybe he could save us. Maybe he could get us out of here. He could take us home."

Norah decided she would offer no false optimism. "I don't know. A few days ago in a dream or maybe while I was praying, I had the strongest impression that Hays was near. But if Hays *was* close, the people in charge would have us killed in a heartbeat. They'd want no complications. Bang, and we would be dead—and our bodies burned, probably—and no one would be the wiser."

For the first time, Roberta stopped looking as if she were on the verge of panic.

"I—I've thought the same thing."

Norah set her cup on the floor and edged closer to Roberta, then placed her arm around her shoulder and held her tight.

"It's okay. It really is. Don't be afraid."

Roberta didn't raise her eyes. "And it's all my fault that we're here," she said. "All because I let myself be taken in by a man I should never have trusted. It's all my fault. If I weren't such an easy mark, such a … such a stupid, worthless person, we wouldn't be here."

Norah stroked her hair, as a mother would calm a child. "You're not, Roberta. You're not."

"He is so handsome, Norah. I couldn't help myself. I looked into those dark eyes and that handsome face and felt that wonderful body against mine—and I melted. I couldn't help myself."

Norah rocked back and forth, cradling Roberta in her arms.

"It's okay, Roberta. It really is. I'm not angry. I'm not blaming you. It's not your fault. It's not. Don't blame yourself for terrible things someone else has done."

"But it's not just what someone else has done," Roberta confessed. "It's me. I've done some horrible things, too. I'm not at all like you—like you and Hays—who have nothing to be ashamed of. I have a lot to be ashamed of. And I mean a *lot*."

Norah wished she knew the right words to say. If she only had listened to Hays more. All she could remember were fragments of what he had told her.

"I know it doesn't make sense, but I don't think God cares what our past is like. I'm pretty sure that one little sin is as bad as a whole lot of sins. He promises to wipe them all clean."

Roberta wiggled free and sat opposite Norah.

"No. That isn't how it works," she argued. "It can't be. That's like saying you and I are starting from the same point with God. You haven't done anything wrong. I have."

"We both have. You don't have anything to make up for. No more than me. Really."

Norah knew the words weren't enough.

Roberta took the last drink of her tea. "I wish what you were saying was true. But I don't know. It just can't be that easy."

Hays continued to add details to his sketch of the laboratory.

Duffy suddenly sat back, the wooden chair creaking under the strain.

"Why don't we go there now? We could figure out what we need, set the charges, blow it up—take care of everything with no one the wiser. Could we do that?"

"No. You could not," Haj said. "The facility is heavily guarded at night. In Quadare, there is much poverty. Unguarded buildings offer to some less honorable men an invitation to loot. And that we couldn't have at the laboratory. As a result, no one goes in or comes out of there at night. Even I cannot get in. I made the mistake of telling Hameed that no one needed twenty-four-hour access. He asked, 'Not even you?' and I told him no. There is now a large contingent of Royal Marines stationed around the building. There would be no way to sneak in—not at night."

Hays brightened. "But what about in the morning? Could we come in with your staff?"

The doctor leaned back. "Maybe ... maybe. But everyone needs a pass—like this electronic key card."

The doctor continued. "The marines leave at eight in the morning—always at eight. I have had to wait for them in the past."

"Are there guards during the day?" Hays asked.

"They come from Fadhil's secret police ranks. They seldom arrive on time. At least I have never seen them come early. They are not noted for their punctuality, nor for their loyalty and honor. If we time our arrival exactly at eight, perhaps the three of us could enter unobserved—if we are lucky."

"We could come with you tomorrow?" Hays' voice was tinged with nervous excitement. "Can we drive by tonight to see the building?"

Haj looked over his shoulder toward the kitchen, then he glanced down the hallway to where his children lay sleeping. "Is it necessary?"

"I think it is," Hays said. "We need to understand the lay of the land."

Haj appeared confused for a moment, until Duffy spoke in Farsi, and then turned back to Hays. "Many things are lost in translation. Many things. No Arab would ever say 'the lay of the land.' It makes no sense to us."

The doctor didn't use his own car, claiming the guards might note the license plate or make and model and be concerned or alarmed that he was driving by so late at night.

"It would do none of us good to arouse suspicion," he explained.

From a cousin down the street he borrowed a rusted and battered Toyota pickup.

As they drove, the neighborhood of small homes and shops gave way to a wide swath of empty land marked with train tracks, pipelines, and power transmission towers. The headlights illuminated dark streets. There was no traffic, and the buildings were dark and desolate.

"They are shells," the doctor said in a hush. "Empty shells waiting for some magic to fill them with machinery and jobs. But there is no magic in the world, and they remain ghosts."

He slowed the truck and pointed. "Up there. Two blocks away on the right. I will not stop, but I will drive slowly. Don't make it appear as if you are interested. People in Quadare have been known to disappear for smaller reasons."

The truck swayed in and out of the broken pavement.

True to his word, several soldiers stood at even paces around the entrance to the facility. A bare light bulb hung on a wire above the door.

"Is that the main entrance?" Hays asked.

"Yes. The card key device is next to it."

Despite being in a desert, despite the summer heat, Hays felt a chill as they neared the building. He didn't turn his head as they passed. "It is all concrete?" he asked.

"It is. Thick concrete. Very thick."

Hays wondered if it was thick enough to contain their plans for the destruction of the deadly virus it housed.

Hameed removed a manila folder from a locked file cabinet. He carefully set the folder on his desk, angling it just so in the harsh light.

He wet his lips and opened the folder. Inside was a thick stack of photos—some black-and-white, some color, of different sizes.

The first few were pictures of an African scene. The foliage was lush and dense, but the subjects of the photos were twisted and gnarled bodies, appearing deformed and deflated in death. Some eyes were open, staring in the direct sunlight. Limbs had begun to bloat.

Hameed held each photo, memorizing the details—the angle of an arm, the glint of moisture on the ground. There was no peace in these deaths, but only a struggle, as if their battle to live had continued to their last breath.

In the next series of photos, the environment shifted to indoors. A bare room with a table, a lamp hanging straight down illuminating a bare back, ropes and constraints visible. The skin was unmarred, pale and delicate white. The next photo showed an angry red gash across the shoulder blades. Hameed could see the tension in the muscle, the pulling against the ropes. Each successive picture showed one more stripe, one more red slash on that pale, lovely white skin.

Hameed felt a drop of perspiration form at each temple. He let it stay, rather than interrupt his mood by reaching for a tissue.

Such a beautiful example of pain, such a wonderful attempt at resistance, such futility.

The next photo was a grainy black-and-white shot from a surveillance camera. It showed two women, with the dark-haired one embracing the other. Hameed wished the photo had been at a closer angle, for it looked as if one of the women was crying.

He smiled broadly, then leered, the hard light showing the deep furrows on his brow.

Such beauty, such wondrous beauty.

Fadhil lifted one pile of paper, then another and another. He muttered an ancient curse under his breath. It was not the way of the faithful to curse, but Fadhil was exasperated. Important papers disappeared with regularity. It was not his actions but those of the incompetent fools who surrounded his life that made his daily routine miserable.

"Come in here," Fadhil shouted at the closed door to his outer office. He pressed the small red button and shouted again, his head close to the intercom system.

After an agonizing wait, the door opened.

"Sir?"

"You didn't hear me shouting?"

"When?"

"Now."

"Just now?"

"Yes. Just now. Didn't you hear me?"

"I heard the intercom sputter. I thought you might have pressed the wrong button."

Fadhil's face grew red, and the veins in his temple pulsed. There were only two buttons on the device—one marked "talk" and the other "off."

"I pressed no wrong button," he shouted.

"Very well, sir," his assistant said and sidled back out the door. Fadhil almost let him make a getaway, but instead shouted again. "Wait. I need you. You have misplaced a file that I need."

The assistant slipped back in, quiet as a shadow. "Sir?"

"I want the latest report from Dr. Haj. I saw that it came in yesterday, and I had no time to review it. I would like it now."

The assistant didn't move.

"Well?"

"Sir, it was on your desk. I placed it there myself. In the upper left-hand corner as you sit, sir, as I have been instructed."

Fadhil reached up and rubbed the bridge of his nose.

"Then find it. It has been covered up by some other drivel. I need to see it. Hameed has been too quiet. If he thinks he will take credit for this, he is sadly mistaken. He will not usurp my authority. Not with this. That I'm certain."

The assistant moved slowly to the desk. He bent stiffly at the waist and began to thumb through the pile of folders, most marked "Top Secret."

Fadhil couldn't be sure, but he imagined his assistant was deliberately trying to sabotage his efforts to stay abreast of this project. He was always slow, but anytime the name Haj come up, his speed was halved again.

As he bent, Fadhil saw a glint around the man's neck. Quadare men seldom, if ever, wore jewelry—unless they were "that" sort of man. Fadhil didn't tolerate that sort of man and reached out and grabbed the glinting object. He formed a fist around it and pulled it hard, nearly causing his assistant to sprawl across the desk.

Fadhil opened his hand. Inside, nestled in a deep fold of his palm, was a small cross made of gold, with delicate scrolling. Fadhil pulled his hand back, dropping the cross, as if he had been burnt.

"What are you doing with one of those? Why are you wearing that cross?"

As he shouted, he pushed his chair back, farther with each word, until he was against the wall. "Why are you wearing that symbol?"

His assistant straightened. A moment of fear flickered in his eyes, then seemed to evaporate.

"It was my father's, sir. He obtained it when he lived in America."

Fadhil was doubly stunned. "Your father was in America?"

"Yes, sir. He studied engineering. He died before I was born. My mother said it came back with his belongings. I wear it in remembrance of him."

Fadhil was about to ask if he was one of them, but realized he didn't really want to know. If this man was a Christian, then his God would have been in this all along and Fadhil did not want to confront that possibility. Fadhil did not want to know if he was truly in opposition to this man's God. It would make success so remote and failure so near.

"Only in remembrance?"

The assistant nodded and handed him the folder with "Dr. Haj" scrawled across the top.

"In remembrance, sir," the assistant said softly, then retrieved the cross and tucked it inside his shirt before slipping out of the office.

35

QUADARE CITY, QUADARE—Norah could look out a tiny slit in the door of the cell and catch an image of the smallest sliver of a window. It was morning—very early morning. The gray light hadn't yet given way to the golds and reds of dawn. The world was quiet for those few moments, and for that narrow slice of peace Norah was grateful.

Roberta remained asleep. Norah prayed and wondered if she was doing it correctly. Nonetheless, she prayed on. Ever since coming to the realization that her days might indeed be numbered, and that only God offered her a way out, she prayed. She asked for wisdom, for grace, for peace, for understanding, for tolerance, for strength, for dignity.

But most of all she prayed for Roberta. Norah couldn't understand how, in such horrific circumstances, Roberta wouldn't break down and admit that God really was their only hope. But Roberta had come to no such conclusion. So Norah prayed that she might find that hope and clarity.

And she prayed that Hays would be safe and that God would offer him protection.

The squeal of a key in the lock of their cell door brought her bolt upright and back into their dark reality. The door opened and the man with the weasel face entered, a hungry, leering smile on his face.

"Have they given you breakfast yet?" he asked.

Norah didn't want to answer, but she shook her head.

He stepped back out and screeched out orders. She heard footsteps hurry and scuffle and further shouts down a long corridor. In the matter of minutes a tray with a plate of hard, sweet biscuits and a pot of tea arrived.

"And here we are—breakfast," he said with an unctuous tone, as if he himself had done the preparation. "You must eat well this morning. And don't take time, for we are to leave here in a few minutes."

"You," he said, pointing at Norah. "Your injuries. They have healed. The doctor said he had found expensive medicine for treatment."

Norah waited as long as she could. "Yes. The wounds are healing."

"Quadare is a poor country. We don't have access to much medicine. Now you must eat. We have only a short time. We must leave here soon."

Norah watched him as he left, noting that his eyes had been filled with hungry anticipation.

Fadhil awoke and sat up. He blinked several times and realized he was in his office. He hated sleeping on the sofa. But he had worked late and had been too agitated the previous night to call for a driver and endure entering his home, dark and silent and intimidating.

He changed into a fresh uniform. He ran his hand across the stubble on his face, decided he didn't want to shave, and instead splashed his face with a palmful of the cologne he had purchased at the duty-free shop in the Paris airport. There was a horse and rider on the bottle—an image that he liked even though he was frightened of horses.

The call for prayers filtered in like a wisp of a summer breeze. Fadhil didn't bother to stop, but glanced at his watch instead. It was early, but he was sure that his assistant was already on duty. He went to the door and cracked it open.

He was correct. He smelled tea brewing.

"I want a cup of coffee," he barked, then shut the door harder than it required.

A moment later, the coffee arrived. Fadhil was sure that it was instant, but he wouldn't make a fuss about it on this day.

"The cross on your neck," he growled. "You are wearing it today?"

The man nodded. "Sir, I always wear it. As I said, in remembrance of my father."

Fadhil waved his hand in dismissal. "It is of no importance."

He pulled a huge book from the bookcase behind him. He let it drop on his desk with a solid thump. "This is their holy book. I believe it divines the future. You will help me with this divination."

The assistant stepped back. "Sir, I cannot. I have no knowledge of such divinations."

Fadhil glowered at him. "I'm not a patient man," he snapped. "You know this God. I can see it now. This book is a book all about your

God. Use it—or you will die. You and your family. I will not tolerate any reluctance."

It was obvious that he meant every word he had uttered—his look was steely and adamant.

The assistant bowed his head for a long moment.

"Sir, this book is not to be treated so lightly. It is not to be used as a charlatan's prop, pretending to foretell the future."

Fadhil slapped his hand on the pages.

"The future has been foretold. The Judgment of Micah has been spoken of within these pages. Dr. Haj is close to producing that judgment. I insist that you use this book to tell me how this terror is to be used."

His assistant didn't move. Fadhil picked up the phone.

"If I dial this number, your wife and your children will be dead before lunchtime."

The room grew cold. The assistant stepped forward and turned the Bible to face him.

"It is no magician's parlor trick, sir. But here, let me read to you. It has your future contained in the pages. It has all our futures so contained."

He flipped through the pages and ran his fingers down the page. He spoke reverently.

"Indeed, sir, this is taken from that same book: Micah. It is not a portent of the future—but it speaks of what you have done and are trying to do."

> Woe to them that devise iniquity, and work evil upon their beds. when the morning is light, they practise it, because it is in the power of their hand. And they covet fields, and take them by violence; and houses, and take them away: so they oppress a man and his house, even a man and his heritage. Therefore thus saith the LORD; Behold, against this family do I devise an evil, from which ye shall not remove your necks; neither shall ye go haughtily: for this time is evil.

Fadhil all but tumbled backward. "It does not say that."

"It does. It is in the same book: the prophet Micah. If you do evil, the Lord will repay that evil. You will be scorned and humiliated."

Fadhil stared at the old book, then at his assistant. "It says that?"

"It does."

Fadhil slumped, then after a small whimper, drew himself back up. He pulled the tails of his uniform coat down and brushed off his lapels.

"Call for my driver. And call for a security detail. Make sure that Lieutenant Assad is in command. I want them all at the entrance to this building in ten minutes."

Fadhil's assistant fairly saluted and hurried through the door and to the phone to detail the arrangements. He stopped and glanced at the clock. It was nearly eight. He knew he had to act—even if he was not yet certain what it was he was acting upon.

Praying the morning shift of guards would be late, Hays huddled in the back seat of the doctor's car, hidden under a tattered blanket. Duffy snugged against the opposite side, holding a pair of binoculars as surreptitiously as he could.

"The marines are leaving," he announced softly, speaking into his shoulder, the words woolen and muffled.

"Any sign of replacements?"

"None."

"Which way do they come?" Hays asked.

The doctor shrugged. "I never watched. I think from the west—the direction of the government security office. From the trash they bring with them, they stop at one of the coffee shops on the Boulevard of the Martyrs."

From Hays' breast pocket came a subtle ringing and vibrating. It was his BlackBerry.

"I thought you turned that off," Duffy hissed. "They can track those things, you know."

"It was off. I—I thought I might hear something more from …"

Duffy offered the slightest nod, as if giving permission. "You might as well see who it was."

Hays flipped it open. He tapped at the buttons. He was silent as he read.

"It's from the CDC."

"What?" Duffy asked, incredulous.

"They say they are considering an official inquiry based on our recent report."

"You're kidding, aren't you?" Duffy whispered.

"I wish I was. They say they will give us a response within thirty days."

"I wish I were in a position to offer my official response," Duffy said. "Now turn the thing off."

Hays agreed and pressed a combination of keys and slipped the device back into his breast pocket.

"The last marine is in the car. They're pulling out," Duffy said calmly. "Dr. Haj, time to go."

The doctor hurried out, with Duffy and Hays at his heels, each carrying a single pack near to bursting, crammed with everything they'd been carrying in four bags.

The doctor nicked his card through the reader. The red light seemed to warble a moment, then glowed green. He grabbed the door handle and hurried in, with Hays and Duffy less than a step behind.

The door shut with a solid electronic latching.

"We're in," Hays said, as if he expected otherwise.

The building was longer than it appeared from the outside, about a hundred yards long and no more than thirty yards wide. Only a few bulbs were lit, producing ghostly pools of light throughout the interior. Almost in the exact middle of the structure was the isolation lab. It gleamed of stainless steel, even in the dark. A bank of red and green status lights blinked from within, monitoring the air pressure, air intake, air scrubbers, self-cleaning filters, alarms and system overrides, and redundancies.

Hays would have whistled in admiration had this been any other time or place. It was a marvel of self-contained protection, a sleek design intended to prevent any sickness from leaking out.

"It's a lot bigger than I thought," Duffy said as he walked slowly toward it. "Do we have enough thermite?"

Hays had been doing the same calculations in his head. They each carried forty pounds of the dangerous explosive and accelerant. Placed at regular intervals around the isolation unit would mean—the lines on Hays' forehead tightened as he concentrated—a pound every ten feet.

Both he and Duffy had used thermite—or at least had practiced with it as Rangers. It was wonderful material if you wanted to burn something down very quickly or blow something up even quicker.

Packed close together, the one-pound bricks would ignite so swiftly, pulling in great gulps of oxygen, that they would rival the heat of a nuclear explosion. But that was the problem, as well. Such an explosion was hard to control. Thermite, a mix of powdered aluminum and powdered iron oxide, had the reputation of blowing up as many of its users as its targets, especially when explosive charges were added—thus spewing an eruption of molten iron. The weapon was easier, safer, and more controllable without the explosive charges if it were simply lit and allowed to burn. The heat would quickly melt just about everything, turning an armored tank into a molten pool within a few minutes.

Hays carefully paced one entire length of the isolation chamber, then one width. His hand went to his forehead and he massaged it with hard strokes. "We don't have enough. We can't risk melting the walls if it leaves gaps."

Duffy nodded in anguished agreement.

"What does that mean?" the doctor asked, close to the snapping point. Hays suspected that the man kept envisioning the faces of his wife and daughters, terrified that the images would be all that was left to him. "You can't do it? It's hopeless?"

Hays shook his head.

"No. That's not it at all. It just means we have to go inside. I hoped it was smaller. We could have done everything from the outside. But we can't. We couldn't be sure it would get hot enough inside if we went from the outside."

"Inside? You have to go inside?"

Hays shrugged.

"It was always our plan B," Duffy said with a self-effacing grin.

"What time is it?" Hays asked. "And where are your isolation suits?"

"In the locker by my office—right there—marked with red stripes. And it's now just eight."

Hays and Duffy were already at a run toward the locker.

Under his breath, Duffy muttered, "I hope they have one that fits and won't mess up my hair when I put it on."

36

QUADARE CITY, QUADARE—Chuck Hild banged on the door to Norman's hotel room.

"Hey," he shouted at the closed door, "I got a response from my e-mail. He picked it up. Where is he?"

Norman opened the door, barefoot and with his shirt only partially buttoned. His hair looked like a swarm of angry bees swirling around his head.

"I don't know yet. I'm still tracking. Everything over here works sort of slow."

Chuck took a healthy bite of an energy bar as he watched Norman move from one screen to another, tapping on one keyboard and then another.

"Okay … yeah, we got him, all right."

"Where is he?"

"Well, just like you said—right here—in Quadare City."

Chuck whistled, as if in admiration of his own guess or Norman's tracking prowess—or even Hays' determination.

"Can you narrow his location down?"

Norman tapped a few keys.

"Maybe. If I had a few more hours. I need to triangulate. Maybe a day." He turned to Chuck and ran his hands through his hair, or at least tried to. "Do we have that much time?"

Chuck didn't answer. Instead he punched in numbers on his cell phone as he chewed the last of his chocolate-coated energy bar.

"It's Agent Charles Hild. From the CDC."

He listened. "Yes. I know when the embassy is open. That's why I'm calling you at home."

Chuck made a rude face at Norman indicating his estimation of the intelligence of the assistant to the ambassador. "Listen, I would call the ambassador but I'm betting he would just tell me to call you anyhow. You know what we're here for, right?" He waited until he got a mumbled affirmative.

"Let me ask you a question. Off the record."

Chuck paused. "Yes. Fine. Very, very off the record. I'll burn the tape. But I need an answer."

He waited again, then nodded his head. "Listen, if you had to put up a secret lab—like a medical lab—with a good-sized isolation unit, and you didn't want anyone to know about it—where would you put it?"

Chuck listened again, then shouted, "Listen, this is serious. If you want, I can call Washington and get the secretary of state on the phone. It's only two in the morning. He will be so pleased that you cooperated fully with me. And I will call him if I have to."

He sighed. "Yes, I told you—off the record."

He listened, shook his head again, apparently in disgust, and then snapped the phone shut.

"I've got the address. Or at least the 'most likely' address. I bet everyone in town already knows where it is. We should scurry. He said it was a few miles from here."

Norman rose and started to follow Chuck.

"Uhh, don't you think you might need shoes?"

Norman looked at his feet as if they had suddenly materialized out of nowhere.

"There any taboo against going without socks in this country?"

Chuck shrugged. "I don't think so."

Norman slipped into a worn pair of black dress shoes and picked up his jacket from the floor.

"Alrighty then—let's go."

Haj dialed the phone, wiping his forehead with his sleeve.

"Listen," he said, his words pouring out in a panic, "this is Dr. Haj. Don't come to work today. The power is out. Stay home. Come tomorrow. Tell Assan, please. He lives near you, right?"

He stabbed at the button, ending the call, and immediately dialing another number.

"Listen, this is Salim—your brother-in-law. I know. I know. I'm sorry for that. We can deal with that later. I have a favor to ask. As a relative. For your sister. Please."

The doctor listened, nodding.

"Fine. That I will do. Soon. But you must help. Call your friend at the Seventh Police Precinct—by my laboratory. You must. Please. It is important. Tell him to send some men to the corners of Dar el Sal and the Boulevard of the Martyrs. They must stop everyone who is wearing a white lab coat. They must be told that Dr. Haj's lab is closed today. There is no power. Yes, they will still be paid. But they must be stopped. Can you do that? Will you?"

Haj closed his eyes slowly and rubbed his forehead, hoping to prevent the headache from starting.

"Thank you. Thank you. And yes, I do owe a large favor in return."

Fadhil waited at the curb until his black SUV pulled up. And he waited until his driver exited the vehicle and opened the rear door for him.

Fadhil was fuming—and yet terrified. The divination—his future foretold—ensured that this day would be different from most. He knew—somehow he just knew that he would find an ominous warning in the pages of that ancient book.

He wouldn't be humiliated. To Fadhil, that fate was worse than any death. No. He would have to stop Hameed. He would have to stop this evil foolishness before it was too late. Perhaps he had already tempted this Christian God. Perhaps he had angered him somehow.

The actions of an angry god terrified him. Clearly, Fadhil had committed a grievous error in judgment by toying with such a power.

Fadhil didn't know how he would explain any of this to his German backers. He began sweating in the back of the air-conditioned SUV. He would have asked the driver to make it colder, but that would be admitting a weakness. A true son of the desert wouldn't mind the heat.

He looked over his shoulder. The two accompanying white vans stayed within a car's length. Each carried seven men, each trustworthy to the death, each skilled in all aspects of weaponry and military combat.

Fadhil worried what might transpire—and if he truly needed to exit the vehicle once they arrived at their destination.

He hoped not.

"What time is it?" Hays shouted. "Can you see the clock?"

The bulky isolation suit covered his wristwatch. The clear plastic visor was being coated with sweat. Seeing clearly had become difficult.

"Ten after eight," Duffy shouted back. From where he knelt, he could see the large clock at the end of the lab.

Both men had hurried into their suits, dragged their packs to the isolation unit, and begun ringing the interior with the bricks of thermite.

For the first time in their quest, Hays knew that a decision they'd made was absolutely correct. Before they left the U.S., the two of them had debated between thermite and plastic explosive—both destructive, both easy to obtain if you knew the right people, and both easy to carry a quantity sufficient to level most any city structure.

Plastic explosive was easier to detonate—but it blew things up. Blowing up a lab was fine, if you had no concern for spreading what was inside the lab throughout the neighborhood. Thermite didn't blow things up with as much destructive force—but it melted them much quicker. It was hard to light, requiring a magnesium fuse. The actual material burned fiercely—fast and dramatic. Within a few seconds, the material would reach temperatures in excess of 4,500 degrees Fahrenheit, hot enough to melt steel, aluminum, even titanium.

Hays knew it was the perfect mechanism for destroying the virus. The isolation unit, equipment, and containers would melt. After a few minutes, even the concrete walls might be reduced to powder. The fire would give off voluminous white smoke—hopefully preventing any firefighter from drawing close before the lab was completely consumed.

Hays packed another brick and added another fuse. They each had forty bricks and two fuses. One brick would light the other in a daisy chain of destruction.

"What time is it?" he asked again.

"Eight fifteen," Duffy shouted back. "Closer to eight twenty."

Hays straightened up, the last brick in his left hand. "When did the doctor say the first staff arrives?"

"He said not until half-past. Then it's only one or two people—if any at all. He said no one shows up until half-past. We have ten minutes to finish."

"Are you almost done?"

"I am. Last one right now."

"Me, too. Let me run a line from the fuse."

The protective gloves were thick and unwieldy, requiring Hays to make a dozen tries to thread the needle—the rounded opening at the end of the fuse. Once the fuse was planted in the thermite brick, a thin nylon rope would be attached to it. A sharp pull on the rope would start the ignition of the fuse. They'd chosen this method so they wouldn't need to depend on batteries or electricity—it was a primitive but effective method. Hays would be able to set the fuse at a safe distance.

The magnesium fuses he'd brought could be set at varying burn times, taking up to two minutes to fully ignite. Once the fuses lit fully, the bricks would ignite, and everything in a seventy-five-yard radius would be consumed in very short order.

Duffy and Hays could get through the first section of the isolation booth exit in no time, strip off their suits in ten seconds, pulse themselves with the ultraviolet radiation for another ten seconds to kill off any stray viruses, and have at least a full minute to get a block away. That was a narrow window of safety, but Hays had considered it more than wide enough for nearly any situation or circumstance.

Finally, after much fumbling and almost cursing, he had the thin nylon cord through the needle trigger of the fuse. He tied it off quickly and began to lay the line carefully on the floor, avoiding any possibility of accidental detonation—or worse, an early detonation. As he unwound the line, Hays allowed himself a smile. *We're going to do it. We're going to destroy this thing.*

He looked over to Duffy, grinned widely, and gave him a thumbs-up signal, masked behind the thick protective glove.

Hameed ordered his personal SUV to pull up to the front entrance, then cursed, seeing that a car was occupying the space that he'd ordered to remain empty at all times.

"Those jackals," he hissed. "Do they think I give orders for my health?"

He stepped out into the bright morning sun, straightening his tunic, pulling on his sleeves, and adjusting the pistol in the hand-tooled leather holster at his hip.

Hameed watched with delight as the two American women exited the SUV that occupied his parking place. The women blinked in the morning sun and squinted to hold the pain of the bright light at bay.

It is going to be a very good day, he thought, as he reached in his pocket for the magnetic card that would open the front door to the laboratory that housed his plans for domination and power.

The phone mounted on the console of the SUV warbled with an annoying tone. The driver reached over and fumbled the phone from its cradle. He spoke a word.

"Sir, this call is for you."

Fadhil grabbed the phone and the coiled cord swung like a child's skipping rope. "Yes." He tried to be as curt and precise on the phone as possible. "What. What. Are you sure?"

Fadhil listened for another moment. He felt another wave of sweat form on his forehead and across his back. He nearly threw the phone back at the driver, not caring if it caused him to swerve.

The two men are in Quadare. We have traced their communication device to the city this morning. And they have come to extract God's vengeance.

Fadhil let his hand slip to the pistol at his belt. It provided scant comfort.

The phone on Hameed's belt chirped. He scowled as he retrieved it. He swore that if anyone interrupted this wonderful day, he would make them pay.

"Yes."

His face went slack. "In Quadare City. That cannot be. You said they would be taken care of."

Norah blinked at her captor. Her eyes caught his, and it was obvious to both of them that the woman saw the sheer terror in his eyes.

He nearly threw the phone into the street. Instead, he grabbed the pistol from the holster, unlatched the safety, and pointed it directly at Norah's forehead. The barrel wobbled, making tiny circles as Hameed fought to control his emotions.

"You. Both of you. Get inside now. I will have no one smiling today. No one."

The door swung open and admitted a shaft of light that blazed across the lab, across the isolation chamber, and across Hays' face.

"Down," he hissed as loudly as he felt appropriate. Both he and Duffy fell to the floor, scrambling to get close to the wall and stay hidden. Dr. Haj had assured them that they would have until half past. They had to have that time.

From the shadows dancing on the wall, at least three people had entered the lab. The door banged shut. Hays caught a reflection in the windows opposite him.

It was a short man, holding what appeared to be a pistol in his left hand. And in front of him, their hands bound, were two women. Hays wanted to shut his eyes and make the hurricane of regret and pain and fear and the waves of anxiety sweeping over him stop. But he couldn't.

Hays pointed to the glass. "Do you see?" he mouthed to Duffy, cowering out of view.

Duffy nodded. "It can't be," he mouthed back.

From beyond the glass, they heard a high-pitched voice shriek, "Dr. Haj! Dr. Haj! Your car is in the wrong space. Get out here. *Now.*"

Hays' eyes darted back and forth. Leaving from the main entrance was now out of the question. Whoever this person was, he wouldn't take kindly to a pair of strangers holding a long fuse and setting fire to a very expensive, very deadly project.

Hays hadn't noticed when they entered, but at the back of the isolation unit was a second entrance. It was smaller, most likely designed to handle small equipment and supplies rather than people. There was an airlock the size of a manhole cover. Hays pointed there. He tried to frame his face in a question.

Duffy stared. Then he nodded. "We have no choice," he mouthed.

"Dr. Haj! Dr. Haj! Get out here." The man's voice was ragged and edgy and forced thin from adrenaline.

Hays took the line is his hand and gently pulled it toward him, then, on his hands and knees, began to edge toward the small, round airlock at the rear of the unit.

37

QUADARE CITY, QUADARE—Duffy slid to the wall, leaning hard against it, and then began to crawl toward the smaller entrance/exit to the chamber. This small access door was used for delivering supplies via a cart system. It was a third of the size of the main opening—but more than large enough for a man to kneel and crawl through. The entire unit curved slightly, creating an elongated oval, but it was cut straight at both ends.

Duffy stopped and pointed to his side of the unit. He had speared a block of thermite with the fuse he carried—the second of the two they had brought inside. "I didn't have a rope in my pack to tie onto my fuse, so I can't light it."

Duffy was a second away from crawling across the floor—a distance of some ten yards. But he would be in plain view.

"It's okay," Hays hissed. "One fuse should be enough. No time for it now."

Duffy nodded, the visor in his biohazard suit fogging from his exertion and, now, his fear. He reached up and tapped in the code to release the small service door. Haj had stressed that there could be no mistakes. If the code was in error, a five-minute shutdown occurred and nothing could be done until the timer reset itself.

"The procedure for all the doors of the isolation unit is the same," Haj had said. "Anyone can enter, but to exit, one must use the correct code." Hays and Duffy understood.

The small LED blinked green twice, and the men heard the subtle sound of a lock releasing. Duffy pushed the door open and slipped into the small service access airlock. Hays followed.

Both heard the screams again. "Dr. Haj. Dr. Haj. You must move your car. It is in an unauthorized spot."

The silhouette of his pistol was caught in a shaft of light. He was waving it over his head. Hays could see the outline of his finger, coiled neatly around the trigger.

The cell phone on Hameed's belt chirped, canarylike and cheerful.

Hameed grabbed it from its clip and nearly banged it into his ear. His face tightened down like a vice closing.

"They cannot be here," he shouted. "Who called? Dr. Haj? But he's not here. He left his car in my parking spot. The Seventh Precinct? What? No. Who gave that order?"

Hameed lowered the phone and slowly turned, making a complete revolution, staring hard into the dim corners of the lab. He saw no movement, nothing that looked out of the ordinary. There was no activity, save the blinking of LEDs from inside the isolation booth.

He looked over at the two women cowering together, nearly lost in the shadows.

I still have the virus. I'm still in control. But the virus has to remain safe. It has to be protected.

He gestured with his gun as he thought, the black barrel catching a glint of light, sparkling like an exposed fissure of coal.

Chuck Hild and Norman Williamson were crammed into the front seat of a well-armored and well-equipped Humvee as it barreled down the Boulevard of the Martyrs.

Norman tapped into the computer, smiling like a child facing a Christmas tree surrounded by presents.

"I love multinational corporations," he said.

Once they knew the address of the lab in Quadare, Norman had cross-referenced it in a number of "top-secret and secure" databases. He quickly discovered that this specific building and the CDC headquarters in Atlanta shared one curious characteristic—they both had security systems installed and monitored by World Security, which was headquartered in Atlanta. It was a simple matter to access the CDC security system, and then to use that access to jump to the headquarters' security system—and find the parameters for this one specific building in Quadare. It was easy—and quite illegal, which didn't bother Norman in the slightest. Firewalls and security coding were just part of an immense game.

"We need to secure it. Can you shut it down till we get there?" Chuck asked.

Norman grinned, tapped another set of keys, and replied, "Done, and done. The outside doors are locked tighter than a drum—although I'm not sure how tight a drum has to be."

Chuck's attention was diverted.

"Ooh—look. A McDonald's," he announced he pointed across the boulevard. "Can we stop there after we're done?"

The U.S. Marine driver—trained to be stoic and unresponsive—turned, his eyes wide in surprise and admiration, and replied, "You bet, sir. Since you're in charge of this mission we can stop. Our CO says it's off limits to us. Something about us being a bad influence."

Chuck wasn't really paying attention. He was trying to figure out if they could be back before the restaurant stopped serving breakfast.

Fadhil's black SUV pulled to a stop just behind Hameed's. Fadhil shouted at the driver, "Who is parking in my space. I was told that the space out front would always be left open for my use and my use alone."

The driver half turned and half shrugged.

Fadhil cursed under his breath. His shirt felt wet and sticky against his skin. He knew he would begin to sweat even more walking out in the morning heat.

"Who are those men?" Fadhil shouted, pointing up the block. A small cluster of men stood, some leaning against the wall, all wearing dark clothes, most sporting identical sunglasses.

The driver shrugged again in reply.

He looked around the driver's shoulder at the car blocking his way. He was certain it belonged to Hameed. That meant that he was already inside—and Fadhil had no idea of what that might mean.

He cursed again and climbed out of the vehicle, striding purposefully toward the door. His squad of security men watched as he pulled out his small key card and ran it through the reader. The red LED stayed red. Fadhil stared at the device, then at his card. He tried again. The light remained red. He pushed at the door. There was no movement. He tried the card again. No change in lights. He tried it upside down and then reversed the direction. He wiped the card on his sleeve. He tried it again, then pushed the door at the same time. He could feel everyone's eyes on him, watching him fail, watching him fuss and fume, impotent at getting a simple door to open.

He banged on the door. "Open the door." He heard nothing. He banged again. The door felt very thick and likely to silently absorb every bang of his fists.

He stepped back and stared hard the blank door, then pivoted and faced his men waiting a dozen steps away. When he stared, all of them averted their eyes, as if uncomfortable with what they were seeing or unwilling to be called on to try another approach.

Hameed heard nothing. He left the two women near the entrance to the lab. He could see no one. He wouldn't go groveling in search of Haj.

He pushed at the outside exit door of the lab. It didn't yield an inch. He pushed again. There was no card reader on the inside. The door was simply supposed to open when pushed. It didn't. It felt as locked as any door Hameed had ever tried to open.

"Dr. Haj, the door is locked. You need to move your car."

Hameed spun on his heels, fully expecting to see the doctor scurrying toward him like a frightened rat from within the lab. Nothing moved.

He wiped his forehead with his sleeve. Apparently he had forgotten about the gun he was carrying, and the hammer of the Glock caught his forehead. He felt a pencil-thin welt rise on the skin over his eye.

Turning sideways, he launched himself at the outside lab door to the street, his shoulder bouncing off, nearly tumbling him to the ground.

He cursed, stood back, raised the pistol, and fired seven shots at the handle and locking mechanism. This technique worked in every movie he had ever seen. The explosions sounded horribly loud in the cavernous structure, and the bullets ricocheting off the metal and concrete caused sparks and flashes. The acrid smoke all but enveloped Hameed. He pushed at the door, first with his hand, then with his shoulder, finally kicking at it with his foot.

The outside lab door remained solid and impervious.

At the sound of the screaming, Hays raised up, the isolation suit halfway removed from his body. He saw the small man struggle as if grappling with an invisible enemy by the lab door. Then he saw the Glock and ducked as the gunfire ensued. If Hays had counted right, the man had two shots remaining.

Unless it was the lightweight sport model. In which case, the chamber was now empty.

Hameed's face flushed pink, then scarlet. His temples throbbed, and a vein in his neck pulsed rapidly. He kicked at the door one more time, then spun about and scuttled toward his two captives.

He grabbed Norah by the arm and yanked her forward. Roberta made a move to protect her, but Hameed raised his pistol and aimed it directly at her face. She stopped moving, but her eyes burned with anger.

He grabbed his phone and scrolled through the recently called numbers. He stopped, pressed Send, and handed the phone to Norah, pointing the pistol square at her forehead.

"When he answers, you tell him to stop. You tell him to leave Quadare now. You tell him to leave me alone—or I will kill you both. You tell him."

His voice grew higher as he talked, almost reaching the timbre of a young girl's.

Norah held the phone at a distance from her ear, uncertain what to do if a connection actually occurred.

A silence fell about the lab like a blanket. Then from the far side of the lab, which was almost dark, save for the pods of light emanating from the doctor's office, came an electronic chirrup—the warble of a cell phone.

Hameed's eyes widened. Norah looked at the phone in her hand, then at Hameed, then at the source of the warbling.

He is in this building. Hameed's eyes frantically searched the area. He swung the pistol around, pointing it about wildly, hoping to find an easy target.

Fadhil was screeching at no one in particular. Sweat was beading on his forehead.

"There must be some way into this building. Get up on the roof. Find a ladder."

No one in his security detail moved.

"Find a ladder," he yelled louder, the sweat now staining his chest and back.

Finally, one member of his security detail ambled off toward the vans they arrived in.

"We need to get on the roof," Fadhil ordered, knowing he had to do something.

Hays slapped at his breast pocket. His BlackBerry was easy to switch on and difficult to switch off. The off button had to be depressed for a full five seconds—otherwise it would remain in its "sleep" mode, only to instantly awaken if a phone call was received.

He found the device and let it clatter to the floor. It bounced, vibrating and chirping as it did.

By the main door of the isolation unit, Hameed stormed to the window and pressed his face hard against the glass, staring inside, his gun resting on the glass beside his cheek.

As Hays reached for the handle of the inner door to the airlock, he pulled hard and fast at the thin nylon rope connected to the magnesium fuse and yanked sharply. Then he clamped the small door shut and twisted the handle to fully engage the lock.

The fuse mechanism snapped open, and a small trickle of battery-supplied electricity flowed to the inside of the fuse, setting off a small powder charge encased inside a thick plastic container coated with polypropylene encapsulated with oxygen bubbles. It would burn for two minutes, then that small flame would compromise the integrity of the case, the combustion having reached 1,200 degrees. That small fire, no bigger than a pencil eraser, would ignite a chamber of powdered magnesium. The extremely volatile powder would burn for only ten seconds—long enough to ignite the solid brick of powdered, pressed thermite. Once the first one lit, Hays figured it would take only thirty seconds for the remaining bricks to ignite.

The fuse started to burn, and a dense, white, choking smoke poured out of the small vent. The air of the interior of the isolation unit began to grow white and opaque.

"Hays—he has Norah!" Duffy screamed, finally realizing the identity of the woman.

"I know."

"But … I don't know if we can get out in time now."

Duffy frantically pulled off the protective Hazmat suit. Any maneuvering was difficult in the small space or the airlock. Neither man could fully stand.

Hays knew that he had no time for explanations. "We have no other choice. Hit the UV-ray switch."

Duffy shut his eyes tight, as did Hays, feeling a twitching against their skin as the high level of radiation poured over their bodies from surrounding UV lamps built into the chamber. If some bacteria or virus had escaped its confinement, the rays would kill any errant cellular assassins.

Normally the decontamination took a full five minutes with pulsed radiation, done in order to eliminate any skin burning. They had no time for such subtleties today and simply set the timer for thirty seconds of the highest dose possible.

Hameed watched in horror as the fuse was lit. He had only one chance to save himself, his future, and the future of a powerful, resurgent Quadare. Just one chance to rescue his vision of a better tomorrow. He turned to Norah, and without the slightest warning, struck her full force against the side of her head with his pistol. She dropped like a rag doll to the floor. In a few quick steps, he entered the isolation chamber. He tucked his pistol into his belt and took a deep breath.

He knew all about the capabilities of thermite. He had used it and knew how to light it, how to pack it, how to destroy just about anything with it. He knew what it would do to his dreams if left to burn. He had only once choice—and only one chance. He opened the second door and stepped inside. The smoke grew thicker. He crouched and hurried toward the source of the smoke. In a moment he was upon it. If he was careful and lucky …

He reached down, grabbed the long vent of the fuse, and wrapped his hand around it. The vent glowed red and seared the flesh on his palm. He screamed out in pain, but didn't let go. He pulled the fuse hard, smooth and direct, hoping he wouldn't break the containment vessel.

He hadn't. It came out in one piece, still smoking and burning. He spun about violently, banging into a wire rack and cabinet, tilting it to the verge of toppling over. A dozen small containers crashed to the ground, spilling a bluish-green scum onto the seamless epoxy flooring. The metal cabinet sprang open from the impact, and vials and bottles spilled out, some breaking on impact, mixing their contents into the oozing puddle.

Hameed paid the crashing no mind. Instead, he ran to the disinfectant shower station and plunged the burning fuse under the water. He knew that burning magnesium could actually be accelerated by exposure to water—while water would extinguish a standard fuse. The water quickly cooled the small chamber, and Hameed grinned as he watched the fire flicker, then die.

He let the fuse drop from his hand, his palm burnt, black and charred.

He faced the window. The vents and air scrubbers had whirred into action and the fog of the smoke gradually began to clear. He could see the two Americans standing a distance from the window. He could see their faces, now shallow and filled with the realization that he had won.

The dust-covered Humvee slid to a stop, blocking the entire street. Within a heartbeat, a U.S. Marine in dark glasses and a flak vest assumed his position behind the fifty-caliber machine gun mounted at the top of the vehicle and protected by a swath of armor plating. A round was chambered and the gun was unlocked from its safety position. It silently pivoted, sweeping the street as Chuck jumped from the passenger door. He was already sweaty and disheveled, yet a startling transformation had taken place. Instead of the laid-back good ol' boy, Chuck had reverted back to what he had once been—a highly trained commando, easily capable of leading men into dangerous situations. He may have been sweaty, but he commanded as though born to it.

He stepped to the curb and six marines silently took positions around the vehicle's perimeter. Rifles were unshouldered and targets surreptitiously acquired.

Chuck hardly glanced about. He walked straight to Fadhil, still blustering and imploring his men to find entrance to the lab.

Chuck spoke in heavily accented but clearly understandable Farsi. "Please, sir, call off your men."

Fadhil whirled about, apparently thinking that if he ignored this new threat, it might simply disappear.

"I don't answer to you," Fadhil snapped back. "You have no authority here. I'm in control here."

No one who first encountered Chuck would think he was a man at ease with assuming authority—but he was indeed such a man. It was apparent to everyone who watched the scene unfold.

"You're right, sir," Chuck said emphatically, his voice gaining force until he was thundering. "We don't have authority here. You have my permission to sue me and the Centers for Disease Control and the State Department and anyone else you can think of after this is all over. But I'm in charge now."

"You have no authority," Fadhil spit back.

Chuck's chest seemed to expand. "U.N. Charter Resolution 12-27-908. Disease and Public Health. The Centers for Disease Control has been given the authority to lead crisis resolution teams in situations of threat to public health—superceding any form of local government or military. Look it up. Today is one of those situations—and I'm now in charge."

Fadhil sputtered. He was being humiliated in front of his men, Hameed's men, and now the U.S. Marines. His eyes registered his chagrin. "The curse is true," he whispered to no one.

"Now if you please, leave this area. Back off—now."

Fadhil didn't move. Chuck turned his back on him, pointed at the machine gunner in the Humvee and held up a single finger. The marine nodded and edged the barrel of his weapon a few inches south.

"I will ask one more time."

Fadhil held his shoulders firm for perhaps ten seconds longer. Then they slumped, as if he were being deflated like a child's flotation toy. He stepped backwards on the sidewalk, away from the door.

"I'm sure the ambassador will gladly entertain all your complaints this afternoon," Chuck said calmly. Without looking, he shouted back toward the Humvee. "Norman, open the door, please."

Hays and Duffy, still in the isolation unit with the UV lights on, felt the burning on their exposed flesh. If they lived past this morning, both would be sporting a painful sunburn—only a few degrees less than a complete blistering.

Then the radiation ceased and the exit door opened, and they tumbled out, scrambling and crawling toward their packs, unlimbering their pistols, grabbing for their packed Uzis.

"What do we do?" Duffy shouted. "I can't get to the second fuse."

Both had weapons trained on the man inside the isolation booth. He, in turn, had his pistol trained on Hays.

Haj edged out of his office, crouching low to the ground, shouting, "Don't shoot. Don't shoot. The virus will escape. The rack that fell contained the samples of the virus. It is out. Don't shoot. It will be released into the ventilation system and into the outside air. For the love of your God, don't shoot."

If the man inside the chamber understood the implications of what had just occurred, he made no indication. "My security forces are outside. You must surrender," he shouted.

Hays felt like closing his eyes and hiding from the pain he knew was to come. He felt like a scared child again, back home in Luxor, Pennsylvania, at the Community Baseball Field when Barry Bioggio and the Herminie Spartans had defeated the Luxor Tigers—all because Hays had flinched. His pistol was still held at shoulder height, he had his target acquired, but he knew he was powerless to shoot. If he did, the man would be dead—but so would everyone else in the room—and maybe an entire city as well.

Duffy sank to his knees in the painful realization of their agonizing defeat.

From the far left, Hays saw a movement—from the area where Norah had been standing. *Roberta. No.*

With deliberate, sure steps Roberta walked toward the main entrance to the isolation chamber. She didn't pause or tremble or hesitate. Hays wanted to shout at her. She saw the terror in his eyes. She mouthed the words, "Don't worry. It will be all right," hoping Hays could read her lips—and her intent.

She paused in the second chamber. If this unit operated like the unit back at the university, it would take the right code to unlock the door. She was sure the weasel-faced man did not have the code.

Hays wanted to shout, *No*. But he didn't.

Roberta took a step forward, placed her hand on the latch to the interior of the unit, looked Hays squarely in the eyes, offered a knowing and pained smile, then stepped inside, shutting the door firmly.

Hameed stood at the far window, holding both Hays and Duffy immobile, taunting them with his call of victory. He pointed at them with his pistol, shouting, his right hand marred by the burnt flesh. He stepped closer to Hays, now only a few yards separating the two men. Hameed's eyes danced with victory. A twisted, triumphant smile filled his face.

"I have won. You have lost."

From over his right shoulder, his eyes must have caught a scrap of movement. His head snapped in that direction.

"Stop!" he bellowed.

Roberta didn't stop, but kept walking. Hameed swung his gun around, trying to acquire the target. A wire rack and a small incubator blocked his sight line. He then saw it—the second fuse that Duffy had placed but couldn't set with rope. The fuse was stuck hard into a brick of thermite—as obvious as a carrot on a snowman's face. He realized she was on her way to ignite it. He couldn't allow that to happen.

Hays wanted to scream. Duffy had his Uzi out, loaded and aimed. Haj jumped at him, pushing the weapon aside.

"Don't you realize what will happen if the glass is broken? We will all die."

It seemed as if Hameed didn't hear a word. He waited. He was nothing if not a patient man. Roberta had another few steps to reach the fuse. He would have a clear shot through the maze of racks and equipment and hoods and vents and cables. Hameed was a superb marksman at short distances.

Roberta would be facing him as she took that last step. Clearly silhouetted by the light, Hameed had a clear and open shot. He grinned, happy again. He pulled the trigger, and the hammer snapped. Nothing.

Puzzled, Hameed yanked the hammer back again, cocking the weapon. He pulled the trigger again.

From the other side of the glass, Hays shouted, "He's got the sports model. With the seven-shot clip. I thought it was nine. He fired seven shots at the door."

Hameed pivoted back around at this infidel. He pulled the trigger again.

Nothing—just the hollow, empty sound of the gun hammer falling against an empty chamber.

Hameed tossed the pistol to the side and began to run around the bank of equipment in the center of the isolation unit and toward Roberta.

Roberta clearly heard his footfalls, but she bent to the fuse, twisted the top, pulled the ring, and leaned back. There was a hiss, a pop, then smoke began to pour from the small black vent.

Hameed was upon her. He had to defuse this as he had defused the first attempt on the destruction of his dreams.

Hays watched in agony as Roberta calmly stood up, almost as if she were oblivious to her attacker. She offered him a grin and almost a wave, then Hameed was beside her, ready to dive at the fuse. It was then that Roberta spun about, raised her right elbow, pulled it back, and released it with the full weight of her body behind it, catching Hameed's nose squarely and cleanly. Smoke began to tax the air filtration system again.

Hameed's feet slipped from beneath him and he toppled backwards, blood flowing over his face, his eyes blank and vacant. The back of his head smacked the cement like a melon rolling off a table.

Hays ran to the glass and shouted Roberta's name over and over.

Through the dense smoke he caught a glimpse of her.

"I never realized my three years in ROTC would pay off this way," Roberta said, her words straining for normalcy. "Go to Norah, Hays," she shouted followed by a cough. "She loves you. She deserves to be saved. I don't. Please, get her out of here."

"Roberta," he shrieked back, "there's time. I know there is. Get back to the rear exit. I can give you the code. You have enough time. Don't worry about the time lock ... we have enough time."

Her words were muffled, indistinct, smoky. "Hays—you should never lie. You're not very good at it."

"Roberta."

"Get Norah out of here. I'm sure they isn't much time left now."

"Roberta." Hays' voice cracked with emotion.

"Maybe this will make up for all the bad things I've done. Maybe—maybe I'll see you in heaven, okay?"

Hays saw the bittersweet smile on Roberta's face—knowing full well her destiny had been sealed.

"Okay," Hays gasped, the word almost constricted in his throat. "Okay—I'll hold you to that."

Duffy grabbed Hays' shoulder. "We have to go, Hays. There's nothing we can do."

Hays ran to the far side of the unit where Norah lay unconscious on the floor. He scooped her up in his arms like a doll and took off toward the door. He knew that Hameed had failed to open it only moments before, but he had no other choice but to try. As they neared the door, the small LED above the lock flashed red several times, then glowed green. Haj charged from his office, shouting, "The lock is on a timer—it must have gone off. The door is open."

Hays kicked at the handle, and the door banged open. Carrying Norah in his arms, he barreled through, followed a second later by Haj, then Duffy.

Chuck Hild was nearly bowled over by the rush of people out the door. As Hays dashed out, he screamed "Thermite," and kept running. From within the structure, a fireball began—a white, round, intense, fracturing light that appeared as if an errant star had somehow fallen into the interior. It blazed like a million flashbulbs all exploding at the exact same moment.

Chuck knew what thermite was. The marines knew what thermite was. They began to run toward the Humvee, frantically seeking safety.

Hays looked over his shoulder as the building seemed to draw in on itself. He was a full block away when he heard the groan. The heat of the conflagration inside was hot enough now to melt steel, and the girders and roof supports would be softening, bending under pressure, beginning to melt. There was a gasp, then a rending, ripping cry as a section of the roof gave way and fed itself to the flames. A ball of fire erupted from the opening, filling the sky. The globe of fire began as the size of a car, then expanded as the air ignited and filled the roof with curling and dancing and clawing flames, growing higher and higher, the white flame at the bottom arcing like a tent inflating from the bottom.

The shriek of metal and concrete and plastic and stone and mortar and aluminum and steel and glass all combined into a cacophony of devastation and annihilation. The concrete walls seemed to pulse and glow, and cracks spiderwebbed along the walls. Chunks of material the size of a man began to tumble inside, as if the building were consuming itself in its death throes. The virus—and everything in the lab—would be consumed, rendered dead and impotent.

It was then Hays knew that he and Duffy had won. And it was then Hays tripped over a curb and fell, holding his right arm out to break the fall and protect Norah.

The two of them lay there gasping, covered with ash and soot.

Hays, his arm throbbing and obviously broken, managed to lift up his head, and then blinked his eyes to clear the ash. Only then did he see the small rising and falling of Norah's chest and knew for sure that she was still alive.

And then he laid back down, closed his eyes, and listened as the wail of the sirens grew closer.

Chuck hunkered down behind the Humvee, which had screeched to a stop two blocks away from the flames. Duffy lay in the shadow of the embassy's Humvee, panting, red-faced, still holding his pistol and the Israeli-made Uzi.

Chuck crawled over to him, his clothing even more rumpled and disheveled than before.

"You know, we should talk about this, don't you think?"

Duffy nodded, then grinned.

Chuck leaned against the Humvee. He looked carefully at Duffy, and then asked, "Do you suppose McDonald's will still be serving breakfast?"

EPILOGUE

FRANKFURT, GERMANY—Hays exited the black taxi. His movements remained awkward and ungainly. The cast on his right arm was only a week old, and his bruises and burns had him limping and a bit off balance. He didn't hesitate long on the sidewalk. He walked briskly up the granite steps, past the elegant and carved marble fountain, and pushed the gleaming steel and glass door, entering a cavernous lobby done in subtle grays, greens, and black.

He walked past the main receptionist to the bank of elevators, and once inside he pressed the top button.

Soft music filled the elevator, an innocuous tune Hays vaguely recalled hearing on the radio some years earlier.

He stepped off the elevator and faced a long, sleek reception desk. A blonde woman looked up. Hays didn't speak to her. He strode directly toward a large walnut door with a gold nameplate affixed to it at eye level.

"Sir, you can't—you must make an appointment—"

Hays neither stopped nor slowed down at the receptionist's protest, but simply opened the door, entered the room, and slammed the door behind him. A silver-haired man behind a desk of rich burled walnut looked up, his eyes weary, almost as if he had expected him.

"Yes?" he said, his hand reaching for the phone.

"Don't," Hays said softly. The word was diamond-cut.

The man behind the desk stopped. "What do you want?"

Hays slipped a finger under his cast and carefully extracted a single folded piece of paper. "This is a copy, of course. The original is in a safe place," he said evenly. "Surprising what you can carry through customs hidden in a cast."

He unfolded it with one hand and slid it across the man's desk.

Hays waited for him to read it completely. It was a signed statement from the new security director of Quadare, addressing the issue of the

Micah virus and the fact that it was financed and supervised by the German pharmaceutical company Huber/Loss.

The man behind the desk showed no emotion. Hays hadn't expected him to do otherwise.

The man allowed himself only to draw a deep breath. "What do you want?"

Hays had practiced this speech a thousand times on the flight from Lebanon to Frankfurt. Now that he was actually saying the words, everything took on a surrealistic edge.

"I want five hundred million dollars from your company for viral research and humanitarian relief."

The man nodded.

"I want a fifty-million-dollar scholarship in honor of Roberta Dunnel."

The man nodded.

If Hays was surprised at the ease of the negotiations, he didn't show it.

"The virus has been eliminated. And I want you eliminated ... I want your resignation."

The man's face grew red and he began to fluster.

Hays kept his voice cold and even. "Don't say another word. You read the letter. It implicates Huber/Loss and you specifically in biological weapon research that led to the deaths of over five hundred innocent African villagers. If you don't resign, this letter will be mailed to several governmental agencies and news organizations. Not only will you suffer, but Huber/Loss will most likely collapse—and that would injure innocent people in your employ. I just want you out. The result will be the same, either way. Consider yourself fortunate that I'm offering you an honorable exit—if such a thing is possible for a man like you."

The only sound was the ticking of a very old, valuable clock on the mantel over the elegant fireplace.

After a long moment, the man looked up at Hays, a weariness clouding his eyes, and simply nodded his head.

Hays nodded in turn.

PITTSBURGH INTERNATIONAL AIRPORT—There was nothing unusual about a man and woman embracing tenderly at the airport. Nor was there anything extraordinary in the way the man bent forward to the woman, whispering in her ear, holding her close, cradling her.

The woman looked up at the man, placed her hand gently on the cast on his right arm, and from her expression it appeared she was inquiring as to the condition of the arm and if there was any pain. The man smiled broadly and dismissed it with a shrug.

There was nothing unusual about any of this. But then the woman held her purse up close to the man's face. She looked around as if making sure that no one was paying close attention, then unsnapped it.

From the depths of the purse came two small snouts, sniffing and testing the air, whiskers twitching in anticipation.

And one might find it curious that this woman brought two rats to greet the man she would spend the rest of her life with.

READERS' GUIDE

*For Personal Reflection or
Group Discussion*

READERS' GUIDE

Over the course of *The Micah Judgment*, Hays Sutton attempts to remedy the disastrous and terrifying chain of events that began when he agreed to hide the terrible secret of the golden skull. Through the many challenges Hays and others face, he ultimately confronts this evil and his own fears. Hays' friends and associates all encounter aspects of Hays' faith in action, and from their observations of these actions, each draws a different conclusion about what it is to be Christian. As you review the following questions, think about your own beliefs and how you live them out through your actions.

1. In the prologue of the novel, the young Hays thinks he has failed a test of bravery by shutting his eyes when an opponent rushes at him during a baseball game, causing him to lose the game. How valid was Hays' youthful self-assessment at the time? In what ways does such a memory affect his future? Are there similar memories and/or humiliations in your past that prevent you from finding peace today?

2. Roberta Dunnel, Hays' newly hired assistant, becomes the pawn of Ayman Qal Atwah. When does she realize that she is being manipulated and controlled? Why does she allow that to happen? Most people have elements in their lives that exhibit control over them without logical explanation. What are yours?

3. Hays promises Tom that he will keep Tom's secret, even though Tom acknowledges he acquired the artifact illegally. How would you have responded to such a request from a friend? How did Hays justify his actions? Which if any of his reasons makes sense

to you? When is it proper to keep a secret like the one Hays keeps for Tom?

4. Both Hameed and Fadhil are world-class villains. What did you find most surprising about each one? How would you describe the moral code each one followed?

5. In chapter 6, Hays says that because he became a believer, he had to end his relationship with Norah. What arguments could you make to support Hays' decision? What arguments might suggest he was wrong? Hays does mention that he tried to share his faith with Norah and she refused to accept it. Did Hays fulfill his obligation as a witness to Norah? How does his decision regarding Norah seem to affect Roberta?

6. After the lab is broken into and robbed, Hays makes a decision to track down the people who committed the crime. Hays acknowledges that he and Duffy will have to break laws in their pursuit of the wrongdoers. When, if ever, does the proper course of action for a believer allow for breaking the law? At what point do you consider it a Christian duty to resist or break a law? What Scriptures support your answers? If Hays and Duffy are doing the right thing, why doesn't God make a way for them that doesn't make it necessary for them to break the law?

7. Hays continues his silence even after Tom has died. How do you think he could fully justify his risking other lives in order to stay out of trouble? How does Hays demonstrate his wrestling with his decisions and actions? How do our wrong choices catch up with us even when we are vindicated or forgiven for them?

8. Norah is by all appearances a strong, independent woman. How does her behavior toward Hays support or contradict this image?

Additional copies of *THE MICAH JUDGMENT*
are available wherever good books are sold.

If you have enjoyed this book, or if it has had an impact on your life,
we would like to hear from you.

Please contact us at:

RIVEROAK BOOKS
Cook Communications Ministries, Dept. 201
4050 Lee Vance View
Colorado Springs, CO 80918

Or visit our Web site: www.cookministries.com

RIVEROAK®
Good News in Fiction

Norah continued to believe that Hays loved her even after their breakup. Why are some romantic relationships able to convert to genuine friendships while others are bitter? How might things have turned out differently had Hays continued a relationship with Norah?

9. As Hays and Duffy travel through Iraq and Iran, they are kept from harm or discovery several times by what appears to be miraculous intervention. In what ways do you think God intervenes in our lives? How often are miracles truly miraculous and how often are they the result of good planning, coincidence, or "luck"?

10. When Norah was being tortured she recalled the words that Hays had told her about Jesus and faith and some of the books she had read. What were some of the barriers that prevented Norah from believing in God? At what point do you believe Norah came to have faith in God? Initially, Norah had a very limited grasp on the truth of God; how true or real can a conversion be under these circumstances?

11. Roberta tells Norah she has done many bad things. How did your perception of the extent of Roberta's wrongdoing compare with her own? When Roberta is trapped in the burning isolation unit, she calls out to Hays and says that she hopes that this one good thing will make up for all the bad things she has done in her past. How does your own belief and understanding compare with Roberta's statement?

12. Some of the evil characters were killed at the end of the story; some remained alive and relatively unpunished. Why do you think God allows evildoers to remain unscathed at times while the "good" are harmed or lose their lives? What more, if anything, should Hays have done to expose Huber/Loss's complicity in releasing the virus?